# *The* ICE-COLD HEAVEN

A NOVEL

MIRKO BONNÉ

*Translated from the German by Alexander Starritt*

OVERLOOK DUCKWORTH
NEW YORK • LONDON

This edition first published in hardcover in the United States and the United Kingdom in 2013 by
Overlook Duckworth, Peter Mayer Publishers, Inc.

New York
141 Wooster Street
New York, NY 10012
www.overlookpress.com
For bulk and special sales, please contact sales@overlookny.com,
or write us at above address.

London
30 Calvin Street
London E1 6NW
info@duckworth-publishers.co.uk
www.ducknet.co.uk

The translation of this work was supported by a grant from the Goethe-Institut,
which is funded by the German Ministry of Foreign Affairs.

Cataloging-in-Publication Data is available from the Library of Congress.
A catalogue record for this book is available from the British Library.

*Book design and type formatting by Bernard Schleifer*
Manufactured in the United States of America
ISBN US: 978-1-59020-140-4
ISBN UK: 978-0-7156-4584-0
1 3 5 7 9 10 8 6 4 2

*The*
# ICE-COLD
# HEAVEN

FOR JULIKA

*Who is the third who walks always beside you?*
*When I count, there are only you and I together*
                                    T. S. ELIOT

## *Part One*

## THE WOODEN FISH

Gumboots and Chocolate
Emyr, Gwendolyn, Dafydd and Regyn
Poste Restante Recalada
Ennid and the Monkey
Shipwreck
In the Swarm of the Gun Crews
Boilerman's Hands
"How are you, Mr. Blackboro?"
Captain Scott's Blanket
Shackleton
Introductions
"Cormorants, Ahoy!"

# 1

## GUMBOOTS AND CHOCOLATE

A GENTLE ROCKING OF HER RIB CAGE, A CRACKING OF HER wooden knuckles, then a bump against the pier to make sure no one falls asleep . . . That's how the ship passes her time.

She's waiting to cast off.

And she's right to be impatient. What are we waiting for?

"We're outta here," was what Bakewell said. But nothing's happening. Just sitting in the dark, the same for hours, rocking. Makes no difference if my eyes are closed or open. It's as black as a night in a black tent.

Christ, the water tastes good.

"Here, drink something," he said, and passed the bottle into the locker. His sooty face in the crack of the door.

"And, shorty, everything okay? Just do me a favor: if you're hungry, don't eat my gumboots. Eat McLeod's."

"Ha ha, Bakewell, very funny, ha ha." I was already suckling at the bottle.

"Come on, we're outta here any minute. The two of us, hey?"

THE LEGEND SAYS THAT KING ARTHUR ONCE SPENT THE NIGHT IN MY village—no idea if that was in a locker, a tent or the Linden Tree pub on the road to Mynyddislwyn. Either way, it's a long time ago. And Pillgwenlly, Wales, is very far away. Today is one of the last days in

3

October 1914 and I'm leaving Buenos Aires. I'm sailing on the British barque *Endurance*. As a stowaway.

Three sailors smuggled me on board and hid me in a locker full of oilskins. The culprits are Bakewell, who I came over with on the USS *John London;* How, who they call Hownow; and McLeod, who's already sailed for the South Pole once before, on Captain Scott's *Terra Nova*. McLeod is nicknamed for the town where he was born, and called Stornoway. And even though Stornoway can hardly be better known than Pillgwenlly, McLeod makes a lot of his home, and if it were up to him, the whole world would know where it lies: "In the Hebrrrides."

McLeod, How and Bakewell belong to the twenty-seven-man crew of Sir Ernest Shackleton's Imperial Trans-Antarctic Expedition. If she ever manages to cast off, the *Endurance* will set a course for the Antarctic continent, which her crew will be the first ever to cross on foot.

My plan from here is to be the twenty-eighth man. And my chances aren't bad. Once the *Endurance* has passed the lightship at Recalada, she'll be on the open sea. Sir Ernest isn't going to throw me overboard, and whether I end up as the seventieth sled dog, like Stornoway predicted during the piss-up last night, is something we'll just have to find out.

This locker could do with a porthole. And maybe a bed below the window while we're at it. I'd only need to lift my head to be in the silver sunshine over the Rio de la Plata. The brand-new transporter bridge must be sparkling in the sun. There's an especially long concert of horns and whistles going on right now, since it's not every day that a British national hero sails under the bridge at La Boca. Hundreds of *porteños,* people from the area around the harbor, must be standing on the pier and wishing Shackleton the best of luck as he sails off.

"Holy ship's gusset, does it smell of rubber in here," was what Bakewell said. It would be the oilskin locker that the three jack-tars picked for me to crouch in, while the three of them are up on deck with the dogs barking and the sun falling on their faces. Farewell, Argentina!

The sirens are howling from the rooftops of La Boca's egg-yellow warehouses. Hooting from all sides. Any minute now and the tug will cast the *Endurance* loose.

Well guessed. They're already cheering. She's off! And I whistle along. Hi-ho! We're off into the ice, into the white, white ice.

We're going to see the Beardmore Glacier and Coats Land and the Larsen Ice Shelf. With a bit of luck, we'll discover the Blackboro penguin or be the first to stand on the ice shelf's unexplored edge . . . Pillgwenlly Land.

Ha ha, no point doing things by halves.

Those are the prospects. The stories I could tell, if I wasn't so completely by myself. I'm a young man from a one-horse town near Newport. More a mother's than a father's son. Unthinkable! But it's true, it's true, and being your mother's son in the time of the Great War is something special. I've never been to any of our enemies' countries, but I know German sailors. Of Great Britain I only know Wales and of Wales only a chunk. To be precise, I know Newport and the southerly villages between the Usk and the Ebbw. The Usk has the biggest trout in Wales. No doubt King Arthur knew that, too.

I've got an older brother, Dafydd, and a sister, Regyn. Her husband, Herman, is a foreman at the oldest factory in Wales, which can therefore also boast of being the oldest factory in the world. Wales was the cradle of the Industrial Revolution, though that, too, was a long time ago. On the day of the general mobilization, my brother-in-law, Herman, and my brother, Dafydd, went to the railway station and on to the new Flying Corps barracks at Merthyr Tydfil.

How says on that day the *Endurance* was anchored in the Thames estuary, waiting for the King to decide if the expedition would take place despite the outbreak of war. Now they're celebrating, my motor-sledding comrades, because we're off into the land of ice. And cheering the King, they'll stick the Union Jack right on top of it. But if King George had telegraphed not just his one regal word—"Go"— but added two others—"to war"—they'd all have obeyed and climbed instead into the dreadnoughts and the trenches: Sir Ernest and Wild, his second in command; Captain Worsley and the two doctors, Macklin and McIlroy; the scientists; the painter and the photographer; Mc-Neish the carpenter; Green the cook; the two stokers; Vincent the bosun and all his sailors. Only Bakewell would have tipped his hat and said, "Not for me. I'm a Yank without a home, and war only matters to people with homes."

You're right, Bakie! And you know what? There are more important things than shooting as many Germans as you can; that's something the King understood, and that's what he meant by just wiring "Go." The King wants us to do something with our lives. He wants us to be the first to cross the Antarctic from the Weddell to the Ross Sea on foot. He wants us to be able to tell our great-grandsons how we did it. And because all that's too much to write in a telegram, the King sent just that one emboldening word.

Go! Get the canvas set, boys!

George V, King of England, is as sensible a man as my friend Bakewell from Joliet, Illinois.

Sir Ernest and the skipper are pacing off the lines of kennels on deck. Orde-Lees is checking the strap rings on the sleds. They won't be needing any dogs, because they're motor powered, made in Wales. Hurley is standing at the gunwale, filming. And high up somewhere on a yardarm, Bakie, Hownow and Stornoway are dancing the tango with the first long-legged gusts coming off Cape Horn.

Away into the south of souths. It's two and a half years since Scott, Wilson and Bowers froze to death on the march back from the Pole. Scott put down in his diary every stage of the tragedy after Amundsen got there first. My brother read it to me out loud night after night, and we tried to imagine what it must have been like in that small tent with a ten-day blizzard howling around it.

Antarctica, Antarctica.

I've been cowering down here for a night and half a day, and haven't eaten anything but chocolate.

# 2

## EMYR, GWENDOLYN, DAFYDD
## AND REGYN

I CAN STILL REMEMBER THE FACE MY MOTHER MADE WHEN MY brother and brother-in-law wrote from Merthyr Tydfil: "Mam, they've actually gone and seconded us to the hangar troop. It's fantastic. We'll be back when we've fixed the problems with the propeller firing."

Until then, Mam hadn't even known exactly what an aeroplane was.

From my perspective, the unsolved problem of propeller firing meant having to find work to help support my family. In the week after general mobilization, I started work in the shipyard where my father, Emyr Blackboro, has been building ships for forty years. He does interior fittings, and it's because of the artistry of his wainscoting in particular that my father is a sought-after, if not famous, man in the harbors on the Usk and the Severn. It wouldn't take him a day to transform this smelly oilskin locker into a richly decorated cabin. It would still be just as dark and uncomfortable, but I'm sure that it would smell as sweetly in here as in our old yard boss's orchard after summer rain.

I did a string of little jobs in the Alexandra Docks in Newport: running messages, stitching, painting. After the end of the shift, I used to sit with the seamen who were smoking their pipes by the waterfront and telling stories about the ports they'd docked at. Not once did they take any notice of me. I used to sit on the mountain of cable rope I'd been splicing since the early morning and feel that I was sinking further and further down inside myself. I was as tired as Checker, the dog that swam the English Channel.

My eyes would be falling shut and it would feel like my ears were, too. With only half of one ear open, I listened to them talk about the houses they wanted to visit in New York, the American friends who'd promised to be on the Hoboken quayside when the tub docked in Manhattan, to take them and their sea chests straight to Times Square, where these fine friends claimed to live. They couldn't have cared less about the pond. That they would first have to cross the Atlantic from Newport to New York, thousands of miles of foaming ocean where, along with everything else, the Kaiser's U-boat fleet was lurking, didn't interest them.

The sea seems not to mean anything at all to most of the sailors I've got to know. They behave like it doesn't exist. Who can understand that? I think of my dad, who loves everything that's made of wood. Imagine if he acted as if there were nothing special about a tree? Here, for example, my cold wall, made of planks. Two or three handsbreadths behind it, there's nothing but water. Even in the dark, he would know what tree it came from. He would smell it, run his hand over it just once . . . "Elm, boy, elm."

After a few evenings on the pier, I didn't know what to make of those sailors. Only one thing was clear: that these men, many of them only a few years older than me, had never been inside a Sunday school. They swore and lied till my head spun. Since then, I've learnt that the one true love these yellow-toothed loudmouths have is the love of embellishment. A few months ago, I still hadn't realized it, which is why I didn't notice that I embellished my feelings just as hopelessly.

My father sometimes sent me to Skinner Street, to pay an invoice at the ship chandler Muldoon's. That's how I got to know her: Ennid.

It took months, or that's how it seemed to me, before I had a conversation with Ennid Muldoon. At first we communicated, other than the usual greetings, only through numbers. When I entered the shop, I said hello like a normal person. Mr. Muldoon inspected me. Ennid returned my greeting. I said my name and Mr. Muldoon clapped open a red-bound ledger, which he handed to his daughter. Ennid took the ledger and limped over to me with it—she's got a weak leg—and said, "Ninety-seven." I opened my father's wallet and counted out the right amount: "Ninety-seven." Ennid re-counted the notes and coins: "Ninety-seven." The next instant, I was standing back on Skinner Street, outside the door and the greening copper plates that encased the building, and didn't know how I'd got there.

Swaying, I wandered down to the harbor. But I didn't even see the ships. I was so happy that I would have given the first sea dog to shuffle past a big wet smacker. And if not that, I would at least have smiled at him the way Ennid Muldoon had smiled at me. That is, if I hadn't been so unhappy.

When it comes to growing up, to maturing in a difficult situation, my dad likes to say that you always stay the same. According to my old man, all that changes in the course of your life is your growing ability to recognize happiness and unhappiness as such. Since I've never heard him change his mind and since that makes him a kind of living proof of his theory, he can't be completely off the mark. But it didn't help me, being the same person before and after the outbreak of war, before and after a day of drudgery over a rock-hard sailcloth in need of patching, before and after Ennid Muldoon. And I thought I *had* recognized where my happiness lay. That's what gave me the confusing feeling that my happiness was making me unhappy.

I didn't understand what was wrong with me. The two people I could have asked for advice had other worries. My brother, Dafydd, and brother-in-law, Herman, were building a machine gun behind the propeller belonging to flying ace William Bishop, and I didn't want it to be my fault that instead of bringing down one of the Richthofen brothers in a dogfight over Paris, he ended up shooting holes in his own aeroplane because his two Welsh machine gun engineers hadn't focused on their work. So I decided to ask Regyn about Ennid Muldoon, but all I got was sisterly incomprehension.

My mam, Gwendolyn, advised me to forget the whole thing and not to mention it to my father. My dad claimed later that he had known at once what hour had struck, and I want to believe it, though he never said anything when we plodded home along the Usk to the village for the weekend, silently. Or I was silent and he whistled one of the tunes he'd invented.

But one morning on the way to the warehouses, he said, "Have a look at the paper today. Everything's in there. Read it and you'll know what's wrong with you."

He cracked the whip and our pony, Alfonso, who had as much distaste for Monday mornings as I did, snorted cantankerously and sped up.

My dad was apparently being serious. How was that supposed to work? I was in love with Ennid Muldoon; I knew that already. I'd been in love a few times before and had even prayed to warm my sister's frozen heart. But fatherly advice is always well-meant. You can't just throw it away.

So after the end of the shift, I bought a copy of the *South Wales Echo* and retreated with the rolled-up oracle into the mess of a steamer that smelled of glue and had just been given the pretty name *Saint-Christoly*.

My eye ran across the headlines:

USA URGES BELLIGERENT POWERS
TO RATIFY LONDON DECLARATION ON NAVAL WARFARE

SCANDINAVIAN COUNTRIES TO RETAIN STRICT NEUTRALITY

JAPAN DEMANDS GERMANY RELINQUISH BASE AT TSINGTAO, CHINA

The course of the war was on everyone's lips. The dispatches in the evening paper only expanded the information that you heard in the harbor during the day. But the more dispatches I read, the more strongly I had the feeling that they applied directly to me, in ways I'd never expected.

Some articles I read time and again. And as I ran my eye over the headlines, the realization that my father had predicted happened:

USA URGES BELLIGERENT POWERS
TO RATIFY LONDON DECLARATION ON NAVAL WARFARE


SCANDINAVIAN COUNTRIES TO RETAIN STRICT NEUTRALITY


NEWPORT BOY MERCE BLACKBORO WANTS TO BE A SAILOR


Sitting in the glue smell of the *Saint-Christoly,* I knew all at once that the reason for my unhappiness was none other than the lure of the sea.

I had wanderlust. I was tearing myself up with the yearning to get away, away from Pillgwenlly, away from my parents and my sister, away from Merthyr Tydfil with its hangars and its oldest factory in the world. Everything seemed as old as the legend of King Arthur, as old as the Welsh we spoke when we were by ourselves, as old as the Celts, who were as old as Moses, who was put out in a reed basket at the waterfront, *yn yr hesg ar fin yr afon.*

I wanted to get away, to go somewhere where everything would be new. Although the reports in the *South Wales Echo* had only one subject, the war, which was spreading around the world, each of the headlines offered me the possibility of seeing that world before it was too late . . . before I made my happiness out of Ennid Muldoon and the artistry of my own wainscoting.

I don't want to accuse my father of wishing that I would join the Royal Navy. I just wish that he would have spoken to me candidly, perhaps about his disappointment that Dafydd, instead of going to sea like a good Welshman, was copying the French and tinkering about with flying machines. In Dad's eyes, an aeroplane is good for only one thing, and that's crashing into the Channel. It's five years since the Antoinette flew from Calais to Dover, and to my father Blériot is still a godless swindler. If, just for a change, we had spoken about my future, I would have said to him that although dreadnoughts do need sailors to go down with them, they've no need of wainscoting, even if it is as nice to look at as Emyr Blackboro's.

But above all, I would have liked to talk to him about Ennid. Particularly one afternoon when we left the cart outside the warehouse and walked home along the Usk, past the meadows of blue bellflowers, past the sawmill and over the little bridge where the Ebbw flows into the Usk. We stopped and looked down at the golden flashes among the pebbles in the water below.

"There. You see it? A big fat one."

He pointed at the trout he'd spotted. Unmoving, it rested in the shadow of the raspberry bushes, its head facing the current. Its spots were red and black, and lightly ringed. Scared by our voices, it beat its tail once before it disappeared under a stone.

I went on and he called after me: "Ennid the Limper? The Jew's brat? Out of the question. Merce, stay there. Merce . . . ! Merce . . . !"

# 3

## POSTE RESTANTE RECALADA

EVERY FLOATING TUB HAS ITS OWN UNMISTAKABLE WHISTLE AND this is one I recognize. There's only one horn on the Rio de la Plata whose tootling is so cheerful and it isn't a coincidence that it's the last one before it's only the wind that's blowing. Where the estuary meets the Atlantic, there lies the Recalada lightship.

The signal means: "Row the man over, *Endurance,* but row him gently. The next lot'll need him as much as you did."

At Recalada, the pilot leaves the ship. From here on, the skipper usually takes charge, and only the skipper. But on the *Endurance* it's different. On this ship, it's Shackleton who has the last word.

And quiet . . . Suddenly there's no more thumping. The engines have stopped. From the way the *Endurance* is gliding, the sea must be flat and calm. The chains rattle and the anchor drops.

"Lower the boat!"

A ship makes the same noises whether she's sailing out or coming home. There's nothing strange about that, because a ship doesn't change, but stays the same as long as her crew doesn't wreck her. A ship can neither jump over her shadow nor slip out of her skin, and it makes no difference how many times she's painted over. Just in Newport, I know a dozen little squirts whose clothes have been made as colorful as flower beds by the endless repainting of hulls. They're all as green behind the ears as I once was, and none of those on the swings that hang above the waterline ever alters a ship just because he paints it sun yellow one day and in camouflage the next. The ship stays the same.

What changes under all the layers and crusts of paint is the boy. He changes because he has time on his swing to dream up stupid ideas. And it's not only there . . . No matter what you're doing, just as long as it stretches out endlessly and stays perfectly the same, your hands will work all by themselves. You wouldn't believe the insights that float into your head when you're sitting on a mountain of cable rope in need of splicing. You become an absolute Buddha. Truths occurred to me by the dozen. I realized the truth about my brother-in-law: he'd taken the first chance he'd had to escape from Regyn. He'd had enough of my sister. I realized the truth about Mr. Muldoon: that by treating me with disdain, he also showed disdain for my dad, who'd been his customer for forty years. Mr. Muldoon needed a solid thrashing. And my dad? He was different. He was different not just from Mr. Muldoon but, above all, different from me. Always the same man, always diligent, always unswervingly focused on doing his bit, he was sure of my love forever. But if there's one thing I'm not, it's unswerving. I'm not the same person two days in a row. On the *John London,* Bakewell and I lived through hours when we were turned inside out, wrung out, chopped up and sewn back together. We looked at each other, asking, "Is that you?" A part of Bakewell became a part of me and some part of me is now a part of Bakewell. Also, you're always in some measure the man standing in front of you. And the man in front of you is always different.

The ship is just the ship. She belongs neither to the sea she floats on nor to the land where she was built and where she'll be scrapped. She's something in-between. Nor is the ship changed by the way her crew handles her. Whether she rides well before the wind or scrapes low through the waves like a plane through too-soft wood, it'll alter nothing about the ship. The next crew will treat her better or worse. The ship never changes, which is why the noises that she makes are the same whether she's coming into harbor or setting out again for the open ocean.

The *Endurance*'s chain rattles and clanks. Because she's going to ram her way through the ice, her bow has been made of wood three feet thick, and her anchor, when lowered over the rail, thunders dully against the hull before it rushes into the water and down to the bottom. The clattering of the winches, the pacing, the stomping, the commands from Worsley and the swearing from a man readying himself for hard work, all that and all the other noises, such as the rumbling of my stomach, are a part of the *Endurance* heaving to.

"Pull! Stroke one, stroke two, pull, pull!"


THE PILOTS FROM BUENOS AIRES, PUNTA DEL ESTE AND MONTEVIDEO disembark on the Recalada lightship. On the morning when they plucked Bakewell, me and the eleven other survivors from the remnants of the USS *John London*, wrecked on a breakwater, and took us down here to pass on to the pilot for Montevideo, there'd been an out-and-out pilots' party happening on the little lightship.

The men didn't drink anything, of course, but they sat in a circle on deck, smoking their golden Virginia or pinching the snuff that went from hand to hand in a circular tin. If I were standing at the railing now, I'd be able to hear them laughing. *Antáricanos!* We towed Scott onto open water and piloted Amundsen and Filchner across the current. Hardly is Mawson back from the Pole but Shackleton wants to set off. What's the Weddell Sea to us? The ocean's made of water wherever you go, even under the pack ice. But it's only the Plata that's made of silver, God's own silver salver.

When it gets dark, the two towers on Cape Antonio light up and the night pilots come. The others all climb on board the last ship going ashore. It's a friendly little boat, Recalada's bright-red lightship.

If a seaman has written a last letter home, he can post it here. For a small fee, the pilot will take it back to port and send it off. And if a seaman has been sent a letter, he can pick it up here. The pilot will have collected it from the harbor post office, for a small fee, and left it on board, poste restante Recalada.

Maybe Shackleton will be getting a last greeting from First Lord of the Admiralty Churchill, written by the lovely right hand of his ministerial secretary. Or perhaps the Queen Mother, Alexandra, has scribbled a note to remind him of the edifying qualities of the Bible she dedicated and placed in Sir Ernest's luggage. Stornoway gets a letter from Stornoway. And Hownow gets a loving telling-off from his wife, Helen, who gives him the news about their baby: it's a boy and he's named after you, Walter. Bakewell, like most of the others, gets nothing. Apart from me, and I'm, firstly, not currently unimpeded, and, secondly, very near him, there's no one Bakewell could receive a letter from.

When he ran away from Illinois, he was eleven years old. Now he's twenty-six and has been a farm laborer in Missouri, a coach driver in Michigan and a railway navvy in Montana before coming to Newport as a topman, where, eventually, I fell exhaustedly into his lap.

No matter if it bothers him or not, seaman William Lincoln Bakewell will be leaving the Recalada lightship empty-handed.

The same goes for me. Even though there are two addresses I could offer:

*Merce Blackboro*
*Stowaway*
*Oilskin Store*
*Endurance*

And, for those whose post isn't urgent:

*Merce Blackboro*
*Seaman*
*USS John London*
*poste restante Davy Jones's Locker*

18

# 4

## ENNID AND THE MONKEY

BEFORE I TOOK SHIP IN NEWPORT, MY MAM GAVE ME THIS storm-proof jacket. I love it. Since then, I've only ever taken it off for washing. Its hood keeps my neck and ears nice and toasty even in this freezing cupboard and, because Mam stitched a double lining into the sky-blue body, I can't complain about a lack of padding, either.

Why should I be sad about there being no post from home when I can dip into the good-bye letter from my parents?

I also have Ennid Muldoon's fish. Ennid's lucky charm has been beside me ever since I sewed a buttoned pocket into the lining of my coat during some time off duty, sitting on the jib boom as the *John London* ran through quiet seas. Hidden in the pouch is a little wooden fish with a note in its stomach that I'm supposed to read only when my courage fails me.

But even if I wanted to, I wouldn't be able in the dark to read the advice of Ennid's wise fish, which feels like a pinecone through my jacket.

And I don't want to read it. Only once have I come close to looking at the note: when we were drifting on the wreckage of the *John London* and I told Bakewell about Ennid. We floated helpless through stormy seas for more than a week, and I still didn't feel like I'd run out of grit. The fish stayed in its pocket then. I'm not taking it out now.

Get some sleep? Yes, sir. Yessir, a quick nap. Don't lose heart, Merce! Build a bed out of gum boots. There's still time to kill before the starting gun. Only when the stub-nosed *Endurance* is on the open sea and her course is set for South Georgia will there be no turning back.

Every day counts in the ice. Even Shackleton can't cross the Antarctic in winter. And Bakewell should sooner or later find a good opportunity to bring me out of the locker and put me in front of the skipper. I've got to get out sometime . . . before I start to lose it down here. But no matter how good Captain Worsley's mood is because all the sails up to the topgallant are swelling in the wind or because Sir Ernest, in his childish excitement, has just put an arm round his shoulders—no matter how good, the captain's going to bawl his own lungs out when I stand in front of him in my sky-blue jacket and rub my eyes, blinded by so much light.

THE *JOHN LONDON* WAS ONE OF THE MERCHANT SCHOONERS THAT sailed the South American route before the war. Mostly three-masters with an underpin, the ships transported large bulk cargo made of steel and iron or sometimes of wood. They were battered rust buckets, always in the dock. The elderly *John London* was under contract to a company in Swansea and she sailed back and forth between Wales and Uruguay with her belly full of railway sleepers. She'd often been in Newport, which is how my dad knew her. Years ago, he'd built her a new fo'c'sle for her crew quarters. When the *John London* moored at the pier of the Parks shipyard, we went on board to take a look at the state of the fo'c'sle and start to arrange whatever needed fixing.

We spent a few weeks on the bulkheads and quarters below deck, which were all in a fairly sorry condition. During all the carrying, sawing, fitting, sanding, filing and painting, I got to know pretty much every nook and cranny of the ship. Everywhere there were signs of neglect. But the three carpenters and I gave the old girl a good sprucing up. And Dad even gave her a new hat to show off in, a new fo'c'sle roof made of gleaming cherrywood.

We were nearly finished when, one morning, life began to pulse again in the usually empty ship. Sailors and stokers came on board. Muldoon's people delivered the parts for the new jib. A motorcar brought the captain to the shipyard, where he spoke to my dad before going below decks. And lastly, there appeared two men, dressed in tailcoats but still not particularly elegant, one American, the other from the Swansea company. The hiring began.

One of the first seamen to come back out into the sunshine from the mess where the procedure was taking place stood next to me and asked about what I did. We talked for a while. He told me that he'd signed up for Montevideo and back. And then he wanted to know, without my having mentioned anything about it, if I didn't feel like coming along.

Maybe, I said. And he laughed, quiet and friendly.

That's how I met Bakewell. Since then there hasn't been a day we haven't put our heads together. If I think about it, there are only three things I miss in my locker: the sea air, the light over the ocean and Bakewell.

"Here, the two of you'd better drink something, you and your wooden fish."

A few days later, I spoke to my father and told him I wanted to go to Uruguay as a sailor aboard the *John London*. I calculated for him that my pay for the three-month voyage was more than I'd earn in half a year working in the shipyard. And I asked him to say yes, because I needed to make my own way.

Captain Coon and his boatswain brushed off my idea of becoming a sailor with tired smiles. This boatswain, who, as on almost all ships where English is spoken, was called the bosun, and whose name was Mr. Albert, was a type of seaman I hadn't known until then. He had nothing in common with the crotchety gasbags who hang around on the pier and have nothing better to do than brag to a woman or threaten her husband with a beating. Mr. Albert, the bosun, asked me if I knew what the sea was.

"Yes, sir," I said. "It's the water between the continents."

"Damned lot of water."

"Yes, sir."

"How good are you at swimming, Blackboro?" he asked, looking at his notebook.

"I think I'm quite good, sir," I said. "Not as good as a fish, but quite good."

"Not as good as a fish?"

"No, sir."

"And how good are you at cooking?"

Flummoxed completely, I admitted I couldn't cook at all . . . I'd never tried.

"So you could do with the practice. Sign here and you're hired as a galley steward."

The mess boy earned only half the pay of a sailor, and I saw my father's reason for letting me go float off downriver.

But it wasn't like that.

My father agreed, and my mam explained how it was he could do it with a calm conscience. While signing over the fo'c'sle, he'd taken Captain Coon aside and let him know that he would personally rip the *John London*'s new woodwork out plank by plank unless Coon gave him his word of honor that sailing under his command would mean that I was under his protection. Captain Coon promised.


I WAS IN A STRANGE MOOD THOSE LAST FEW DAYS BEFORE PUTTING TO sea. On the one hand, I'd no chance of thinking about anything else. Tears jumped to my sister's eyes every time she looked at me, and my parents were in a flap because the news that their son was setting sail for Uruguay seemed to have been spread by the wind. I noticed that people were speaking about me, and all that together made me so nervous that sleep was impossible.

On the other hand, I suddenly felt a gnawing unwillingness to go. When I thought about it, and I did nothing else, my decision to go to sea seemed embarrassing and stupid. What had I been thinking? I hadn't been! It had just been a feeling, and now there was a whole armada of other feelings, protecting and strengthening one another and sinking every sensible thought-process on the spot. Sometimes I considered myself as ridiculous before erupting again in cheers and congratulating myself on my limitless courage. I combed through my parents' and siblings' bookshelves to find descriptions of shipwrecks and felt a superstitious shiver when I read that Jack London had actually been called John London, just like my own ship. And when I read the first sentences of his book, I felt as though I was already rowing far out onto the ocean.

It was only thanks to those books that I stayed halfway sane in the days before we set sail. In one sleepless night, I read the whole of *Robinson Crusoe*. In another, I wrote Ennid a love letter that climaxed in an ode to her limp. Luckily, I read it again before posting it.

But throwing away the letter was a lot easier than unsigning the signature I'd left on the hiring list. As it became clear to me that there'd be no way out, I was sick with fear. I remember coming back along Dock Street after running an errand for my dad. I saw the ships lying at the pier at the end of the alley. The *John London* wasn't one of them, but my knees still went soft at the sight. I couldn't move. People stared at me. I must have looked dreadful. Wild-eyed and my head burning, I pressed myself against a wall. I felt as though I'd been driven into a corner, horribly alone. Yes, that was the worst moment. It didn't get any worse than that. I ran away home, and after that it began to get better.

On the last day before sailing, I went into Muldoon's shop to say good-bye to Ennid, but she wasn't there. She was sick. Mr. Muldoon asked whether he could help, and I made up some story about Ennid and Regyn.

"Good-bye, sir!" I reached out my hand.

He shook it without looking at me.

23

"I've got a question," I said. He lifted his gaze and, so it seemed, only now did he clearly see me standing in front of him.

"I love your shop, sir. Everything"—I pointed around the stuffy, dark storehouse where Ennid had become Ennid the Limper—"everything here, I love it. I'd like to . . . I mean, when I'm back, sir, I was wondering if you might need an assistant?"

Mr. Muldoon clapped open his ledger and stared into it as though it might contain an answer.

THERE'S THE BELL. FOUR STRIKES.

On a small barque like the *Endurance,* you can hear the ship's bell even in a tiny cubbyhole below decks. So even the stowaway knows what time it is: fourth bell. It can't be much brighter out on the sea between Patagonia and the Falkland Isles than it is in my locker.

I don't want to second-guess how Shackleton does things, but, including me, there can't be more than half a dozen members of the twenty-eight-man crew awake right now: one helmsman, three on deck watch, one lookout and the man in the oilskin locker. The rest will be asleep with wax pellets in their ears. When I close my eyes, I see the big chestnut in the square outside Muldoon's shop and think about how I walked through the harbor streets to say good-bye to the things I actually loved, like the trees where my dad pointed out the unmistakable characteristics of each wood. The fear and all the other feelings that had weighed so heavily on me had vanished. On my last day in Newport, all that was left was wistfulness. I felt my arms and legs moving, and the air was so mild as it flowed around me that it was like I was swimming in it, walking along Rodney Street to the warehouse, but swimming upright.

Our old warehouse boss Simms told me that the *John London* was loaded, equipped and provisioned.

He jollied me a bit: "Crew all present and accounted for, as long as Blackboro makes it on board in one piece." And he told me when we were sailing: "Start of rat watch."

Meant nothing to me.

"Midnight, Merce."

We chatted about time on board being split into bells and watches, and Simms, who spent years as a helmsman, warned me to be careful not to become the patsy.

While he sorted his bills, he explained that every ship has its patsy. "A patsy is a kind of black sheep. The scapegoat on board, that's the patsy. Everything's his fault. If a yardarm comes loose, it was the patsy. If there's a fire in the coal bunker—the patsy did it. Every skipper sometimes has a bad day, and he has a go at the helmsman. The helmsman goes to the bosun and shouts him down. The bollocking gets passed down the ranks until everyone agrees: the patsy's got to pay. There are ships with more than one patsy, on those you have to be careful you don't become the patsies' patsy. And there are ships where they're all . . ."

He got no further. In front of the alcove where Simms was doing his best to warn me about the patsy's lot, there stood Ennid. She smiled quickly as she saw us and raised her hand tentatively.

"Little Muldoon," said Simms.

I took her into my dad's empty office. It was the first time we'd been alone together. She looked beautiful in her raincoat with her umbrella hanging off her arm. She wasn't ill at all, Ennid, she was standing right in front of me, and I began to count compulsively, compulsive counting. I counted the windows in my father's office and the buttons on Ennid's coat. I flashed through the numbers: I'd seen her five times in her father's shop and once outside, on the Alexandra docks halfway to Pillgwenlly. But even there we hadn't been alone. And it had been our fathers who'd spoken, while we shot each other looks that couldn't get meaningful enough. She stood at one of the windows. There are four, I thought, exactly four. And I sat on one of the desk's corners, of which there were also four.

The newly built warehouse across the way, on the other hand, had so many windows that I could only guess their number. It was a massive place.

"It's like this," she said. "I'd like it if you wouldn't speak to my father that way. Maybe you can understand that since this afternoon, he thinks you're totally bonkers. What were you thinking, Merce Blackboro?"

She had a mouth on her; that ran in the family. All right then, I thought, let's fight. You'll be sorry; I'm sailing at midnight. Start of rat watch. On the wall above the chair in the corner, I saw the gold-framed picture that I've thought was mysterious and significant since I first saw it as a boy. It's of Napoleon, standing alone on a beach and looking out over the sea. My father claims it's the south coast of England, which Bonaparte once landed on by mistake.

Ennid was silent. There was no fighting after all. She searched her handbag for something and pierced me with a look when she found it.

"I've got something for you." She held it out to me. It was colorful, colorfully painted. I took it and saw that it was a little wooden fish.

"It's a lucky charm." She came over to me and took the fish from my hand. She turned it over and opened its belly. There was a note inside.

"If you ever run out of heart, then read it."

She gave me the fish back. She was less than an arm's length away from me. I pulled her close to me, buried my face in her neck and kissed my way upwards towards her mouth.

"I have to go," she gasped, and freed herself. I had the feeling that she was going to crumble under my lips.

"Stay."

"What for?"

My father left workers waiting on the chair under Napoleon until they were almost mummified. I'd once sat there with toothache until I almost passed out. Ennid sat on my lap. I kissed her and she said for the first time, "You monkey." Again and again, in each break between kisses, she said those two words. She opened my belt, reached under her dress and panted, "You monkey. Monkey!"

When she stood up and pulled her clothes straight, I still had the fish in my hand. My pulse was racing while I told her about the ode to her limp and that I had thrown the love letter into the Usk.

"Lucky you" was all she said. "You were lucky there, my little monkey."

Of course I wonder what's written in the note. I ask myself each time I cross my arms and feel the fish against my chest.

One, two, three, four, five. Fifth bell.

Bakewell thinks that, just for reasons of space, all that can be on the piece of paper is a quote from the Bible, a phrase like "Remember me!" or a single word, like the telegram from King George. And he says I should let him read the note so that he can tell me what it says in case I ever lose the fish.

Clever, Bakewell. But not clever enough.

# 5

## SHIPWRECK

I
F I LIE ON MY SIDE AND PULL MY LEGS UP TO MY BELLY I MIGHT
be able to sleep a bit after all. I'll take a jacket off the pegs for a
pillow. I don't know if it's because I'm tired or because it's nighttime, but I'm colder and colder. The floor of the locker is covered in
oily-smelling cloths and towels. I tuck them between my joints and
under my limbs and it's all right like that; I'll just lie here for a while.
If only I could stretch out my legs.

Each watch is four hours long. Monkey watch from 16:00 to
20:00, donkey watch from 20:00 to midnight, rat watch until four in
the morning and then finally dog watch. Monkey watch, because at
that time nearly everyone's hanging in the rigging. It's called donkey
watch because of the slog of getting the ship ready for the night. Rat
watch firstly because of the rats, of which, if you're unlucky, there'll
be more running around the deck than there are men, and secondly
because on rat watch you start to feel like a rat yourself, sniffing the
air in the dark, always on your guard, scurrying round corners at
every noise. And why dog watch? After four hours' sleep you've got
to make the ship ready for the day, climb up to the crow's nest and,
what's worst, wake up the men on the day watches without them
chewing your ear off. At the end of the dog watch you ask yourself
who's more tired, you or the man you're waking. You should really
be kissed and stroked and bathed at the end of dog watch. Instead
you just feel like you've been beaten.

Six bells.

That's exactly the time it was when the *John London* put to sea: six bells. We left Newport with a three-hour delay that no one could explain and no one ever learned the reasons for. Something like that creates a bad atmosphere right from the off. The watches get mixed up and already there are sections of the crew who've got some bile in their guts.

No chance, I won't be able to sleep like this. Where's the bottle? Almost empty.

When was Bakewell here? Probably just after the watches changed, so not long after midnight. Should I just go out and get some water myself?

Better not. Even though these memories are pressing in and I can see all the faces in front of me. The men standing on board and waiting for it to begin: thirty-two men above more than eight hundred tons of timber in the hold, all needed to build the railway in Uruguay. And two of those bleary-eyed lads Bakewell and me.

Mr. Albert had the grumblers well in hand despite everything, and at first, discipline on board didn't seem to be the problem. But that the *John London* did have a problem was soon obvious, even to me. It started with a rumor that the coal we'd loaded was shoddy quality. I'd wondered why it was that a shower of soot rained down on you near the chimneys, and this was the explanation. Bakewell's face got darker every day, in both senses. As we lay in our bunks when both off watch, he explained that the slick of dirt dragging behind the ship was a sure sign that the boilers weren't delivering enough power. The *John London* would be in trouble if she had to move what must now be far too heavy a cargo through any bigger storm.

But I also remember how happy I was. There were hours when I forgot any and all fear and felt only the freedom I enjoyed. I was rushing along under full sail with fewer than three dozen men, and for miles, for hundreds of miles all around me, there was nothing but water. It's wonderful not only to watch the rising and falling of the sea but at the same time to feel with your body the ocean's breathing in and out. Sometimes, when I'd finished my work in the galley and wasn't needed on deck, I stood at the gunwale by myself or with Bakewell and couldn't see enough of the breadth and stillness of the deep green sea.

What's best is the way this stillness gets carried over into you. I began to miss the wind when I was below decks. I felt strong, free and sound. I wished fervently for nothing more than this happiness to hold and for everyone everywhere to sometimes feel like this. There's not much left of those moments now. The unrelenting work and the crew's constant fighting over the pecking order mean that you soon become numb to it. You don't even notice it anymore. And when the sea turns against the ship, not a syllable of that happiness remains. The ocean knows no language and there's no negotiating with it. Its breakers come on deck and whirl their freezing chains like lashes.

After nine weeks at sea, a few hundred nautical miles off the South American coast, we met the first outriders of a powerful storm and began to get an inkling of what was coming our way. Since the storm seemed to be moving landwards, Captain Coon gave orders to strike out for the open water opposite Porto Alegre. We'd hardly reached Uruguay's territorial waters when we found ourselves in the hurricane. The ship climbed to the crest of mountainous waves and would come almost to a complete stop at the summit, listing crazily from side to side; then she would right herself and for a moment pause, as though frightened of the abyss. But the sea struck her astern with all its force and plunged her downwards. The bow plowed up to the catheads in the milky tumult, which burst over the railing and in through the scuppers. The heaviest of these rollers lifted the *John London* so far out of the water that her bow rose, dripping, into thin air.

In a sea like that, it's only a matter of time before all the fury comes together into a single wave.

When it came, it hit the midships, which were lying far too deep, and flung the hull over onto its side. Planks shot from the cargo hatches and smashed themselves a flight path out and down into the sea. The ship, listing strongly, raced into the valley of the waves. The railing went right under until the water reached the shattered hatches and poured inside, into the hold, while swell after swell broke over the gunwales and an icy current swept the deck. Every second there could have been lethal. Those who hadn't had time to tie themselves fast clung with feet and hands to a rail or a capstan and hoped.

We were all completely helpless, but most of the men also seemed paralyzed and confused. All they seemed to want was not to obey orders. Most of them just wailed. Some were still screaming curses, but that small defiance no longer brought any respect from me. Because neither Mr. Albert, who they otherwise listened to, albeit grumblingly, nor the captain, who they had nothing left for but mockery, could convince them to go to the pumps and set a sail to turn the ship with the wind, we capsized within an hour, and all the idiots, braggarts and slackers climbed up the side and hung in the rigging. Finally I crawled over there as well; it was the only halfway-safe place left. When the hull tipped, Mr. Albert wasn't able to get out of the fo'c'sle and drowned. I saw the cook bobbing in the sea like a cork before he suddenly went under to follow all those who hadn't even made it out of the ship's belly.

Without Mr. Albert, the captain was as helpless as we were. He swore meaninglessly at us good-for-nothings. Bakewell and the ship's carpenter, a gorilla from Liverpool called Rutherford, had to cut the foremast and the mizzen. They heaved for two hours at the thick trunks while the wreck reared up and down, breaking herself into pieces. Freed of her masts, the *John London* righted herself again. We were in luck it was wood in our hold; any other cargo would have dragged us under. It was only during the night that the mizzenmast finally pulled clear of the shrouds. Like the ax Bakie had hacked it down with, the fallen mast struck and struck against the hull.

The next morning all that jutted out of the water was the stern, a splintered mast and some uneven framework where the railing on the afterdeck had been. I was soaked through and felt close to death from the cold. There was nowhere to rest. Each swell broke right across the wreck. We stayed in Coon's cabin, where the water lapped at our knees, but at least the walls sheltered us from the wind. The captain managed to convince the mutinous group that had formed around Rutherford that the only way any of us would survive was if we took turns on watch. In the afternoon Bakewell called down that there was a ship in sight. Everyone rushed up and clung to the railing or climbed into what was left of the rigging to keep the cruiser in sight. But its course wasn't in our direction, and after that none of the others wanted to go up the mast anymore. And after the second day, Coon, Bakewell and I had also had enough. From then on the wreck drifted through the storm without a lookout.

Of the thirty-two men, thirteen were still alive. We were freezing, had nothing to eat and only a couple of bottles of wine to drink. All the stores of food and drinking water were below decks with the fish. We managed to get tiny rations of water by using an upturned lid we'd fished from the flotsam to collect rain. But it hardly rained. When it did, we caught the drops with our shirts and wrung them either into the lid or straight into our mouths. Once the weather had quietened, I mopped up some water on parts of the deck that the salt-water hadn't contaminated. But there was nothing to eat and no way of getting anything, even though the sky was full of birds.

# 6

## IN THE SWARM OF THE GUN CREWS

SEVEN BELLS. WHOEVER'S STANDING UP ON THE GLOOMY DECK HAS to ring the ship's bell for the last time before he's allowed to crawl into his bunk and sleep. Then dog watch starts and for four unending hours the ship will be steered by the moaning and grumbling of men who can only think about one thing: coffee.

Yes, that would be just the thing. A mug of coffee, tar-black and as oily and fire-smelling as the stuff on these rags.

It must be at least ten pairs of rubber boots that I've piled into a heap at the other end just to make some space. One of the heavy boots keeps sliding down onto my legs or suddenly sticking between the planks and my back. There's an incredible amount of stuff crammed in here with me. An arm's length beyond the boots, there are jackets and anoraks, leather gloves, rubber gloves and fur gloves lying all mixed up, and everywhere there are rags and towels that smell like the machine room in a dead man's ship.

It's not quite as bad as that. But if the *Endurance* were to run on a reef and turn her insides out like the *John London* did on the breakwaters off Montevideo, where our wreck finally and unspectacularly ran onto a sandbank ninety nautical miles from the coast, never to move again, anyone with the opportunity to do so would wonder at all the things being washed out of Blackboro's locker. Gloves upon gloves. And so many rags, cloths and towels that you could mark out the entire route across the white continent with little black-smeared flags. On the day the *John London* ran aground, the sea was calm, the sun was shining and we were hunkered down on deck like starving cats, waiting to be spotted. All our possessions drifted in and out of the rocks around us. Five corpses, too, were given up by the wreck. Mr. Albert's wasn't one of them. It stayed in the fo'c'sle that my father had built and went down with it.

I NEVER WOULD HAVE MADE IT OFF THAT SHIP, NEVER TO MONTEVIDEO, then Buenos Aires and finally onto the *Endurance* if the ship's carpenter, Rutherford, hadn't, luckily for all of us, come to his senses. Without his moderating influence, there were at least a couple of others who wouldn't have hesitated for long before tossing those of us who'd stuck by Captain Coon into the sea.

Eight days after our shipwreck, a coastal fishing boat brought us aboard and carried us to the harbor at Montevideo. They fed us up for a few days before one morning the police arrived in the courtyard to arrest Rutherford and his gang. I remember going into the small poplar wood that belonged to the hospital and running into Captain Coon, who was taking a walk, and thinking that I'd have liked to speak to him about what had happened on board and about the arrests. But that would have been out of the question for a galley boy.

"Well, Merce, you out and about as well? Better walking than standing still," and already he had passed me. I hadn't even had time to say my "Yessir." I carried on. He called and I noticed that he was coming after me.

He had, he told me, promised my dad that he would look out for me. I didn't owe any explanations to a captain who'd lost his ship, but would I please tell him what my plans were.

I told him the truth: I had no plans.

Coon said abruptly, "Those men will have to answer to a judge for the fact that their misconduct cost the bosun and the others their lives. That'll take a few months. But if you're in agreement, I'll write to your family and tell them you're well."

I asked for time to think about it. The next day the six of us left got our pay. As we were leaving the hospital I asked Captain Coon not to write to my parents. My decision didn't surprise him. He didn't even ask for a reason. Perhaps he suspected, as he clasped my hand in the rain, that I wouldn't have been able to give him one.

MY VERY FIRST SHIP WENT UNDER. A REAL SEA DOG WOULD SAY: THIS IS A shadow you'll never shake off. Forget the sea! But I'm a sea dog as little as I am a carpenter or a lad who wants to follow in Daddy's footsteps. And if my father could see me now, cowering in a locker with a chocolate-smeared mouth, he'd use the gloves and boots to box me round the ears.

And he'd be right to do it. Why didn't I join the Navy and sign on to the *Invincible* or the *Inflexible,* battle cruisers with dorms for eight hundred sailors to hang up their hammocks? There's no loneliness there; no one gets caught up in stupid ideas. You have your gun barrel you crawl into once a day to clean it, you have your shore leave, your naval action, your burial at sea and your notice in the *South Wales Echo:*

NAVAL BATTLE WITH GERMAN FORCES
OFF THE COAST OF ARGENTINA

AMONG OUR HEROES LOST AT SEA
WAS MERCE BLACKBORO,
SON OF THE WELL-KNOWN SHIPBUILDER

That's the eighth bell sounding: rat watch is over. Now they're scampering below and shaking dog watch out of their sleep.

IN THE HARBORS ON THE RIO DE LA PLATA I DIDN'T SEE MUCH SIGN OF the war. If you believed what they wrote in the papers, it was just a matter of time before Argentina and Uruguay were infected by this spreading madness. But our euphoric animosity was something alien to the people I got to know there. Hatred for a tsar, a pair of old kings or two strange emperors who not only look alike but speak the same language, that was something they couldn't understand and that they thought of as a disturbance. And so what they called us there was troublemakers, *perturbadores*.

In La Boca, the day's business is postponed until the cooler hours of the evening. In the afternoon it's so hot that your head starts buzzing after only a few steps along the birdlime-white alleys. In our attic hotel room, Bakewell and I slept from six in the morning until six at night, and when I looked out of the window, I saw a plane tree that had no leaves but was full of tiny green birds. When there was a noise in the street, the tree's whole canopy rushed up into the air only to sink back down onto the naked branches a few moments later. Surrounded by things like that, we forgot about the war. We had better things to do. Because even if it didn't look that way, we were very busy.

We were keeping watch. Bakewell had a plan for what to do with ourselves next. The ship belonging to Sir Ernest Shackleton's Antarctic expedition had made a stop in Montevideo on its way from London to Buenos Aires, supposedly in order to take more fuel on board. But a rumor was going around the port that the real reason for the stop was that without Sir Ernest, who was going to join the crew in Argentina, discipline on board had fallen apart. How quickly that can happen—and how you only need a few to make it happen— was something I now knew from personal experience. In fact, Bakewell found out from two of the sailors, Hownow and Stornoway, that there'd been a fight on board too serious for the instigators to go unpunished. It looked as if the four responsible for the brawl would be put ashore in Montevideo. We resolved not to let the explorers out of our sight.

Our disappointment was as large as you'd expect when we came down to the pier on the day we said good-bye to Captain Coon and saw that Shackleton's ship had set off without McLeod or Hownow letting us know. The *Invincible* and the *Inflexible* had come up the Plata overnight and were riding at anchor in the center of the estuary. They lowered ever more boats that pulled, fully crewed, across to the pier. The alleys were soon swarming with gun crews and other candidates for a watery end. We took the next ferry to Buenos Aires. Two days later, in a pub called the Green Monkey, we stumbled as if by accident into a gang of men from the *Endurance*. How and McLeod were so happy to see us that they didn't think twice before pulling the bosun over to our table.

John Vincent was preceded by the reputation of being anything but a barrel of laughs. With an unpleasant grimace, he let us know that although Shackleton's second in command, Frank Wild, had struck the four brawlers off the hiring list, only Sir Ernest could decide who was going to replace them. Then he fell silent and began to hypnotize the tabletop.

When was Shackleton coming, Bakewell wanted to know.

Vincent didn't even look at him but instead turned and said to McLeod, "The boss gets here when he gets here, right?"

McLeod nodded. "Course. But they're good lads, the pair of them. They were on a coffin ship and put in an excellent show when it went under. You could put in a good word for them."

Vincent looked at me, and for the first time his broad, eerily smooth face was right in front of mine.

"This one's far too young, first of all." He stood up. "If the two of you are excellent seamen, make yourselves excellently useful until the boss gets here, and he'll decide if he wants to hire you or not."

For his part, Bakewell could be fairly sure of having a job on the *Endurance* as good as in his pocket, but I, on the other hand, had to worry that Shackleton would leave me behind. Not long after this first conversation with Vincent, Bakie told me openly that he'd fallen in love with the idea of going to the Antarctic. He didn't hide the fact that he'd go without me if he had to.

In the meantime, we put the finishing touches to the ship. The *Endurance* got a coat of black paint and was reprovisioned. The noise started when the sled dogs arrived. A Canadian freighter so dirty you had to wonder if it had sailed through an ocean of filth made fast alongside and brought out its crane. The beasts were swung on board two to a cage and locked into the kennels, sixty-nine mongrels from near the North Pole, no two of them alike, unless you count that they're all enormous and only halfway tame at best. The strongest are part-dog, part-wolf, and the two pack leaders are called Shakespeare and Bosun, which, at least in the harbor at Buenos Aires, never led to any confusion.

Vincent must have soon recognized that he'd made a find in Bakewell, who lent a hand everywhere and was always in the right place. With the arrival of Frank Hurley, the Australian expedition photographer, the crew was at full strength, with the exception of Shackleton himself, and they moved into quarters on board. The first officer, Greenstreet, asked me if it was true that I'd sailed as a mess boy and, when I said yes, asked if I'd like to be the cook's assistant for the time being. But I still didn't get a berth on the ship, and even though they would have set one up for him, Bakewell, too, continued to sleep at our small hotel. It was nothing to do with me, he said. He just needed his daily whiff of bird crap.

Which reminds me that I'm starting to need to go to the toilet myself. For water I've still got the empty bottle, but I get the sense that the chocolate, too, would like to make an exit, the way it's making these rumbles in my belly. The sea has somehow got into my guts overnight, mixed itself with the smell of rubber and the knowledge that we're out on the waves, and given me a greasy, queasy sense of seasickness. My face must be verging on green by now, just like Green's does when he stands in the full heat of the galley stove and, spotted with a light sprinkling of sweat, stirs his genuine turtle soup.

Push it away, don't think about it.

If need be I'll crap in a boot and then stuff it with towels.

The turtle soup is served in the Ritz. The Ritz is the former cargo hold and the current mess. It's the biggest room on the *Endurance*, her heart, her center. It would easily pass for a corridor if there weren't tables and chairs for thirty men in there. The Union Jack and all the Empire's other flags are hanging from the walls, which is lucky, because the wainscoting is one big bungle. After a couple of days of lugging pots I knew every raised threshold and every not-quite-flush screw from the far end to the galley. But the Ritz's clientele greeted our turtle starter with loud cheers, and Captain Worsley asked the room what Shackleton would say if he found out how Green and Black were spoiling the men.

A few days ago, everyone was waiting to see Shackleton, and now I'm the only one who still hasn't. I haven't laid eyes on him yet, and that's not likely to change while I'm crouching in this locker. It's pretty unlikely that Sir Ernest will come on deck during dog watch to get himself an oilskin jacket or a piece of chocolate.

Rubber boots? Take these ones, sir. They're still warm.

But I wouldn't even be sitting here and the heroes of the Antarctic wouldn't have me round their necks if Shackleton hadn't been too fine to tell me to my face: "Boy, I can't take you with me. You're not grown up."

Everyone knew that once Shackleton arrived, it would only be a matter of hours before they cast off. But no one was waiting for him the way I was. I tried not to make it obvious, something I couldn't quite manage. I kept being overcome with self-pity while clearing the plates. Then it was usually the biologist, Bob Clark, who clapped his hand on my shoulder and said, "It'll be fine." Or Green shouted, "Get going, lads. You've all had enough. Make sail for somewhere else. Let Blackie clear away the wreckage, or do you want to do it yourselves instead?"

One evening I got drunk with Hownow. He told me his whole life story and dragged me off to a brothel that, thank God, was fully booked. The others wound me up about it when we ran into them in

La Boca and got a vicious tongue-lashing from the skipper for their trouble.

I'd have accepted anything, because I had already pictured every single possibility, just not what actually happened, which was suddenly finding out that Shackleton was already on board. I heard it from Green, who assumed I'd known like everyone else, and the first thing I did was tell Bakewell, who was flabbergasted.

Shackleton had come aboard early that morning. He was said to have inspected the provisions and the equipment, taken a look at the dogs and the motorized sleds and then disappeared into his cabin to rest. Since that afternoon, he'd been meeting the men there one at a time.

And almost all of them had already been in to see him: Green, How, McLeod, the researchers, the doctors and the boilermen. When those still left were signaled over with a nod or a quick call, they put down their glasses and left the Ritz wordlessly. I'd finished my work and sat at the table. Mrs. Chippy, the cat that belonged to the ship's carpenter, Chippy McNeish, was running across on the tabletop to make her evening rounds. Frank Hurley was dismantling a camera and cleaning its parts. A trio were playing cards. The giant Tom Crean, bearer of the Albert Medal for courage on Scott's last expedition, my brother's idol, gave me a wink. These men who had been all over the world, who knew Amundsen himself and who, had there been only a handful of them on board, would have made sure the *John London* didn't sink, did everything they could to make me feel that I'd soon be one of them.

Despite that, I could think of only one thing. I thought of old Simms and his warning. That's what I've become, I thought. Despite everything, I've become the patsy.

When Bakewell returned to the Ritz, I saw from his face what the verdict was going to be. We went on deck. He said he'd signed on. And that Sir Ernest didn't want to take responsibility for me. He was sorry, but at seventeen I was just too young.

"Fine," I said, as coldly as I could. "When are you off?"

We were standing in a dark corner by the gunwale. In the gloom I could see only Bakewell's silhouette. He was looking out at the water, not saying anything, and in the quiet I could hear the dogs scrabbling in their kennels before they balled themselves up to sleep.

Suddenly he said in a different voice, "Listen, Merce. Just listen and keep your mouth shut while I tell you something. We're casting off tomorrow morning and when I say *we,* I mean you and me. I already spoke to McLeod and How—they're in on it. You go get your stuff and wait on the pier at three o'clock. How and me come on watch at four. You two go below decks and McLeod'll show you the oilskin locker. You stay there until we're out at sea and I come get you."

I didn't have much time to think about it. There was no more reason for me to be on board and the night watches were about to begin.

"Okay, it's down to you," he said. "It's a tricky thing, I see that. Listen: I've gotta go below because otherwise the bosun'll wonder what's going on. Let's do it like this. You count to a hundred and think it over. Then you either come below and say good-bye like a good boy to your old friend Bakie, who loves you dearly, which you hopefully haven't forgotten, or . . . you get your little wooden fish and the rest of your stuff and make sure you're on the pier at three sharp."

"I've got the fish with me," I said truculently.

"Well then, you've only got half as much to think about."

With that, he ran his hand over my scalp and went.

And I began to count.

But . . . it's impossible to think something over while you're counting. All you have in your mind's eye are erratically dancing numbers. What's more, counting always makes me think of Mr. Muldoon's red book, then I think of Ennid and am already feeling sad. And I didn't want to be sad or to feel sorry for myself. I didn't want it!

So I forgot about counting and instead asked myself what I'd have to do to make myself content and perhaps even happy.

Two things occurred to me: firstly, to sail with Bakie to somewhere where there's no war. And, secondly, to get to know the man everyone talked about with lowered voices: Shackleton.

# 7

## BOILERMAN'S HANDS

I MUST HAVE FALLEN ASLEEP AFTER ALL. WHAT WAS THAT? SOMEONE'S fiddling with the lockers.

What did he say . . . the coal bunker?

Coal bunkers . . . It must be one of the stokers or, no, both of them. Yes, by their voices I'd say it's them, Holness and Stevenson. If they're both here at the lockers that means they've put out the fires and the ship is running under sail.

We're far out at sea now, no land for miles and miles.

"Or do you want a heap of coal to come pelting towards us the first time we slosh about a bit in the soup? Let me tell you, if a ton of those clinkers decides it wants out of the bunker to stretch its legs, that means only one thing."

"And what's that?" Holness is the younger of the two, and because Stevenson is allowed to call himself the chief stoker, Holness, whether he likes it or not, gets the title of ordinary stoker. "Come on, then, give me some advice, Stevie. You know I can't live without your little bits of wisdom."

"Just laugh, you rat. Take a look at this . . . my trousers. Brand-new and already ripped, and what a rip. What filthy rotten luck."

"So what do you do when all that coal's coming towards you? You run away, don't you? I mean, standing still probably wouldn't work out so well."

"Wouldn't work out." Stevenson's laughter is like the bleating of a goat.

45

He's standing directly in front of my locker. I have to hide. But where? The best I can do is put myself behind the jackets.

"You really think you can run away from a ton of coal? You think it'll be tired from lying down so long? You know what I'm going to be doing while you're running away?"

"Why don't you tell me?"

"I'll be wondering which shovel I'm going to use to scrape you off the wall."

"Oh, yeah, and where will you be wondering it?"

"That's what you'd like to know. Tell me instead what I should do with these trousers. Take a look at that. I must have caught them somewhere."

Stevenson mutters a word that would have sent my mother bright pink with embarrassment.

And Holness mumbles, "Sew it. Patch on, then sew it up."

"You know what, I'd thought of that, too. And where am I supposed to get a patch from?"

"Have a look at the oilskins. There'll be some clean cloth in there."

The game's up. They'll open the door any minute. And there aren't even any clean cloths in here. They're all covered in tar.

"So what're you going to do?" Holness wants to know. His first name is Ernest, like Shackleton. He's only a couple of years older than me and once told me that he has twelve brothers and sisters. I've got nothing to fear from Holie. Stevenson, on the other hand, you have to be careful with, and not just because he belongs to the bosun's little gang.

"I'm going to take my trousers off, what does it look like?"

"What are you going to do when the bunker breaks, I mean. If you don't run, what are you going to do instead?"

"Jump, Holness. Jump up to the ceiling and hold on somewhere, that's the only chance you've got. Those damn clinkers'll roll through the whole room and bury everything they can, believe you me. So have a look at the ceiling next time you're in there feeding the boiler and make sure you know which pipes you can hang onto without them burning your hands off. If you don't do that straight away—oh . . . which one's the oilskins?"

"This one."

The door opens. All at once it's bright as day. So bright that tears jump to my eyes even though I'm squeezing them shut. And I really need to see how it looks where I've been lying.

"So if you don't do that straight away, you might never get another chance, because . . . Wait, have a look at this. It's a pit in here. And what's that?"

Holness says, "A water bottle. And it's smeared in something. It's not . . . No, it isn't, we'd smell it. Looks like tar. Or chocolate."

"Chocolate," repeats Stevenson. "In the wet-weather locker. There hasn't been someone eating in here, has . . . Hang on. I don't believe it. There's someone in there."

"What, where is there someone?"

"There, look! That's a pair of feet, or are those not feet?"

They feel my feet, then the jackets are pulled aside and I open my eyes.

Holness and Stevenson stare at me. Holness seems relieved, as though he'd been expecting something worse, maybe a body. Stevenson is anything but happy, judging by the glowering of his face and how tightly he's gripping my upper arm.


"BLACKBORO," IS ALL THAT HOLNESS SAYS BEFORE GRABBING ME UNDER the other arm and helping me out of the locker. My knees wobble, I feel ready to throw up and Stevenson is squeezing my arm off.

"Jesus, how long've you been in there? You're as green as a leek."

"Just wait and see how he looks once Vincent's through with him."

Stevenson finally lets go. He plants himself in front of me and watches Holness prop me up on the bench below the row of lockers.

He chucks me under the chin and smiles, Holness from Hull, Holie the cinder monkey, who's just stopped being the youngest man on board.

"Where are we?" I ask up at Stevenson, but he doesn't answer.

"Eight days from South Georgia," Holness eventually says, while aiming a vague nudge at Stevenson. He shakes his head and has to laugh. Stevenson doesn't share his sense of the absurd. He just stares.

Holie says, "You haven't missed anything. Except I suppose that a motor sled went overboard when Orde-Lees was—"

Stevenson interrupts him. "Stop that. It's got nothing to do with him. Creeping on board. Needs a good leathering." While looking again at the hole in his trousers, he leans down to me. "Where did you get the grub from, huh? Don't you know that everything is rationed, dickhead?"

"Simmer down," I say. "It was my tack."

"It was my tack, it was my tack," he mimics me and bleats out his goat-laugh again. "Sits here in a locker and stuffs his face with chocolate like a little brat while we're lugging coal day and night. Makes me sick. I'm getting the bosun."

"Come on, Stevenson, be fair," I say to him. "I haven't done anything to you. Get Bakewell instead."

He doesn't even think about it. But before he can catch his breath to really bawl me out, Holness says, "That's not going to happen, Blackboro. We're fair, but we're not going to risk that. If Stevenson agrees, you can choose between the bosun and the skipper. What do you think, Stevie?"

Stevenson mumbles something but doesn't disagree. So it's up to me.

"Get the captain," I say.

Once Stevenson's gone, I try to stand up. But my legs have fallen asleep.

WHILE WE WAIT FOR WORSLEY, HOLNESS TELLS ME THAT THE SHIP LEFT Argentinian territorial waters a few hours ago. We're currently about seven hundred nautical miles northwest of the Falklands. Shackleton's quite worried, says Holness, because the weather's unusually damp for this latitude, a sign that summer hasn't yet begun in the Antarctic. The Weddell Sea must still be frozen solid. No chance of getting through that.

"People are saying," Holness says while he stretches my legs and kneads my calves, "that we'll be stuck in South Georgia for at least four weeks before we can even think about getting further south. And even then it'll be pretty bumpy."

He's talking about the pack ice. In the course of the Antarctic summer, which begins in December, the ice withdraws to far inside the circumference of the Antarctic Circle. The later the summer, the slower that mass of ice melts and retreats.

Holness, too, has caught ice fever. I saw it in my brother when he read Scott's diaries and I also saw Bakewell let himself get infected by Crean and Cheetham and by all the stories from the other Antarctic veterans, to the point where he couldn't talk about anything but glaciers, depot tents and leopard seals. One night he sat bolt-upright in bed and, as though it were running under full sail straight through our attic room, shouted the name of Shackleton's previous ship: *"Nimrod!"*

"How's that?" asks Holness, meaning my legs.

"Good," I say, meaning: wonderful, never stop.

I ask him after Bakewell. Bakewell's doing excellently. In the last few days, he, Stornoway and Hownow have often seemed like they were cooking something up together.

"And now I know what it was."

For me, the Weddell Sea, the pack ice and the leopard seals are as distant as Wales. Crabeater seals seem as real to me right now as King Arthur or flying ace William Bishop. In that sense, Stevenson's right to treat me as if I don't fit in and am therefore not one of them. The Antarctic means nothing to me in comparison with Ennid Muldoon. In fact, I'd happily rename the whole thing Ennid-Muldoon

Land. But I'm getting an inkling that that'll change as soon as I'm standing in front of Shackleton.

I ask Holness if he's ever seen an iceberg.

"Come on, let's walk a few paces," he says, and I stand up. Of course he's seen icebergs, but in the Northern Atlantic, where they aren't the same as they are here, they're smaller and a different color.

For my first steps after two days of cowering and crouching, the *Endurance*'s slight port-side roll makes me feel like I'm walking on marbles, and instead of knees I have hinges halfway down my legs. That many icebergs aren't white but blue, blue like a summery sky, or green as a bottle or even as red as sunburned skin, is something Tom Crean told me one evening in the Ritz. Holness lets me sit down again. I make an old-man noise and he laughs.

"You'll be fine. In a couple of hours you'll be dancing up the rigging. And you'll see your first iceberg soon enough. I hope so, anyway. I'd like it if you stayed aboard."

"That isn't up to me, unfortunately. But thanks all the same, Holness."

Because he's got nothing more to do, he starts to knead his hands against each other.

"Because it's not just in the water that there's a heap of icebergs," he says. "The ship's full of them. If you know what I mean."

# 8

## "How are you, Mr. Blackboro?"

I KNOW WHAT THE GENTLE BOILERMAN HOLIE MEANS. FOR ALL that I wouldn't have a clue about what makes icebergs different colors—until Tom Crean explains to me that the green and red ice is because of two different species of microscopic algae, while blue ice is pure glacier ice that consists almost completely of water, whereas normal ice is white because it contains so much air—I know precisely, without an ice giant like Tom Crean having to tell me, which three types of iceberg I've got in front of me when Stevenson, Vincent and Captain Worsley come in the door.

The stoker is green from the poisonous coal dust, the bosun is red from high blood pressure and Captain Worsley's whole demeanor is as blue as his jacket: he's a cold-blooded man. His friendliness is as cool as his authority. The few times that I've had the opportunity to observe the skipper of the *Endurance,* I've felt the need to talk to him. I would so gladly have got him to speak to me for once instead of just sizing me up in passing. Well, I suppose I've got my wish, though I don't feel particularly chuffed to have his eyes on me in this instant.

"Thank you, Holness," he says without moving his gaze off me, and steps closer. Holness gives me a clap on the back before squeezing between Stevenson and Vincent and making himself scarce.

"How are you, Mr. Blackboro?"

"Thank you, sir, I'm fine."

"You must be half starved. And it's quite cold down here." He goes over to the locker. "You were in here."

51

It isn't a question, it's a finding.

He bends over into the cupboard and looks around it. "Fine. So now you're here."

Nothing else occurs to me. I say, "Yes, sir."

Vincent, who doesn't dignify me even with a glance, considers himself required to help the skipper along: "Who's supposed to clear out the muck in the locker?"

Worsley pulls his head out of the cupboard and says, "Stevenson—" so that the boilerman misunderstands and starts to protest: all he did was find me. He didn't have anything to do with smuggling me on board. Why should he be responsible for my crap?

"Stevenson," Worsley calmly begins again, "you're off duty. Use the time to get some sleep. I have to speak to the bosun and Mr. Blackboro. Have you passed your report on the defective coal bunker on to the ship's carpenter?"

"Aye, sir. McNeish is taking care of it."

"Then go and get some sleep."

Stevenson imagined this turning out differently. He went to Vincent anyway despite what I asked for, and now he's not even allowed to watch him chew me out. He gives me a last glare and then walks away.

"John, would you repeat your question, please," says the skipper, and Vincent repeats his hostile formulation. Now that he's alone with the miscreant and the executor of the law, which on the high seas is the captain, the blood rushes to his head in rage that I've dared disregard Shackleton's refusal to take me along.

But that's not the real reason for the bosun's fury, which must be as predictable as it is transparent if even a simple soul like Stevenson can manipulate it. In truth, what makes John Vincent furious is that I didn't pay attention to the rebuff he gave me in the harborside pub. How does that make him look? Shackleton's got nothing to do with it, even in the pub that was just a secondary consideration.

"But it's not even about that," he says. "If it comes to that, I'll wash the locker out myself just to make sure the oilskins are ready. Do you know what it can mean at this latitude?" he roars into my face, "if the rough-weather kit isn't ready? Well, do you? Or does a little fool like you not have any idea about things like that? What's that stupid grin for? If I put you over my knee, boy, you'll be standing in that locker, you'll be standing as straight as a brush."

At this unconventional image, the captain, who's pacing up and down between me and Vincent, has to laugh, only briefly. It almost sounds like a cough, but it's a laugh.

"John, John," he says, "you can be very funny."

Worsley stops walking and looks at me. "Of course the one who's going to clean up this locker is you. That's clear, isn't it, Blackboro?"

"Yes, sir."

"Most of the time, the oilskins are just lying around, but that doesn't mean that they aren't sometimes vitally important. Once one of the doctors has looked you over and once you've eaten and slept, our bosun will show you the brush he was just mentioning and you can scrub and tidy the locker. Shall we leave it at that? John?"

"Fair enough, Frank, sir. Does that mean he's joining my troop?"

This prospect runs a flush of heat through me and I'm just about to protest myself.

Worsley says, "That's not for me to decide, John."

He goes over to the door and opens it.

"Come with me," he says in a way you could almost call happy, and he even waves me over. Whether I can or not, I have to get up on my wobbly legs and reel around Vincent, who's standing in front of me.

"Now, get out of his way, you stubborn bastard!" the skipper calls to the bosun and, when he brings himself to do it, Worsley asks seriously, "What do you want me to do? Have the boy flogged?"

And Vincent: "I . . . No, sir."

And Worsley to me, just as seriously: "You're an Englishman, Mr. Blackboro?"

"Welsh, sir."

"Welsh! Not that, too. You know where I'm from?"

"New Zealand, sir?"

"Christchurch, right. Since you and I are both from the Empire, Merce, I can't treat you as a prisoner of war. While we go to Sir Ernest's cabin, I'll decide whether I think that's a shame. All right, get moving." He shakes his head. "Little fool, is he? A bunch of little fools, the lot of you."

# 9

## CAPTAIN SCOTT'S BLANKET

I FOLLOW THE CAPTAIN DOWN THE NARROW CORRIDOR THAT DIVIDES the lower deck of the *Endurance* lengthwise in two. We pass the entrances to the various magazines and cargo holds. In the middle of the ship's belly are the dry stores, where barrels and crates of rice, flour, sugar and salt are kept, and the bread store, which is lined with lead to keep out the mice and rats. Just next to it is the bubbling of the freshwater kettle, in whose little room there are also crates of beer, wine and spirits. We go past the sail locker, where the big spare topsail and the far smaller replacement topgallant sails are folded like shirts in a cupboard. Directly opposite is the tiny paint room, whose shelves are stacked with pots of gloss and varnish, and beneath them lie the hawsers, ropes and cables not needed on deck.

Each of these spaces is so small you can hardly turn around in it. Because Green showed me all of them, I know where Vincent's workplace is. The door to his room is open. In the dull light of a lamp hanging from the ceiling, you can make out the shelves full of marlines, yarns, plies and other whipping twines all laid out by thickness. Vincent, who's walking close behind, punches me in the back before disappearing into his pen.

Even though I can't get any air after the blow and I have to hold onto the wall so as not to fall into the captain, it'd be a cold day in hell before I let anything show.

Worsley hasn't noticed. "Come along," he says, standing on the ladder leading up to the next deck.

Or did he see the punch after all? Because once we get upstairs, he says, "The bosun and you are going to have plenty more opportunity to enjoy each other's company."

The stairs lead up between the galley and the Ritz, and I, having just climbed up from the underworld, run straight into the arms of my chief cook.

When Green sees who it is, his jaw drops and he stops dead.

"I thought you could do with some help, Charlie," says Worsley, who seems to be amusing himself more and more. "The stew yesterday evening tasted like minced dog meat."

"It was minced dog meat" is the retort from Green, who takes every criticism of his cooking personally. But seeing me on board makes him forget even this slander of his cooking. "And where's he appeared from?"

While he fills Green in, the captain pushes open the swing-door into the Ritz. I see Wordie, the geologist, and Clark, the biologist, who are meant to be scouring the floorboards but are actually just kneeling on a carpet of suds with brushes in their hands, because both are staring at the doorway where I'm standing.

"Oh ho," says Green quietly, before he calls across to the others, "This is how it works now: piss on the hiring list. Whoever wants aboard comes aboard. Where have you two hidden your assistants?"

Clark and Wordie look at each other.

"Don't have any," mumbles Clark. "You think we'd be on our knees if we did?"

And Wordie grins. "But Merce is more than welcome to take over."

"No chance. Let us through, men." Worsley points at the exit and lets me go first. "I can already see that Blackboro's in great demand. I'm just afraid there won't be much left once Sir Ernest has finished with him. Charlie, you make a coffee that'd wake the dead and take it to the boss with two cups. And we'll go have a look at what the weather's doing. Go on then, Mr. Blackboro! I've other things to do than give tours of the ship to young stowaways. Particularly Welsh ones."

There's the daylight. That's where the air's coming from. I'm not even all the way above decks before the wind blasts me in the face as if in welcome. I close my eyes and let it pull through my hair . . . Yes, it's a good feeling. Air that feels like water, cold, clear and fresh. I open my lips, swallow a lungful of it and step on deck. What a relief. Rain spatters onto the planking, I'm immediately soaked, and it seems to me that I've never experienced anything more wonderful in my life.

Where's the captain? He's standing under the canopy of the deckhouse and discussing something with Greenstreet, the first officer. The latter's upper lip stays stiff. On every side there's the sea, ruffled by the west wind and rolling deep gray for as far as the eye can see. The *Endurance* is running at full speed, battering along through the rain. They've got every sail aloft, the topsail, the upper topgallant and even the moonraker are billowing out. They look like migratory albatrosses perching up there and spreading their wings.

McLeod has noticed me but pretends to go on feeding the dogs. And only now do I see that a group of men are working on something in the bow.

"Oi, oi," I'd like to call out. "Bakewell, look over here! I'm here! Look over here, you Yankee idiot."

And I'd like to hear him say, "Holy Mary, holy keelhauled Gabriel, boar's teeth and virgin's claws. Hell's biscuits, my Blackboro's back and swearing again." And I'd like to see him, my friend, stomping over to me through the rows of snapping dogs, wringing wet, grinning widely but questioning with his eyes if I've ratted him out. You better not have . . . eh, sunshine.

"Brace the halyards," thunders Greenstreet two paces behind me, so loudly that I flinch in shock.

And I see the gang in the bow jump apart to spring up into the rigging, and now Bakewell has seen me, stretches out an arm and waves his hand in greeting.

But Greenstreet says so quietly that only I can hear, "Go see the skipper, Merce."

WORSLEY IS WAITING FOR ME AT THE ENTRANCE TO THE DECKHOUSE AND throws a woolen blanket over my shoulders. He's not too stern to mention it's one of those donated to the expedition by Scott's family. So it's a special blanket, not just because it's warm, but because Scott froze.

We go in. The deckhouse is divided in half by a narrow corridor. At the forward side, it has the captain's cabin, abaft it has Shackleton's. The doors to the two rooms are opposite each other. Worsley would like me to wait in his cabin while he speaks to Sir Ernest. He closes his door and I hear him knocking on the one opposite.

On the narrow shelf above the berth there are five blue books, all by Dickens. The rain slaps against the porthole. Outside lies the ragged surface of the sea and above it the unending milky sky. A single picture hangs by the door. The small drawing is of a rider who, as his horse rears up beneath him, is turning back and leaning far out of his saddle to pull a child up onto it.

Worsley comes in. He closes the door, takes off his jacket and hangs it on the chair by his writing desk.

"Sit down," he says, and turns the chair around. "We're waiting. He'll let us know when you're to go over."

He doesn't seem to know what to do with me now. A discussion of what happens next would be superfluous; that's for Shackleton to decide. Worsley looks at the spots of chocolate on my clothes and watches the water dripping from my hair onto Scott's blanket. Then he hands me a towel.

While passing it to me, he says, "There was an advert in the papers that Sir Ernest placed. Ever hear about it?"

Crean told Bakewell what it said, but since it seems smart to avoid mentioning Bakewell right now, I lie and say no.

Worsley picks up a leather briefcase from the desk and pulls out a cutting from the sheaf inside, which he holds in front of my nose.

### NOTICE
Men wanted for hazardous journey.
Small wages. Bitter cold.
Long months of complete darkness.
Constant danger. Safe return doubtful.
Honor and recognition in case of success.
Ernest Shackleton

"More than five thousand people replied to that," says Worsley, and puts the briefcase away. "Aside from a few he already wanted to have with him—Frank Wild, Tom Crean, Alf Cheetham and the sailor McLeod, who've all been south before and gathered plenty experience there, as well as George Marston and Frank Hurley, whose painting and photography he admires very, very highly—aside from them, every man on this ship responded to that announcement and was personally chosen by Sir Ernest himself."

With that he lets me know that even he, the captain, has had to pass through the eye of a needle in being interviewed by Shackleton. Is that meant to demonstrate how hopeless my situation is? Or, on the contrary, does he want to encourage me by making it clear that Shackleton treats everyone the same way, from the lowest navvy to the captain?

"Sir," I say, "can I say something?"

"Go to it. But would you be good enough finally to dry yourself off? I'm not going to do it for you, you know."

"No, I'm doing it. Thank you, sir."

I towel my hair, neck and face dry.

"I didn't see the advert when it came out in the paper, and even if I'd read it, I wouldn't have put myself forward. I'd have thought what all of you are thinking now, that I'm far too young and inexperienced. Not to mention that my father would never have let me go if it said 'Safe return doubtful.' The towel, sir, where shall I put it?"

He hangs it over the doorknob. Worsley's expression has turned serious and he looks at me in expectation.

"But now everything's different," I say.

"The dangers, Blackboro, are the same as they were, and you are not an adult. Someone will have to take responsibility for you. Though that, in my opinion, needn't be the deciding factor. I went to sea at fifteen." At the thought of that, his expression lightens again.

"I know the men, I know the ship, I know the plan and want to help achieve it," I say, and realize as I do that I sound pathetic.

Worsley notices, too. He shakes his head. "I don't believe it."

"I thought it was unfair that I was the only one Sir Ernest wouldn't speak to. That's the real reason I sneaked on board and I'm not scared of telling Sir Ernest that to his face, either. Also, I really do want to help him."

"You should mind your temper, that's the advice I'll give you. You shouldn't speak to Sir Ernest like that."

"He's the hero," I say, and already wish I hadn't.

Luckily, Worsley doesn't allow himself to be provoked. He just asks whether I doubt that Shackleton is a hero.

"No."

"No, sir," he corrects me.

I'm afraid I've annoyed him, and he doesn't say anything else. And then there's a knock at the door. On the threshold stands Green, dripping rain, holding the coffee and saying in his high, whistling voice that I'm to come across. Behind him, the door to Sir Ernest's cabin is open.

I pull the blanket off my shoulders and am immediately cold. Worsley takes it from me but doesn't look at me as he does so.

His face seems frozen, as though it were the tip of the iceberg he has turned himself back into. The rider in the picture, I wonder, what's he saving the child from? Both faces show the same panic and dismay.

"You can carry this yourself," says Green, and pushes the tray into my stomach. In the drafty corridor, I can hear the rain thrashing against the deckhouse doors.

# 10

## SHACKLETON

TRAY IN MY HANDS, I TAKE THREE STEPS INTO THE ROOM. I
don't want to spill anything, that really would be a disaster.
But right at that moment the ship rolls heavily to port and it
takes all my balance to keep the pot and cups horizontal.

As soon as I'm past him, Green wheezes behind me, "Here he
is, sir."

I hear the door close and am alone with Shackleton.

The walls, bed, table, chair and shelves are white. Pale light falls
into the cabin through a large porthole above the berth. Shackleton
is standing at his desk reading a book. He's wearing heavy, laced
boots and thick trousers with suspenders over a dense gray jumper.
He's older than I'd imagined, much smaller, too, so that even without
stretching I can see the skin gleaming through the thin hair on his
scalp. I thought he'd be a tall, long-bodied, fine-limbed man full of
energy and vigor, lithe and comfortable in himself, one whose experiences I'd recognize instantly in his bearing. Not at all. Suddenly I
realize that imagining Shackleton, I'd been thinking of Mr. Albert, the
bosun on the *John London*. Shackleton is completely different—
stronger, stockier, almost slightly bloated looking. In front of me
stands a mature man in his middle years, a man like my father, who
also seems at first glance to be dour and sluggish, though in fact he's
not like that at all—quite the opposite. Shackleton turns around, anything but tired, while I try to catch my breath, and before I can stand
up straight and greet him properly, he hurls the book he's holding in

my direction. The tome flies past my head and crashes into the wall behind me.

"Put that down," he roars, advancing on me with his sparkling light-green eyes wrenched wide open. For an instant I don't understand what he means. I've totally forgotten the tray I'm still holding.

"Put that down or I'll knock it out of your hands."

"Yes, sir! Where, sir?"

He doesn't stop shouting. The tray with the steaming-hot pot of coffee on it makes him doubly furious. He curses me along with the pot, the cook, the rain, me again, my getup, my age and my shameless impudence, boys who dare disobey him, the cook, the pot, me, my long hair, this God-awful weather, my stupid face, the idiot sailors who dare to . . . , his cabin, where there isn't even space for a pot, my parents, the two boilermen, my bottomless cheek and the weather that makes it impossible to take the ship . . . , me and the pot . . .

"Sir, if you please, I'll put . . ."

"Do not interrupt me!" he roars, before falling silent.

He paces the cramped white room. I retreat towards the door and can't tear my eyes off him. What a scene. Here, throwing a tantrum right in front of me, is Sir Ernest Shackleton, one of the most famous men in England, Scott's only true rival, and somewhere in this small, swaying, water-surrounded room we're encountering each other in, there'll be a Bible dedicated by the Queen Mother in her own handwriting, the former Queen of half the world, and all of us, Shackleton, the men, Her Majesty's Bible and I, are all on our way to the Antarctic. Let him take the whole *Encyclopaedia Britannica* from where it's stacked here and there on the floor and the shelves and lob it at my head one volume at a time. What wonderful luck. I can't believe it.

"What are you goggling at?" he shouts. "Are you an idiot? You must be an idiot. Who do you think I am that I would . . . How old are you?"

"Seventeen, sir."

"What have you been trained to do?"

"I was trained by my father, sir. He's a shipbuilder in Newport, Wales."

"Have you been to sea?"

"On the USS *John London,* sir. She went down in a storm off—"

"As what?"

"As what, sir?"

Shackleton responds in Gaelic, because Gaelic is both our language. The only thing is that he speaks Irish Gaelic and I speak Welsh, Cymric. So I'm not quite sure if I understand him correctly when he asks, "Nach dtig leat na ceisteanna is simplí a fhreaghairt, a amadaín?"

It sounds like he's asking, "Can't you answer the simplest questions, dummy?"

"Any, sir."

"Any what?"

"I'll answer any question, sir."

"But not any question correctly."

"No, not that, sir. But I'll try."

"Because someone who can answer any question correctly, that person would be omniscient!" he roars again. "Are you omniscient?"

"No, sir."

"As what did you sail? As a dummy? *A amadaín?*"

"Perhaps, sir. Probably, sir. And also as a kitchen boy."

The last thing he needs, says Shackleton, is a kitchen boy who disobeys instructions. What he needs is men with brains and experience, men who can take responsibility for their own lives as well as for those of their comrades, strong, brave men with heart and with wits, men for whom *comradeship* is no empty word, who are ready to put themselves at the service of an effort, an effort whose aim is nothing less than sounding the deeps of hope.

"Hope. Understood, sir."

Whether I know what his motto is. "Never lower the flag! Or, in Tennyson's words: To strive, to seek, to find, and not to yield!"

So with a bit of luck I might be able to piece together why the ship I've crept onto uninvited, which used to be called *Polaris,* has been renamed *Endurance.*

I say, "Yes, I can see why, sir," but am thinking, those are just words, what bollocks is this? And again he flies into a rage.

You could never give anything up, nothing, not the least. Neither yourself nor any other person, nobody! That was the aim, and that aim was untouchable and inviolable. You could live without arms, without legs, without eyes, without any faith or a single penny in your pocket as long as you held onto an aim with which you did justice to yourself and to everyone around you. The aim didn't have to be impressive, not everybody could be a Wright or a Pasteur and, ultimately, crossing the frozen end of our planet was as quotidian an ambition as millions of others when you considered how easily an albatross would do it. Whether I have a girl in Wales, he wants to know.

I hesitate but nod.

"The miserable creature," he mocks. "What's her name?"

I tell him.

So what am I doing here? he wants to know. Love is always an adventure. Because I've got it all backwards if I think he wants to be the brainless head of a gang of adventurers. The last thing he needs are egotistical, fame-obsessed renegades, but that's exactly what I am: a renegade. And an enormous cretin, too.

What's wrong with me? I can't put up any resistance. I feel the need to howl climbing up my throat.

Just keep it together a little longer, Merce. Can you do that, Merce? Can't you do that?

"Sir, if you please, I'll put the tray down on your bunk. Shall I serve some coffee and leave you alone?"

Shackleton stands at the porthole and stares out of it. He does not make a satisfied impression. He has left as good as none of my happiness intact. If it were my father I'd say, Shame, Dad, shame you're such a stubborn git.

Shame, Sir Ernest, we could have enjoyed each other's company.

"The greatest problems out on the ice," he says quietly, "are all determined by the cold. It'll go down to seventy degrees below, if we're unlucky. Our tents and suits are made of the best material that there is, and the cold shouldn't be able to reach us. But that's only true as long as we're able to keep ourselves warm by having enough to eat. Do you understand what I'm saying to you?"

"I know what hunger can do, sir. Not on the ice, but on a wreck. After eight days some of the men were all but ready to fall on the others."

He makes no reply to that. Instead, he moves abruptly and in two paces is directly in front of me. I can't go any further back. A quiet clinking from the tray betrays me: I'm shaking, and not only with cold and exhaustion.

"Are you afraid?" he asks, and looks me in the eye before bending over to pick up the book.

"In the locker, sir, I was afraid," I say, as he stands up and inspects the book's spine for damage. He takes the book over to his desk and puts it down beside the typewriter that glints in the light from the porthole.

"You've got good reason to be afraid." He comes back, takes the tray out of my hands and puts it on his berth. "Young man, I swear to you by bell, book and candle that when we run out of food you'll be the first we butcher and carve into steaks. Is that a worthwhile ambition for this life of yours?"

"No, sir, but I'll take my chances."

"Report to Captain Worsley."

"Yes, sir."

"And stop grinning this instant."

"I'll never grin again, sir."

"Now, get out."

There is a smile playing across his lips. Shackleton is smiling, and in the same instant it seems to me that the rain stops, as though there were no longer any reason for even the heavens to be weeping.

# 11
## INTRODUCTIONS

THE RAIN OVER THE SEA TURNS INTO SNOW. THE WANING east wind scatters thick flakes before it, and because it isn't cold enough, they don't stick on deck, but melt almost at once, coating everything and everyone with a cool, damp glaze. There's a Christmas-like quiet over the dark, calm water as the flakes melt soundlessly into it, and if you look up the masts, it really seems that you're looking into the crowns of three fir trees in a whirl of snow. The ship holds a steady course on this almost magical sea, and I don't think I'm wrong in suspecting that the other men, too, are more thoughtful than a couple of days ago, that each of them is in his own way performing his duties in a festive mood. Those on watch on deck or taking care of the dogs and, of course, the angels above us who become invisible in the white swirl after only a few yards' ascent into the rigging, all of them are wearing oilskins from my former hiding place. My hiding place, something it isn't anymore . . . though on a few of the yellow hoods hurrying past me on deck I do now and then see a dark stain, a remnant of Bakewell's chocolate that must have eluded me on the cleaning detail.

Captain Worsley has assigned me a bunk in the same space as Bakewell, How and Holness. After being examined by Dr. McIlroy, who declared me "basically healthy, fairly exhausted, and clearly suffering from delusions of grandeur," I slept a whole day before starting my kitchen duties beside Green in the evening. He still doesn't have a

69

good word to say to me but is beginning to thaw out upon seeing, to his surprise, the happiness almost everyone on board greets me with. Some come past the galley as if by chance, marvel at me like at a delicious steak and probably wouldn't hesitate to jab me with a fork if Green had more of a sense of humor and didn't drive them back into the Ritz.

As I come through the door with my first official terrine, a deafening noise of jubilation breaks out. Apart from Shackleton and Worsley, who listen smiling, and Vincent and his hunched companions, everyone joins in the hooting. There's a well-intentioned hail of claps and nudges from all sides, and it's difficult for me not to spill anything. Part of the crew starts singing "God Save Our Gracious Merce." Eventually Worsley brings the jamboree to a close by calling out: "Gentlemen, enough! Let's taste what Green and Black have conjured up for us."

Finally, Green himself appears in the doorway and shoots me a stern look across Shackleton's round table, ordering this false Merlin back into the galley.

"How is it, sir?" he asks the captain with an unmistakable undertone. Just because he holds his grudges so tightly, it's better not to get on the wrong side of Mother Green in the first place.

"Excellent, Charlie. What is it? It can't be minced dog meat."

"No, sir. It's wolf ragout."

The jibes go back and forth a few more times between the cook and the captain until Shackleton exercises his authority and asks for quiet.

He stands up. Leaning slightly forwards and moving his gaze around the tables, he gives a little speech that is interrupted only by Dr. McIlroy and, later, by Mrs. Chippy. "Well, the baptism has been done. Gentlemen, I thank you for accepting Blackboro. In my estimation, he's a fine lad, and he has promised to pitch in diligently wherever he's needed. That, my dear Mr. Green, will initially be in your galley. But because I am an old man . . ."

70

"You're forty, sir, hardly over the hill," says McIlroy, and I think: Forty! He looks ten years older.

"If only you knew," says Shackleton. "But be that as it may, as well as serving in the kitchen, Blackboro will also lend me a hand personally. Treat him well. All of you! The best would be for you to see that we are now twenty-eight, a crew like a February, and we even have the snow to match it. Would you be so kind, Mr. Hurley, as to take a photograph of the illustrious company that will now come to its feet."

We all stand up simultaneously from the chairs, which makes such a racket that the cat spits and leaps in a single arc from the table into the corridor's entrance. His glass raised, Shackleton watches her go.

We toast the King, everyone drinks a glass of port and then we disperse into our berths, to watch on deck or, like Green and me, to do the dishes.

Since then it's been there, this festive atmosphere on board. And who can be feeling more festive than I am? Shackleton announced it: only with me is the crew complete, and my being not the last one but the one who brings the crew up to strength, that's a message even the bosun must have understood, albeit that not so much as a single wrinkle in his face betrayed any kind of attention or interest.

I'm the twenty-eighth man, the twenty-eighth of February. Depending on how you consider it, Antarctic or non-Antarctic, I'm either a summer's or a winter's day, a warm breeze or a cutting, freezing headwind.

THE SNOW WORKS CONSCIENTIOUSLY AT PAINTING THE SHIP WHITE. Every day a slightly thicker coat sticks to the deck, and if you aren't careful, large shovelfuls of snow fall out of the topgallant and down your neck. Every day it becomes more distinct, the maps say it, the air says it and more than anything our mood says it: we're approaching Antarctic waters. Three more days and we'll reach Grytviken on South Georgia.

In the meantime, at least a dozen snow-dusted jack-tars have pulled me aside when believing themselves unobserved and tried to interrogate me. Every one of them is burning to know how I pulled it off, how I won Sir Ernest over and soothed him so completely that he made me his personal steward right off the bat.

I don't know, is what I say to them. Shackleton and I just talked for a while. I shrug my shoulders and wear an impartial expression. And that's not a pretense.

"I don't have the foggiest of what I'm supposed to do for him," I say a dozen times. "Maybe keep his cabin clean. What more can I tell you?"

Jock Wordie, our geologist, is in the process of labeling a compartmentalized rock-sample box that McNeish has made for him. His metal-rimmed glasses have been pushed up onto his bald head and the tip of his tongue sticks out of his mouth as he glues the strips of paper, each printed with tiny letters, down onto the wooden frame. He presses them home with his fingernails and sometimes makes a rumbling noise of agreement when I speak about Shackleton.

The walls of the cabin that Wordie shares with Clark, the biologist, and that both of them call "Auld Reekie," is hung with myriad small photographs and postcards of whale flukes, mountain peaks, still lifes and scantily clad, exuberantly voluptuous young ladies. Hundreds of enigmatic objects often smaller than my thumb are heaped around the frames of both berths. Are they stones or bones? Maybe both. They look like the splinters kept in the miniature glass coffins that are embedded into the walls of St. Woolo's Cathedral in Newport, near the back entrance from Gurney Road.

Jock Wordie is the first to tell me the story of how he became a member of Shackleton's crew: on the recommendation of his Cambridge supervisor, Raymond Priestley, who was Shackleton's geologist on the 1907 Antarctic expedition on the *Nimrod*. It slowly dawns on me that there's a kind of Antarctic line of succession.

"He probably doesn't know himself yet what he's going to do

with you," Wordie says phlegmatically, and tips the box over so that he can weigh down its reverse with a couple of books. "But you can count on it that the time'll come when you know all there is about what he wants you to do. So, I'm finished here and have to take a look at the dogs. Do you need a book?"

There's a rumor on board that Wordie advanced Shackleton money from his own pocket to buy fuel in Buenos Aires. In general, there's a lot of talk about money, mainly about the lack of it. Somewhere below decks there's meant to be a crate with a radio receiver, but, according to the rumor, it might as well be as empty as Wordie's rock box, because the money didn't stretch to a transmitter. A plausible explanation for why there's no radio operator: no radio.

If there were one, our physicist, James, would probably also operate it. Jimmy James is a reticent, endearing man who can explain something to you thirty times in a row without ever giving you the feeling that you might just, not to put too fine a point on it, perhaps be too damn thick ever to get what he's on about. Under the pretext of showing me the new wind gauge he's built, he steers me into the "incubator," the workspace under the foredeck that he shares with Hussey.

Hardly have I wiped the snow from my face but the two of them begin to grill me for a blow-by-blow telling of how the conversation with Shackleton unfolded. James nods, his guesses confirmed. He presses his lips together, and his eyes flick happily back and forth. He shows me the anemometer, which looks to me like the framework for a miniaturized umbrella, but that might just be because I always have to think of umbrellas when I see Jimmy James, ever since he told me that his father manufactures them.

"Nice," I say to the glittering thing.

And James says, "Blow on it, then."

I blow and the little wheel turns a few times, totally silent and so light that it doesn't seem possible that it's made of metal.

"It goes up on the roof," says Hussey, who's standing in front of some ovenlike apparatus bedecked with indicators and dials. He winks at me and says, "Jimmy, tell him why Shack took you on. How did it go again?"

James is reluctant at first but then tells us that the whole thing was essentially a joke. He'd almost finished his studies at Cambridge when one afternoon, a neighbor he hardly knew leaned out of his window and asked whether he didn't fancy going to the South Pole as expedition physicist.

"Without having to think twice, I said no. I few days later one of the professors called me in to see him and told me that Shackleton, the Antarctic explorer, was searching desperately for scientists who could do the first crossing of the continent on foot. He asked whether I might be interested. I said no, but asked how long the expedition would be en route. Professor Shipley didn't know. But he told me that if I was really a physicist, I must be able to work out how long it would take to cover two thousand miles on foot."

Hussey laughs quietly while tapping a fingernail against the glass casing of a dial.

"And that's just the start of it," he says.

James continues, "Three weeks later I had a telegram from Shackleton himself. He asked me to come and meet him at his office in London. So I went and the interview was over in less than five minutes. All Shackleton asked me about was the condition of my teeth, whether I had varicose veins, whether I was good-natured and whether I could sing. That last question I thought was quite strange, not knowing him yet, and when I asked what he meant, he said, 'Oh, I don't mean like Caruso. It's enough if you can bellow along with the others.'"

We joke and banter with one another for a while until Hussey actually starts a song so that I can get to know the tuneful bellowing of Jimmy James. Then it's his turn. He tells me that he was an anthropologist on the Wellcome Expedition in the Sudan when he read Shackleton's announcement in an old newspaper. He applied and was invited for an interview. It went much the same way. Shackleton looked him up and down a few times, paced up and down a few times and then finally said, "I'll take you. You look funny." That Hussey knew next to nothing about meteorology was totally unimportant. Shackleton wanted him to complete a crash course, which he did.

"I think what he's looking for," says Hussey, "is versatility. He doesn't want to have specialists on board, he wants men with talent for as many things as possible. He has a clear idea of how to balance the crew, believe me. It's supposed to be equipped for any situation."

"Not to mention that he's quite right," says James. "You are funny-looking, Uzbird."

True. Everything on Hussey is smaller than usual. He looks like a diminutive representative of a species of which he's the only exemplar. But he's not just the smallest on board, he's also the quickest, with his head as well as his tongue. He plays the banjo, too, something that maybe isn't everyone's favorite, but that no one wants to miss, because Uzbird knows so many sad and beautiful melodies. He accompanies me a little way across the snowy deck and explains that, as far as the weather is concerned, we'll soon have the worst behind us. The *Endurance* is now on the edge of the wild forties, the latitudes that delineate the earth's stormiest seas. Between Tierra del Fuego and South Georgia, the ocean rushes unhindered by land on its circular course around the globe's southern ice cap.

"We're in luck," shouts Uzbird as we catch our breaths at the railing. "We're striking it nicely. At least for the time being." Standing next to me, his head only reaches up to my chest.

A few hours later, we run into a hailstorm that drives most of the men below decks. In the thunder of lumps thudding down from the skies, Bakewell and the other sailors on duty strike the topsail before it can freeze solid and be torn or punctured. Greenstreet bellows through the noise and gives the command to lock all the dogs into the kennels, with no exceptions, not even those who've proved they're trustworthy and are now allowed to wander around freely on the foredeck. The bosun comes dashing across, barges me out of the way and growls, "Out of the way, dipshit."

He turns around briefly and bares his teeth.

But as quickly as the hail began, it has stopped again. Between one second and the next, the gusts, strong enough to launch blocks of ice like cannonballs through the air, weaken to a cold breeze. Snow falls as quietly and constantly as before. Suddenly Shackleton is on deck. In a black winter coat and wearing a woolen hat, he stands alone at the railing of the quarterdeck and watches the spectacle. The turbid sea is cobalt blue. You can't see even a patch of sky because a canopy of snow clouds is hanging above the ship and over the sea for as far as the eyes can reach.

Sir Ernest goes over to Greenstreet and gives the order to hoist the topsail again. Without complaining, with entirely undisturbed expressions, Bakewell and the others climb back into the rigging, where the ice has frozen ankle-thick on the ropes.

"Someone on lookout," shouts Greenstreet and, an instant later, I think I recognize McCarthy, a young Irishman beloved by everyone on board for his no-holds-barred humor, clambering from the topsail yardarm up to the topgallant and then onwards and upwards until I lose sight of him in the driving snow. McCarthy will still have another third or so of the mast to climb before he reaches the crow's nest.

"Doesn't exactly look overjoyed, does he?" says Holness, and nods in the direction of Sir Ernest, who has taken up his former position at the railing. Holness is sticking his head out of the door that leads below decks. He's been looking for me; Dr. Macklin would like a word.

"What's going on?" I ask, meaning if he knows what Mack wants.

Holie misunderstands me. "Icebergs. That's what's going on. In this weather it's not impossible that one's floated up to this latitude. Is there someone in the barrel?"

The *Endurance*'s crow's nest looks like a narrow white barrel.

"Yeah, I think McCarthy's up there."

"Icebergs," says Holness again. "From up there in this weather, you'd only see them if they were waving right at you, and even then they'd have to be house-sized above the waterline. No wonder the boss looks worried. So, you coming below?"

I follow him below decks. As soon as we're alone in the corridor, Holie stops me and says, "Hey, I've been wanting to ask you all this time: how did you actually work it out with Shackleton?"

# 12

## "CORMORANTS, AHOY!"

MICK AND MACK COMPLEMENT EACH OTHER FULLY, NOT ONLY in their role as ship's doctors. Dr. McIlroy is tall, slim, handsome and a bone-deep cynic while Dr. Macklin, on the other hand, isn't tall, isn't slim and is no beauty, but does have a rare friendliness. Mick and Mack are more or less the same age, in their late twenties at a guess, and both are equally highly esteemed by the men because they love their craft and practice it without unnecessary fuss. There's also another love that the two men have in common: India. Macklin because he was born there and McIlroy because he lived there for years.

They're sitting over tea and cigarettes at the long table in the Ritz, which is otherwise empty. Only in the galley do you see Green going back and forth, but he's busy or at least pretending to be.

"Here comes the man from the cupboard," McIlroy calls happily when I come closer, "the maggot in the chocolate."

There's nothing Mick doesn't have a phrase for, nor is there anything that would put him at a loss for words, though his witticisms do always have an edge to them.

There's a brief conversation about my well-being, and all three, Mick, Mack and Merce, concur that I'm completely restored.

So the boss hasn't knocked me off-kilter. Speaking of which . . . How did it actually pan out, my little tête-à-tête?

Bit by bit I'm getting some practice in giving a report of my remarkable job interview. And I'm no longer surprised that everyone who wants me to tell my short tale then volunteers his own in return.

McIlroy came back to London from India while suffering from malaria and had an interview with Shackleton. Sir Ernest wondered why the young doctor standing in front of him wouldn't stop shaking and finally couldn't think of anything other to do than call another doctor. The young doctor who hurried to McIlroy's aid was Macklin. He's supposed to have won Shackleton's favor with his answer to the question of why he was wearing spectacles: that "many clever heads would look pretty silly without any glasses."

Once McIlroy had recovered, Shackleton offered him a contract on the condition that he convince Macklin to come, too. And Mick persuaded Mack by promising to travel to India with him once they were back from the Pole.

A few hours later, Wild draws me into conversation in exactly the same place. I'm setting the table for the men off duty, and Shackleton's second in command is sitting over a chart that he explains he's noting weather conditions and depth soundings on.

He answers my question by saying, "No, there's no ice in sight," but we do need to be cautious nonetheless, because the driving snow and banks of fog make it difficult to regularly establish our position. Wild wants to know if I understand anything about calculating longitude.

"No, sir, I'm afraid not. But I've borrowed a book about navigation from Wordie, *Logs, Depth and Longitude*."

"Oh ho, *Logs, Depth and Longitude*," he mumbles, smirking. "A good book, honestly. If anything's not clear to you, just come to me and ask. Here . . ." With his compasses, he points at two tiny dark points lying right next to each other on the chart. "These are the Shag Rocks, which we should be passing soon. Six cliffs in the middle of the ocean, the tallest two hundred feet high. Look like a group of black icebergs. We'll all sleep a bit easier once we've got them behind us."

Not everyone likes the slightly inhibited, also perhaps truly devious, bundle of energy that is Frank Wild. Some say Wild's bitter because he's no more than Shackleton's second in command, and bitter above all because he knows that he, in contrast to Shackleton, who himself was nothing more than Scott's third man, lacks the courage to make his own plans, to say nothing of the ability to see them through. Even Bakewell, who's usually tolerant to the point of naivety, doesn't like him and thinks his manner is both bootlicking and tyrannical. Since he's also hardly bigger than the midget Uzbird, Wild's nickname among the sailors is "the mini-boss," though of course only when they're by themselves. There's a joke that was making the rounds until Worsley heard it and had the bosun place it on the forbidden index. It goes like this: "Why is it that you can only hear Frank Wild and not see him when Sir Ernest is up in the barrel? Because he's up there with him. He's standing in Shackleton's back pocket and shouting, 'I'm the greatest.'"

"Back pocket" being the cleaner version of the joke.

I like Frank Wild. Not only because his sometimes melancholy haggardness reminds me of my brother, but also because, except for Tom Crean, he's the only one who doesn't tell anecdotes when talking about Shackleton.

And not even Crean dares to question Shackleton's point of view, but Wild does, and he does it regardless of it being attributed to his jealousy. No one knows Shackleton better. No one loves him as much. None of the crew, who are almost all good at heart but who become mocking and envious when the talk turns to the onboard number two, none seem to ask themselves why it might be that Shackleton has chosen the introverted, unimaginative and obstinate Frank Wild, of all people, to be his right-hand man.

For a while I'm standing close up to him and my nose is full of the sweat-smell streaming off him. He lets the compasses wander across the chart. A monstrous white shape is drawn on it with a single, rising, sharply pointed horn: Antarctica and the peninsula it sends curving up to the northwest. The bay between the back of the horn and the monster's forehead is divided on the chart into hundreds of tiny splinter- or shard-shaped sections. They represent a water surface clogged with ice floes, an area "as big as France," Wild says, and puts down the instrument.

"The first person to sail into that"—he taps the bay with a brown fingernail—"was Weddell, and that was only in 1823. That's where we're going, into the Weddell Sea."

"Merce, the glasses, the bottles! Move it!" Green shouts from the galley.

Wild continues undisturbed. "Look here: there's a little cove on the south coast. That's Vahsel Bay. If the sea's clear, we can sail all the way to the ice shelf and moor the ship against the barrier. Then we unload all the stuff directly onto the ice. What do you think of that?"

I'm impressed but can't imagine it clearly, and instead of saying something stupid, I just say nothing. Right then, Hudson, the navigator, comes in and reports that the latest sounding gave a depth of just eighty fathoms. The lead came back up with black sand and shingle on it.

Wild turns back to the compasses and the chart. "So, the Shag Rocks," he mutters. "Here we are."

And I toddle off to Green, whose furious whistle is threatening me with a boot to the back pocket.

After the off-duty gang have eaten their fill and peace has returned to Green's kingdom, I find myself a quiet corner under a porthole and gaze alternately out at the whirling snow and down at Wordie's book about logs, depth and longitude. Gray, black and white, a perfectly striped and four-legged embodiment of chaos, the ship's cat comes out from under the table and rubs herself, purring, against my legs. I lift her onto my lap, where Mrs. Chippy makes herself comfortable and glances for a while at the pages with about as much understanding and interest as I can muster, then falls asleep.

What the author, Commodore Robert FitzRoy, captain of Charles Darwin's *Beagle,* has put together as a guide to nautical navigation is as dry as sawdust in summer. By page seven I've reached my own personal ice barrier and jettisoned the paraphernalia of quadrants, sextants, chronometers and lunar tables for good.

My passion for calculations is limited. The distance from fingertip to fingertip of an averagely sized man stretching his arms out to the sides is equivalent, says FitzRoy, to one fathom, i.e., about six feet. Wild's fathoms must be a touch on the smaller side.

The ocean the snow is tumbling unceasingly, unstoppably into is eighty fathoms deep at this point. Five hundred feet, which is really not a lot, when you consider that we're out on the high seas.

I close the book softly so as not to wake Mrs. Chippy, and look outside. Everything can be elucidated with numbers: the depth of the sea, the size of the ship, the density of the flakes. Five years ago, the daily ration of the men Shackleton tried to reach the South Pole with shrank to four biscuits, a couple of grams of dried fruit and a nibble of pony meat. A hundred miles from their destination, they turned around so as not to starve to death on the way back. And when Wild had reached the end of his strength, Shackleton gave him one of his own last biscuits.


AFTER THE MEN OF THE SECOND SHIFT HAVE EATEN, TOO, THE CAPTAIN has me sent to him again. It's getting dark over the sea, but the snowfall is relenting as I stomp across the deck. The lights are on in both quarterdeck cabins. Worsley would like to know how I'm fitting in and whether I'm happy with my bunk, my duties and so on.

I am.

"Good. And as all of us heard, Sir Ernest is happy with you, too."

He beams at me for a moment.

I seize the opportunity. "Sir, I want to apologize. I shouldn't have made that comment even if I'd really thought that—"

"You've got nothing to worry about," he interrupts me. "Let it go, Blackboro. There was something quite heroic about your little comment."

"It was stupid."

"The two aren't mutually exclusive. Each of us has his own experiences of the boss. By now some of them must have reached your ears. Am I right?"

"Yes, sir."

"Have you spoken about Shackleton with Crean?"

"No, sir."

"Then do that. Though, if you can, you should keep your thoughts on heroes to yourself around Crean. After all, he's a hero, too. I'm sorry to have to say this to you, Merce, but you're surrounded by heroes. Do you think you can cope?"

"I'll try, sir."

"Excellent. Do you know how I met Sir Ernest? I dreamed about him. Or rather, I dreamed I had to steer a ship down a Burlington Street that was barricaded with blocks of ice. Do you know Burlington Street? It's in the West End, in London. A fine street, no pack ice to speak of. The next morning I went down there and found a plaque outside number four: Imperial Trans-Antarctic Expedition. I hypnotized Shackleton and gave him no choice but to make me his skipper. That's how it was, you understand? And don't believe everything these sea dogs tell you, Merce."

I promise not to. And I'm already leaving when land is sighted, land starboard ahead. Through the ship thunders the tramping of running men who storm onto deck and rush up to the railing alongside Shackleton, Wild, Worsley, Greenstreet and all the others. From bow to stern, the *Endurance*, sheathed in a layer of snow that glints with white stars, is in a state of blazing excitement. Even the dogs howl as though celebrating as we swish past the six black spurs of the safely distant Shag Rocks, which jut upwards out of the water in utter silence.

"Ahoy!" shouts one of the men amidships I'm standing next to. "Cormorants, ahoy!"

All the others fan out against the railing and watch unspeaking as a cloud of birds rises from the cliffs and moves across the darkening sky, storm petrels and cormorants that sailors used to call shags, which is why the rocks that belong to these birds have been named after them.

I see Bakewell. He's gazing out over the water with glowing eyes and marveling at the group of cliffs no man has ever set foot on. And rightly so: what would anyone do there? I press myself against my friend's back and hold onto him as tightly as I can so that he doesn't jump overboard. Not even a piece of paper could have slipped between him and me, not even one signed by the King himself. There's only one thing between us, and even that is a lucky charm.

## Part Two

## THE UNEXPLORED COAST

Grytviken
"Where'd the pig come from?"
The Excursion
A Young Hero
The Order of Jonah
The Library
Skipper's Pet
The Sermon
Captain Cook, or, We're Not Sure Where We Are
In the Ice

# 13

## GRYTVIKEN

T HE BLACK HILLS, THE WHITE LAND AND THE WATER THAT'S LIKE a crystal between us and the bottom of the fjord we've sailed into all remind me of a dream. A couple of years ago, I dreamed it for a few nights back to back, probably because my sister was sleeping next to me in bed

I remember that it was midwinter. There'd been an accident in Pillgwenlly's old fish factory and the foreman, Alec Garrard, had had both of his hands cut off. A young mechanic came from Cardiff to replace him. And because my family were friendly with the family of the unlucky foreman, my parents temporarily gave the young man Regyn's room to sleep in. So one afternoon, swaddled in an overcoat, hat and scarf, with little icicles hanging from his eyebrows and beard, Herman tramped through the garden and, without knowing it, moved into the bedroom of his future wife.

I hadn't slept under the same cover as Regyn for years, the last time being when we were still children and didn't think anything of swimming naked and diving for crabs together in the Usk near Mynyddislwyn. I lay there in the dark, my eyelids clapped open like a vampire's, feeling and disliking the warmth coming off Regyn's body. My sister's breathing was calm and regular, and for a long while I wondered whether she was just pretending to be asleep. I, for one, heard every step taken and every noise made by the unknown man pacing up and down behind the wall, and I couldn't imagine that it was any different for Regyn.

The strange thing about the dream that I had for the first time that night was that it didn't consist simply of images and sounds, but it seemed like the images and sounds were concatenated parts of a mechanism like a musical organ that I operated myself with any, even the slightest, movement of my body. I still remember running up a circular staircase made of white stone, hearing the slapping of my footfall, and that, having arrived at the top, where there was nothing but a white wall, I woke up and found myself curled against Regyn's back, curled like the staircase in my dream.

Herman spent a whole week sleeping in Regyn's room, and during each of the six or seven nights that she and I shared my bed, I dreamed the same dream of myself as a kind of organ. The dream had no real story. A group of dwarfs appeared in it, a dozen faceless, totally identical little men dressed in hooded robes. I watched them marching one after the other along a river and across a snow-bedecked landscape encircled by black, treeless peaks. And there's nothing there but the dwarfs and me. The land is so white and the hills are so black that they look like a script I can't read and whose meaning is indiscoverable. There's no water in the river. It's simply empty. I'm insolubly bound to the dwarfs. They move when I move. They stop when I stay still. With sounds that are sometimes shrill, sometimes muffled, a quiet, piercing call or a rumbling bass grumble, I'm steering them, as abruptly becomes clear to me, towards myself. But I can't remember if I realized then what I'm now sure of: that each of the dwarfs represented a part of my body, one an arm, another a leg, a foot or a finger.

The landscape always stayed the same; it was always just empty. The hills with their white-capped peaks and the black, naked cliffs ran on endlessly behind shores that bordered nothing. Only once the dwarfs had marched in a wide arc towards me and were coming closer did I run away and up the stairs to where the sudden stop woke me again. Then I shifted away from Regyn, turned to face the wall and listened. Sometimes I heard Herman snoring. And in the last night with Regyn, I woke up and was again lying alone in my bed. The dream had vanished like my sister had, and didn't return.

I never thought that one day I might arrive at a country that looked like the one in my dream.

We've done a day and a half's sailing since passing the Shag Rocks. The weather's still unpredictable but has got steadily colder. The lookout spotted land this morning. We passed the islets Willis and Bird and then sailed with our topsail reefed at a respectful distance down the north coast, as it disappeared and emerged again from behind gusts of snow.

The black hills, the white land and the water that's like a crystal between us and the bottom of the fjord we've sailed into . . . the country I imagine I recognize is South Georgia.


IT'S DEAD CALM WHEN WE CAST ANCHOR OFF GRYTVIKEN IN CUMBERLAND East Bay. A mighty old whaler, whose Stars-and-Stripes banner has Bakewell's heart beating faster, lies within hailing distance, and the houses and the flensers' barracks on shore look like they've slid from the black cliffs and tumbled down into the snow. Cheetham and Hurley, who've both been here before, point out Grytviken's attractions with sweeping gestures: that's where the whales are dragged on land, there under the cranes that look like churches topped with fishing rods, that's where they're carved up, and there in front is the real chapel, where Pastor Gunvald, who Cheetham implies is not exactly the easiest man to deal with, carves up the souls of the whalers and sticks them back together in line with God's instructions. The dirty yellow tower of Grytviken's little church isn't even as high as the mast that has the same flag drooping from it as has been flying at the South Pole for the past three years: the Norwegian cross.

Two of the three tenders are ready. Once Sir Ernest has decided who's going to keep watch on board and feed the dogs, the rest of us will row over. I'm bursting with excitement because the head of the whaling station is supposedly Roald Amundsen's brother-in-law.

Wild and Greenstreet stay behind with six others, including, luckily, the bosun and Stevenson, but unfortunately also Holness, who I've really got to like. The rest of us, ten in each tender, push off and row, hooting and laughing, eight versus eight, since the boats only have that many rowlocks. In mine, Shackleton is standing at the bow while Captain Worsley steers. In the other, the veterans are letting the whippersnappers tucker themselves out. While the oldies' boat glides ahead and extends its lead, Crean fills his pipe with his spare hand. He glances over, and though I can't be sure, I think I see a smile like a slow flash in the corners of his mouth.

The island's mountains appear to belong to neither the earth nor the heavens. The sky is uniformly white, and equally white are the hands and fingers of the glaciers that reach down from the cliffs into the water of the bay. The black ridges and the peaks above them seem to be hanging in midair, and the air is so trenchantly cold that you might accept a floating mountain just because you can't look up for too long. The cold makes our eyelids blink incessantly.

By the time our boat has covered half the distance to the pier, I've got more used to it and can see more clearly how the island is formed. Along the whole convoluted coastline, land and sea meet in a jumble of shadowy-blue pressure folds and glacier furrows. The rock walls around the fjord reflect the soft light, and there's a glittering mist of shimmering blue over the water we're crossing. It smells like a snowy pine forest.

But not for long.

"Two strokes to port, Captain," calls Shackleton, not agitated but very distinct. I pull and can't see what it is behind me that's making him call instructions. Until I smell it. Until I see the water around us go first violet and then red, bloodred.

A sickening stink of decay hovers above the middle of the bay.

"Jesus, that's revolting," Hussey says next to me, and pushes his oar out of the water. Our blades at head height, we slip silently through the red surface, twisting our heads around to look in front. The whales are floating side by side, five or six of them lashed together and bound to a plank lying flat across them, the heads under water, only the mouths partially visible, jaws with teeth each as big and thick as a man's thigh.

"Pull," shouts Shackleton. "Come on, this is unbearable, pull."

We pass another group of carcasses and then the stench gradually fades. Crean's boat is already tying up and the Norwegians are welcoming them onto land.

"It's a great honor, Sir Ernest," one of the gaunt whalers says to Crean, who goes pink at once and tries to correct the error by bending over to help Sir Ernest up onto the landing.

"May I present Tom Crean," Shackleton says as soon as he's upright and before he's presented himself.

The water splashing against the pier is just as red as before.

WE SIT UP TILL LATE AT NIGHT IN THE HALL OF THEIR MAIN BUILDING with a dozen hard-drinking Norwegians. The floor is carpeted in sawdust, like the one in my father's workshop. On the walls hang whalebones, harpoons and a photo of the King of Norway posing beside a harpoon gun. A deep rumbling, then a crack and a long susurrus . . . Some of the noises from my dream also seem to be here in South Georgia. The sudden racket, which sounds menacingly close and chills me to the marrow, comes from a glacier where for days ice has been breaking off and tumbling into the sea. Each crack means a new iceberg. The louder the crack, the bigger the berg.

"No fear." Fridtjof Jacobsen laughs into my ear and smacks one of his paws against my shoulders. No, he isn't Amundsen's brother-in-law. "That's how it sounds when the glacier is calving. And that"—again we hear the drawn-out susurrus; it sounds like a biplane, a Sopwith Camel diving from a great height—"that's the avalanche that comes down the Nordenskjöld Glacier to see the iceberg off."

The dandily neat Captain Jacobsen gives me a gentle box around the ears and kisses me on the back of the head. No, Amundsen's brother-in-law is called Sørlle, Thoralf Sørlle, and he's head of the Stromness whaling station fifteen miles further north.

The continuous rumbling has nothing to do with calving glaciers or fjord-bound avalanches; it's coming from the generator that provides Grytviken with electricity. Even the pigpens and the chicken coops, they tell us, are illuminated. And yes, when we step back out into the open air, a ribbon of yellow and red lamps lights the way through the darkness and down to the harbor. The generator housing originally stood in Strømmen, the village in Norway where most of Jacobsen's men are from. Strømmen's church, too, was dismantled into portable sections, shipped here and rebuilt. It's temporarily abandoned. Pastor Gunvald is currently on the Falkland Islands but will be back in time to give a service in our honor before we set off.

Our group stops outside Jacobsen's house—even if some of us find coming to a halt harder than usual, what with all the swaying. I've never seen Bakewell as drunk as he is on this Norwegian beer. Wordie and Hussey can't stop giggling, pulling each other's hats off and ruffling each other's hair. The house is brightly lit. The blank night sky is far above it, and in the distance we can hear the glaciers again.

Captain Jacobsen introduces us to his young wife, the only woman on the island—actually, he proudly tells us, the only one in the whole Southern Ocean. Mrs. Jacobsen gives each of us her hand and introduces herself to each with her first name, so that she ends up saying the same two words twenty times in a row: "Stina, hello," "Stina, hello . . ."

And because he seems to have an unerring sense for rarities, Captain Jacobsen draws our attention to another curiosity: outside his house's bay window are boxes where geraniums are blossoming. They're the only flowers on the island, the only flowers in the whole Southern Ocean . . .

"Stina, hello," "Stina, hello." Mrs. Jacobsen, who is pretty but already slightly withered, has now greeted each of us. So we have to say good-bye.

The Jacobsens and a small troop of whalers who haven't gone to bed yet come with us to the pier. Every Norwegian wants to embrace every one of us. There's no time for that. Boys, it's just too cold.

"You'll have to be our guests a little longer," says Captain Jacobsen to Shackleton and Worsley, "but don't worry, we'll help you make the time go quickly!"

He laughs like a glacier and slaps his hand against Sir Ernest's arm.

Shackleton thanks him in his own way, saying, "I will never forget your generosity and hospitality, Fridtjof Jacobsen."

There's nothing celebratory in his tone, only this overwhelming candor and such surprising seriousness that Jacobsen is visibly both moved and irritated. As he shakes Tom Crean's hand, the mustachioed leader of the whale hunt bows as if before a knight of the Holy Grail.

We cast off and row slowly across the icy bay. At some point, I see, over the shoulder of the man in front of me, the colorful bulbs and the lights in the Jacobsen house go out. It's dark on South Georgia. Without anyone saying anything, we raise our stroke rate and drive the tenders on through the stink. And because I can't hold my nose shut, I try to think of sawdust, of the aroma of sawdust from my father's workshop in Pillgwenlly in winter.

# 14

## "WHERE'D THE PIG COME FROM?"

W E'VE GOT TO SPLIT UP. JACOBSEN WARNED SIR ERNEST AS insistently as he could against venturing into the ice before the start of December and Shackleton eventually acquiesced. Since it now looks like we're going to stay on the island for at least a month, the dogs have got to be transported ashore. Twelve men directed by Wild have been detailed with erecting a kennel complex on the edge of the settlement and, since the impetuous creatures are finally going to receive some training and can't be left unguarded for even an hour, the men Shackleton has appointed dog leaders and assistant dog leaders also have to be housed on shore. A foggy day is spent constructing kennels and fences, loading the dogs and rowing them across, and then with mucking out and cleaning the cages on deck. Meanwhile, the Norwegians have cleared out Strømmen's fire station in the blink of an eye and furnished it with bunks for their guests. Someone has scrawled "God shave the King" in chalk over the entrance. You can hear their singing through the fog. Bakewell says they're standing with their legs planted wide apart, belted onto the bloating whales floating in the bay, and using knives with blades longer than they are to slice chunks out of the carcasses.

For us sixteen Antáricanos left on board, a few relatively relaxing weeks are beginning. Sir Ernest and the skipper have retired to their cabins to study their charts and weather maps. The scientists and artists leave the ship early in the morning to explore the country. They measure the speed of the downdrafts and the temperature of the hot springs; they collect stone samples, mosses and lichens. Marston draws elephant seals, tussock grass and glaciers. And Hurley lugs his camera, which perches on his back like a man-sized, three-legged spider, up into the hills encircling the bay. Motor sled expert Orde-Lees, who's nicknamed Aunt Thomas on account of his moodiness and snootiness, has managed to convince Shackleton to have the three machines, which were built in Wales and are yet to make a single movement, shipped ashore. Orde-Lees wants to test the sleds on a snowfield above Grytviken. While he's on deck removing them from their wooden crates, Aunt Thomas explains to me what a wonder it is that's being revealed before my very eyes.

"The biggest is nearly fifteen feet long and three feet wide. They've got sixty-horsepower motors and aircraft propellers, motors from Anzani, by the way. Does that mean anything to you?"

"Anzani motors are what Blériot flies with."

"Clever lad. This one here can get up to thirty miles an hour and pull a ton of cargo." He points out a boxlike structure in the middle of the sled. "The exhaust fumes flow into this. It's a kind of heated store-box," he says. "You can dry out sleeping bags and clothes in there if you need to."

Orde-Lees is convinced that his Welsh motor sleds will revolutionize polar exploration. And he's not the only one to think so. I've heard Shackleton, too, say that dog teams in the ice will soon belong to the past as completely as the pony sleds that turned out so fatefully for Scott.

"Incidentally," says Orde-Lees, "in 1907, Sir Ernest was the first to take an automobile into the Antarctic."

I don't dare ask whether he knows what happened to the sled in the end, but I'm certain the machine must have been left behind somewhere right at the start of the starvation march across the Beardmore Glacier, and that it's still there, sunk under ten feet of snow and ice waiting forever to rattle back into life. Aunt Thomas smiles proudly.

I say, "I'd like to have a go on one."

And he: "No problem. Give me a hand and they'll be in the boat all the quicker."

"Um, the dinner. I've got to go call the others for dinner." And I get out of there as fast as I can.

I also have to tell Chippy McNeish, the ship's carpenter, who's nailing together an extra coal bunker in the rig, and our machinist Rickenson, who's busily knocking and blowing through the innards of our steam engines in the belly of the *Endurance,* that Green and Black have conjured something up again. Apart from me, since I'm always hurrying up and down, back and forth through the ship, they're the only ones on board who are at work all day. No wonder they want to know what's on the menu. At Shackleton's request, we're having Irish brawn. Neither McNeish nor Rickenson can imagine what that might be.

I tell them truthfully that it looks like bread but is actually a pig's head in jelly.

"Where'd the pig come from?" the skipper wants to know when we're at the table. And since no one answers, Shackleton has to come out with it himself. "Bosun, Songster and two of the other dogs escaped from the kennels this morning and brought down one of Jacobsen's pigs. Bon appétit, gentlemen."

On some days Green and I have only ten hungry mouths to fill because all the other men are out and about. We use the time to inspect the stores and put in more of them. We salt penguin and seal meat, I stack yards and yards of hero-biscuits in the bread store. Meanwhile, Bosun, Songster, Sue and Roy kill three more Norwegian pigs. A few hours later the meat has been salted away in storage. In Mrs. Chippy's hunting ground around the magazines on the lower deck, it's as cold as it was in my parents' living room when I used to come downstairs on winter mornings to have breakfast and set off for school. One of the boxes of Belmont stearin candles has "Ideal for warm climates" printed on it. On the wrapping is a picture of some kind of chieftain preparing himself a delicious meal over a fire on a palm-fringed beach. Looking at the other tins and boxes on the shelves makes me homesick. I grew up with orange-blue packets of Huntley & Palmer biscuits, green-and-gold tins of Lyle's syrup and that strange shape of the label on bottles of Heinz ketchup. With the yeast that had the sun on the packet, my mam, too, could trust that "This one always rises."

Green trusts it as well, even though he doesn't possess the inexplicably accurate body clock of Gwendolyn Blackboro. But he manages by other means. Green's got an incredible imaginative richness in his own narrow field. He places a thin metal lid on top of the yeast. When it has risen to the correct height, the lid touches another piece of metal, closing an electrical circuit and ringing a bell up in the galley. That's where Green sits, dozing or reading last year's *Illustrated London News*.

WAR WILL NOT BREAK OUT . . .

is the title of an advert, under which is printed in much smaller type:

BUT IF IT DOES, STOCK UP IN TIME
WITH STINGER'S FLOUR!

Hardly anything is more important to the men than food. Uzbird says it's because only food is close to being a substitute for sex. That's something I still need to think about. The fact is, though, that the cook's resourcefulness has secured him respect on board. The men downright revere Green for his ability to give his peas a light taste of mint. Only I know that when cooking them he stirs a dollop of toothpaste into the pot.

"You'll soon see," he says to me. "They's soon be playing 'who's portion is this?'"

When food is being handed out after long weeks in the ice, every man in turn has to close his eyes while a filled plate is put in his hands.

Without knowing how much is on it, he's got to decide whose portion it'll be.

"That way they can't accuse us of any favoritism, you see? Oh, just wait, just wait for when the rations start to get smaller. Then they'll start dreaming about food. Then the moaning'll start and they'll start berating themselves because of one time, years ago, when they didn't feel like having seconds."

Leaving aside that I can't imagine men like Tom Crean and Alfred Cheetham behaving like that, I find it strange that Green always speaks about "them." Why is he counting himself out? And why me? Why don't I count, either? All this is another thing that Green has in common with Mam. "Just wait" is what she would have said. "Just wait till you're eating nothing but dust bunnies and air pie."

"Those fine gentlemen," Green squeaks malevolently. "They're still spraying themselves with eau de cologne and hiding their chocolate so they don't get fat."

There'll be something to what you're telling me, Green, you miserable old pot-washer. It's not for nothing that they say everything important that happens on a ship can be felt first in the galley.

That's where I'm kept occupied throughout the morning, tipping the aspic from one pot into a larger one, until Greenstreet appears in the doorway and orders me, with the inimitable impersonality of a man who is the onboard regulations made flesh, to report on deck in twenty minutes, combed, clean and without bits of food on my pullover. I'm to row Shackleton to Grytviken.

"Sir? Me, sir? Why?"

"Don't ask questions, Mr. Blackboro, just do as you're told. It won't hurt."

"Are you sure, sir?"

It's impossible to wrest even the beginnings of a smile from the *Endurance*'s first officer. He just looks at you till you look somewhere else. If you don't, you start to think you've become your own ghost, inhabiting the husk of someone who's already departed without permission.

This morning, the breakfast table in the Ritz resembles a flea market stall. Wordie has spread out his hunks of rock. Alongside them are gray-green scraps of moss and lichen that Clark is examining through his magnifying glass while nibbling contentedly at a slice of marmalade toast. The grim Marston is examining a sketch pad and then writing on it, and Hurley, who isn't nicknamed the Prince for the blueness of his blood, smells of aftershave again. He's polishing either one, two or three dismantled cameras. Frank Hurley is in the highest of spirits. The Norwegians want to take him on a whale hunt. I put his fourth coffee down beside him.

Suddenly there's a commotion among them. On one of Wordie's dark-gray rocks Clark has made a discovery of what looks like a bit of rock.

"Where did you find this?" Clark asks as innocuously as if talking about a hat. But his excitement is obvious. Whether moss or lichen, whatever Clark has spent days searching for in the South Georgian scree, it's on this lump of Wordie's. He takes the bull by the horns. "In this stone," he says slowly, "is located a précis of the whole of Antarctic history. Its microorganisms divide it stratum by stratum, like a salami. It takes ten thousand years for a single layer to form. It's here that you can see clearly the manner in which biological and geological time frames overlap. Fantastic. May I have it?"

"No," says Wordie without looking up. "You can look at it."

Clark puts the rock back on the table and Marston and Hurley laugh.

One of them says, "Hit it with a hammer, then you can both have a chunk."

"No, no, it's fine, forget it."

Aggrieved, Bob Clark takes his glasses off. He stands there blind and defenseless, breathes on his glasses and polishes them so meticulously that it seems like he's happy not to have to see for a while. Then he quietly gathers up his scraps of lichen.

"I'm probably mistaken anyway," he says. "But I can live with it. I know they say science always has to be optimistic, but I think that's fundamentally false. Properly understood research is built on mistakes."

"Hear, hear," mocks Marston. "Just one more step, Bobby, and you'll go head over heels into the abyss of art. Then you'll be one of us, the doubters."

"He just shouldn't exaggerate so much," says Wordie, who has put all his stones back in his box apart from the one Clark is so keen on. "Here, take it, Bob. I've got more of them."

"Doubt doesn't indicate art, George," Hurley says quietly in Marston's direction. He has assembled all the pieces spread out on the table with astonishing speed. There are now three cameras in front of him. "What you have to be able to do is play skillfully with doubt, don't you? It's the same with the Eskimos; they practice the art of understatement. The more seals they've caught and piled on their sleds, the more they seem to let themselves droop."

"But I'm not an Eskimo," says Marston.

Clark takes the rock, squeezes Wordie's shoulder briefly and says to Marston, "No, but you look like one."

When I come to clear the plates, miniature crumbs of Clark's lichen are scattered across the table like green sand. One of my dad's mottos is: always understate by twenty percent. To which Mam used to say, "Forty. Forty is better."

I've got to go wash and get changed.

# 15

## THE EXCURSION

THE SUN IS HIGH OVER CUMBERLAND BAY WHEN I COME UP ON deck. The ice sparkles on the glaciers that have been sitting quietly for the last few days and there's even a shimmer in the distance as if from heat. The water is rippled by little silver waves that carry tiny, knurled lumps of bobbing ice.

It's so quiet that I hear the blood rushing in my head and get the feeling, like when diving, that I'm gliding through another world. But what kind of a world is it? I walk loudly across the planking to drive off the feeling that it's one I don't exist in. Much more than Clark's microorganisms, to me this silence seems like a précis of the whole of Antarctic history, a history that has always followed one century of solitude with another. An albatross circles above the cliffs of Duce Fell, far too far away for me to hear its call. Around the mastheads of the floating whale oil factory that has moored at Jacobsen's pier, a swarm of terns swoops just as quiet and reckless as the bats at night on the avenue by the Usk. Frank Hurley stands at the ladder with his arachnid camera on his back and waves at me to hurry.

"Quickly now, Mr. Chief Steward."

Two boats are bobbing in the water. In one of them the Vikings are sitting and twirling locks into their beards. In the other waits Shackleton. I get myself down the rope ladder. Hardly am I sitting opposite him on the thwart but Sir Ernest raises a finger and lets it fall in the direction of Grytviken.

"Southwards, ho!"

I row. This isn't my world, rowing. There are rowers who row you to death and rowers who row themselves to death. I'm the latter. Whenever I row, the water always wins.

Opposite me, the Norwegians row Hurley across to the pier. There are only two men sitting at the rowlocks in front of the Prince and pulling, but they're more than twice as fast as me in my dinghy.

The carving platform comes into view between their boat and ours. A handful of flensers in leather aprons to their ankles are cutting up two exemplars of some smaller whale species and greet us as we pass them.

"Don't look," Shackleton says calmly.

But his warning comes too late. There's no narwhal species that's snow-white and only a couple of yards long. What the men on the platform are cutting up are two just-formed fetuses, two unborn narwhal babies, and though I look away quickly, look at Shackleton, I get the sick feeling suddenly in my mouth.

"Everything all right?"

"Thank you, sir."

"Listen, Merce. The *Sir James Clark Ross* is paying a visit to old Grytviken. What takes the men here a month to handle, they can do in a single day on the ship. And that's how progress is . . . If it weren't, it wouldn't be progress."

Shackleton runs his expert eye from bow to stern of the ugly factory ship. He seems like a boy marveling for the first time at the traffic in a big harbor. "Strange, isn't it, that we always give our new monsters the names of our pioneers. If Ross knew that something like this had been named after him . . . You know who Ross was?"

I don't know Sir James Clark Ross, but I mention my guess that it could be the same Ross that the Ross Sea and the Ross Ice Shelf are named after.

"Well done," says Shackleton. "You really aren't an idiot. Surely you must be able to tell me what the two highest mountains beside the Ross Sea are called."

"I'll have to pass, sir."

"Mount Erebus and Mount Terror. And why would they be called that?"

"I don't know; because someone named them that. Maybe Ross, sir?"

"Damn it, Merce, you're right! *Erebus* and *Terror,* those were Ross's ships." He wrinkles his forehead. "What's that?"

We're rowing past the stern. An enormous steel plate mounted into it has been left slightly open, and the head of one of the sailors keeps appearing and disappearing. Rubbish flies out through the gap and slaps down into the disgusting bay water next to our boat.

"Hoy!" Shackleton shouts through funneled hands. "Wait till I get up there! I'll cut your damned ears off!"

While I heave with all I've got, tongue between my teeth, to speed the dinghy across to the pier with as little rocking as I can manage, Sir Ernest gives free rein to his dissatisfaction. What he wouldn't do in front of Jacobsen or his harpooneer Larsen, he does in front of me: he swears at the whalers who should be too ashamed even to give themselves that title once they hire aboard a ship like the *Ross*. At least the men who hunt seals have had the decency to get used to calling it seal clubbing since they started slaughtering them in their thousands.

I get the boat alongside on my second attempt and jump up onto the quay.

"What name would you call them, sir?"

"Butchers in a whale factory," he says so seriously that I immediately regret the glibness of my question.

We go up to the houses. The sky above the flensing area is teeming with birds. Skuas, petrels and shearwaters chase one another in competition for stolen chunks of meat and wheel above the ramp the men are hauling the carcass of a humpback whale onto, its flukes already hacked off.

"White-chinned petrels," says Shackleton in passing. "You don't often see them here." And since I don't react: "They really do have a white chin. Trust me."

The whaler Hurley's riding in comes out from behind the *Sir James Clark Ross*. We can see him standing on deck next to Larsen, the chief harpooneer. The ship is called *Star X*. Its horn hoots and then a roaring starts in its engines and its screws begin to churn the water. The white-chinned petrels complain loudly and leave the bay to the departing ship.

AROUND THE LIBRARY TABLE, WHERE CAPTAIN JACOBSEN HAS SPREAD OUT a map of the continent, stand Tom Crean, Alfred Cheetham, Frank Wild and Shackleton. Stina Jacobsen has baked biscuits, which she serves with tea and Madeira. As she's leaving the room she points at a chair between the bookshelves and gives me a smile. It means that only she is supposed to be able to see me. Could I please make myself invisible to the others.

The debate around the chart turns on two pivots. Jacobsen makes no secret of the fact that he can't wait to be initiated into Shackleton's plans for crossing the continent. Shackleton, on the other hand, needs to draw out everything that the head of Grytviken knows about the current state of the ice in the Weddell Sea. And Sir Ernest is clever enough to make the first approach.

"We'll come at it with two ships, in two teams," he says. "While you're being kind enough to host and resupply our *Endurance,* the *Aurora* is—"

Jacobsen interrupts. "The *Aurora*? Mawson's *Aurora*?"

Shackleton: "Sir Douglas has sold the *Aurora* to me. But as I was saying, while my crew is pushing on into the—God willing—open Weddell Sea, Mackintosh will have taken the *Aurora*—"

"Aeneas Mackintosh?"

"Just so. Mackintosh should have already landed his men on the other side of the continent. Or, to be precise"—he leans forwards over the chart—"here. Near Scott's hut in the north of Ross Island."

"So, if I understand you correctly," says Jacobsen, "the continent isn't, after all, as was being announced everywhere, going to be crossed by a single group. Instead, there'll be two teams who come from north and south to meet in the middle. Where exactly will that be?"

Shackleton responds uninflectedly. "Nowhere. The two groups won't meet. My plans are for my men and I to complete the whole crossing of the ice, from the Weddell to the Ross Sea. The Ross Sea group's task consists exclusively of setting up depots, northwards up to the Beardmore Glacier. Those depots will keep my men alive once we've run out of provisions."

Jacobsen gazes silently at the chart for a while, then says, "Bold. Bold and with a Shackletonian elegance. I congratulate you."

"Thank you. I appreciate the compliment, Captain."

How many men are to take part in the crossing? Fridtjof Jacobsen would like to know. Instead of crossing, he says "transversale."

"Six," says Shackleton. "Six sleds with nine dogs for each of the six best-suited men."

A shock goes through me, a rip in my thoughts. Until now I'd assumed that we'd all attempt the transversale. How stupid can I be? Of course it'll only be a handful of men and of course only the best-suited . . .

But who? Which five with Shackleton?

Frank Wild pipes up: "As fantastic as Sir Ernest's plan is, its success depends on ensuring that we get as far south as possible into the Weddell Sea. Would you be so good, Captain, as to give us your estimate of the ice conditions at present? We're aiming for Vahsel Bay."

"Ha!" says Jacobsen, laughing and turning away from the table. He's a real popinjay, Captain Jacobsen. His is probably the only waxed handlebar mustache in the Southern Ocean. He has the eyes of a gander, small, dark and alert, and so he sees me sitting on the chair immured by books and asks, "Are you going along, young man? That's something I would reconsider, if I were you."

I smile and he turns back to the discussion.

"The Vahsel Bay, Mr. Wild, Mr. Crean, Mr. Cheetham, Sir Ernest! You are talking about sailing down to the seventy-seventh parallel in the coldest summer in the Antarctic since men have lived here, and doing so in a wooden ship! With respect, I advise you not to. There were good reasons why both Amundsen and Scott and why you, too, Sir Ernest Shackleton, started your attempts on the South Pole in the Ross Sea. The Ross Sea's ice shelf is an area of unearthly desolation, as you all well know, a place of strange notions induced by losing the horizon over a borderless expanse of ice. But you know also that the Ross Sea is comparatively predictable as long as you can endure its emptiness. In the Weddell Sea, however," says Jacobsen, rushing towards the chart so that Crean and Cheetham have to dodge out of his way, "the ice does not stay in one place, you understand? It's in constant movement, in itself and also on the water. There are unimaginably large ice floes containing thousands of bergs, each of which can easily be several miles long, and they all melt, then refreeze, break up and freeze again. I've seen a pressure ridge in the Weddell Sea ice, gentlemen, that looked like the Great Wall of China. Pack ice, drift ice and the bergs themselves are all spinning clockwise at the speed of a racing steamship. More or less at the latitude of the Vahsel Bay, Mr. Wild"—he laughs—"the ice is then squeezed together and neatly folded into stacks. There are bergs stretching hundreds of meters up into the sky and also, unfortunately, down into the deep, where you can't see them. And then this whole mess of shards and splinters is pushed northwards again and builds up even more momentum than before. Of course, you're quite right, Sir Ernest, it is entirely possible to sail across the Weddell Sea. After all, Weddell has shown us how it is done. But we know today how lucky he was to do it. He must have come across a patch of open water a hundred thousand square kilometers across, probably because he stumbled into an exceptionally warm summer. This year, the opposite is the case. Ask my men if you don't believe me, Mr. Cheetham; I can see that your opinion differs from mine. Ask them and these simple whalers will confirm it for you: the Weddell Sea is frozen shut." Jacobsen clasps his hands behind his back. "As elegant and audacious as your plan is, Sir Ernest, and although you've gathered the very best men around you, giving me the singular good luck of having you all as my guests . . . I'm afraid you're taking too great a risk. I advise against it. It would be irresponsible of me to do anything else."

Shackleton leaves the table and comes across to me. Once he has come so close that I could count the holes punched into his suspenders, he changes direction and begins to pace along the wall of books. He is again wearing the dark expression he wore on the boat. Now and then he runs a finger across the spines of the books until he abruptly, and without looking at Crean, asks, "Tom, what's your opinion?"

Crean rubs his palm against the back of his head. To the impatient Jacobsen, it must seem like hesitation from this bearer of the Albert Medal, this silent giant whose chest is at the height of Jacobsen's head. But the few words that sound in Crean's bass are anything but hesitant. They're unequivocal. "We want to cross the Antarctic. That means accepting a maximum of difficulty at every stage."

Crossing an open Weddell Sea would have been a stroke of luck, yes, but making it through the pack ice would be even better.

Shackleton seems to take no notice of Crean's words, and as he passes me for the third or fourth time, he whispers, "A real luxury, these books, don't you think?"

I nod.

And Shackleton smiles at me. He is as if transformed.

He slowly turns around and says mildly, "Thank you, Tom. Perhaps, dear Captain Jacobsen, I shouldn't throw your caution to the wind so thoughtlessly. What do you make of going together to visit Thoralf Sørlle in Stromness and asking what he thinks?"

Jacobsen holds up his palms but says nothing. What would Sørlle know better than he does? Eventually he says, "I'll gladly lend you a ship," which means more or less that he'll continue to do everything in his power to help us, but unfortunately won't be able to accompany us personally to Stromness. The lord of Grytviken is offended. The corners of his mouth, turning down in the shadow of the mustache, are not the only thing to reveal it.

OUR MEAL IN THE EARLY EVENING GETS FROSTY. THIS TIME I'M ALLOWED to sit at the table, eat Stina's crab soup and look down her top when she serves Falkland turnips or another Adélie penguin steak to Cheetham, who's sitting next to me. It was definitely worth being brought along.

Even if only because it's brought me back to reality. This much is certain: I will not have to endure a two-thousand-mile march through a mountainous desert of snow and ice behind a sled dragged by nine beasts half-crazy with hunger. Since her spouse is choosing to eat in silence, Stina asks the table what the other twenty-two men will get up to while their shipmates are crossing the continent.

Jacobsen can't resist adding, "If they even get that far."

Wild waits for Sir Ernest to nod before answering the question. At the other end of the table, I learn that the rest of us are to construct the first-ever Weddell Sea station. A base that, according to Wild, will provide a staging post for decades of future exploration, the largest station in the north of the continent.

Stina would like to know whether the planned base has already been given a name. Shackleton shakes his head.

"Stina's Hut," says Crean, of all people, and flushes. Even Jacobsen has to smile to himself. I see the hut in my mind's eye. To me it already has another name: the Blackboro Hut on Ennid-Muldoon Land.

"A little more penguin, Mr. Cheetham?"

Which six will it be? Sir Ernest, Crean and Cheetham—that's already three sleds occupied. And the other three? Wild? Will Shackleton take his second in command with him? Or the skipper? Hurley . . . ! Shackleton will have to pay his debts with the earnings from Hurley's photos. And he'll also want to have a doctor with him for the men and the dogs . . . It's going to be damned hard for Bakewell to bag himself a place on one of those six sleds bound for that hell.

Stina's penguin is delicious; Cheetham thinks so, too. But he still can't bring himself to laugh at Wild's joke that visiting a penguin hatching ground is like running onto a football pitch halfway through a game. Cheetham is breathing loudly. And he can't find a vent. He's been fuming since Captain Jacobsen, in the space between two bites, made the claim that Scott lost the race to the Pole solely because of his deficiencies of character.

"The way I hear it," Jacobsen continues, "it's now considered proved that Captain Scott pressured the weakest of his three companions, by staring at him uninterruptedly, to leave the tent during the snowstorm and go to his death."

No one contradicts him. And Fridtjof Jacobsen seems willing to stick out the embarrassing silence.

"Can I ask a question, sir?" I say to Shackleton. He nods briefly. You can see how hard he's been hit by this remark that Jacobsen has pulled out of thin air. I'm quite surprised to realize that he's helpless in the face of open malice. "I'm sorry, Captain Jacobsen," I say, "but isn't it true that no one can know what made Titus Oates leave the tent? Everyone who was there froze to death a month later: Wilson, Bowers and, you'd assume last of all, Captain Scott."

Jacobsen's gander eyes glint at me. Now he's angry. He'd bite my head off if it wouldn't make him look ridiculous. He controls himself and eventually goes back to eating his dinner as cool as you please. I feel a warm hand on my back. It belongs to Cheetham, who says, "Everyone who knew Scott knows that the well-being of his men came first. Let's leave it at that."

I look across at Crean. He was one of the last to see Scott and his companions alive. Rumor has it that Crean still hasn't got over not being asked by Scott to go with him on the last leg of the march. Crean doesn't react. He seems not to have noticed that my contribution was partly an attempt to come into conversation with him. He just carries on scratching around on his plate.

"Exactly. Now there's going to be a change of topic in Stina's Hut." Mrs. Jacobsen stands up from the table. "First the topic and then the plates. Which of you would like dessert? There's strawberry ice cream."

WE SPOON THE PINK ICE CREAM OUT OF BOWLS WITH CHIPPED RIMS AND listen to Stina. She's put on a knitted jacket and is telling us about the event she can't wait for, the arrival of the post boat. It's expected in the coming week.

There's a knock at the door and Holness appears, visibly shaken. He pulls off his bobble hat and begins to turn it in his hands. "Sir, the dogs." Holie comes closer at Shackleton's command. "Some dogs have escaped again."

A rumbling emerges from Crean. He stands up and wipes his mouth with the back of his hand. "And?"

"This time it's really bad. Songster and three others, we couldn't catch them."

Everyone has stood up. The get-together is over. Holness reports that the dogs haven't only torn open two more pigs, they've also wreaked havoc in the darkness of the whalers' cemetery. It takes a while before Holie gets the word out. Eventually he says, "Limbs," and looks at his feet.

# 16

## A YOUNG HERO

HURLEY'S WHALER HASN'T RETURNED YET, BUT YOU CAN already hear its foghorn in the distance. At the pier, Wild, Crean and Cheetham wish us a good night and disappear into the darkness with Holie. A little later comes the news that the dogs have been caught. Shackleton orders that the damage to the graves be repaired at once.

"The Imperial Trans-Antarctic Expedition is leaving its mark," Jacobsen says in a caustic but not actually unfriendly tone, and Shackleton shows with a smile that he, too, is willing to leave dinner's pointed exchange behind. He does, however, insist on making compensation for the pigs while Jacobsen counter-insists on their being a gift. Shortly after it has begun to snow, four men appear out of the dark carrying the two carcasses and load them into the dinghy right away. Shackleton thanks them. He kisses Stina Jacobsen's hand. I've again become invisible.

"Sir Ernest," Jacobsen calls from the pier once we're already in the boat, "do you know what Amundsen said—or is supposed to have said—when he heard about Scott's death? It was: so he's won!"

"We'll wait until the fifth of December," Shackleton calls back. "If the post boat hasn't arrived by then, we'll set off."

"You absolutely must wait for the post boat. Pastor Gunvald will be on board, and I won't let you sail without his blessing."

"Good night, Captain Jacobsen."

"Good night, Sir Ernest."

115

I lower the blades into the water. We've got a week till the fifth of December, not much time to bring a pack of dogs to heel, bunker several tons of coal and visit Amundsen's brother-in-law.

I begin to pull. Rowing alone in the darkness, rowing alone with a national hero and two dead pigs on board—not my world.

WE GLIDE THROUGH THE BLACK AND SILENT BAY TOWARDS THE LIGHTS of the ship, quickly putting distance between ourselves and the stink of the cutting platform. I can't see Shackleton's face, but his voice sounds tired when he says that an idea came to him while I was defending the dead Scott against Jacobsen.

"That was brave of you, Merce. It pleased me very much."

And Jacobsen's library pleased him, too. Whether I wouldn't like to organize the books in his cabin while he's in Stromness.

"I have everything, not just the whole encyclopedia. I have the complete history of Antarctic exploration from the Greeks to the modern day knocking around in there. But it's all fairly useless at present because I have to search for an hour before finding anything. Ross, for example. You don't know who James Clark Ross was. He wrote a wonderful book: *A Voyage of Discovery and Exploration to Southern and Antarctic Regions, During the Years* . . . from when to when, that's what I would have to look up. But I can't because the book has disappeared."

Wordie's prophecy occurs to me: Shackleton suddenly knows exactly what he wants me to do for him.

"I'd be glad to help, sir."

"Good. You're the right man for it. That is of course assuming that Mr. Green can spare you from time to time. You've read about Scott?"

"My brother, sir. He got Scott's diaries as a present last year and read me a lot of them."

We come within hailing range. From the deck of the *Endurance,* the watch calls out for the password.

"You tell them," says Shackleton, and again he sounds very tired.

"Queen Mother Alexandra," I shout. "Sir Ernest returning with Blackboro from Grytviken."

"Come aboard," they shout back to us. And you can hear Greenstreet's whistle.

"I didn't know him very well," says Shackleton while we slide alongside the ship's rump, "Titus Oates, I mean. Lawrence was his real name. Oates came from an old family, was highly decorated in the Boer War, a young hero who wouldn't let anyone divert him from a kind of cheery pessimism. Scott writes very movingly about him. Your brother, you said? Also an adventurer?"

"No, sir. An engineer."

"In the forces, I assume."

"Royal Air Force, sir."

The rope ladder comes clattering down and we moor alongside. Shackleton doesn't say any more. He wishes me good night and climbs aboard.


HOWNOW, UZBIRD AND I HEAVE THE CUTTER ONTO THE DAVITS AND THEN drag the two pigs on deck before I go and tell Green about them. The food prepared for tomorrow is waiting in the galley: pork chops. A pot of Yorkshire pudding cools on the stove, a tray of pasties beside it, and the usual six loaves of bread wait in the oven for the shrilling of the yeast-clock. No sign of the head chef, nowhere in the kitchen, where a cake and a bowl of Green's special biscuits are standing under cloths. Sometimes when Green is bored after finishing his work, he appears in the Ritz armed with scissors and a comb, looking for someone who'll submit to a haircut.

And that's exactly where he is, scraping over the black stubble on Bobby Clark's head. "I've brought extra supplies of pig," I say with satisfaction, and lift my bloodied hands. The same gang who was sitting together at breakfast stare at me dumbfounded. Only Hurley is missing. He isn't back yet.

It seems that not enough blood has flowed this evening. One hedgehog-haircut later, I've fallen asleep several times in the chair and snapped up out of dreams of strawberries and Mrs. Jacobsen's breasts whenever Green's scissors nicked me. I know how short the bristles are by the cool breeze that's running across my scalp and by the mountain of wool I can see lying before me on the table.

There's a tramping on deck and on the stairs, the swing door flies open and a man soaked from head to toe in gore staggers into the Ritz. He doesn't have Hurley's locks, he isn't perfumed, he has no camera, and yet it is still Frank Hurley. Everyone sitting jumps to his feet. "Frank! Holy shit."

The Prince collapses into a chair. He really smells bad. We keep away. He doesn't seem injured. Instead of saying anything, he holds up a circular object hanging from a cord around his neck. It's about as large as a saucer and made of leather.

"What is this?" We don't ask Hurley; he asks us.

No one knows.

"This is the Order of Jonah, you idiots," he says. "They've conferred it on me."

"Who has? And what for?

Frank Hurley explains while Green cleans him up and, since he's already at it, shears off the Prince's hair.

# 17

## THE ORDER OF JONAH

WHILE THE TENDER THE NORWEGIANS HAD COLLECTED HIM IN was bearing down on it, Hurley noticed the unusual shape of the *Sir James Clark Ross*, whose stern was fitted with an enormous hatch that could be swung open and shut. As the rowers pulled their boat past it, this steel door, which was standing ajar, looked to him like a gateway to the underworld. From the scuppers of that floating abattoir blood was purling out into the oily, greasy water. Hurley found it so nauseating that it didn't even occur to him to take a photo.

But there was no way to avoid contact with that ship, because the Norwegians made fast alongside it, and he had to carry his equipment across a flensing deck strewn with strips and chunks of flesh and fat. The small whaler *Star X* was squeezed in and moored between the *Ross* and the pier. He climbed down to it and was greeted at the railing by the fleet's master marksman, first mate Als Larsen.

As soon as he and the cameras were on board, the long-beards who'd rowed him over cast off, the engines jumped into motion and the *Star X* navigated a course through the whale carcasses floating in the bay like partially inflated balloons. They made off at a quick twelve knots.

From his voyage with Mawson, Hurley knew Carl Larsen, the mate's famous father, who founded the whaling stations on South Georgia and captained Otto Nordenskjöld's expeditionary ship, the *Antarctic*. So they already had something to talk about while

Larsen's son showed him around the *Star X* and led him up to the firing platform in the bow, where he explained how the harpoon gun worked.

Hurley would soon see for himself. The ship had passed Barff Point and the Nansen Banks and was maneuvering at lower speed through the first ice floes. They looked like enormous floating plates of white stone that some blow had shattered into pieces. And from the crow's nest came the call: "Whale, there she blows—whale on the starboard side."

They turned and the hunt seemed to begin. A fountain of spume hardly visible to the naked eye rose at the horizon and, at the sight of it, the men came to life. They cheered and laughed and some of them sang the same eerily beautiful melody time and again.

Larsen was indifferent. "A sperm whale," he said. "He's no use to us. But we'll go closer; the men can have their fun and you can take your pictures."

Sperm whales haven't been hunted for a while because their oil doesn't mix with oil from other species. The *Star X* was only looking for blue whales and razorbacks.

They could soon make out the outline of the whale through the calm sea. It swam as slowly and leisurely as if sleeping through the blue water. Only every minute or so did its tail fluke rise and fall just below the surface to maintain the animal's forward movement. Hurley shot a series of unrushed photos. The eye on this side seemed to be watching him. The whale was almost as long as the boat. A third of it was made up of the boxy head that underwater battles with giant squid or killer whales had left with deep, gleaming scars.

The helmsman managed a few times to give the doubtlessly already ancient giant a bump on the stern. Upon which the whale would descend out of sight, seeming more weary than frightened. The tail fluke lifted itself up out of the water, and from the two jet-black sickles two dense curtains of water rained back down into the sea. The men on the firing platform cheered every time the helmsman managed to bump it.

The school of blue whales appeared in the early evening when they were already on the way home, more or less opposite Hound Bay. On the northern horizon, perhaps five miles distant, a whole cluster of high silver jets rose out of the water. "Grazing blue whales," said Larsen. "We're in luck." Once the ship had come within a mile and a half of the animals, Hurley could hear the noise of their blowing. It sounded like a range of whistling pressure valves.

All around them, the sea was shimmering pink with swarms of krill, a bounty of food for the dozen or so whales in the school. They swam singly or in twos and threes, scooping the crab soup into their gaping mouths with the layered combs hanging down from their upper jaws, then pressing the filtered water back through them and into the ocean with a loud huffing. Shortly before the *Star X* came into firing range, the whales sensed the danger and dived.

A shining stream of eddies showed the whalers their route. Larsen went up to the firing platform and patiently followed the string of whirlpools hurrying away across the sea. Until a jet of spray shot up in front of the bow, followed by the dark and rapidly growing mass of a surfacing whale. Larsen aimed the gun and fired it with a thunderous explosion. The harpoon's rope hissed through smoke and vapor into a mess of blood-drenched foam, and they heard a muffled thud as the dynamite detonated inside the stricken animal. "Hurrah," roared the men, and Hurley roared with them. He was intoxicated by it and for a while forgot all about photography.

The whale began to tow the ship. It dragged the *Star X* to the south, in the direction its school had disappeared in. It was still managing more than eight knots, so Larsen fired a second charge into it. The men reckoned its length at twenty-six meters. The whale slowed and an hour later it climbed to the surface and spurted bloody mist out of its blowhole. It was no longer moving. Just before it sank into the deep, the great eye fell shut. To Hurley, who had captured every stage of its final agony on camera, it seemed like the eye of the slain giant in the fairy tale who'd been able to crack coconuts with his eyelids.

A hollow harpoon was used to pump air through the blubber and into the whale's insides. The carcass swelled and returned to the surface. The Norwegians fastened it to the stern, and two younger long-beards put on nailed boots, clambered onto the whale and hacked off its worthless tail.

It was dark and snowing by the time they tuckered into Cumberland Bay and tied up against the cutting platform. The whale was left in the water and made fast while they carried on to the pier.

Hurley took his equipment ashore, said good-bye to Larsen and his crew and went across to the fire station. Most of our men were already asleep, and when Frank Wild told him that some of the dogs had escaped again and what they had done, Hurley decided not to disturb Crean and the others but to find a boat down at the harbor and row back to the *Endurance*. He left the cameras in the fire station and set off carrying a storm lamp.

To clear his head, he walked along the edge of the water. When he reached the flensing area, there was a horrible scene waiting for him. Sawed or chopped chunks of whale and seal had been piled into heaps. Flippers, jaws, tongues and eyes glittered with crystals of frozen blood, and the wind whipped through the alleys between mounds of dead flesh and exposed skeletons as light snow fluttered into them.

The carcass of an as yet undissected humpback whale lay across the stone ramp, blocking his way. In the weak light of the lamp, he tried to find a way around its head, but since it lay half in the water, Hurley retraced his steps and tried again at the tail end. It was buried deep in a hillock of waste that he'd never be able to cross.

He decided to use a flensing ladder to climb right over the whale and did manage to reach the top unscathed. But as he pulled the ladder up behind him, he lost his footing, slithered down the other side of the carcass and plunged a few feet through the dark before landing in something soft and sticky, where he stayed lying.

It was the most disgusting moment of his life. Whenever he moved, there was a sucking noise, and on his face and hair were oily threads that could only be coagulated blood. Where was his lamp? He could see only the silhouette of the meat pocket he'd tumbled into, and outside it the snow whirling through the night. Eventually, he began to scream.

The worker who heard him shone his light into the whale only briefly, and when he saw that there was a man lying inside it and swearing in English, he swore himself in Norwegian and ran off. Shortly after that, half the factory's workforce was on the scene. The men dragged Hurley out of the belly, wrapped him in a blanket and carried him to Jacobsen's house. There he insisted on being brought to the *Endurance* at once, which Captain Jacobsen had them do.

The Order was handed to him by one of the monosyllabic long-beards he'd spent the day with on the *Star X*. Like a polar bear pondering what he might eat and what not, carefree, content and as happy as the first light of morning, he pinched Hurley's cheek and wordlessly hung the leather pendant around his neck.

# 18

## The Library

S HACKLETON HAS FIXED OUR DEPARTURE INTO THE ICE FOR NOON in three days' time. He's been in Stromness since yesterday with Cheetham, Crean and Wild, speaking to Captain Sørlle, and while almost all our crew are spending the time on land and sitting in the fire station writing letters home for the post boat to carry back to the Falklands, I've stayed on board with Bakewell, who's doing what needs to be done before the mast; Holness, who's keeping the boilers stoked; and the skipper, who's enjoying his one day in total command of the *Endurance*. We're sailing across to Leith Harbour to bunker the last of the coal and other provisions. No one can tell me why the Russian whaling station at the foot of Coronda Peak has exactly the same name as the harbor at Edinburgh. But all that matters is that Sir Ernest has managed to agree to a good price with the Russians. The whalers, directed by Worsley, carry aboard the timber, flour, condensed milk and forty-one crates of potatoes that are going to give a moment of truth to the idiosyncratic bunker construction that Chippy McNeish has nailed together between the deckhouse and the mainmast. And while the Russians, who are black with sparkling dust, lug the coal into the rig for hour after hour, I stand in front of the empty shelves in Shackleton's cabin and consider where I should put which book. I rummage in boxes, pick my nose and do a little reading.

How am I supposed to arrange a library that might not be very extensive but where the only books I know out of at least a hundred are the Bible and Scott's diaries? Alphabetically, you would think. But I shouldn't make it that easy for myself, especially since it won't be what Sir Ernest is after.

What will he be expecting? For a while I toy with the idea of arranging the tomes by size or by the color of their bindings, the way that the nails, screws, tools and wood in father's workshop are neatly arranged on shelves of tins and boxes so as to be quick to locate. While in Muldoon's chandlery there are whole areas taken over by a single color: red yarn, red ropes, red canvas. It startles you when Ennid is wearing a red dress behind the counter and limps over the border from the red area into the blue. But that would hardly help Shackleton when he's searching for a certain book. Arranging the books by size or color would mean having to memorize the appearance of each one and always remember the color of, say, this two-volume paperweight *Voyage autour du monde* by a certain Louis-Antoine de Bougainville, i.e., a fairly threadbare black. Or he'd have to remember that the slimmest book in his collection is by Fridtjof Nansen, *Crossing the Mountains on Snow-Shoes. From Bergen to Kristiania*. And it would mean having to separate Nansen from Nansen, because the other book of his that Shackleton owns, *By Night and Ice. The Norwegian Polar Expedition 1893–1896* is easily among the fattest of all his volumes and would therefore have to be at the other end of the shelves. I'm not sure that's the general idea.

Whenever there's a lull in the racket of coal clattering into the bunker, you can hear the cries of birds dipping over the bay. The Russians rolling the coal aboard across a gangplank seem not to get tired of laughing. For an instant I wish I could change places with one of them. But then I say to myself that while I'm finding the first step the hardest, every step is a hard one for those lads on deck. I move into the light falling into the cabin through the narrow window and open the slim Nansen volume.

I read: "I had finally overcome the worst of it. My word, was it hot! It attacked my arms and legs and the sun was baking. I felt a burning thirst and the snow hardly quenched it. In delight at having made it this far, I took out the orange that I had been saving for so long. It was frozen and as hard as a coconut. I ate it whole, peel and flesh. Mixed with snow, it was very refreshing."

After I've pulled several books out of the boxes and crates and stacked them beside Shackleton's table, I impulsively decide to approach the matter differently. What I'll do, I say to myself, is arrange the books by when they were written or, better yet, chronologically by the period they describe. Then I notice that on almost every spine there are two dates printed after the title, one for the start and one for the end of the voyage the book describes.

Merce, this is something you should check. Books with years after the title in one pile, others in the other. I put the fat Nansen on the first stack, the slim one on the second. Then to the first pile I add F. A. Cook's *Through the First Antarctic Night. A Narrative of the Voyage of the* Belgica *Among Newly Discovered Lands and Over an Unknown Sea About the South Pole;* to the second I add *The Narrative of Arthur Gordon Pym of Nantucket* by Edgar Allan Poe, as well as *The Life and Adventures of Peter Wilkins, Relating Particularly His Extraordinary Meeting with a Flying Woman and His Shipwreck in the Antarctic,* inside which I read that it was written by a man called Robert Paltock in the year 1784. Which gives me another idea. I take a book from the stack of those without dates and have a look to see if it, too, has a date of publication: Alexander Dalrymple, *An Historical Collection of the Several Voyages and Discoveries in the South Pacific Ocean.* I find it right on the first page: London 1770. And to be completely sure that each of the books can be chronologically ordered, I reach again for Poe's *Narrative of Arthur Gordon Pym.* No date in the front. But at the back, hidden on the rear flyleaf and tinily printed, there it is: New York, 1838.

Shackleton's boxes contain two books by his former boss and subsequent rival: *Robert Falcon Scott: The Voyage of the* Discovery,

*1901–1904* and the one that my brother also owns and that he used to read to me: *Last Voyage. Scott's Diaries, 1910–1912*. I know at once where to look, because the entry where Scott describes the death of Titus Oates is one of the last ones before he, too, takes his leave from the world: "Should this be found I want these facts recorded. Oates' last thoughts were of his Mother, but immediately before he took pride in thinking that his regiment would be pleased with the bold way in which he met his death. We can testify to his bravery. He has borne intense suffering for weeks without complaint, and to the very last was able and willing to discuss outside subjects. He did not—would not—give up hope to the very end. He was a brave soul. This was the end. He slept through the night before last, hoping not to wake; but he woke in the morning—yesterday. It was blowing a blizzard. He said, 'I am just going outside and may be some time.' He went out into the blizzard and we have not seen him since. We knew that poor Oates was walking to his death, but though we tried to dissuade him, we knew it was the act of a brave man and an English gentleman. We all hope to meet the end with a similar spirit, and assuredly the end is not far."

It's the first time that I've read it myself and, just like when I lay in bed listening to Dafydd, a cold shudder runs down my back. I again see in my mind's eye the inside of the hump of tent with the three men lying in their frozen sleeping bags, emaciated, semiconscious with hunger and thirst, and incapable of speaking a single clear word because their tongues are so thickly swollen. Scott, Bowers and Wilson can't hear anything but the tireless, deafening howling of the storm that's pulling at their tent, ripping and tugging at it, the wind's only obstacle for hundreds of miles. And Captain Scott has his pencil stump wedged between his fingers to write. He's scribbling something like "the act of a brave man and an English gentleman." Incredible. Like standing in front of a bellowing dragon that's about to swallow you up and straightening your tie. Dafydd always said that no act of courage would ever match that bravery in the face of death. To me, on the other hand—and this is what sends the shudder down my back—it's the writing of a dead man, someone who has already put everything behind him, even courage.

I put the diaries on the stack. There are four book towers: one built of the twenty volumes of the *Encyclopaedia Britannica,* one of the books with dates in the title, one of those that only have the date of publication and finally a small stack of five books that have neither one nor the other and that, as far as I can tell, are all history books, books about how Ptolemy and other ancient Greeks and Romans imagined the Antarctic. I'm still thinking about Scott. While I empty out Shackleton's boxes and sort his books into either this or that pile, I'm suddenly spooked all over again by the sentence in my head, the one that moved me so much when Dafydd read it to me that I bawled my eyes out as soon we'd turned off the light and I was alone under my cover: "Well, we have turned our back now on the goal of our ambition," Scott wrote on the morning before their march back from the Pole. I pull out the book again. There it is: "and good-bye to most of the daydreams!"

Among the last books to be fished out of the wooden box is the one Shackleton mentioned. It's green and battered and has got dates after its title: *A Voyage of Discovery and Research in the Southern and Antarctic Regions, During the Years 1839–43.* The others are a threesome backed in thin white paper: three copies of Shackleton's own book, *The Heart of the Antarctic. 21 Miles from the South Pole. The Story of the British South Polar Expedition 1907–1909.* It contains numerous pictures, drawings that seem both gentle and grim, just like their creator, George Marston, who I ate breakfast with this morning! There are portraits of Shackleton in a pullover standing in front of a vast ice field; there's one called, "The *Nimrod* moored before a tabular iceberg," another shows a gramophone standing in front of a group of penguins who are craning their necks at it curiously, and there's also a self-portrait in there: "The inventive Marston at his reading" is lying in his bunk, a burning candle in a porcelain holder balancing on his temple.

With that I'm over the hill. The rest is easy. I throw another glance into the empty boxes and suddenly notice that everything is quiet. There are no laughing Russians, no swearing Bakewell and, as I go out into the corridor, I don't hear the skipper stomping up and down behind his door. My towering work is still in Shackleton's cabin: four stacks that don't look like much but were quite the slog. I lock the door with Sir Ernest's key. And I haven't even reached the deck when I realize what I'd forgotten: Where the hell is the Queen Mother's Bible?

# 19

## SKIPPER'S PET

THE SIGHT AWAITING ME IN THE RITZ WOULDN'T HAVE BEEN possible under Scott's command. Scott thought it was important for the officers and men to be quartered separately and that the soldiers and civilians not eat together.

In contrast to his former third officer Shackleton, who comes from merchant shipping, Scott worked his way up the ranks of the Royal Navy. Despite all the affection in him when, for example, he wrote about little Birdie Bowers that he'd never met a man who was so brave, so hard and so undaunted, his watchword was always order. I'm not sure how much I'd have warmed to the great Captain Scott. Sitting in the Ritz over mashed potatoes and pork, which it should actually have been my job to reheat, are my sleepy-seeming captain, my leg-massaging stoker and my best friend, and beside the plates for Worsley, Holness and Bakewell, there's a laden plate waiting for the ship's boy, for me.

Of course, they can't resist winding me up for making it within a few weeks from the oilskin locker to Sir Ernest's cabin. But even though there's no malice to their jokes, I notice that Bakewell seems to be taking it pretty seriously. He gives me an odd look a few times, a searching one, as if among the general mockery there were something important that I'm missing.

Before the skipper retires to his cabin to, as he puts it, write letters to New Zealand, he lays out the plan for the rest of the day. As soon as the supplies we've just taken on board have been counted and the rest of the coal has been bunkered, we'll cast off and tucker slowly down the bay to Stromness to collect Sir Ernest and the others.

"The supplies will be checked over by Mr. Bakewell. Holie, you can go back to your boilers."

"Aye, sir."

"And you to your special mission, I suppose," says Worsley to me, not without a grimace.

I reply that it's as good as finished and ask permission to help Bakewell. He's got nothing against it.

The three of us go down onto the lower deck. Holness accompanies us to where the provisions are stored then goes on alone in the weak yellow lamplight of the corridor that leads astern to the ladder down to the boilers. He looks pale, quite an achievement for a cinder monkey, and he's got thinner, like a dried herring. It's more with his big, blank face than in words that he says, "See you," before stalking off.

It's the first time since Buenos Aires that Bakewell and I have been alone together. I see right away that he's avoiding my eyes. But I don't let on that I notice something's up. It's his job we're doing, so I let him lead the way and wait for him to tell me what to do.

We start with the vegetables. He wrenches the first potato crate off the stack, digs his hand under it, jerks it to the side and reaches for the next. He is furious. But he doesn't say a word. He wouldn't be Bakewell if he just came out with what his problem is. And since I've got nothing to feel guilty for, at least in what concerns Bakewell, I don't say anything, either, but leave him to his Russian potatoes and wander over to the dry stores to count the tins of milk.

Of course he does them all himself, all forty-one crates, that's how it is when a pissed-off jack-tar has a bee in his bonnet. And it's his own stupid fault if the sweat's now pouring off him as he stands in the doorway.

"Twenty pallets," I say innocently; the numbers are my witnesses. "Twenty times forty. That makes eight hundred tins of milk. Have you got something to write on?"

"Go write it in your books." He comes across, panting, and although there are other things in the way, leans over the milk I've just counted. Yes, he's doing what I think he is: re-counting the tins of milk.

Fine. I love him. He's got credit with me, not unlimited credit but enough for now. When Bakewell's in this mood, he'll bang in nails with his elbow. I wait to see whether he regrets it. He's kneeling on the floor and running his fingers across the pallets. But he'll never say anything off his own initiative.

So I tell him to his face that the reason he's making such a stink doesn't have anything at all to do with those books. Other than a couple of knuckleheads, he's the only one on board who hasn't asked me once in all the days since I appeared out of the locker how it is that the boss has taken such a shine to me. And I also know, I say to him, why that is. Because he's jealous. Because he's letting himself be eaten up by a crummy, mean little grudge. I might have expected that from some of the men on board, but not from him.

Bakewell stands up and says, "You're right: eight hundred." And he turns to the next stack of pallets.

I'm already wondering if I should jump on his back and bite him in the shoulder, like I always used to do to Dafydd when I wanted to bring him down a notch, when he says, more to the tins in front of his face than to me, "I just wonder what's going to become of you, Merce. You know, as far as I care, you can shine the boss's shoes as much as you want. You can feed and wash him and then you can even read him a nice bedtime story while you tuck him in. You can do all of it as far as I care. And why it is that you're bending over, why it is that you're arranging his books and why it is that, as well as the big Antarctic heroes, he takes you, of all people, with him to supper with Jacobsen and his lady, none of that's got anything to do with me, that's entirely your affair, Mr. Chief Steward." He gradually unfurls his index finger to point at me and quietly says, "But let me tell you just one thing. No one on this ship knows you as well as I do. None

133

of them knows that you're usually all right. Think about it: how are the brothers supposed to know that you're not like that?"

The Russians are back to the coal. Every time they push their wheelbarrows on board, you can hear the gangplank thwack off the gunwales, and every shovelful of dropping coal sends a fine tremor running through the ship.

"Who are you talking about?" I ask. "And what am I like?"

"As if I'd stand here and rat someone out," he says at once. "The fact that you don't notice who you've made your enemies should be enough of a warning, don't you reckon? These aren't the kind of guys to muck about. Remember Rutherford? They've got a very fine line of what they'll take; you put one foot across and they'll go off the deep end." He turns his back on me. And as he crouches to carry on counting, he says, "What you're like? You want to know what you're being?"

"Go on."

"A bootlicker."


I'D ACTUALLY COME TO A FINAL DECISION NOT TO SEND A LETTER HOME. But as I climb up to the noise- and dust-filled air on deck, feeling the choking lump in my throat, I'm aching for someone I can sob it all out to, someone I know where I am with. They're frightening creatures, these ten or twelve Russian whalers who, each blacker than the last, are shoveling coal into the last free spaces between the kennels, the tenders and the crates that the motor sleds came in, strange brethren who flash me beaming yellow smiles as I slip past. Just as I close Shackleton's door behind me, a deep rattle goes through the ship. Holness is banking up a fire under the boilers down in her belly.

"Dear Mam, dear Dad and dear Regyn, I know it's terrible but unfortunately I've got to tell you . . ." There would still be enough time to sit down at Shackleton's writing desk and explain everything, really everything.

No. No matter how tempting it is to help myself to Shackleton's writing paper, I won't be writing a letter home. For three reasons: Firstly, because it would be wrong to scare and worry Mam, Dad and Regyn with the news that I'm on my way to the South Pole. Secondly, because I'm relatively sure that Captain Coon will have placed his duty of care and the word he gave my dad high above my own wishes and will have written a letter not only about the wreck of the *John London* but also about my rescue. And thirdly, because I've got no desire whatsoever to write my family an apology letter. Perhaps I am as gullible as Regyn says and as presumptuous as Ennid thinks. That I'm far too easy to impress and that my bravery is really bravado are things I already know about myself. But submissive is one thing I'm not. Bakewell would have kept his head down on the *Discovery*. I, on the other hand, would have driven Scott berserk. Not a good trait. Not good, but I don't think I would have got down on my knees even for King Arthur, no matter how much he waved his Excalibur around.

Outside, the rocks of Grass Island are passing by. Although she's running much deeper in the water, the *Endurance* is making good speed. It must be good coal that the Russians have sold us. I'd better make sure I finish up, so I go back to my book towers.

Just the way that the cloud of coal dust that has been hanging over the ship dissipates into thin air as we steam out of Leith Harbour, my annoyance vanishes as I begin to put away the books. The volumes of the encyclopedia go alphabetically onto the top shelf. But I'm still thinking about Bakewell. He's wrong. And even if he isn't, what can they do to me, these brothers he was pontificating about and who can only be some of the unfriendlier onboard animals, like the bosun and the chief stoker? They'd be risking endless trouble with Sir Ernest and the skipper and then they wouldn't have anything to laugh about for the rest of the voyage, that's for sure. But he's wrong anyway. What's much more likely is that the men are getting nervous because we're about to set sail. It's only normal that there's a bit of tussling over the pecking order.

And what if he's not wrong?

The middle shelf is occupied first by the Greeks and the Romans, then the books about the Middle Ages, until Magellan and Drake appear for the first time in the tables of contents . . . Yes, it'll work like this. And right after these two I should have the first of the books with dates.

1768. Cook.

No, Mr. Bakewell, you can't put one over on me. For you, too, it's ultimately all about getting a place on one of the sleds. The rumor has spread as fast as wildfire that there'll only be three men going along with Sir Ernest and the two most experienced veterans, Cheetham and Crean. Worsley will be joining the group as their navigator. Two left. Only two! And one of those will have to be a doctor. McIlroy's prospects are looking dim at the moment, because Dr. Macklin has been taking care of the dogs and generally making a better impression. So it'll be Sir Ernest, the captain, Cheetham, Crean and Macklin. Which leaves just one space free. And I'm afraid that Hurley will probably get it for the sake of his photos. But let's wait and see. Hurley can take some pretty photos of the hut instead, or the scientists, the dogs, the frozen ship.

Then all the volumes with dates one after the other onto the next shelf. What comes right at the end? 1912. Scott's diaries. Less than three years have passed since the deaths of the five men who reached the Pole. A lifetime of fame awaits the six men who manage the crossing. Nothing for those who stay behind. I can't hold it against Bakewell if he hopes that Sir Ernest will choose him.

And he is very fit. No one's tougher. And despite all his drive, Bakewell's a peaceful presence to have around, at least for the most part.

Shame that he won't be going!

BRITISH TRIUMPH OVER THE ETERNAL ICE OF THE ANTARCTIC

*The Imperial Trans-Antarctic Expedition Succeeds*
*in Completing the First Land Crossing of the Sixth Continent.*
*The 1,800 Miles from the Weddell Sea to the Ross Sea were Traversed*
*by Sir Ernest Henry Shackleton with his Companions*
*Cheetham, Crean, Worsley, Dr Macklin and*
*Blackboro.*

Done.

SHACKLETON'S IN HIGH SPIRITS WHEN HE, CHEETHAM, CREAN AND Wild climb out of the Stromness motorboat and come clambering up the rope ladder, joking relaxedly among themselves. The sky is darkening over the bay, and I'm holding up the only storm lamp, so it's difficult for us to read the outcome of the discussion with Captain Sørlle in Sir Ernest's expression.

But he doesn't keep us waiting for long. In the Ritz, I haven't even finished giving everyone a glass for the port he's requested when he takes the bottle in his hand and raises a toast. There's good news and bad news. What do we want to hear first.

"Good news first," everyone says. I see Shackleton's gaze. It's so wild that I have to drop my own when he looks at me.

"We're doing it," suddenly says not Shackleton but Crean, looking around the company. No one says a word. It's absolutely silent but for the ship creaking under the tons of coal the Russians have carted onto her back. Shackleton lifts his glass.

"Let's drink to it," he says, and all reserve goes out the window. The cheering and yelling are so loud that we forget everything else. His big bonce gone bright red, Bakewell stands in front of me, his whole face beaming, and squeezes me against his chest.

The bad news is about the post boat. Pastor Gunvald arrived this morning on board a whaler from the Falklands—in a state of total exhaustion and limitless outrage, as Sir Ernest puts it. He doesn't know precisely why that is. All that's certain is that the post boat won't reach Grytviken before mid-December at the earliest.

"Unfortunately, that's far too late for us. I know we're all waiting for post from home. It's no pleasant thought to be away from the world for months without some friendly words to take along. But I'm afraid that the weather conditions, as Captain Sørlle has explained them to me, leave us no choice. The summer is ending before it has even really begun. The pack ice is at its furthest spread in ten years. In principle—"

He interrupts himself and musters us, who are hanging on his words and who both know and don't know what he's about to tell us. I'm sure that it's not his intention to unsettle. But he seems to be the only one not to realize how irritating his notion of honesty really is.

"In principle, it's already too late."

LATER I STAND WITH HIM IN FRONT OF HIS SHELVES AND EXPLAIN HOW I thought I'd do it. He seems very impressed and pulls a book out here and there before neatly slipping it back where it came from. Three or four times he strides back and forth along the shelves, letting his eyes run across the spines.

"Ah ha, very good, I see," he mumbles. "Chronological sequence, very clever, Merce. Because it runs parallel to the progress made in the discoveries. If you'd organized them by southernmost latitude, you would have ended up with the same order, isn't that right? Amundsen and Scott are at ninety degrees south. Very nice. Thank you, I'm very grateful."

"There was no book by Amundsen there, sir. Otherwise I'd have put it next to Scott's, of course."

"It's not there because I'm reading it." Shackleton opens the lid of his desk and hands me the book. It's called *The South Pole:*

*An Account of the Norwegian Antarctic Expedition in the Fram*
and is followed by two dates, the same as those on *Scott's Diaries:
1910–1912.* "Put it on the shelf," says Shackleton. "But put it in
its proper place."

I think about it briefly, then place it on the right-hand side of
Scott, at the end.

Shackleton nods.

"Sir, there was another book I couldn't find, that is, the
Bible . . . the Bible from the Queen Mother, sir."

"What do you mean? It was on the shelf. How have you managed to overlook the Queen Mother's Bible, eh?"

"I've got no idea, sir."

"You haven't thrown it overboard in a fit of Welsh pique, have
you?"

"I . . . sir, for the love of God, no!"

Shackleton steps closer. Once he's right in front of me, he puts
his hands on my shoulders. "Just a little joke, Merce. I left the Bible
in the keeping of Captain Jacobsen. He would like Pastor Gunvald to
give his sermon in English, presumably so that we don't misunder-
stand it. So, and now to bed. I have to write a letter to my wife if I
don't want to let things with her deteriorate completely."

Before I can creep into my bunk and wail under my covers, I
have to endure one last bit of onboard humor. To celebrate the news,
the captain has had Hussey bring his banjo into the Ritz. Accompanied by his feverish plucking, Cheetham and Bakewell are warbling
and bellowing the "Shanty of Lorenzo," the skipper's pet.

> Oh Ranzo was no sailor—Ranzo, boys, Ranzo . . .
> He went on board a whaler—Ranzo, boys, Ranzo!
> And he could not do his duty—Ranzo, boys, Ranzo . . .
> So they took him to the gangway—Ranzo, boys 'n' sailors!
> And they gave him five-'n'-thirty—Ranzo, boys, Ranzo . . .
> That made poor Ranzo thirsty—Ranzo, boys 'n' sailors!

Now the captain was quite good—Ranzo, boys, Ranzo . . .
And he took him to his cabin—Ranzo, boys, Ranzo!
And he gave him wine and water—Ranzo, boys, Ranzo . . .
And Ranzo loved his daughter—Ranzo, boys, Ranzo!
And he taught him navigation—Ranzo, boys, Ranzo . . .
To fit him for his station—Ranzo, boys, Ranzo!
Now Ranzo is a sailor—Ranzo, boys, Ranzo . . .
And chief mate of that Whaler—Ranzo, boys 'n' sailors!

# 20

## THE SERMON

THE ORGAN GOES QUIET. PASTOR GUNVALD GRIPS THE SIDES OF the lectern and lets his gaze wander across the heads of the whalers. He waits until Jacobsen's men are quiet before he raises his voice to speak.

"Good to see all of you looking well! Let's offer our thanks to God, each with the Lord's Prayer in the language of his homeland. Then I'll continue in English."

Once the Norwegians' murmuring has trailed off after ours, Pastor Gunvald turns his attention to us. No greeting. Without any further preamble, he begins to read from the Bible, and hearing the Gospel in our mother tongue doesn't fail to have the effect he intends. Bakewell, Holness and How lower their eyes and bring their hands together. I'm the only one who can't look away from the reddish beard with the words coming out of it about Jesus calming the waters in a storm.

"'And there arose a great storm of wind, and the waves beat into the ship, so that it was now full. And he was in the hinder part of the ship, asleep on a pillow: and they awake him, and say unto him, Master, carest thou not that we perish? And he arose, and rebuked the wind, and said unto the sea, Peace, be still. And the wind ceased, and there was a great calm. And he said unto them, Why are ye so fearful? how is it that ye have no faith?'

"Men of the *Endurance*," says Gunvald, "a few weeks ago, you completed the same crossing that I have in the past few days. But how

141

different your journey must have been from mine. You knew nothing of the storm that was roaring behind you and onto whose periphery I strayed, as unconscious and afraid as the fishermen of Capernaum with whom the Messiah crossed the Sea of Galilee. I want to speak to you about this storm, to make clear to you what is waiting on the other bank for those who do not heed the might of the Lord."

An *Amen* rolls through the ranks of the whalers. On our side there is nothing to hear but whispering, boots shifting and the wooden pews creaking under our weight.

The pastor strokes the beard that hangs down below the neckline of his jacket. "Since I left the Falkland Islands, I have not been able to forget the question that the fishermen ask: 'Master, carest thou not that we perish?' How can it be that the Redeemer remains silent in the midst of noise and ruin?"

Captain Worsley is sitting two rows ahead of me, wearing a white pullover and surrounded by his officers. Of Shackleton, I can see only the back of his freshly shaven neck. Sir Ernest sits unmoving in his place beside the Jacobsens, who've joined us on this side of the church. For a while, everything is quiet; we listen to Pastor Gunvald's observations, and outside the church the quick snow tumbles past the windows.

And yet there's something in the air. I don't know where it's coming from: from the God-botherer up there at the lectern or from the taut stillness of the men who, in this church, suddenly seem as alien to me again as if I'd been a stranger driven in here by some coincidence or the inhospitality of the weather. I'm fumbling for Ennid's fish when Bakewell gives me a nudge and points his chin in the direction of Worsley.

The skipper seems to have fallen asleep.

"He's just pretending," I whisper.

Bakewell has another look and decisively shakes his head.

And in the same moment it all kicks off. With the next sentence that the pastor carefully delivers in our direction, the taut stillness snaps. Everything he's said so far has been to bump us with the bow; now come the harpoons.

"It is thirty-three days since, on the first of November, a large part of the British Royal Navy was sunk in battle off the coast of Coronel in Chile. The victors, the German fleet under Admiral Graf Spee, suffered no significant losses and were, when I left the islands, some few hundred sea miles from the Falklands, preparing to take them into their possession. The storm of war has reached the South Seas. And I say to you, men of the *Endurance,* that this is a storm such as no man has ever experienced."

Not one of our men has stayed sitting quietly; everyone is bolt upright and looking at the others in shock. A muttering runs through the pews while the Norwegians stare from the other side and the old red-beard at the front drinks from a glass of water.

"Quiet!—Men!" is barked in quick succession by Crean's bass and the thick rasp of the bosun.

Shackleton turns around and briefly lifts his hands.

"Holy shit-house!" says Bakewell beside me. That calms me down a little.

"Thousands of your countrymen lie dead in their wrecks at the bottom of the sea off Coronel. The storm, uncalmed by any Redeemer, has pulled them into the deep. It seems that God is sleeping. And not one of you asks whether He doesn't care. Nothing on earth can calm this storm. And not one of you believes that this sleeper is the one to do it!"

"Get to the end," heckles someone very close to me.

Vincent stands up and turns around threateningly.

"Who was it?" I whisper to Bakewell.

Vincent sits down again.

"We are all sailing on this ship on which Jesus is soundly asleep, all of us. And if this is any consolation, let me tell you that in the heart of Europe it will not be thousands that this Godless storm will drag down with it, but that alone in the battle for the Flemish town of Ypres it is already hundreds of thousands who are being thrown into

143

the grinder for a few yards of mud. No!" roars Gunvald, leaning forwards over his pulpit. "I do not have to get to the end. I am already there! And you no less than me."

"Just wait and see!"

The same voice. Vincent is on his feet at once. There's nothing he can do. The whalers say a resentful Amen.

Pastor Gunvald directs his words back towards them. The longbeards nod after every sentence and at the front, next to Shackleton, Jacobsen and the wonderful Stina lower their eyes.

Meanwhile, the Imperial Trans-Antarctic Expedition plays dumb. Holie whispers the message into my ear: "Strict order from the boss: no heckling!" I lean over to Bakewell.

Gunvald switches back into English. He says that what he has just advised his countrymen to do is remember King Sverre, who, as Abbot Karl Jonsson tells the story, was forced by a superior enemy to retreat with his men, the Birkebeiners, deep into the Raundal. "King Sverre took five guides who knew the way. And they were bitterly needed, because the weather had become as bad as happens only rarely, even there. The snowstorm was so furious that they lost a hundred and twenty horses with golden saddles and bridles, cloaks, weapons and other precious things. For eight days all they ate was snow. On the eve of All Hallows' Day, the storm became so powerful that one Birkebeiner was killed by the wind hurling him down and breaking his back in three places. All that King Sverre's men had left were their shields. They dug themselves under them and into the snow. And only the Birkebeiners' shields ever returned home from the Raundal . . . Thus is it written in the history of our country, which has known the ice for thousands of years, just as it has known death in the ice. We have known the ice longer than we have known God, and it was despite the ice that we found our way to Him. Amen!"

"And you're done!"

This time it's Greenstreet who jumps to his feet. "Who said that? Stand up at once!"

No one stands up. There's only Lionel Greenstreet, upright between the pews, arid as ever in his first officer's uniform, and, up at the pulpit, Pastor Gunvald stands and waits.

A shoe, a flenser's boot, comes flying from the other side of the church. It lands with a crash between Mick and Mack.

"You missed!"

"You're blind!" shouts Bakewell before my elbow hits his ribs.

And I'm sure it's Orde-Lees who yells: "Birkebeiners!"

Shackleton gets up, motions Greenstreet to sit and comes towards us along the aisle. He passes wordlessly and sits in the first empty pew behind us.

There is still some noise coming from the other side, then everything again goes quiet but for the wind piping around the church. Before the pastor carries on, I quickly turn my head: Shackleton looks back at me; his eyes are bloodshot red, as though mirroring the beard and mane of the pastor.

"Be advised: do not provoke the icy storm of the Almighty! Do not carry the storm of Godlessness into the storm of God! Do not carry this war into the ice! Turn back, if you do not want to suffer the same fate as King Sverre! Turn back and think of the lessons that the ice has taught you. Three years ago and within a single month, it took from you your greatest hero and your greatest ship. Think of Scott, who froze at the South Pole, and of the *Titanic,* which lies at the bottom of the Atlantic."

Pastor Gunvald brings his palms together, rests his hands on the lectern and closes his eyes. He seems to be praying. I, for one, pray that it's over.

But it isn't.

Gunvald slowly lifts the green leather-bound Bible above the edge of the lectern.

"What awaits the fishermen from Capernaum on the other bank? A man possessed! A man who lives in graves and calls himself Legion, for, as he said to Jesus, 'We are many.' And he besought him much that he would not send them away out of the country. Now there was there nigh unto the mountains a great herd of swine feeding. And all the devils besought him, saying, Send us into the swine, that we may enter into them. And forthwith Jesus gave them leave. And the unclean spirits went out, and entered into the swine: and the herd ran violently down a steep place and were choked in the sea."

Pastor Gunvald claps the Bible shut with a bang and lowers the book. Nobody moves. Gunvald says, "Commit yourselves happily to the harbor that is faith in Jesus Christ, for it is he who calms the storm and saves the possessed."

"Amen," say the whalers.

"No expedition, no matter how skillfully equipped . . ."

"Enough now!" shouts someone, Cheetham or perhaps even Wild, the shout comes from right at the front. And others follow it. Bakewell jams two fingers between his lips and starts whistling shrilly. And it's Captain Worsley who shouts through his hands, "When the hell does the music start?"

Gunvald carries on speaking about the banner of possession that Shackleton must not carry into the ice until the whistling and stamping drown him out. The whalers on the other side have stood up and look less than happy with what's going on. But Jacobsen and Larsen have their men under stricter control. Standing forwards and back in the aisle, they make sure that it doesn't become a brawl.

The service is over. The pastor descends from the pulpit. He has the Bible in his hands and lays it carefully in the space in the first row where Shackleton was sitting before he moved behind us. As the noise lessens and the first muted laughter travels back and forth between us and the long-beards, I walk along the pews and look for him. But he's nowhere to be found. Shackleton has gone.

# 21

## Captain Cook
### or
### We're not sure where we are

GREENSTREET'S COMMANDS THUNDER AND CLASH WITH THE ear-bursting yowling of the winches and the clattering of the capstans. Yard after yard of green chain rattles on board until, with a double thwack on port and starboard, the two monsters break the surface of the water and thunder against the bow.

"Anchor weighed. Bring it up!"

Apart from the stokers and the man in the wheelhouse, everybody is on deck as we make a last curve around the cutting platform. The sirens wail from the shore and there's a seventy-strong howling from the kennels as we steam slowly out of Cumberland Bay. The afternoon we set off on course for the Sandwich Islands, only stop before the Weddell Sea, is a cloudless example of sub-Antarctic summer, five degrees above freezing, the fifth of December. Holness has bequeathed me a lilac pullover, not so thin that I'm not warmly swaddled, but not so thick that I can't fit Mam's jacket over the top.

A small troop of Viking whalers has arrived at the pier and is waving us lunatics good-bye. "Ahoy, you Birkebeiners! Cheerio!"

WE PASS THE HOBART ROCK AND COME OUT INTO THE MAIN BAY, AND hardly have I checked below to make sure that Green isn't already on

147

the warpath, but we've passed Sappho Point, which recedes behind length after length of open gray sea. Stornoway, Hownow, Bakewell and the others race up into the shrouds, stand on the footropes and let the freshly ironed sails drop with a crack into the wind.

"All up!" bawls Greenstreet, meaning his men.

"All down!" screams the bosun, meaning the sails. Because when Vincent means a man, it sounds very different: "McCarthy, get your arse up that mast! Bakewell, stop looking for your brain, you haven't got one, move the tackle instead! Blackboro, go read something, and piss off!"

We rush along under full sail, hugging close to the island's jagged, snow-covered coast. In the gaps where the breakers aren't surging high up rocky cliffs lie bays named by Captain Cook, all of them desolate, with beaches of black sand that glaciers creep across until, when their own weight gets too much, the end snaps off into the water and floats away as a berg. For at least an hour I stand at the railing, shivering despite my lilac pullover, and can't see enough of this outer edge of the last outpost of civilization, the powerful crashing at this last tip of the world that I, Merce Blackboro, am sailing off. How is it supposed to make me feel? James Cook named the southernmost end of South Georgia Cape Disappointment because he realized that it was an island he'd found and not the fabled southern continent that it was his secret mission to locate. When you read about what old Cook did to himself to be the first man to go so far south, you can sympathize with his sense of dejection. Right up to the point where the island again vanishes under the sea, it's no more than colorless waste, naked of trees, just the way you would imagine the end of the world: there's less and less of everything except for water. And then all at once there's nothing at all, nothing but the sea. The reason I still don't feel disappointed is probably because, in the whole month on South Georgia, I never had the feeling that I was standing on uncharted territory. It felt like someone had given me the opportunity to land on the coast of my dreams and explore its interior. And that was wonderful. But in contrast to Cook, I know for sure that the enormous southern continent really does exist, and that it's no dream, but as solid as South Georgia itself.

Vincent is right enough in his own unpleasant way when he spits his sarcasm into my face. In the free hours I have between meals, it's now rare to see me without a book in hand. But what can I do about it if Shackleton doesn't order me to sit cross-legged at my bosun's feet and mend old signal flags, but instead demands that I read the books as conscientiously as I arranged them. When he came aboard after saying good-bye to the Jacobsens, he wordlessly pushed the Bible against my chest. And I was just putting it in its place in his cabin when he stormed in, banging the door, and began to complain. He was in a foul mood and I was back to being an idiot.

"Take a book and read it. There will be a test in three days' time."

"Yessir, with pleasure, sir. Did you have a particular one in mind?"

He did. After all, for the next three days we'd be sailing the same route that was taken in January 1775 by Cook's *Resolution*.

While we follow a course southeast towards the Sandwich Islands, accompanied across the ocean by an ever smaller number of birds, Shackleton's tension gives way, thank God, and so does that of the men. The conversations in the Ritz focus ever less often on Pastor Gunvald's indications about the apocalyptic war raging in Europe, and the men also slowly forget their sadness at having missed the delayed post boat. Now that we're out on the ocean, it's the predicted ice conditions that again occupy the bulk of our interest, at least for the time being. But since the ship proves herself to be unexpectedly well-trimmed and since we make good speed across the equally unexpectedly peaceful seas between the fifty-fifth and fifty-sixth parallels, with no ice in sight, not even the smallest chunklet, calm descends on the ship. Each of us gradually buries himself in his work, just as I bury myself in Captain Cook's logbooks of the voyages from

1768 to 1779. Halfway between Cape Disappointment and Zavodovski Island, the northernmost of the South Sandwich chain, on a hazy morning when the dividing line between sky and sea can only be guessed at in the white fog, I notice that the birds that had followed us from South Georgia and perched in our rigging when they wanted a rest, have all gone. The departure of the birds feels to me like our final good-bye to the island, and my melancholy this morning gets stronger and stronger until tears push out of my eyes when I read about where we are in Cook's logs: "Countries damned by nature to eternal cold, that never feel a warming shaft of sunlight and whose wild and terrible appearance I cannot describe in words; such were the countries we discovered. How will those appear that lie further to the south? Whoever possesses the determination and the stamina to illuminate this question by sailing further than I have done, I will not envy him the honour of his discoveries, but will instead have the audacity to say that there will be nothing for humanity to gain from them."

PERHAPS IT'S TRUE THAT HUMANITY HASN'T YET DRAWN ANYTHING useful from the exploration of the Antarctic, apart from the opportunity to kill millions of seals, walruses and whales for their pelts, fats, oils and bones. A whole century owes its progress to blubber, to the layer of fat encasing the animals butchered in the Antarctic, whose oil lubricated machines all over the world and burned in the streetlamps even in Wales, including in the three in Pillgwenlly, burned brightly enough at night for my dad to walk my mam safely home and conceive me by the light of a whale-tallow candle. Cook saw it coming: men who sailed further south than he had, explorers who didn't think it was all about profit or progress but who, as it turned out, managed very well to extract some benefit from the eternal ice. Shackleton, for example. His expedition brought him so much fame and admiration that the King made him a Commander of the Royal

Victorian Order. That must have been a slap in the face for his old teacher. Scott wasn't even knighted.

If our Sir Ernest really intended to test my reading like some controlling schoolmaster, I could reel off the symptoms that Cook's men suffered when scurvy went round the *Resolution:* "Foul gums, blue-gray spots, rashes on the skin, shortness of breath, contorted limbs, murky green slime in the urine, sir!"

It amuses Dr. McIlroy when I read him this passage from Cook's notes. "Yes, when it gets to that stage, you can forget about carrot jam and barrels of limes."

While his colleague Mack uses the quiet days at sea to train the dogs, Mick is one of the few on board with nothing to do. He's no good at concealing his boredom and is the first to confirm what Green had predicted: as soon as he's scoffed down a meal, he starts to ask about the next one. So we're both often lurking in the vicinity of the kitchen. It's just a shame that you can't really speak to him, because he keeps what he thinks to himself, for example, about the war, about whether England and Wales might be the next battleground or how likely it is that the battle will also be fought in the air, and prefers instead to make an obscure joke of it: that the British redbreast may well whistle the last post for the German blackbird.

So, I suppose, yes, in his opinion there'll definitely be a war in the air.

There's still time before the evening meal. McIlroy is pleasure-lessly smoking a cigarillo to distract himself and asks more in passing than out of interest if I see parallels between Cook and Shackleton. This is Mick's other aspect.

I'm not sure. Shackleton, too, when he was Scott's third officer, was almost killed by scurvy. So I tell Mick about how Cook broke down on his return from the ice. The mild commander of before had become a thin-skinned, temperamental bully with a fondness for draconian punishments and the cat-o'-nine-tails. And he was hiding the murderous pain of a gallbladder infection.

"Ouch," says Mick, and blows a smoke ring.

Cook starved until he was skin stretched over bone. It was only when the scientist on board, the German Reinhold Forster, sacrificed his beloved dog to strengthen the gaunt captain with a scrap of meat, that the longed-for recovery eventually began.

McIlroy considers. "Well, at least we've got plenty of dogs," he says eventually, and runs his palm along the cat, which is sleeping between us on the sill of the porthole.

The cigarillo is smoked out and there's no sign of dinner. Perhaps Shackleton does have a certain resemblance to the young Cook, the stiff and selfless pioneer full of scruples. But the harried obsessiveness that drove the older Cook up and down the oceans of the world is more reminiscent of Scott. Mick neither agrees nor offers a differing opinion.

"*Discovery,*" is all he says, glancing from the corner of his eyes at Green, who, although he's moving around, still has nothing in his hands, no bread basket, not even a stack of napkins. Outside Mrs. Chippy's porthole, gray twilight is sinking onto gray seas. Dinner can't be that far away.

"It can't be a coincidence that Scott's first ship had exactly the same name as Cook's first ship," says Mick, bored.

He doesn't know and probably wouldn't even be at all interested in knowing that there have been seven *Discovery*s and that Scott's ship was no more than the latest to bear that name.

Listing the captains of these seven ships might be a way to win Shackleton's respect. For that to happen, he would first have to act on his threat and check through what I've learned. But I'm sure he's got other worries.

IN FACT, WE ALL HAVE THE SAME WORRY. ON THE NEXT MORNING, JUST as on the others, the fourth since Grytviken, there's no ice in view. As soon as the cloud cover tears open, Worsley and Buddha Hudson establish our position, but they always both come to the same conclusion: according to the information from both Jacobsen's and Sørlle's men, we should have been in thick pack ice for the last day and a half. And yet all around us there's nothing but water.

Shackleton personally climbs up to the barrel a number of times and keeps lookout in the dry and biting wind. In the Ritz, where they go to warm up, Sir Ernest and the highest-ranking officers discuss where the mistake could have come from. Worsley rules out a navigation error, but still tells Uzbird and James to examine the equipment.

It's in perfect shape. And in a few hours we'll know for sure whether our calculated position—56° 10 south and 28° 30 west—is accurate, because either Zavodovski Island will appear on the horizon or it won't.

The smallest person in the room sees it differently. Uzbird Hussey has been collecting the barometer readings of the past few hours. They seem to indicate that a heavy storm, a real tempest even, is approaching. Shackleton thinks fastest: if Uzbird is right, the storm could be the explanation for why we haven't encountered any ice. Although it really would have to be a big one to sweep the icy seas this clean.

"There's also another problem," says Worsley. "If we're going to run into heavy weather, it's far too risky to pass close enough to Zavodovsky to sight it. I suggest we set a more westerly course."

Shackleton agrees for the eventuality that the storm does indeed appear. He doesn't yet want to give up the best chance we have of being sure of our position. With that, he dismisses the group and goes back up on deck. Shortly afterwards, I see him up in the lookout barrel. In the ice, Cook had red caps handed out to all the men, as well as red fleece jackets and red flannel trousers. Shackleton's hooded jacket is black, and the sky soon turns blacker. Hussey's storm has arrived.

That night, I see men heave who I thought had never heard of sickness. A month on land is enough, it seems, for even an old shellback like Vincent to find himself clutching the railing and spewing his guts into the sea. In the water live fish and everything else with fins. Above the sea fly the creatures with wings, in the home of all free birds. But there's nothing that lives *on* the sea, nothing and no one. All that floats is dead, algae and flotsam, rubbish and carcasses. And somewhere west of the South Sandwich Islands, which are as hidden from us as they were for thousands of years, there floats the collected dinner of the men of the *Endurance*.

The storm is violent. Hail-bearing gusts shred two of the sails, and How and Bakewell have to go aloft and hack them from the yards. The wind races with a boom into the sheet of sailcloth swooshing up and down above the mastheads, carrying it off. And just as the two lads are back in the rigging, the yardarm they'd just been balancing on, out above the waves, snaps from its brace and crashes into the rig bunker, pulling spars and shrouds down with it.

But Hussey's Zavodovsky storm is not as violent as the killer that fatally wounded the *John London*. In comparison with that, this is a light breeze. You notice that this one has a will. It wants to show us what a polar storm looks like, and does so assiduously, bringing in all the elements at its disposal, downdrafts, house-sized rollers, and hail like grapeshot that's followed home by blinding flurries of snow. It's a tempest that finishes what it started but also ends just as quickly as it began. The hurricane off Montevideo was an inferno, an undeclared war between water and sky where everything between them was obliterated.

When Captain Worsley manages to recalculate our position, just as the weather is beginning to clear up, he tells us that the storm has driven us almost exactly two degrees of latitude further south. If he's calculated correctly, we've already passed Zavodovsky, Leskov, Visokoi and Candlemas without having sighted any of the four, and should now be between Saunders and Montagu Islands. Having already passed half the volcanic islands in this sickle-shaped chain on the way to the Weddell Sea would be the best news since the start of our voyage. But we still haven't seen any land and there still isn't any ice. Worsley takes it with humor but has to admit that we still don't really know where we are.

We repair the storm damage. Parts of the rig have fallen onto the foredeck and smashed one of the kennels. Two of the dogs have been crushed, and Crean and Dr. Macklin have to dispose of the bodies. It isn't much consolation that three of the bitches are now pregnant. They sew the carcasses into two old sacks and lower them over the railing into the sea. They were two of the more inconspicuous dogs, who behaved well in the kennels and who, because they looked almost identical, Crean and Macklin had named Jake and Jones.

I'm sitting with the cat by the porthole and reading when land is sighted. I already finished Cook days ago and am now deep in the nineteenth century with seal hunters who became scientists and explorers, with Weddell and von Bellingshausen, who, a hundred years before Scott and Amundsen, fought out a very similar rivalry and finally divided the glory between them: Weddell's *Jane* and *Beaufoy* were first to reach the sea named after him; von Bellingshausen's *Vostok* and *Mirny* managed the second Antarctic circumnavigation after Cook.

You don't always have to be first. I'm one of the last to have my jacket on and be standing at the ice-sheathed railing, marveling at the picture that has risen out of the gray seas to the east: an enormous rocky plinth.

Is it Montagu? The bosses aren't certain. Some of the Antarctic veterans sailed past here years ago, but none of them ever took a particularly close look at Montagu. Cheetham grabs Greenstreet's telescope and, the instrument to his eye, declares this rock Montagu Island: it has three more or less equally large south-facing bays, each with one large rock; also, there are colonies of chinstrap penguins all over the place. Saunders Island, further north, has no south-facing bays, while Bristol, in the south, is easily recognizable by Freezland Rock, which stands just off it. What could this be but Montagu?

Shackleton strokes his already quite impressive polar beard and exchanges a look with the skipper.

"Chinstrap penguins, eh, Alf?" mocks Worsley, and gives Cheetham a clap on the back in wandering off.

Alf Cheetham is gobsmacked. "Chinstrap penguins, yes. What's funny about that?" he calls after Worsley. "Have a look yourself if you don't believe me. They're right there, millions of them!"

Shackleton is ready to classify the island as Montagu for the time being. He puts an arm around Cheetham, who's all of a dither. "If we sight Bristol Island tomorrow, he owes you a drink, all right? Don't be angry."

But as soon as Cheetham has left to find solace with the dogs, Greenstreet directs his telescope at the island for a second time and Shackleton makes a murmur of agreement when he says, "Could also be Bouvet Island, sir. Which would mean that we've really made a pig's ear of it. I don't think that's what's happened, but it is possible."


ON THE MORNING THAT WILL REVEAL TO US WHETHER WE'RE ON THE best ice-free course to the Weddell Sea or have for the last week been sailing bravely into nowhere, a morning when most of the men have lost their appetite, I'm again sitting alone in the Ritz with McIlroy, who's nibbling his breakfast as placid as a dairy cow. But not even he can be entirely unmoved by our uncertain state, which is why he asks me if I know why the South Sandwich Islands are called that. Is it because the island chain lies between South America and the Antarctic, not unlike a slice of ham?

I don't know if he means the question seriously or if he just wants to wind me up. By now, it's begun to get on the nerves of some of the gentlemen on board if I mention while clearing the table what Cook's men had to eat, or respond to the advice that a ship's boy shouldn't do so much to risk a fat lip by telling them that it was Nick, the boy on Cook's ship, who discovered both Australia and New

Zealand. Even though Green found it amusing when I told him that Cook's astronomer was also called Charles Green, he hasn't wanted to hear anything about my books since I told him in an argument that Cook's Green died at sea, of dysentery, and that he should, to put it politely, mull that over.

I don't see any ulterior intentions in McIlroy's expression. He seems happy to have the breakfast table to himself and get the opportunity for a bit of a chat.

So I say, "As far as I know, the bread and the island are both named after some earl."

"Ah ha," he says, his mouth full. "Why's that?"

I just shrug and start to clear up. The fourth Earl of Sandwich, the great man behind Cook, will have to wait his turn. I suddenly have an urge to go up on deck, perhaps because the ship has suddenly gone dead quiet.

I slip into my jacket, leave—"What's up with you?"—Mick sitting alone, and go on deck. One glance over the shoulders of the men gathered at the railing is enough for me to know what's happened. An island is soaring out of the mist, smaller than Montagu and with a large, pointed sea stack lying just off it. Bristol Island and the Freezland Rock. But behind them, there at the mouth of the route that Cook named the Forster Passage after the German scientist and his son, there's something else. Resplendent white, with crevasses that pulse blue with sudden light, it lies there like a forgotten, uncharted coast.

The edge of the pack ice.

# 22

## In the Ice

For half a day we steam south along the ice's border, our engines just turning over. It must be running straight along the middle of the Forster Passage, since in the clear light you can see that the peaks of South Thule and little Cook Island are precisely as far off the bow as Bristol Island is from the stern. Giant petrels are traveling unceasingly between the clusters of rock and don't seem particularly interested in the ship that's crossing their route. In contrast to the skuas, who have found their master of ceremonies in Green, as the one who tips kitchen waste over the gunwales, these gray-blue giants zoom towards us just above the waves, sail leisurely through our rigging almost as if we odd fish, ducking our heads, didn't even exist. Sometimes, the sea and the ice shimmer red when a swarm of krill passes below. Often weighing hundreds of thousands of tons, it is these collections of innumerable little crustaceans all swimming in the same direction that attract the petrels. Bob Clark tells me in a gruesome voice that I can be sure of one thing: that as much as the birds are picking at the krill from above, the whales will be helping themselves from below.

The barrier has opened in many places to form fissures that would be wide enough for the ship, some of them even wide enough for her to turn around in if she reached a dead end. But since the edge is leading south, Shackleton has given the order not to sail into the ice. He and Wild are taking turns in the barrel, keeping watch until darkness descends around midnight, in case the drift changes direction. But even in the gloom of night, when I sit up every couple of hours to listen, I can hear the engines turning quietly and evenly and the *Endurance* continuing slowly on her way, just as if we were traveling up the Severn towards Newport in the gray hours of morning before the fishing fleet arrives.

The moment comes on the following day. The barrier sweeps in a long curve up towards the northwest. We follow it until midday to make sure that the direction doesn't change again, then Worsley orders us to heave to. We about turn and search for a suitable entrance. The lead that Frank Wild eventually spots from the barrel is fully three beams wide. Since it doesn't significantly narrow for as far as we can see, the fissure is probably a canal between two otherwise undamaged floes. There must once have been a single enormous ice plate, a white moon-landscape stretching over who knows how many square miles, floating steadily for years if not decades until at some point it split along this line running south. When Sir Ernest gives the captain, and the captain passes on to his first officer, Greenstreet, the order to make half speed ahead, the whole crew but for the boilermen has assembled on the foredeck. Everyone peers past the bowsprit and follows with his eyes the blue-black wedge that pushes its way through the white plateau until losing itself as a hairline crack on the horizon.

Only I look back over Bakewell's shoulder, across the afterdeck to the open sea. In the minute that it takes me to go back to the stern, the open sea has gone, as have the rushing gusts of wind sweeping across the water and the cracking of the surf against the edge of the pack. Now all there is in every direction is ice. And to me, clutching the frozen railing, it seems as though I'm standing not at the stern of the boat, but at the stern of time.

I THOUGHT IT WOULD BE QUIET IN THE ICE. BUT IT ISN'T. THE ICE IS constantly in motion. Where it hasn't been pressed together and forced up into ridges, the floes are a few yards thick. When the underlying swell knocks them together, you hear the dull crash of the collision and the long grating sound of the two floes grinding against each other. I notice by contrast just how much racket that's making a few hours after we've steamed into the belt of pack ice. We reach an open stretch of water the size of a small lake where, once we've stopped the engines to let Stevenson and Holness recover a little from the graft of feeding the boilers, you really can't hear a thing. We skim along under full sail, and while the sailors on deck make a game of taking turns to climb ever further out along the bowsprit and shout to the others to declare an arm, a hand or a finger the southernmost body part on earth, I use this quiet day on a pack ice lagoon to read up in Weddell's *A Voyage Towards the South Pole: Performed in the Years 1821–24* on what the captain of the *Jane* had to say about the "stinkers." That's what he calls the giant petrels after seeing a flock of them "eat around ten tons of elephant-seal blubber in a matter of hours."

Weddell estimates that after thirty years of seal-hunting in the Southern Ocean, twenty thousand tons of elephant seal blubber have been sold at the London market and that more than 1.2 million fur seals have been killed by British and American hunters. Bob Clark's lips press themselves into a disconsolate line when I present him with the figures, and the others don't want to have their mood spoiled by finding out.

But the time for quiet is soon over anyway. When we reach the other side of the lake that evening, the rising and falling sound of grating on all sides announces the presence of a huge ice field. How large it really is is something we discover over the next two days, when it sounds like we're sailing through gravel regardless of where on board you hide yourself to read or just to cover your ears without anyone seeing.

In the week after Christmas, we're between the sixtieth and sixty-fifth parallels and steaming cautiously through a fleet of gigantic icebergs. Some of them must be a few square miles across, all are at least a hundred yards above the water and so flat on top that I see with my own eyes how the most experienced navigators and geologists used to believe themselves to have discovered land that, no matter how conscientiously it was inscribed onto the charts, could never be found again. An apparently motionless tabular iceberg floats in the sea, the swell breaks against its white or blue cliffs and the waves spray upwards against it like breakers on a reef. There are icebergs the sea has drilled tunnels straight through or dug caves into deeper than we can see. Every wave breaking into them echoes thunderously in the ultramarine chambers. In the water, you can see the shadows of the bergs, but you can never be sure if this dark shape stretching towards the ship isn't actually the iceberg's underwater rump, tightpacked ice and rock swimming silently below the waves. "The wrecks of a demolished world" is what Forster called the Antarctic icebergs. When one passes safely behind us, we all breathe easier and listen for a while in relief to the raw slapping of the waves against the gently bobbing pack.

The days go by in finding leads we can squeeze ourselves into and in making the sober realization time and again that even the broadest canal ends at a barrier where we either turn around to search elsewhere or have to ram a way through, repeatedly steaming forwards and back, shredding our nerves. Since the wonderful day on the lagoon, our useless sails haven't been taken out of their lockers. We're moving exclusively under steam, which means that every spare man, be he an officer, a scientist or jack-tar, is given coal-shoveling duty. And so, in making the precisely calculated drives that ram the rounded bow against the ice before we recoil and are again steered against the squashed and shattered fracture, we've already used up more than half the coal in McNeish's bunker. And we haven't breached the Antarctic Circle.

Shackleton wanted us to have moored in Vahsel Bay by the end of December. We were going to celebrate New Year's in the first of the huts we'd constructed. But on Christmas Day there are still three hundred miles separating us from the entrance to the Weddell Sea, and after that we still have to cross half the sea itself. No one knows how much ice is waiting for us there. With his characteristic sobriety, making no allowances for celebration, Greenstreet calculates by the light of the candles in the decorated Ritz that if we maintain our current daily average progress of thirty miles, we'll reach Vahsel by the end of January. And all of us know that Greenstreet, in his own stiff way, is trying to give us some encouragement. But that doesn't change anything about the reality that his calculation, which affects all of us equally, is wrong: by the end of January, no previously averaged daily progress will be made anywhere. By the end of January, the southern Weddell Sea will be frozen solid.

To avoid any gloom, however justified, Shackleton divides the watch over the pack ice into hour-long shifts, so that everyone can celebrate and enjoy his helping of the Christmas feast. We raise a toast to the King and Queen, another to our comrades in the war, and then start singing. The tablecloths have been specially reversed and the men pass around the menu I've concocted with the help of our onboard specialist in all matters epicurean, Dr. James A. McIlroy. When I stop to think about it, it's the first effort from my pen since the never-presented ode to Ennid's limp:

*Christmas Menu*
*On Board His Majesty's Unglaciated*
*Expeditionary Sailing and Steam Ship*
*ENDURANCE*

*Entrée*
*Skilligalee (oatmeal porridge) or*
*Cracker Fricassee*
*(ship's biscuit, steeped and salted)*

*Main Course*
*Served on Carrots, Parsley, White Beet and Onion*

*Baked Forktailed-Petrel (pork) or*
*Emperor Penguin á l'anglaise (pork) or*
*Sirloin of Roe Deer (rat)*

*Dessert*
*Hard Cake (ship's biscuit with corned beef)*
*Soft Cake (white bread and butter—officers only)*

The real Christmas dinner comes out of tins. There's turtle soup, fried fish, braised rabbit, Christmas pudding, terrine and candied fruits. *Madam Butterfly* tootles along on Orde-Lees's gramophone a few times before we forget about it, and Crean's well-meaning suggestion that I declaim something from Cook unfortunately falls on deaf ears amid the flash and bang of Hurley's camera. I'm sure they'd all have listened spellbound: James Cook on Tahiti, his men in love with the island beauties who asked nothing more in exchange for their devotion than a handful of nails. After which, the proud *Endeavour* soon threatened to fall apart.

I do my stint of watch in the dark hour between midnight and one o'clock. I stand alone on deck for a long time and listen to the ice. Whenever Uzbird's lugubrious banjo takes a breather in the Ritz and Worsley and Bakewell don't have a shanty immediately to hand, I can hear the floes creaking and yammering, and sometimes it really does sound like out there in the unending darkness there's a shed where my dad has set up a little workshop just the way he used to—just for fun, to do a bit of sawing and planing after work.

Clark comes up and stands beside me. A little drunk and with a Scottish accent that I've never heard so strong, he explains to me about his favorite animal in the ice, the macaroni penguin. We look up at the Christmas sky, where Canopus is blazing above the long band of stars that make up the Hydra, and Clark says he hopes he'll be able to show me a colony of macaroni penguins.

"The very first time I saw them," he says with a slight slurring, "their coloring seemed to answer every question that's ever occupied me. I don't mean the gold on those bizarre crests, which is how you can tell them from far away and which looks like each of them has stuck some bits of straw to its head. It's more the black and white of the plumage, because in there are really all the colors you can imagine, and each of them is present in all the others. Well, I don't know if that means anything to you, but that's how it seems to me."

I'm pretty sure I don't understand what Clark is trying to say, but since I don't really know, I say, "Yes, of course, I think I get what you mean."

And Clark says, "Yes. That's why I told you. I can understand why Sir Ernest likes you so much. You're something special. You don't ask yourself any more about what you know about horses since someone taught you that in Latin it's called *equus*."

A long, difficult sentence, but Clark manages it.

"Thanks, Clark."

"Anyway, I hope that we get the chance to have a look at one of these colonies together. But I've just thought of what I forgot to tell you . . . The macaroni penguins have a peculiarity. You'll laugh when you hear the sound they make. You see, it sounds as though they're calling my name. No joke! Honestly, their call is: Clark, Clark! Clark, Clark!"

ON THE FIRST MORNING OF THE NEW YEAR, I FULFIL A WISH THAT I'VE kept as secret as Ennid's fish ever since my liberation from the oilskin locker: I climb up the mainmast rigging and clamber into the barrel on top.

Up there, you can't hear anything except the wind piping round the yards and stays. Despite the carefree feeling warming me from within because I'm thirty yards closer to the glorious, empty sky than anyone else, it's still brutally cold. So as not to end up freezing into place as an extension to the topgallant's ice-encased yardarm, I wrap the light-blue jacket around myself just like King Arthur did with the cloak that had twenty-seven dragons stitched onto it. Seen from above like this, the *Endurance* resembles a long arrowhead pushing itself down a narrow runnel in a jumble of waterways. Plates of gleaming black, blue and silver, those are open water, small ice-free spaces between the floes that are keeping us moving forwards despite everything. Far below me on deck, our skipper is standing wrapped up behind the new windbreak on the bridge, one hand on the engine room telegraph, the other on the semaphore that McNeish built with slats from Jake and Jones's splintered kennel. The signaling system that the captain uses to communicate the constant course corrections to the helmsman without shouting himself hoarse reminds me of clock hands broken off from their face. But sometimes, when I see Worsley standing there like that, his hand on the wood, his head turned until Greenstreet reacts to his signal at the helm, I think of my brother: Dafydd in front of one-eyed Mick Mannock's aircraft, waiting tensely to spin the propeller and leap out of the way.

Bewitched by the view, my thoughts wander and I daydream about the past and about what we might encounter in the ice. The new year's starting well. We've managed the longest distance since entering the pack ice, a hundred and twenty miles in a single day.

But there's still the usual back-and-forth. On the sixth of January, we're so tightly wedged that Sir Ernest decides to give the dogs a change from their daily existence of kennels and medical examinations, Spratt's dog food and Lysol baths. They're led out onto the ice in their sled groups and allowed to let off some steam. Only five fall into the water and are rescued. Then another two days of steaming powerfully, crossing the sixty-ninth parallel, where, shortly before sunset, a glittering white line on the horizon announces the next obstacle. In the morning, we pass an iceberg of such unimaginable proportions that Shackleton gives it a name. He baptizes it Mount

Rampart. Although we keep several lengths away, Wild spots its out-runners under water and estimates that they stretch three hundred yards into the deep beside us. But Rampart also holds a surprise that makes all of us who witness it break out in cheers. Behind it, the ice and the bergs, the endless white puzzle, have disappeared. There's nothing but water, the water of the Weddell Sea.

It takes a while before the lads manage to stamp the frozen sails down from the yards, but once they've fallen and been lashed fast, the breeze rushes into them. The Weddell wind fills them out, breaks the crust from their skins, and we, unleashed, rush south under a rain of tiny ice crystals tinkling onto the deck.

On the following day, the tenth of January, a Sunday, another giant iceberg comes into sight. It looks like Rampart's doppelgänger and puts us into a panic that the ice will begin again behind it. But then we hear what Shackleton, Worsley and Wild have to say about the berg. Its position is checked: 72° 10 south, 16° 57 west. It's certain: the mountain stretching up out of the light-green water is no iceberg. We've reached Coats Land, discovered by the *Scotia* expedition in 1904. What we thought was an iceberg is a coast of sheer cliffs, a piece of the ice shelf attached to Queen Maud Land. It's the Antarctic.


WEDDELL NEVER SAW IT AND FOR DECADES NO ONE BELIEVED HOW FAR south he'd come. The smug Dumont d'Urville called Weddell a vulgar seal clubber, and the man in whose book I read "Observations on the Sea-Voyage around Cape Horn" and "Observations on the Conditions of the Poles" as well as "Observations on the Calculation of Longitude by Means of Chronometer," in which I find myself marveling at the care he put into his charts of anchoring spots, natural harbors, promontories and easy landing points, died in poverty as the subtenant of a Miss Rosanna Johnstone. But we're sailing through his sea. For days on end, we watch seals playing in the water and lolling around upwind of the ice floes without the slightest notion that for the rest of time they'll be called Weddell seals.

On the fifteenth of January, which is celebratorily designated Greenstreet Day, there are only about two hundred miles between us and Vahsel Bay. In the shadows of the steep white wall we're sailing under, seals are jumping and diving, racing one another in our bow wave and plowing their snouts through the water like a herd of pigs; but none of them will follow us a single yard south. They're all heading north. The departure of the Weddell and crabeater seals is a sure sign that winter is coming.

But as long as the sea is clear, we carry on sailing. The following day is also a special one. Sir Ernest gets the opportunity not only to baptize another iceberg but to name a newly discovered stretch of land. In honor of the expedition sponsor who has dug deepest into his pockets, Sir Ernest names the cliffs that stretch five hundred yards into the air above our ship, which have an enormous glacier tumbling down them, the Caird Coast. Its covering of ice seems bleak and unfriendly and is split by unbridgeable fissures. Nowhere can we see any bare rock. Which is completely different from the bay we reach less than six hours later. Its ice falls sheer into the water, and as we heave to and have the engines bring us up close, it becomes clear why there's suddenly so much agitation on the bridge.

The height of the ice offers a perfect landing opportunity, and we'd be able to construct our winter station on the glacier above it. Shackleton, Wild, Worsley and the other Antarctic veterans retreat into the Ritz for discussion. Even the cat is banished. Worsley spills her into my arms in the doorway of the galley. I'm not even allowed to serve them coffee.

In view of the distance that the transcontinental sled journey will have to cover, Shackleton decides to try it a little further south. If we meet pack ice before reaching Vahsel Bay, the plan is to come back here. Worsley calculates our precise position: 76° 27 south, 28° 51 west. It confirms that we've covered more than a hundred and twenty miles in the last twenty-four hours. We sail on.

On the next morning, a storm approaches from the northeast and gets up to damaging strength by midday. We go for cover from the driving snow in the lee of a stranded iceberg, not least because we're not really making any distance. The stokers and the men on the bridge are kept hard at it all night, maneuvering the ship forwards and back while the rest of the crew shovels snow from the deck and breaks off the gathering ice, which within a few minutes recloses over everything.

The snowstorm lasts two days and the *Endurance* lies hidden behind the grounded iceberg as though behind the knee of a crouching giant. When the storm abates and we venture out, we see that for as far as we can make out, in every direction, the bay has filled with pack ice. Since it now hardly makes a difference what course we plot, we try to get further south, where there's a dark line on the clouds, indicating open water with the promise of a broad lead onwards. And we manage twelve miles in six days. The ice is differently constructed from what delayed us before. The floes are thick and soft and seem to consist mainly of snow, which sinks sadly into a mush of ice that the dull, colorless water can hardly wash through. There's nothing left for us but to watch the sea gradually freeze around our ship.

I notice how much Shackleton is reproaching himself for having passed over the one coast we could have landed on, and I see his excitement when, at midnight on the twenty-fourth of January, Greenstreet reports that a crack is opening in the ice around fifty yards ahead of us. We set all sail. The engines are stoked. For three hours, we stand on deck and shout ourselves warm, shout ourselves nearer to the coast of Vahsel Bay, now less than twenty-five miles ahead of us.

Two hours' sailing through open water and we would have reached it. But we don't get even a single yard closer to the lead. And eventually, we watch it freeze up again.

## *Part Three*

## THE FROZEN BOOKS

# 23

## "WE NEED A LEAD!"

HIS SKY-BLUE EYES, WHICH ARE A LITTLE CLOSE TOGETHER, gleam like a pair of new-minted coins. Sometimes they sparkle so much you might almost think he'd just been crying. During a few conversations with Frank Wild, I've noticed the way he suddenly takes me into his confidence just because it pleases him to talk to someone one-to-one in a friendly way. His position as Shackleton's mouthpiece makes all of us, including Wild himself, forget all too often that he's really a cheerful and obliging man. Perhaps that's why Wild usually seems quite miserable when he has to address the crew as a whole. He'd much rather throw out a couple of quick, funny commands and communicate the rest with a meaningful look.

Why isn't it possible to use either the motorized sleds or the dogs to travel across the pack ice to Vahsel Bay?

That question can't be answered with just a look. Frank Wild is in the middle of describing the state of the ice between us and the mainland, and the mortal dangers concealed by the snow, when the ship, which has been locked in for four weeks, is struck by a single tremendous blow. The bass thud is followed by an awful screeching rising shrilly in pitch.

My first thought is that another ship is firing on the *Endurance*, a German destroyer whose steel hull, three times higher than ours, is cutting loudly through the ice as it prepares to ram us.

"Everyone out!" roar Shackleton, Greenstreet and Vincent.

Lunch is forgotten, the seal roulade with potatoes abandoned, we throw down our cutlery and rush on deck.

The sight that greets us is completely other than expected and makes me, along with all the others who hadn't already been on deck, break out in wild cheering. Directly in front of the *Endurance*'s bow, the floe has cracked in two. A lead has formed and there are only two hundred yards of ice separating the ship from open water on which we could escape to the south.

No one has to tell us what to do. We leap overboard armed with shovels, picks and saws. I attack the white field until the numbness creeping up from my fingers and toes reaches my shoulders and hips. Gasping, I fall into the snow and it slowly dawns on me why all the ice veterans have stayed so calm.

I can see it from where I'm lying. Hardly has the water begun to flow but it becomes sluggish, goes porridgy and resolidifies. It really looks like it's dying. Water that perishes. There's no point working to keep the lead open. The cold is faster.

And it isn't even autumn.

You're an important day, you, the twenty-fifth of January 1915, I think while I lie there in the snow in front of the ship, looking at the hoarfrost encrusting its surfaces. Today, not only the water, but the whole expedition has died. Fancy that.

It's been a week since Sir Ernest had to declare that the drifting ice landscape between us and the receding coast was impassable, and now, for better or worse, we also have to recognize that we won't be reaching the open water under our own steam, either. We're stuck in the Weddell rotation, which is turning clockwise towards the north and, just as Captain Jacobsen said, carrying everything, including us, away from Vahsel Bay and away from the route to the Pole.

"We're stuck as fast as an almond in a chocolate cake," says Orde-Lees over dinner. And although no one's in the mood for laughing, Sir Ernest rewards this attempt at lightening the mood by asking

Aunt Thomas whether he'd be disposed to take on the quartermaster's responsibilities instead of looking after the motor sleds.

"Thank you, sir, it's a great honor; I thank you kindly" is the response. And then there is a little laughter after all.

Since the *Endurance* has stopped being a ship and since we now have to face autumn and winter, eight months in the cold and dark, the onboard routine has been officially suspended. We're transforming ourselves from a marine vehicle into a floating research station, the southernmost on earth. Not only Orde-Lees, all of us are assigned new duties. We take night watch in alphabetical order, twelve hours where you're responsible for the safety of the ship, for firing the boilers and recording the meteorological data. The thankless first watch falls to Bakewell. He has everyone's sympathy as they clamber into their bunks and wrap themselves up while he tramps onto deck in the cutting night wind. No one would want to swap with him, but I'm going to have to. It's the second B's turn tomorrow. If only my name were Zackboro.


IN THE LIGHT OF THE LAST SMALL LAMP BURNING IN THE RITZ, IT LOOKS like he's fallen asleep. His elbows are angled out on the sea-chart he's rolled across the table and his head is bedded down in the crook of an arm. The shiny skin on his bald pate reflects the lamplight. I ask myself if I should wake him and, with all due respect, send him to bed.

But Frank Wild isn't asleep. His eyes are wide open and fixed on the chart, red, sagging, dog-tired eyes, just the way all of ours are after breaking our backs out there on the ice. Now and then he nibbles at the skin of his lower lip, and when I go around the table and enter his field of vision, he looks up and briefly raises his eyebrows.

"Ah, Merce, it's you. Aren't you sleeping?"

"No, sir. I thought I'd see how Bakewell's doing and keep him company a bit. I was going to bring him some tea. You want one, too?"

He isn't listening. His thoughts are elsewhere, in a space in his imagination whose size is bounded by the coordinates of the chart in front of him and where time is determined by the length of the polar night. Frank Wild shakes his head almost imperceptibly, and I'm sure that this small, silent *no* doesn't only apply to the offer of a cup of char, something he wouldn't allow himself anyway in the presence of others. No, no, the situation we're in is as incomprehensible and unendurable for Wild as it is for Shackleton.

He more than anyone else has been trying all month to work the ship free. When the rest of his troop has already long been huddled around the stove, rubbing their fingers, Wild has stayed out with the next, and with the group after next, on the moguls of pack ice before the bow, shoveling snow to expose the frozen swell. And when, after ten hours of shoveling, he was too weak to hack up the ice in the runnel or to swing the pick even feebly, he stomped back to the ship and fetched replacement axes for whoever lost his to the icy soup, so that at least someone else could continue in his place.

"Come on, men, come on, keep going!"

In mid-February, the temperature sank to minus fifteen degrees Celsius. And although any open lead froze shut faster than we could squeeze the *Endurance* into it, Wild didn't give up hope. In his opinion, the speed the ice was drifting at meant a small crack might at any time widen into a lead broad enough for the *Endurance*. All we had to do was make the crack.

That's why he screams at least a hundred times a day, "We need a lead! Make sure you keep that crack open!"

Coming back from the galley, I pour him a mug of tea. He smiles, sits up and clasps it.

"That's nice of you," he says. "But now take one to Bakewell. He's got more need of warming up."

So I go up on deck and tramp to the bridge, whose light falls forwards onto the foredeck and its rows of kennels before losing itself in the darkness beyond the bowsprit.

There's a crash somewhere out there in the ice desert, but you can be certain there's nothing out there that's alive, that breathes, that could be awake or sleeping. The noise comes from the water wrestling with the ice, and is as cold as that sounds. In the small command cabin, the air is thick with the smoke from Bakewell's cigarettes.

"Well?" His drifter's face looks out at me from a fur hood.

"Wild's awake, no one else. He's totally spent." I have to cough. "But he still doesn't want to believe it."

We talk about what's happened today. I wait until Bakie's drunk the beaker empty and then quietly, so as not to wake the others, go down to my bunk.

But I can't sleep. And I'm not in the mood for reading. So I get up again and go through the gloom of the midship corridor back to the Ritz.

Frank Wild is still sitting over his map.

"*Logs, Depth and Longitude*?" he asks as I sneak past him towards the porthole.

That's the thing that makes the mini-boss's life so hard: he really doesn't catch what's happening around him because he's so fixated on avoiding, preventing and resolving all the ship's problems. Since ingloriously giving up on Commodore FitzRoy's navigation bible, I've dug my way through more than fifteen hundred pages of exploration history.

"Something like that," I say.

I'm reading the logbooks of John Biscoe, the most cunning of all seal hunters, who even Weddell wrote about with deep respect. Biscoe was in the Southern Ocean from 1830 to 1832 with his brig *Tula* and the cutter *Lively*. He was the third man after Cook and von Bellingshausen to manage the circumnavigation of the Antarctic, and Biscoe was the first to recognize that the horn of islands, reefs and rocks stretching towards Tierra del Fuego were a peripheral part of the mainland that people had been searching for for thousands of years: the Antarctic Peninsula. Almost his entire crew either died of scurvy during the voyage or wasted away in the cold belly of the *Tula*, but

Biscoe, with only two seamen and the ship's boy to hand, sailed onwards. His ship, he writes, was "no more than a mass of ice." Convinced at one point that he'd found some rocks that were set off from the mainland and frozen over, Biscoe fired his cannon at icebergs, let down a boat and searched the wreckage under clouds of panicking storm petrels. After two and a half years at sea, he returned to London with a booty of thirty sealskins. I would have liked to read Frank Wild what John Biscoe wrote at the end of his voyage. "I did everything in my power to keep up the spirits of the men on board and often put on a smile when in truth I felt quite differently." But when I look up from the yellowed pages of the eighty-year-old *Geographical Journal,* his head has finally nodded onto the table.

# 24

## A BICYCLE, A PIANO
## AND A BALLOON

WHEN OTTO NORDENSKJÖLD'S *ANTARCTIC* WAS CRUSHED BY the pack ice in 1902, the Swedish geological expedition took shelter on one of the Antarctic Peninsula's northernmost points, the minute Paulet Island. The men built a hut that should still be there and held out for months on the bare rock before they could be rescued. One day, while hunting seals among the cliffs, they found a topmast festooned with scraps of a Union Jack clinging. It was from John Biscoe's cutter *Lively*, which had sunk seventy years earlier in the Drake Passage. The Weddell Sea's drift had carried the topmast around three thousand miles of a circle, and no one could say if it had done so only once.

Captain Scott made a similarly almost unbelievable chance discovery. While digging in a depot for the march to the South Pole, on an ice field stretching for miles in all directions, the men hit metal fifteen feet below the surface and finally pulled out a sled. It was the same motor sled, drawn by George Marston, that I saw in Shackleton's book. Since his *Nimrod* expedition, the sled had been four years under the Ross Ice Shelf. And it's still there. Since Shackleton's affairs were no business of his, Scott had his men re-bury it.

For our new quartermaster, Orde-Lees, there's no joking around when it comes to motor sleds. He's quick to explain that, from his perspective, it was Scott himself who took the most ridiculous things with him to the Antarctic and then left them there. Nat-

179

urally not including himself. He grins. Standing between us is the bicycle he's just pushed down the gangplank. In the bright light reflected off the ice, I can see that its coat of black paint remains only in dapples. A deep-brown layer of rust has grown across the first Antarctic push-bike.

"For example, they left a piano in the Ross Hut," he says, and checks the spokes, none of which seems to have broken during the months of storage in the anchor locker. "No one ever played it, because neither Scott nor any of his men ever learned how." Aunt Thomas tilts his head to the side and smiles. "So why did he bring it with him?"

I've got no idea. Maybe because he was planning to learn.

"Hold the handlebars a minute." He crouches and searches for a valve.

"Looks like they're solid tires," I say to him.

"Hm." He stands back up. "So they are." He's as tall and almost as massive as Crean, but he gives the impression of not trusting his own muscles and bones. It's like he's standing on stilts in his own body. He mounts cautiously. Anyone else his size would see that this bicycle is too old and too small for him, that it would be both dangerous and ludicrous to take it even only for a quick spin along a harbor wall. But not Orde-Lees. For him, the fact that no one would dream of cycling this fragile contraption onto the ice is half the appeal.

"All right. You can let go." He pushes his snow goggles down over his eyes. "Let's see what these bludgeoners are up to."

He climbs onto the pedals. The rear wheel spins; he pedals harder and wobbles off. In his Burberry snowsuit, his boots and his snow goggles, he looks like an aeroplane mechanic darting across a snowy airfield. Two men stomping in the opposite direction along the path marked in the snow applaud and move to the side as he skids past.

My lord and master is calling me, so I go up onto the foredeck, where Green is tipping white strips of a butchered seal into a cool-box, the last of yesterday's meager haul.

"More ice" is all he says, which means that I should go cut another block to store the meat. At minus twenty, Green's mouth seems to freeze shut. His chin is as white as the seal meat, and he speaks as if he's just come from the dentist. So, back down onto the ice, might go have a look see if Orde-Lees is still cycling.

WE DRIFT. BUT BEING ON A THREE-YARD-THICK LAYER OF SNOW AND ICE that's floating on the Southern Ocean is something I notice just as little as that the earth is spinning and flying through space. Everything seems to be standing still. It's only when an iceberg doesn't even need the four remaining daylight hours to overtake our ship that a fear that grows with the approaching berg reminds you that all this white expanse is actually in motion. At the end of February, when we were newly locked in, the pack ice was shifting imperceptibly westwards, parallel to the coast. At the start of March, it turned towards west-northwest and picked up its pace. Worsley and Hudson made depth soundings and found that the ocean floor dropped sharply from around a hundred and twenty fathoms to more than five hundred. With that, we knew for certain that the drift was carrying us in its main current, northwards alongside the Antarctic Peninsula, and that the ice shelf and Vahsel Bay would be further behind us every hour. The day of Orde-Lees's bicycle patrol is the sixth of April, the seventy-second day since we were frozen in, and the two men who encountered him on the path and are standing by the ship to report to Sir Ernest are Worsley and Hudson. They've just calculated our position from in front of the bow, and it shows that we're drifting north at a rate of two and a half miles a day. Although the *Endurance* herself hasn't moved an inch, she's been shifted more than a hundred miles by the massing ice.

Shackleton takes the news nonchalantly. He's standing directly above me at the railing and seems almost cheerful as he asks Worsley to relieve the man in the barrel—it's Hownow—and keep a lookout for seals. I know this cheerfulness by now. Shackleton is taking great pains not to let anyone see his worry and disappointment. His real cheerfulness is very different. When we're talking about a book he's given me to read, all the tension softens out of his face, a mischievous glint dances in his eyes and he can't stop smiling, something he always apologizes for at least once.

I use the opportunity to ask up to him if I can take one of the blocks from the pyramids of ice used to construct the dogloos.

"To freeze the meat, sir."

He looks down and gathers himself like he's seeing me for the first time. "Yes, take one, take as many as you like," he says cheerfully.

GREEN SHATTERS THE BLOCK OF ICE WITH A SINGLE MALEVOLENT BLOW from an ax, and the light-blue shards and bright splinters skitter down into the spaces between the meat in the packed crates. Hownow stalks past, frozen stiff in his yellow snowsuit after just an hour in the crow's nest. Green lifts the ax in his direction, bares his ruined teeth and then pulls his grin at the attempted joke into a disgusted grimace when How shows him the finger. How is having difficulty taking the steps. His knees won't bend. And he knows that he'll need twenty minutes by the stove in the Ritz before he can detach his cap from his head.

"Seal two degrees southwest," Worsley cries down from the barrel through his fire-engine-red megaphone, which, from deck, is all you can see of him. "Correction, three degrees. Seal three degrees southwest!"

They're hunting less than a mile beyond the double ring of larger and smaller ice-block structures that surround the ship like circled wagons: the thirty dog-igloos, the dogloos, on the inside and then, a snowball's throw further out, a line of pennanted markers that are meant to help you orient yourself in driving snow and blizzards.

They're hunting out there, on the open ice, two dog teams with five men and a quartermaster on a bicycle. From here, they're only small, slow-moving figures, indistinct in the fine snow dust. Worsley directs them from the mast, Crean and Macklin steer the sleds, McIlroy and Marston keep the dogs' panting bloodlust leashed and Frank Wild hurries on foot or on skis to wherever the seal is lying.

A quiet bang floats across to the ship.

"Hear that, dreamboat? Seconds," says Green, and sits on the finished crate to close it. "You can forget about your three hours today."

Apart from last night's watchman, who is at liberty the following day, each of us is on duty for three hours daily, shoveling coal, hacking ice. The rest of our time is at our disposal. But that's naturally outweighed by the importance of laying in as large a store of provisions as possible before the polar night descends in three weeks' time, and so, in practice, the hunters, the quartermaster, the cook and I are busy all day with catching, preparing and storing meat for ourselves, the dogs and the cat, as well as separating out blubber and oil to be used in the stoves and lamps. And since it turns out that no one has as good an eye as the skipper, Worsley is up in the barrel far more often than he should be, directing the hunters with shouts and flag-waving or warning them when he spots orcas or leopard seals approaching swiftly up cracks in the ice. According to the calculations that Shackleton carries out every night in the Ritz, we've taken on five thousand pounds of meat and fat stores in this way, enough to last us ninety days without touching our tins and dry rations.

Ninety days . . . By the start of July, we'll already have been living in the dark for months.

Outside on the ice, two groups have formed. While half the men keep the dog teams at a distance and try to stop the animals going for one another's throats, the rest take on the hardest part of the work, hauling back the seal carcasses, some of which weigh more than five hundred pounds. The twilight thickens, and I can't see Wild and

Crean leaning over the dead seal as McIlroy puts his surgical training to use. But I know, having watched it plenty of times, that they'll be gripping it tight so that McIlroy can work fast: as long as the seal stays warm, the men skinning and butchering it don't get chilblains on their hands.

The first thing that eventually appears out of the graying landscape is neither a sled nor Frank Wild on his skis. Aunt Thomas comes cycling up as calmly and leisurely as if he were Reverend Hackett returning home to Pillgwenlly on a warm summer's evening from someone who has just gone in peace to the Lord.

"Don't cycle into a tree!"

Worsley is hanging in the rigging, halfway down from the barrel, and roaring into his megaphone. Orde-Lees tips his cap and waves.

Shortly afterwards, the bicycle is leaning against Green's cool-box. Orde-Lees is almost completely encased in a thin white sheath, and hundreds of tiny icicles hang from his goggles and the brim of his hat.

"Good for thinking things over on, these velocipedes." He's speaking very slowly and his voice is hoarse. Since the dogs' barking covers everything else, you have to shout on the ice to make yourself heard.

"Something has occurred to me, the strangest thing that anyone has ever brought into the ice: it was a hot-air balloon. Scott flew it over Ross Island. Read about that, have you, Blackboro?"

I haven't, and I don't believe him.

"It was called *Eva*, if I remember correctly. Scott went up once and then never flew it again, because the valve broke. He's supposed to have gone up a few hundred feet. He was probably so excited that he couldn't stop throwing sandbags overboard."

He chortles and the icicles in his beard tinkle and chime.

"And did you know that before the *Flyer*, Wilbur and Orville Wright made bicycles?"

"Aaargh," says Green, "get out of here with your gossip, the pair of you."

# 25

## FEELING THE WEIGHT OF LIFE

O N A SUNDAY, OF ALL DAYS, THROUGH THICK FLAKES OF SNOW, we see the sun for the last time. For a while, there's a dim, deceptive twilight and you can make out the ship's stark outline against the horizon. But it's not enough to judge distances by and even the ice in front of our snowshoes gets so blurry that going for a walk around the perimeter has become a dangerous undertaking. Bobby Clark has drilled a hole into the ice in front of the bow and is using an outrigger attached to the sprit to pull up all kinds of sea creatures. He's already fallen into a few hollows and tripped over a ridge that he thought was still a yard ahead of him. But it hasn't put a dent in his mania for collecting. In dozens of honey jars that are lined up along a skirting board in the Ritz and that gleam green and blue in the light of the oil lamps, he keeps a plethora of strange little creatures and plants, organisms that have never before been exposed to so much as a glimmer of light, that have always lived in complete darkness, just like we'd have to if our ancestors hadn't discovered fire.

We don't grieve for the departed sun. It'll come back. It might take half a year, but that doesn't matter. Nothing you can do about it. McNeish says that if he has to he'll make us a sun out of wood, and Alf Cheetham senses the moment is right for his monthly joke. As the ice swallows up the last of the sunlight, he asks McNeish to make him a pair of wooden swimming trunks.

In the company that comes together that evening in the Ritz, I'm not the only one to notice that Shackleton doesn't seem so somber and gloomy now that the ship has been made winter-ready in time for the polar night. His better mood improves the mood of everyone else. He knows himself what an example he is to the rest of us. But no one holds it against him if he shows some weakness from time to time. Because, just like his wrath, his self-directed anger is a sign to us that he cares just as passionately as ever about our situation and isn't ready to give himself up to the bitterness he tends towards and, frankly, would have good reasons for.

For Tom Crean, a decision made by Sir Ernest stands beyond the shadow of doubt. Crean sits two seats further along, and I would never contradict him, even if only because the profile I can see to my right also hung framed for years in my brother's bedroom. But still, I do disagree, and I think that, in reality, Shackleton's ability to motivate us is founded not on certainty but on the deepest of doubts. It's not true at all, what he likes to say about himself, that he hates ever to deviate from a plan once it's made, or to leave off from a goal once envisaged.

I don't think he's got either a fixed plan or a definite goal. Shackleton doubts. He doubts at the start and is still doubting when he reaches the end. For Crean, Cheetham, all of the veterans, it's about exploring, overcoming, conquest, triumph. For Shackleton, it's about happiness. He's the adventurer, not me. After a short, heated wrestle with himself, he'll welcome any outside misery. Adversity—which Wild moves heaven and earth to avoid or undo with all the exuberant energy of a man obsessed with order—only spurs Sir Ernest on to greater enthusiasm, to a confidence so exuberant he's got to share it with us, and, despite our shock, it's that that gives him the greatest satisfaction. Once he's enjoyed it, the doubt comes back.

After the customary toast to the wives, to the girlfriends, and may they never meet, which Worsley always brings out, Sir Ernest takes the floor and embarrasses us all within a few sentences. He apologizes unreservedly for the expedition's failure. And he admits that he made a mistake by not dropping anchor and going ashore on the Caird Coast instead of sailing further south.

"In the hope of coming across something even better. What an idiotic delusion! I wish I had listened to the skipper that day and to you, Frank, Tom, Alfred."

He looks each of them right in the eye, and I get an idea of what it must mean for him to say that in the same room where he convened his ice council on that day three months ago, and overruled them.

"I go hot and cold when I think that we could all be sitting in our hut right now, the scientists working on their studies and the rest on making preparations for the march. And I would almost rather not imagine what hardships Mackintosh and his men have put themselves through in the Ross Sea to lay depots that it's likely we will never see. I cannot value all of your efforts highly enough. Be assured that I will do everything I can to get each and every one of you safely home to your wives and children. Or to your lovers." Laughter. "I thank you. Despite all the disappointment, it is a constant pleasure to spend this time with you. I would not like to be without any one of these faces."

"To Sir Ernest," shouts loyal Alf Cheetham, and raises his glass.

"Sir Ernest" thunders back, and I find a lump in my throat and tears in my eyes.

Shackleton stands up. He asks those who do the same to remain seated. He stands alone. He has finished what he has to say about the past; now he'll turn his gaze to the future. I lean back. Might there be another glass of port . . . ?

But what he says plunges down on me like Green's ax, smashing my calm into splinters. He'd like me to stand up.

And, while I hesitate and look questioningly around the company that smirks back at me, he'd like me to tell everyone something about the polar night. Right now. He sits down. My vision goes black.

"Sir Ernest, the polar night, I just don't know anything about it; I haven't ever lived through one," I say. "And the one that's just starting, I don't know . . . It's bit short so far for me to say . . . to say anything that might be interesting . . . or amusing for everyone."

"Bravo," says Mack. "A murky start. Very appropriate."

Everyone laughs.

"Quiet, gentlemen, please!" Shackleton smiles but doesn't laugh. He's being serious. "All right, Merce, no one wants to show you up. I thought you might tell us what you've read about it. It's important that one of us read the books. And that he tell the rest of us what's in them . . . but you don't have to if you'd rather not."

Of course I don't have to; I know that myself. I say that I'd like to sit down, and I sit.

"Very well." Shackleton nods his close-cropped head. He'd thought that would work out differently. He interlaces his fingers. Awkward silence.

I know that I could do it. And ask myself why I'm not. Then I hear that I'm already talking. And the others are quiet.

"The first thing that I think of when I think of the polar night is a word that Hurley taught me. It's an Inuit word, I don't know if I'm saying it properly: *perlerorneq*." I look across to Hurley, and the Prince nods. "It's a word for the depression you get in the long polar night and means something like 'feeling the weight of life.' Yes, exactly, I just read a couple of reports from people who were on the *Belgica* expedition, which spent the winter here sixteen years ago. But there's not really that much to tell. That expression describes everything I've read pretty much spot on. The men were the first who ever wintered on the pack ice, and one of them, Frederick Cook, wrote in his diary that there's a black curtain that drops between your own icy loneliness and the outside world, and that it quickly drapes itself across the soul. It's horrible, it's like a vampire story, like when, for example, he writes about how week by week the night drains more color out of their blood. And there's a bit somewhere where he says that he couldn't imagine anything that could have been more disheartening and destructive for himself and his shipmates—is that enough?"

"Haven't you got anything about polar ice maidens?" shouts someone. "About women?"

"Oh, God, leave off!" Stornoway lets his head fall forwards. "My trousers'll start bursting."

"And that," says Shackleton, "is something none of us wants to risk, Mr. McLeod. Carry on, Merce. Perhaps you could get to the temptations as a conclusion."

"Yes, all right, then. The other book of yours, Sir Ernest, about the *Belgica*'s voyage into the Weddell Sea, is by someone called T. H. Baughman and is called *Before the Heroes Came* . . . Honestly, Captain, that's what it's called. In what I read, there was none of that funny Dracula stuff. After three weeks in the dark, the crew all gave in to melancholy and depression. The men couldn't concentrate on anything, and even eating turned into a kind of ordeal."

"Was Green on board?"

"Go to hell."

"Shhhh. Don't interrupt."

"To fight the signs of madness that they were all recognizing in one another, they started to take walks in a circle around the ship. They called it the nuthouse promenade. One man died of panic, someone else had hysterical fits until he went deaf and dumb, and another one wedged himself into a tiny nook on board because he was convinced that the others were out to kill him. There were men from seven different countries on the ship, and Baughman wrote that it was like a nightmare in seven languages. After a while, everyone built himself a little cave in a different corner of the ship, where they ate and drifted in and out of waking. They couldn't even talk to each other, and the whole crew completely fell apart."

Since Shackleton makes no indication of preventing him, McLeod reminds me about the women. He wants to know whether there have ever been any in the ice, and if so, when, how many and, above all, how young?

I explain that I've never read anything about any women in the ice. Stornoway wouldn't be Stornoway if he didn't mix up when people were joking and being serious. First he pretends to be disappointed, then is for real, and finally, affronted, he says, "Then at least pull out your fish and read the note from your . . ."

"Shut your face, McLeod," Bakewell says across the table.

And right away, Vincent: "Easy, easy, Yankee Doodle."

The atmosphere in the Ritz is no longer jovial, and I'm not sure that that isn't what Sir Ernest intended. He doesn't comment on what I've said but lets it have its effect on the men, and it's only once the company gradually breaks up that he takes me aside and apologizes for the ambush.

"That's all right, sir."

He is very serious and almost whispers, "Merce, you know it's possible that we'll lose the ship. If we do, we won't be able to take any books with us. Then you and I would be the only ones who'd read them."

"Yessir."

"By when will you have read all of them?"

I don't know what to say. There are books I'd have to read again and some that I keep putting off because I know how bleakly they end. There are plenty men on the *Endurance* who appear in those.

"Work on the assumption that you have another half year," he says to me, with a look that gives me to understand he no longer doubts it will happen.

I go with him on deck. There's a pale light in the southerly sky, and the shine of two storm lamps illuminates the port-side semicircle of dogloos, where Macklin and Hurley are going about the night feeding.

"You know who the man in the nook was," he says after he has already turned to go. "The one who was afraid that the others on the *Belgica* would kill him."

"Yes, it was Amundsen, sir."

"It was a fine thing you did not mentioning that. Good night!"

Shackleton won't be getting to sleep anytime soon. In the four-man cabin that's been refitted as an officers' mess, which the four men housed there, Wild, Crean, Marston and Hurley, have nicknamed the

Stables, the blind-drunk Greenstreet is showing his musical side and presenting a duet, both of whose parts, Lord Effingham (with a beard of soot) and Mr. Charcot (with a soot beard and a monocle), he has decided, for simplicity's sake, to play himself. He's being barracked by a colorfully dressed mob of roughnecks. Uzbird Hussey has used some jam to paint himself a black eye. He's dragging around a small boy with a piping voice, who is reminiscent of Frank Wild and is coincidentally played by Frank Wild himself. A bottle of malt whisky makes the rounds. Once it's been emptied and sent flying out of an open porthole, a majority decision is made to relocate to Sir Ernest's cabin, where a further store of spirits is suspected. Shackleton is treated to a serenade and gives an ovation, but he isn't prepared to distribute any alcohol. He buys us off with chocolate instead and eventually drives us away by threatening to start declaiming sonnets.

# 26

## THE ANTARCTIC CLOCK

AT A TEMPERATURE OF BETWEEN THIRTY AND FORTY DEGREES below, unexpected things start to happen. I pour out a beaker of boiling water and it freezes before it smashes on the ground. If you blink for too long, your eyelids freeze shut, a shock that's momentary but terrifying. After spending a long time outside, we snuggle up to the stove like a gang of cats. And if you lick the clothes you've taken off and press that spot against the cabin wall, the jacket or the pullover stays hanging there as if by magic. You shouldn't think that after a certain temperature it stops making a difference whether the air is at minus twenty or minus thirty-seven. It's a difference equivalent to that between spring and high summer, just at the end of the scale where there are no seasons.

At the close of May and in the middle of June, between the 125th and 145th days in the ice, we put on two contests that draw in the whole crew despite the ever more bitter cold. For days, the men have been leveling a playing field on the lee side of the ship, and once the six storm lamps on deck have been directed onto it, Sir Ernest, who couldn't pass up the opportunity to be the referee, blows the whistle for a full ninety-minute football match in the crepuscular floodlight: the Vahsel Bay Wanderers, wearing white vests over their snowsuits, versus Weddell Sea United, the strong favorites because their team has got one more pair of snow goggles.

## VB WANDERERS

Manager: F. Wild—Substitutes: A. Kerr, G. Marston, H. McNeish

Goalkeeper *T. Crean*

Right center half *R. James*     Left center half *J. Vincent*

Right back *T. McLeod*     Left back *F. Wild*

Center midfield *A. Cheetham*

Right midfield *M. Blackboro*     Left midfield *L. Hussey*

Right wing *H. Hudson*     Left wing *J. McIlroy*

Center forward *W. How*

*Center forward *W. Bakewell*

Left wing *T. McCarthy*     Right wing *A. Macklin*

Left midfield *F. Hurley*     Right midfield *E. Holness*

Center midfield *L. Greenstreet*

Left back *L. Rickenson*     Right back *J. Wordie*

Left center half *R. Clark*

Right center half *F. Worsley*

Goalkeeper *T. Orde-Lees*

## WS UNITED

Manager: F. Worsley—Substitutes: C. Green, W. Stevenson

Weddell Sea United don't initially manage to profit from their advantage. But it quickly becomes clear that the match is going to be decided on the right wing, where doctors Mack and Mick are fighting an exciting duel. However, when Weddell Sea's most reliable bastion, player-manager "Wuzzles" Worsley, subs himself off at halftime, at 4–3 down, and pushes Charles Green into his position for the restart, the team's shape begins to come apart. Other than a few isolated counterattacks led by the unsynchronized strike-duo of McCarthy and Bakewell, United aren't able to string anything together. Green stubbornly refuses to move more than a yard in any direction. The departure of goalkeeper Orde-Lees (after taking a ball in the temple from Vahsel Bay center forward How) completes the debacle. Wild, Hussey and I score twice each for the Wanderers, and the match ends 9–4. A walkover. No one is shown a yellow card for dangerous play, but everybody gets one for complaining. The victory ceremony is canceled: Shackleton, who has been a largely absent referee, thinks he's spotted an orca's fin in the water behind the Wanderers' goal.

A week before the winter solstice, the bearer of the Order of Jonah, Frank Hurley, brags over lunch that his dog team is the fastest. Even leaving the other eight out of it, no one else's mutts could ever keep pace with his lead dog, Shakespeare.

Ridiculous!

Fierce indignation breaks out among the other five sled drivers in the Ritz and, stoked further by Shackleton, it builds to a deafening tumult. And even though the brawling is only in play, a handful of plates get broken nonetheless. No one, not even Mother Green, seems to mind. But I sweep up the shards and wonder to myself.

A racecourse is marked out. Eight hundred yards in length, it leads once around the perimeter, starting and finishing at the football pitch, which now has a stand of ice-block stools. The six dog teams are allowed one more day's training. Every driver chooses an assistant, receives a storm lamp and goes out onto the ice to practice, each at a favored spot somewhere in the dark.

Dog commands ring out from the night:

"Mush!"

"Haw!"

"Gee!"

"Whoa!"

"Haw!"

As early as the start of April, Frank Wild had to shoot one of the dogs, called Bristol, who was suffering from some enigmatic illness. Bristol lost almost half his body weight in a few days and, tormented by the invisible torturer inside him, the poor creature crawled apathetically into the dogloo, his eyes creamy, gloomy and unbearably sad, until Wild came to fetch him. In the last weeks, twelve more dogs have fallen victim to Bristol's disease and been put down. With the loss of two dogs off the South Sandwich Islands and the thirteen shot on the ice, only fifty-four of the original sixty-nine are still alive, and at least three of them are already in bad shape. And since no dog has yet recovered from the disease, Wild will probably have to make a few more trips out onto the ice with a dog and come back alone on blood-spattered skis.

Each of the six sled drivers knows his animals well and maintains a tender relationship with the monsters. I keep myself as far away from them as possible, because I know the only thing that works on them is demonstrating physical superiority. They leap on one another on a whim and bite their sled-mates bloody. I'm sure that if no one stopped them, they'd tear such shreds out of each other that within a few hours we'd be completely dogless. Amundsen devotes many, many pages of his book to the dogs that were with him on the ice, and he describes many of them in more detail than he does the men. When the hunger came on them in winter, when it was time to kill the dogs, Amundsen turned his Primus stove up to full blast so as not to hear the shots. He took a photo of one of his men and wrote on the back: "In the absence of ladies, Rönne goes waltzing with the dogs." Amundsen is the great-est, and Shackleton is right: you shouldn't undermine his achievements by telling stories about nooks he crept into when he was a young man and scared of being torn apart. He left a letter for King Haakon behind in the tent at the South Pole for Scott to deliver if the Norwegians didn't make it back. The request must have aggrieved Scott almost as much as his defeat, but it was only a consequence of Amundsen's insecurity. On the way to the Pole, he photographed himself almost every day: a man with the long, querying face, enormous nose and sadly sparkling eyes of a basset hound.

All of those who feed or wash, treat or ruffle the dogs, but par-ticularly the six who have to cope with them day in, day out, have been altered by the experience. McIlroy is again as thin as he was in Buenos Aires, because he isn't hanging around in the Ritz all day looking for snacks. Marston is still drawing, but every time he decides to tackle an iceberg, it comes out in the shape of a dog's head. Hurley no longer smells like a prince, he smells like Shakespeare, whose side he hasn't left since they both fell into a crack where the black-and-white snout of a curious orca surfaced a few minutes after they were rescued. Macklin the Gentle has to separate two beasts who are locked in a tussle and gives each a clean punch to the jaw. And Wild is wrapped in cotton wool and handled with kid gloves when he again uncomplainingly takes on the job that no one envies him.

But no one looks after the dogs with as much loving care as big Tom Crean. He has spent nights in the dogloos and kept alive the eight puppies that are now almost grown. Greenstreet, who seems through some magical elixir to be steadily losing his officer's rigidity, is going to take over their training and then drive a seventh team. Before that, however, he has to study at Crean's school of kindness, until, I assume, he no longer needs that panacea.

The Antarctic Derby starts on the sixteenth of June. We are all off duty on this 143rd day in the ice, and many of the crew have got dressed up accordingly. Holie, How and Kerr are in bookmakers' costumes and offering odds in Antarctic currency: chocolate and cigarettes. But their odds—6:4 on Wild, evens on Crean, 2:1 on Hurley, 6:1 on Mack, 8:1 on Mick, Marston no return—aren't accepted by anyone.

Shackleton gives the start signal by blinking a lamp. Urged on by the cheering of the fans and the shouting of their drivers, the teams storm out across the ice, which shimmers blue under the faint lights. Macklin goes out in front. Bosun and Songster are almost equally extraordinary lead dogs, and they drag Sue, Judge, Steward, Mac and the three others in their team up to racing pace. But the other dogs can't keep up with Bosun and Songster for long, and Macklin's sled keeps falling back. Two others are quickly left behind: Marston, led by Steamer, and Dr. McIlroy, whose dog Wolf is the only one we think really might be purebred wolf. As such, he takes no pleasure in this whole circus and sheers off right at the start. Crean can keep up for a while, but then his lead dog decides to live up to its name. It seems to be to Sourly's chagrin that he can't hold the pace, so he doesn't even try. He snuffles around in the snow instead. The derby is between the sleds of Hurley and Wild, neck and neck until the perimeter course ends in front of the bow.

| | |
|---|---|
| Shakespeare | Sailor |
| Soldier | Lupoid |
| Martin | Owd Bob |
| Jerry | Samson |
| Bummer | Bony Peter |
| Rugby | Horre |
| Rugus | Tosse |
| Hackensmidt | Helge |
| Noel | Saint |
| ———— | ———— |
| Frank Hurley | Frank Wild |

TWO SLEDS WITH EIGHTEEN DOGS AND TWO MEN COME TEARING ONTO the football pitch. We've all sprinted over to the finish line and are cheering and whistling them down the final spurt. Hurley, in a red jacket that he's dug out of God knows where, with a small Australian flag wrapped around the sleeve, stands upright on his sled while Wild crouches low on his. And Wild wins. Hurley is second, followed by Macklin and Crean, then McIlroy and, finally, Marston. Wild's sled covered the eight hundred yards in two minutes and sixteen seconds.

Quartermaster Orde-Lees, shuddering with cold next to me, is not satisfied. "Wild's beasts are an average eleven pounds lighter than Hurley's, so, for me, Hurley is technically the winner. I'll be interested to see whether the mini-boss offers him a rematch."

The second round takes place a few days later, and this time the sleds have passengers. Hurley wins with Hussey on board, but only because Shackleton falls off Wild's sled during the final spurt. Sir

Ernest is so disappointed in himself that he pays all bets from his own pocket. Either way, it's an unlucky day for Frank Wild. In the evening, Crean reports that three more dogs have collapsed, and although Wild takes the news hard, he doesn't leave anyone else the job of putting them down. It's Dr. McIlroy who eventually insists that Wild bring the carcasses back on board for autopsy. The investigation takes three hours in the anchor locker they've commandeered, three hours when a general despondency settles on the crew. But Mick and Mack have found the cause of Bristol's illness. It's a worm, a red tapeworm that they've discovered in each of the three carcasses, almost a foot in length and practically eating the dogs alive from within. Macklin is desperate as he tells us that there's nothing we can do to treat the dogs. There's no deworming medicine on the *Endurance*.

Tom Crean claps his hands to his face. When he takes them away, his eyes are closed. Crean is crying and, before going away, says quietly, "We've got five thousand gramophone needles on board, but not a single tube of wormer, is that it?"

Cheetham is distressed by Crean's tears. "No, damn it, Tom's right, isn't he? Are we a dog-sled expedition or a pleasure cruiser?"

Shackleton lets them go because he knows that Crean's criticism is directed at him and that it is accurate. Looking into a distance that isn't there, not in the Ritz, he has been the first to understand what the doctors' discovery means. With that devil in their bellies, the dogs would never have covered the two thousand miles to the Ross Sea.

The knowledge that we're going to lose the dogs and that, if we lose the ship, we'll be thrown back only on ourselves, weighs heavily for a while on the whole crew. That's why everyone's happy when there's something to celebrate, even if two of the dogs don't touch the extra portion of seal meat allocated to them on the day.

On this, the twenty-second of June, we've reached the middle of the polar night and we mark the winter solstice with a modest feast and a concert to follow. Chippy McNeish has built a stage in the Ritz to host it. It's decorated with streamers and flags, and Hurley's acetylene lamps, propped up in coffee tins, bathe everything in white light. "God bless our beloved dogs" is written on a piece of cardboard pinned above the center of the stage.

Shackleton takes on the role of master of ceremonies, presenting the performers to the crowd. The first on is Orde-Lees. Dressed as Pastor Gunvald, he warns the congregation against accepting the wages of sin. Jimmy James takes the stage as the Prussian Herr Professor Doktor von Schopenbaum and conducts a circumlocutory lecture, consisting only of words of one syllable, on the properties of blubber. Macklin intones a tropical melody in honor of the irascible Captain Eno, an homage to Captain Worsley, who strongly denies being its subject. In costume as a tramp, Kerr is announced as Spagoni the troubadour, but forgets his text and becomes Stuberski the toreador, and his public shouts at him, "He's going to die! He's going to die!" Marston is drawn, Wild recites Longfellow's "Wreck of the Hesperus" and Greenstreet, portraying himself as a boozer with a red tomato nose, makes the last performance we let on stage before the start of the ladies' program: Hudson as a Haitian beauty, Rickenson as a London streetwalker and Bakewell as a limping sweetheart who keeps shouting, "Monkey! Oh, my little monkey!" something he's lucky he asked my permission for first. McIlroy gets the largest hand as a Spanish lady with a deep décolletage and a slit up her skirt. For four hours we forget all our worries, and when it gets to midnight, we've laughed ourselves across into the long night's second, waning half.

# 27

## MACHINIST WATCH

LITTLE BY LITTLE IT DAWNS ON ME WHAT IT WAS THAT TURNED THE *Belgica*'s crew into shadows of their former selves. Perhaps it was the scurvy that finally made them believe they were vampires who could survive only by finishing each other off. But what was the reason for the scurvy? There was plenty of fresh food on board that they could have eaten to stop it breaking out. But the *Belgica*'s men took no notice. The vegetables moldered in their tubs. Instead of slaughtering their animals and building up their strength by eating the meat, they let them freeze to death in their pens.

Something completely and utterly senseless happens to you if you live through a monthlong night. I'm sure it was nothing other than lack of sleep that atrophied the strength in Amundsen and the others. I can see with my own eyes how the polar night is turning us into ghosts. Pale, frozen, morose figures are what most of us have already become, and if we didn't all have the same beard dangling from our chins, you might really think we were a lost tribe of bloodsuckers. Especially if you saw us all lying rigid in our bunks, eyes open. At least we know what Hurley read somewhere: firstly, vampires don't have beards and, secondly, that they've got to stay out of the light because it burns them down to ash. So we aren't vampires, since all of us are longing for the daylight to come back. And yet, none of us has had a wink of sleep for weeks.

Mainly because it's too cold. Almost all of us are forced to spend the last period before the sun's return below decks. At the end of June, a terrible blizzard begins that just doesn't stop and in whose rising and falling whirling and wailing the temperature outside falls to minus fifty-seven. Only the seven men responsible for feeding the dogs ever leave the ship. Shackleton insists that they all be attached to safety ropes, and so as not to be swept away regardless, they crawl out to the dogloos on all fours. The snow driven on by the hurricane-strength gusts is like dry, sharp sand. It penetrates every layer of clothing to burn your naked skin like boiling water. Crean's chest is as red as a lobster when he reports that giant furrows of snow have formed on the windward side of the ship. In the lee, on the other hand, the wind sweeps the ice clean. Marston says that, as far as he'd been able to see in the light of the storm lamp, the swell was frozen into shape, a black-green sea of glass. Jimmy James's miniature umbrella, his homemade anemometer, which is fixed to the roof of the bridge, measures two hundred miles an hour one morning before snapping off its socket and disappearing into the screaming dark.

The supplies of blubber and oil gradually begin to run low, and Worsley gives the order to fire the cabin stoves as little as possible. So there are always at least twenty of us sitting together in the overheated Ritz when the clock says it's day, whiling away the time until we have to crawl shivering into our bunks. We don't take off any of our clothes in bed. We put on whatever we've got, pullovers, jackets, overcoats, hats, scarves and boots. And at least once during the night, trembling with cold under three layers of clothes, one of us stalks stiffly back to the stove in the Ritz, where he takes the cat onto his lap, warms himself up and collects the reward that awaits the perambulant ghost. Whoever's on watch has got to give him a mug of hot tea and a biscuit.

On one of these nights, a dry cough steals what small chance of sleep I had. So as not to disturb Bakewell and Holness anymore, I get up, grinding and popping, and finally, after an eternity, shuffle down the corridor.

What's all this smoke in here? I wonder, before I realize it's the air I'm coughing out. I've already done six watch duties, and the alphabet is already back at R. It's Rickenson's turn. His friend and colleague Kerr is sitting by him at the oven and keeping him company. Machinist watch. The two of them are drinking tea and fraternally sharing Mrs. Chippy, who wanders purring from one to the other while they screw up their eyes. The fifth bell has been and gone, another hour till the end of the watch. And the blizzard howls. While I slowly thaw, we listen to its voice. The snowstorm has been tearing across the ship for weeks now, but no matter how much it volleys into the superstructure or how much, up there in the dark, it chases through the rigging, it always sounds the same, now higher, now deeper, higher and deeper. I sometimes almost feel sorry for it, because nothing in the world should be that lonely, not even this wind that seems to tear in off the stars.

My cough has fallen asleep. I slurp the tea that Rickenson has brewed me and dunk my reward biscuit into it. Completely full of pleasant warmth and the delicious taste, I'm pleased that my ghostly appearance gives Kerr and Rickenson a topic for discussion: washing. Washing clothes at minus fifty . . . can it be done?

While Kerr squanders his time thinking on how to get the clothes dry before they freeze into clothes-shaped boards, Rickenson reveals himself as a proponent of dry cleaning. "Once every two weeks, you turn all the gear inside out, and that's it."

Kerr looks at him uncomprehendingly. What Rickenson is proposing, whether he means it seriously or not, isn't reconcilable with a machinist's professional ethos. Divesting himself of the oil and grease, the traces of work, belongs as much to the job for Kerr as does caring for the valves and driving rods. But Rickenson is just as much of a machinist as he is, and a good one, too. Tired and confused, Kerr searches his friend's face for a sign he's winding him up.

"You're off your rocker," he says in a tentatively joking tone.

"No, not at all. But I'm only talking about the last phase before you just leave the dirt on your skin, when you've got nothing left to change into."

"Right. But we do have enough clothes, and that's how it's going to carry on."

"Let's hope so." Rickenson sips his tea. He strokes the cat and as his red-rubbed eyes linger on me for a second, I realize that he isn't joking at all. He's speaking from experience. A hefty shudder runs through the stern. The storm throws itself against the ship, and we wait for it to find the corner and speed off again.

The old howling returns. Rickenson says, "You've got to decide for yourself how you want to approach it. I reckon what you do is tidy away the dirtiest clothes until the ones you're wearing are even dirtier, then the old ones almost seem clean in comparison and you can put them on again happily."

Is that a piece of advice or a memory? Kerr and I hesitate. Kerr chews the end of his thumb, giving me the chance to say something, and when I don't, he asks, "What do you think, Merce?"

Difficult question. No matter what I say, they'll assume that I'm revealing my own clothes-changing habits. That we have as good as no opportunity to do so is well-known to all three of us. As is that this conversation is steering itself towards a certain point. So spit it out! Kerr and Rickenson look at me. They don't look that tired anymore.

I admit that I think Rickenson's approach is inventive, and both of them nod. I say that coats, jackets, trousers and actually even socks aren't really the problem. Nodding.

"Where it gets difficult, well, and that's where you've got to choose one way or another, that is, from where I'm sitting, and stop me if I'm getting this wrong, is with underwear."

Kerr: "Quite right."

And Rickenson: "Good. Let's talk about it."

And I . . . cough, because I've lost this night anyway.

"Okay, who's going first?"

• • •

68° 43 SOUTH, 51° 17 WEST, DEPTH 1,000 FATHOMS, DRIFTING AT THREE knots, 185th day in the ice. That's Worsley's logbook entry for the twenty-sixth of July, the day when, around noon, the sun first twinkles above the horizon for a good minute. The storm has weakened and is now only a tricky wind racing low across the ice from the southwest. A couple of hundred miles away, as invisible as it is unreachable, and yet certainly just where Biscoe left it, is the Antarctic Peninsula. Slowly but surely we're scraping northwards along its eastern flank.

"Imagine we're standing on the beach in Sicily," Bob Clark says to me in the whirling snow at the railing, where I'm sucking in the wonderful fresh air.

"Okay, good, I've got it."

"Fine. Now imagine that there's Egypt over there, except that here it's called the Larsen Ice Shelf."

I'm not the only one lacking the nautical know-how to make a mental image of the course of our odyssey. Some of the crew have studied the maps in the encyclopedia. Others who'd have fallen asleep a few weeks ago now listen more or less enthralled to a slide show that Worsley and Green present one evening in the Ritz. To keep the rest of the crew up to date as well, Shackleton gives an interdisciplinary team the task of building an Antarctic clock. Wordie the geologist, James the physicist, Marston the painter and Hurley the photographer really do manage to work it all out together. The clock is strikingly simple: a wooden disk the size of a small wagon wheel represents the more or less circular outline of the Weddell Sea. The numbers on the face are marked as geographical points where the *Endurance*, at the end of the clock hand, has found herself on particular dates. South Georgia is at twelve o'clock. The chain of South Sandwich Islands stretches from half past one to half two. And we passed Coats Land, the Caird Coast where Shackleton didn't land, at four. The ship was locked in at half past and since then, the drifting ice has carried us along for three and a half hours. The Larsen Ice Shelf lies at precisely eight o'clock.

When it's unveiled, Sir Ernest starts raving. He's completely beside himself. "Make sure you get it! Another two hours. We must manage that. Our little pointer just needs to travel another two hours on this damned clock face and we'll have reached the peninsula's northern tip." I keep imagining the day when the ice suddenly lets go and the *Endurance* slips free. "If she makes it, gentlemen, she'll ease very gently into the water. Perhaps she'll heel over at first and then rock pretty violently from side to side. But then she'll float. Then she'll be floating!"

We nail up the Antarctic clock next to the imperial flags in the Ritz. Every evening before dinner, Wild or Worsley moves the pointer a finger-width further along. But we haven't even reached nine o'clock when we start to hear the noise and blows of the Weddell Sea applying itself to the task of crushing our ship.

# 28
## ENMITIES

HARDLY HAVE WE WITHSTOOD THE WORST OF THE COLD BUT the squeezing of the ice again prevents most of us from sleeping. With the end of the blizzard at the start of August, the temperature rises to a spring warmth of minus twenty. Hatless, their faces protected only by their beards and manes, those who still have the strength to work take a week to clear the huge weight of snow from the decks. There's so much that it's only after a few days that the amount visibly decreases. When the bridge and the kennels eventually reappear, the *Endurance*, freed from a weight of tons, rides a whole yard higher out of the ice.

Pale blue shrouds shimmer in the sky. They stretch to the horizon in every direction, pulsing, swelling and shrinking before they melt into the dark. Bright viridian light reaches from star to star, and red flames flicker within what seems like grasping distance above the mast tops, occasionally sending tongues of flame out into the cloudless space around them. A slow reddening of the light returns the color to Bakewell's face and brightens the apricot-tinted fog in the east. And when we turn our heads, there isn't one sun above the ice in the west, there are three, one real and two mirages.

Not even Bakewell's aptitude for swearing is untouched by it. He sucks in his cheeks and his eyes widen. The skin around them is dry and taut. He can't suppress a yawn, but he's truly impressed. "Hell," he says, swallowing the rest.

As incredible and beautiful as they are, the southerly light and phantom suns show us how bad a position the snowstorm has put us in. Before the blizzard, the pack ice was a fairly even, solid mass. The storm has broken it up into countless fragments. Twisted, raised and tightly wedged, they provide the wind with innumerable new surfaces to push on. Hussey calls it the behemothic swing, this force of wind and swell that propels the movable floes incalculably onwards. Visibly flattered that his speciality is moving ever closer to center stage, he does say that the ship has nothing to fear for the time being, because she's fixed in the middle of a thick, hard floe. But how long that will be the case not even little Uzbird can predict. He shrugs his shoulders and reaches for his banjo. And behind the soporific-sweet melody, you can hear the rumbling and the thunder.

The brighter the days get, the more distinctly they show us the extent of the destruction wreaked by the shifting ice. The perimeter path doesn't exist anymore. To starboard it's been shaved away by the edge of a passing iceberg, and to port, where it used to lead to the football pitch, a canal extends through the ice, sometimes gray, sometimes a cloudy silver, depending on whether it has just pulled itself open or again frozen over. A small black flag, a towel from my oilskin locker, which had been stuck into one of the ice blocks to mark the way back to the ship through dense snow, is now hundreds of yards away, snapped and sticking out of a pressure ridge formed by a blue and a gleaming green floe pushing into each other.

At night, in the sixteen hours that are still pitch-black, you can hear them, the floes yammering and groaning as they drive their way through the older ice. They sometimes howl louder than the dogs, who may still be in the dogloos but seem to know they'll soon be brought back on board. Everything suddenly goes dead quiet. Then our dozing shatters as the soothing hush in our cabin is burst by an ear-splitting crash.

Bakewell jerks upright and moans, "What the hell is that? For the love of Christ!" And while we listen in the dark, I can hear Holie's teeth chattering.

There are nights filled with the clattering of a train on squeaking axles, while a ship's horn toots and some nearby surf crashes unendingly. It seems to me once that there's an old woman screaming on the floe, and again and again I can hear drumrolls where there can't be anything, on the other side of the planking, deep in the ice across from my ear.

In the first longed-for night when the temperature in my bunk is endurable without fur gloves, my fists turn the pages of Shackleton's copy of the *Belgica* reports by the light of a candle. I read what Amundsen wrote about that winter: "Gripped by a laming horror, I found a nook all the way forward in the bow, which I barricaded with stinking potato sacks. It was no use. Although I was now free of the others, there remained the noise, the blows, the fear and the bottomless exhaustion. These all kept me loyal company in my hole."

There it is: bottomless exhaustion. When I read this section for the first time, I assumed the noise and blows were what Amundsen had been so afraid of. Now I know that it was really the squeezing ice that filled him with such horror, even in his nook, that he stopped going to sleep.

Agitated by this discovery, I take my book and candle and sneak out. In the corridor, I can still hear the ice's distant crashing. Only in the Ritz will it be blocked by the mumbling of the watchman and his visitors, the crackle and hiss of the stove.

But the poor devil sitting there is by himself. I'm just about to say what all ghosts say, "Hey, what're you up to? You brewing me a cup of tea?" Then I see how far through the alphabet we are. We're at V . . . Damn it!

"THERE'S A DRAUGHT. IN OR OUT," SAYS VINCENT, AND MOVES HIS STOOL to the side. "And you don't always have to act like I'm going to eat you alive."

I put my book on the table and place the candle next to it. But I don't blow it out. Might be that I go back right away.

"If it seems like that, I'm sorry." I sit down next to him and look around for Mrs. Chippy. "It's not on purpose." Even the cat has scarpered.

"Fuck it," he says. He opens the stove, the heat of the burning blubber springs out at once and he closes the door again by kicking it shut. The strips of fat are stacked up the wall behind him, right next to Bobby Clark's battery of honey jars, and give off a musty aroma, our Antarctic perfume. Vincent rumples his nose and turns to look at them. Anything, it seems, so as not to have to look at me.

"And now I have to brew you a tea, is that it?"

"You don't have to."

He bares his teeth. "I do have to. It's an order from Sir Ernest, or have I missed something there?"

"How do I know what you've missed?"

He stands up, and for a while I have his giant rear end in front of me. You could almost feel sorry for the trouser seat that's stretched across it, so mighty is Vincent's backside. He melts some ice, boils water, adds the tea, lets it brew, washes a mug and pours the tea into it. Silent minutes.

"There."

I slurp and while I slurp I sink slowly back into thinking about my book. The bosun, too, carries on with what he was doing before I, of all people, chased him out of his absorption. He's rolling his ciga-rette supply for tomorrow. Tobacco on the paper, then once to the left, once to the right, fold the paper over and up to the mouth. A colossal tongue slides across it. How does this man have such an incredibly smooth complexion? His skin looks like it's been poured. Not a blem-ish in sight, not a scar or a wrinkle, nothing. Vincent's hands look like work gloves, but his face is still that of the baby he once was.

"And your fish," he says. "What's he up to?"

"No idea. Not thrashing around."

"Always with you, eh?" The way he says it almost sounds tender.
"Yep."

Vincent snickers, quiet and mean, and shoots a look at me. Perhaps he would have let himself get carried away and said something more. But it gets louder outside. We hear something break in the distance, and the fine shiver of a shock wave runs through the ship. Rivets creak in their braces. If it were anyone else, I would ask how he rates our chances of escaping the ice.

He stands up and blows out the candle.

"Or were you planning to set the whole place on fire?"

"I forgot. Sorry."

"Fuck it."

"Fine by me."

"That's all right, then, isn't it, Blackboro?"

There's no point getting into an argument with him. All of us sitting here in the ice are as pigheaded as a herd of swine. But he, our bosun, is the piggest-headed of us all. I can't remember ever hearing him speak about something that wasn't work, duty or doing as you're told. By now, everyone is talking openly about women, girls, about what they're going to do or would like to. Not him. Behind closed doors, they say the bosun bats for the other side. Unlikely. The ones who think he's one of those are making it too easy. They're the same ones who say that Holie is a girl, or at least that he feels like one. The ones who recommend a night in a dogloo or, for those who can't do it with a bitch, taking Chippy, little ship's tiger, with them to their bunks. Or a properly cut chunk of seal meat, because "it's warm, soft and doesn't cry afterwards." Vincent knows about it but doesn't join in; he stays silent. A real bosun doesn't tolerate any chitchat before the mast, but when they're off duty, he lets his sailors do what they like. Vincent picks his nose and, behind his blank forehead, he seems to think: as long as these goons do their job, what do I care?

"It's all about reading, isn't it?" he says, interrupting my thoughts. "Reading books and making yourself important."

Exactly, that's the point. The work. The crux where everything balances for him. Do the work, finish the job. When it's finished, new work, hop to it. That's why he doesn't like me. Or maybe he does secretly like me after all—who can tell with him? But still he's disdainful because he can't chase me up the foremast to where you have to stop daydreaming simply because every handhold is either the right one or your last.

"My job is bring you your food."

He doesn't consider that worthy of comment. Even Vincent is tired. All he has for a response is a look from the corner of his eye, a twitch of his lips before he licks the next rolling paper. I have to take him as he is. Arguing with him leads nowhere and being friendly will get me no further.

The devil take him. I don't like the way he expresses his insults, like they're just a part of the conversation. At first, he seems to be speaking in general and just adding in a malicious little joke here and there. But then his nastiness suddenly starts to come in total earnest. He thinks he has to tell me something. In Grytviken, a couple of his people were planning to teach me a lesson. But unfortunately they had to forget about their plan because he got wind of it. "Rotten luck, kiddo."

He's regretting that they didn't put one over on me, and I'm supposed to be grateful to him.

He's finished with his cigarettes and lays them carefully in a small tin, where they lie perfectly flush with the sides.

"Actually didn't make much difference to me if they put you in a sack and let you have a good look at the bottom of the bay," he says. "No, really, when it comes to stowaways who slime their way in and chum up to people and try to put themselves ahead of the seniority, that's the sort of thing those black-hearted jack-tars'll do; even someone like you knows that, or that's what I assume in my tiny brain."

The malice is neither here nor there; what does he want to know? If I knew anything about it? Well, if I tell him that Bakewell told me, things will be rough for Bakie, who's under Vincent's command. And if I act like I knew nothing, I'll again be the daydreamer who doesn't have the foggiest about anything that really matters.

The cleverest would be to say, "What do you mean, forget about it? Overboard in a sack and three dunks down to the bottom, that's exactly what they did to me!" And then see who gets a thrashing from the bosun tomorrow morning for insubordination.

"I thought something like that might happen," I say instead. And to put some distance between us, I stand up, go over to the table and pick up the book. "Thanks for being so open, Vincent. And for the tea."

"Open, of course. You're very welcome. Christ, you're not all there are you? Take your candle with you. But it doesn't get lit, you hear me?"

"Doesn't get lit, I promise. Good night."

"I promise, good night," he mocks me. "That game won't work on me. And just so you know: no one cares what you read in those books. Nobody gives a monkey's, are you getting that?"

"Got it."

"Boy, I'm telling you, what matters in the ice isn't in the books. You've got to have it in here, in the blood. My granddad was in the Southern Ocean in 1839 and drowned here, nobody knows where, nor when, and especially not why. But I know what I'm talking about; I don't need any books to do it. Oh oh, 1839, hear that? What bollocks. I hate that explorer crap."

"That's your business. But Vincent, before I forget: next time you're on watch, I'd prefer my tea with a biscuit. You got that?"

Time to leg it.

"Next time!" he shouts after me. "Next time there won't be a ship to drink it in. Aye, piss off, you idiot!"

No, we're never going to be friends. But do we have to stay enemies forever? Why not? There's not much you can learn from the ice, but you can learn this: even enmity is a kind of bond.

# 29

## THE QUIVERING WRECK

IN THE FIRST DAYS OF OCTOBER, THE POINTER ON THE ANTARCTIC clock in the Ritz passes the nine o'clock mark. Outside, on the ice, there are distinct signs that spring is coming. Bobby Clark's daily water samples show an increase in the level of plankton, then Wordie spots the first solitary emperor penguin. He tempts the curious bird out of the small, ice-free pond it's paddling in and onto our floe. He kills it with his knife, just the way, a few days later, Wild kills the first crabeater seal that dares come close enough to taste Green's kitchen rubbish. The animals are back. For half a year, they've been in the South Orkneys, South Georgia or Patagonia, while we've circled the ice in darkness, putting on theater and shooting our dogs.

The despondency that's taken up residence on board since the July blizzard isn't driven away by these first harbingers of warmth. When we bring the dogs back aboard, there are only twenty-nine still alive, at least a dozen of them emaciated down to their bones. And early one morning, when the ship suddenly slips free without our assistance and floats in the center of a small floe-enclosed lake, we don't even succeed in firing the boilers, because the ice has burst a leak in the water pipes. Hours go by before we manage to set all the frozen sails. And we move about a hundred yards before the almost imperceptible swell thickens back into porridge and calmly seals us in.

The squeezing doesn't let up, but becomes ever more powerful as the opening water gives the drifting ice wreckage more and more room to maneuver. Sir Ernest, the skipper and the veterans hold unwaveringly to the belief that we're going to make it nonetheless and they miss no opportunity to encourage anyone whose head has begun to droop. But even the most obstinate and defiant of us, the ones who are always sure of their own opinion, cheerful Hussey, tough Bakewell, Aunt Thomas, Marston, all of them now only shake their heads if you ask them about the ship's chances. They snooze through the days, yawn through the watch and vacillate between equanimity and surrender. It's bitter, but it does seem to be true that when everyone around you thinks they can see the writing on the wall, it gets next to impossible for you to believe in a positive turn of events.

What use is hope when no one wants to hear about it? I never doubted that the *Endurance* would escape from the ice in one piece until that night in the Ritz when Vincent told me what chance he gives our ship: none. In Bakewell, Holness or How, in friends or shipmates, I'd have shrugged it off as their expecting the worst. But with Vincent I can be sure that he knows when his enemies are unbeatable.

So, hop to it, lads! Let go all hope!

On the tenth of October, day 259 in the ice, two blows strike the ship and presage what awaits us. The first is also the first to attack the hull directly. There's no longer a buffer floe in the way and, in a matter of seconds, a rising pressure ridge lifts the bow several yards into the air, clasps the hull, which is held fast at the stern, and, amid screeching and yowling, crushes it. Below decks, you can hear the braces and frames moaning into a loud snap like a firing gun. Whether it's to protect or seek protection from him, a small group gathers around Sir Ernest on the bridge. Clinging to the helm, I can see the foremast sagging, sagging like a sapling in the wind. Greenstreet is standing close to it in the rotted white remnants of his first officer's uniform. He's holding on to a capstan and can't wrest his eyes from the spectacle. Tom Crean jumps down and pulls him away.

But the mast doesn't break. Her bow lifted above the divided horizon and her stern pressed deep into the ice, the *Endurance* resists until the pressure abates. And with the coming of darkness, it peace-fully begins to snow.

The second blow that day hits us no less hard, but it doesn't come from the ice. It's homemade. Equipped with the few lamps that are still intact, we spread out across the ship to make a list of the damage. Green and I tidy up what's left of the kitchen. We throw out the cupboards that have burst off the galley's bent walls, along with the shelves and everything that was on them and is now broken. The boards and shards are spattered with a mess of flour and ketchup mixed with glass splinters. The heap that we pile up in the flickering of the galley lamp shines red and soon starts to stink.

As usual, we don't speak a word to one another while we work. But there's something itching at me, I want to know something, and that's why I, as if in passing, ask Green a question that's got nothing to do with cooking or cleaning.

"Vincent told me his granddad drowned at the Pole. Do you know anything about that, Mr. Green?"

Mr. Green makes a noncommittal noise.

I try again. "It was 1839, Vincent said. I wonder if his granddad sailed with Ross or if . . ."

Green just walks out. And when he comes back, it's as usual: we don't speak while we're working.

Stevenson and McCarthy come past. They examine the state of the outer walls unenthusiastically and scuff their snowshoes through the sauce on the floorboards to check for cracks or warping.

"Have you heard?" Stevenson says when they're finished. "It's going about that Sørlle told the old man back in Stromness not to take this rotten tub into the ice. Thought you'd like to know."

While McCarthy is already on the stairs, Stevenson the stoker with nothing to stoke fills his pipe. He's grinning. He doesn't need to tell us what he thinks. He knew it all along.

"Ah ha." Green isn't impressed. "And you're the little gossip who's having a smirk about it? Get out the way."

"I'm just saying that this tub can hardly be built for pack ice if even the Norwegian thinks the same. They sold us a lemon, those gentlemen, and now we're standing around looking stupid."

"Urgh." Green's hands are red with ketchup. "This mess. Do you want to help? No? So make yourself scarce. Go tell your gossip to the other jessies."

Stevenson distorts his mouth into a disgusted grimace. He scuffs the planks he's standing on a few more times and then goes without saying anything else.

"And what are you smirking about, eh?" Green asks me. "Have you seen the applesauce?"

I nod. "We've still got a whole crate of it."

"So. Applesauce for dinner. That bastard. Stands there and bad-mouths the boss. I'll put the rats onto him tonight!" Green wipes his hands on the towel wedged between belt and belly, which is flecked red with seal blood and ketchup. "Good for nothing except gabbing. They're all good at that. Vincent and his damned granddad. Yes, he always jaws on about it when we're at sea. If he was with Ross I've got no idea. Ask him yourself."


WHAT THORALF SØRLLE REALLY SAID IN STROMNESS WE ALL FIND OUT A few days later from Shackleton himself. It's one of the few daylight hours without waves of pressure, and we all huddle together on the foredeck. The air feels almost warm, it's only ten degrees below, and many of the others don't even have a hat on. Sir Ernest is wearing a felt hat and a white pullover. He's cheerful. And he lets us know that it was him who prompted Wild, Crean and Greenstreet to circulate Captain Sørlle's opinions on the *Endurance*'s suitability for the ice among the crew.

The men are surly. The gleam in their eyes isn't coming from the light; it's discontent. Our faces are black with blubber soot, many are puffy with chilblain, and while we listen, we scratch our stringy, matted beards.

Shackleton speaks quietly and carefully. He raises his voice only when there's a groaning from the ice. He starts by saying that there's no one who knows the ship better than Sørlle, that that's why he went to see him on South Georgia.

"Captain Sørlle was in Sandefjord when the *Polaris*, which became our *Endurance*, was being built. Originally she was designed for use in the Arctic Ocean, in the breaking ice off Spitzbergen. So the question was to what extent the ice conditions in the north are comparable with those in the Weddell Sea. To cut a long story short: we agreed that the *Endurance* would be able to navigate any ice as long as she retained her freedom of maneuver. Captain Sørlle, however, was of the opinion . . . No, that's not right. In truth, Sørlle predicted that the *Endurance* would be caught in the pack ice and then crushed."

"How's Sørlle supposed to know that?" asks the ship's carpenter.

"Well, Sørlle thought that because she doesn't have the same rounded stern as Amundsen's *Fram,* she wouldn't be able to roll up and down between the pressure ridges. The captain said word for word—Tom, you were there, correct me if I'm wrong—he said that the ice would get us in its vise and then squash us, because . . ."

All eyes flick across to Crean. He takes the pipe out of his mouth, looks tiredly around the company and says, ". . . because once the ice has got something, it doesn't let it go."

"I didn't disagree with him. I just thought that we wouldn't encounter the pack ice in the first place. And that if we did we'd be comfortably able to sail around it on the way to Vahsel Bay. I've always worked from the assumption that we would have an average Antarctic summer; I never took into consideration that it would be twenty degrees colder than normal for months on end. Gentlemen," says Shackleton, lifting his hands and pointing both thumbs at himself, "this was my mistake. I have to recognize, without begrudging him it, that Sørlle took this possibility into account."

"No one could have known!" shouts Wild. Leaning on the gunwale to one side, he makes no bones about disliking Shackleton's willingness to put himself on the defensive.

Shackleton nods. "That's very true, Frankie. But it isn't my intention to make a list of for and against in retrospect. Everything, right from the start, has gone against us on this voyage. The money, the war, the stop in Buenos Aires, the month in Grytviken and then the ice always being where it wasn't supposed to be. Jinxed! Do it anyway, I said to myself—I want to tell you this, even if most of you will be surprised: I never had the feeling that we were going to fail. I don't have it now. Because we've left nothing untried. And we're still on our way. Dr. McIlroy, do you find that amusing?"

"No, sir. Well, yes, because it's true, sir. But the voyage *is* taking a different course than expected."

You can hear murmurs of agreement and there is a glint of anger in the eyes of the ones looking for a scapegoat.

"Quite right. The six of us on the sleds, at least, would be long dead by now. With these dogs? Another error, another example of the miserable planning for which I alone am responsible. Enough about that. There'll be others to talk about it. What matters to me is the following: there is something entirely extraordinary about this voyage. Because it never should have been able to take place, because everything that could go wrong has gone wrong, because every doubt has proved itself justified. It seems to me that we haven't sailed into the Southern Ocean but have disappeared right off the edge of the world. As though we'd been driven away from everything human and into a realm of absolute unreality. Sometimes I look at one of us and think, this man isn't really doing that; I'm only dreaming that he's been unconsciously cutting and recutting a crack into the ice while it freezes and refreezes. Whether we'll be able to keep the ship, I don't know. I don't believe so, but I'm sure that each of us will do his best to try. I want us all to be agreed on one thing independent of success or failure: we mean to get home. We mean to sail back to our lives. To put an end to this lucklessness.

Tell me, men, whether we're agreed on that. I'm open to all other suggestions."

Three days after Shackleton's speech on the foredeck, heavy ice masses scrape, squealing, along the hull and tear parts of the sternpost out of position. Water and ice fragments pour into the ship from starboard, flooding the boiler room and most of the loading spaces. All available men are ordered to the bilge pumps but can't do anything: the pipes and valves are frozen shut. Worsley's attempt, with Hudson and Greenstreet, to make it through to the bilge is blocked by an impassable bulwark of coal that has tumbled out of the bunkers and cascaded across the stored blubber of sixty seals. McNeish, Vincent and three others construct a cofferdam in front of the sternpost to shield the rest of the ship from the invading water. Hurley gathers a troop that saws cracks into the ice ahead of the bow to relieve the pressure on the hull. The rest of us pump. Fifteen minutes pumping, fifteen minutes rest, for twelve hours, interrupted only by an hour's break when Green provides us with porridge and tea under the gruel-gray sky. As we get back to it, Shackleton gives the order to prepare the dogs, sleds and two of the three tenders in case we have to abandon ship in a hurry.

But it takes another ten hours before we reach that point. We pump. When the ice pulls the rudder off the stern, McNeish says, "Doesn't matter. I'll build another." When the ice encases the cofferdam, crushes it and presses the shards through the whining corridors, McNeish begins a new one. We pump. Enormous pressure ridges tower up on the port side. When they roll against the shaking hull and catch on the bulge of the gunwale, the *Endurance* makes animal sounds; her wood howls and yelps before her beams snap and another deck gives way. As the stern rises ever higher out of the ice, until it's finally seven or eight yards above the surface of the floe, and as the freezing soup creeps up the walls and begins to toss about on the deck, you can still hear McNeish and Vincent hammering at the second cofferdam and McNeish shouting, "That might do it."

Wild takes both of them off the ship. He finds How and Bakewell at the pumps. The dogs, sleds, boats and all equipment of any value have been moved onto the floe to starboard, which seems stable. Shackleton and Wild nod at each other. Then they, too, leave the quivering wreck.

# 30

## A Mountain of Possessions

I T'S LONG BEEN CLEAR WHAT'S RESPONSIBLE FOR OUR SHIP'S destruction. Superstitious as you get at sea, we all noticed that the ice's squeezing was always at its most powerful when someone, whether out of boredom or to see if it still worked, turned on Orde-Lees's gramophone. I experienced it for myself when Jock Wordie told me that he had a recording of songs from Purcell's *King Arthur* opera in his sea chest. Hardly had we started the record, but such a brutal squeeze began that Jock and I wordlessly found it right and proper that one of the many things it broke was the Purcell record itself, scratching it to pieces. Because neither of us dared to say out loud what everyone was thinking and whispering to one another, the gramophone stayed where it was. It was no longer used in the Ritz, but it continued to silently exercise its power. Whenever the ice began to squeeze, there was always someone who asked whether the others below decks were by any chance listening to music.

Worsley puts an end to this curse. As our disconsolate captain, he's the last to step off his sinking ship and climb onto one of the sleds that are going to carry us out onto the ice. Before the caravan sets off, the skipper calls so that all of us can hear, "Does anyone want to take the music box? It's floating at the top of the cabin. Well, anybody?"

But he doesn't get an answer, not even from Orde-Lees. Worsley's lost an entire ship; Orde-Lees isn't going to start about a gramophone, though his expression shows that he's just as unhappy as the captain. All of us have to say good-bye to almost everything. Two

223

hundred yards from the wreck, we put up our tents and spend our first horrible night on the ice. The groundsheets aren't waterproof and the fabric tents are so thin that the moon shines through them. Three times the floe breaks close to our encampment and each time we have to dismantle the tents and rebuild them somewhere else. In the morning, Sir Ernest wakes each man by passing mugs of hot milk into the tents. Worsley and Wild have been over to the wreck in the dawn light, salvaged a petrol canister and constructed a temporary galley. Most of the men take this as a matter of course and don't think it necessary to thank them.

Wild, who is completely exhausted, loses his rag. "Would those gentlemen who'd like their shoes polished please be so good as to place them outside the tent!" His face shiny red, he stomps off through the sleet.

Shackleton has us form a circle. He stands in the center and begins to empty out his pockets. A gold cigarette case, a gold watch, a couple of gold coins, everything that he's managed to stuff into his snowsuit to make this demonstration as dramatic as possible, all lands on the ice. I'm standing very close to him, rigid not so much from tiredness and cold but because I don't dare move with the Bible in my hands. While I wait for Shackleton's signal to pass it to him, he explains seriously that it's absolutely necessary to reduce both the loads on the sleds and the weight of every individual man.

"It is only by doing so that we will at all manage to drag the boats. It's for the dogs, too, that we have to make the sleds as light as possible. I can't say how far we'll have to march before we can switch into the boats, but . . ." Shackleton motions me over to his side and his eyes twinkle at me as he carries on with his lie, "but since Blackboro and I have again gone through all the various expeditions that went on foot across the ice, I've reached the conclusion that those who carried equipment and instruments for every eventuality did far worse than those who jettisoned anything superfluous in the interest of speed. Every man should ask himself what he really needs. Throw the rest away. You can take what you're wearing, plus two pairs of gloves, six pairs of socks, two pairs of boots, a sleeping bag and a pound of tobacco. As well as two pounds of personal equipment. Do not think about monetary value when making your selection. Compared with you and your survival, none of that is relevant. Merce, please open the Bible and read out what guidance the Queen Mother has inscribed for us."

I do as I'm bid and read truthfully. Though it would be a good opportunity to build in a little lie of my own.

Dedicated to the Crew of the *Endurance*
by Alexandra, 31st of May 1914. May God
Help You Do Your Duty and Guide You
Through All Dangers on Land and Sea.
"May You See All the Works of the Lord
and His Wonders in Eternity."

Shackleton takes the Bible, rips out the page with the dedication and throws the book onto the ice. He gives us eight hours to decide what we need and what we're leaving behind.

I don't have to think for long, since I don't have anything except the clothes on my back and the few things I inherited from Holie and Bakewell on South Georgia: pullover, boots, snowsuit and goggles. And since all the books that I've taken to heart have been left on the wreck and are going to go down with it, I stay easily under my two-pound limit. All I have to add is Ennid's fish. And that weighs next to nothing.

All kinds of things end up on the heap of objects unnecessary for our survival: watches, pens, tins, shoes, rope, chisels, magnifying glasses, pots and a deck of cards. For a while I think about what of the particularly nice stuff I could take with me to give back to its owner later, but then I say to myself that it would be unfair to the others to do this favor for only one of them and decide instead to leave everything where it is.

Bob Clark cries when he has to give up all his jars of water samples, mosses and creatures after having managed to save them from the ship. Marston does the same when he leaves behind all of his equipment, his canvas, paints, finished and half-finished pictures, all but for a little sketch pad. Nor does the Prince get any special dispensation. To make room on the sleds for his cameras, Hurley left his boxes of negatives on board, only to now have to mutely add the cameras and tripod to the mountain of possessions. A small silver hand camera is all that's left him. Like most of the others, I haven't really warmed to him in nearly three hundred days on the ice, but I hope it consoles him to see how many photographs are eventually lying beside his in the snow: pictures of wives, children, parents, siblings, friends. Of innumerable ships. And among them I see the little drawing from Captain Worsley's cabin, the rider saving a child in mid-gallop. I look at the picture again and try to make out the reason for their shared panic and shock. But the drawing doesn't reveal it to me this time, either.

Sir Ernest makes two exceptions: Mick and Mack are allowed to take almost all of their medical supplies in the small tender, and he lets Uzbird store his banjo in the whaling boat.

Stornoway has three sets of glasses on top of his hood and is so thickly swaddled in his snowsuit, jacket and wrap that I only recognize him when he stalks up to me: "Give us a look at that pocket you sewed for your wee trout." He nudges me with his elbow.

I unbutton my jacket and let him feel the fish pocket. He's visibly impressed. "Backstitch, eh?"

"Yup."

I've got an idea. I offer to sew a similar pocket into his wrap if he gets some information for me in return.

"All right. What do you want to know?"

Five minutes later he comes back. He says just one word: "*Sabrina.*"

"Are you sure?"

"The name of the ship his granddaddy went down on. Vincent said it was the *Sabrina*."

Several of the others also take their cue from my pocket and sew their valuables into their clothes: cutlery, toothbrushes, combs, nail scissors. Orde-Lees even adds a store of toilet paper. Soon there are pockets bulging from all over Burberry snowsuits whose torsos, arms and legs end up with lumps within and boils without.

Shackleton, Hurley, Hudson and Wordie make up an advance party. They go ahead on their sled to determine the route. When they come back, Sir Ernest stands on the sled's frame. He calls to us, "Gentlemen, let's get started for Robertson Island."

Since it's wet, cold, windy and snowing, we don't all rush at once. Crean and Macklin shoot three puppies and a young dog called Sirius there wouldn't have been any space for in the teams. There's a vote on whether McNeish's cat should be left alive. It will. We put the remaining dogs in the traces, and we yoke ourselves to the boats.

IN A FIFTEEN-STRONG TEAM, WE DRAG TWO SLEDS WITH THE WHALER AND the tender securely lashed on top. Each weighs nearly a ton. Twelve men drive the sleds or help the dogs pull them over cracks or ridges. The sleds go back and forth. Once they've covered a certain stretch, they're unloaded and driven back to the camp beside the wreck to take the next load. The boat draggers and the sled drivers switch jobs every hour. Sir Ernest goes on foot. He tests the ice, checks the ramps we build over the pressure ridges, brings us drinks and encourages us with little stories. Whenever a sled gets stuck, he's there right away to help push or pull it.

At one point I hear him say to Bobby Clark, "Come on, old boy, you can do it. Another ten minutes, then Frankie's sled will come along and take you with it. I've given him enough biscuits for everyone. Here, I'll give you a hand and we'll do this last little bit together.

Or you go up ahead and test the ice." He puts his arm round his shoulders. "Sound all right, Bobbly?"

Robertson Island is northwest of us, off the coast of the Antarctic Peninsula. Shackleton and Wild's plan is for us to slog our way in that direction as long as the ice holds. The floe we're creeping across is still twenty feet thick. Once the summer progresses and the ice breaks, we'll switch into the boats and row the rest of the distance through the drift ice. And once we've reached the island, a small group will cross to the peninsula and march over the mountains to the bays in the west where lots of whalers go to hunt in the summer. While the rest of us build a hut and stay put until the rescuers arrive.

A bold, elegant, Shackletonian plan. With one tiny catch.

Robertson Island is more than two hundred miles away. After three days, our baggage train has covered just over one single mile. The floe we're creeping across isn't drifting to the northwest, but to the northeast. It isn't doing an inch of the journey for us. Again it's the weather that's making a nonsense of our calculations. At three degrees below, it's far too warm for this time of year. It snows all at once, and the new snow lays itself in layer upon wet, slippery layer over the older ice. When they try to trot across it, the dogs sink in up to their bellies. Sir Ernest on his skis vanishes up to his thighs. And we, yoked to our two giant nutshells, sunk in up to our waists, drag ourselves forwards one footstep at a time.

On the first of November, day 281 in the ice and a week after abandoning the ship, Shackleton declares the plan to reach Robertson Island under our own steam to be impracticable. We take the news indifferently. Especially because Shackleton sees no need to despair. Our aim as of now is Paulet Island, off the peninsula's northern tip, the same small island where Nordenskjöld's expedition were able to save themselves twelve years ago and where they found the mast top from Biscoe's *Lively*. Sir Ernest announces enthusiastically that there'll be a large store of emergency supplies in the hut that the Swedes constructed on the island, he'd bet his hat on it. After all, he himself helped enlarge the Paulet Hut into an emergency station in the course of the Nordenskjöld rescue.

As tired and disappointed as they are, as torn back and forth between hope and fear, some of the men for the first time openly voice their doubts. McNeish the carpenter, Stevenson the boilerman, Green the cook and a few others finally want to air their anger: they don't believe him anymore.

Shackleton leaves them be. He consults with Worsley, Wild and Crean, and after a while Greenstreet pulls me into the little circle that's retired into the lee of one of the boat sleds.

I'm to confirm to everyone that Shackleton was one of the rescuers of the crew of the *Antarctic* in 1903. "Yes," I say and look Shackleton right in the eye, "that's what I've read."

There are no hurrahs as the order is given to unload the boats and sleds and set up a permanent camp. When it stops snowing, I see timber and a squint black funnel reaching above the ice at the southern horizon—the sorry remnants of our *Endurance*'s mast and chimney. For three days we've hauled ourselves away from the direction of our rescue, and we still have to watch from a distance as the ice finishes crushing our ship spar by spar. Shackleton holds a vote on what our new home should be called. "Ice Camp" and "Floe Camp" only get a handful of votes. After the sea we're all waiting for, the overwhelming majority decides on "Ocean Camp."

Once the tents and dogloos are up and the first evening meal has been distributed, I go into Shackleton's tent. He's lying stretched out on his mat, his hands clasped under his head. He opens his eyes. When he sees me, he says my name.

"A quick question, sir."

"About the Paulet Hut, I assume. Come in, Merce, I'll explain it to you."

"No, sir. You don't need to explain that. But please tell me: which expedition in 1839 had a ship called *Sabrina*?"

# 31

## THE BURNING EFFIGY

ONCE AROUND, CALLOOH CALLAY AND AROUND AGAIN!
The tips of his boots touch mine, we sometimes hold each
other's hands, sometimes each other's shoulders, and whirl
around Ocean Camp with all the other greasy, sooty couples, How
and Holness, Hurley and Wordie, Cheetham and Crean, Bakie and
Blackie: once around, once under and around again! Uzbird's banjo
twangs and Worsley and Greenstreet belt out a shanty in honor of the
orca that appeared from a fissure a few days ago and helped itself to
two of our dogs. The warmer November days fly past as we wait for
the ship to go under. And in the distance, the sled teams fly back and
forth between the wreck and the camp, salvaging whatever we can
use to shore up our melting homestead: the ten-man tents, which
we've put plank flooring underneath; the new oven made of parts of
the former galley, which is now even under a roof. Callooh Callay!
To everyone's happiness, we managed to rescue the last dinghy before
it was buried by the ice. We're dancing around it. Welcome, dinghy!
When the time comes, we'll divide ourselves into the three boats and
have room to take a third more provisions with us onto the water.
And we dance around Sir Ernest, who frowns earnestly but claps. He's
named the boats in order of his most generous financial backers: the
whaler is called *James Caird*, the tender *Dudley Docker* and the little
dinghy *Stancomb-Wills*. There's McNeish. Pull the carpenter in!
Come on, Chippy, don't be a such a wet blanket. But he doesn't want
to. Too busy! Making the boats ocean-worthy, raising their gunwales,

equipping each with a mast and sea anchor . . . No, you're right, Chippy, the work won't do itself, quite right, you old misery-guts.

"Just keep on dancing."

"We will. It's Guy Fawkes night. Come on, Chippy, put it down, we're about to light the guy."

The jib boom that's snapped off the *Endurance* is too big to be used on any of the boats, but Sir Ernest had it brought to camp anyway and had Chippy anchor it securely into the ice as a watchtower. Since it's been up, there's been lookout duty again, keeping watch for cracks in the ice or for more orcas. The last one only needed a couple of bites to swallow the dogs. That's faster even than Sailor and Shakespeare sling down a baby penguin. One of those thirty-foot monsters wouldn't even know any better; it would take us for a strange, presumably delicious type of bird: not a king or an emperor, but maybe a devil penguin.

What else would one of these killer whales, crazy with starvation after a long voyage across the Atlantic, make of us, if he pushed his piebald snout up through the ice and saw that we've hung a puppet made of scraps of cloth from a wooden frame and that we're dancing around it? He wouldn't know anything about Guy Fawkes, wouldn't even know what music is, and certainly not why we strange birds have linked arms and are yelling and jumping around the burning bundle.

> "Och, hungry orca, don't be blue,
> I'll drink a beaker rum to you
> And if the thinning ice should break
> Don't take me for a penguin steak.
> So trust me, orca, it ain't fun,
> I'm pickled up in Bombay rum."

One of those who's bawling it out with the rest of us actually has no idea, either, of what we're celebrating. Bakewell doesn't care.

He can properly let himself go for once, "knock it out," as he calls it, forget the drudgery and the cold.

"Join in, Chippy! Sing along!"

Bakie whirls me around by the shoulder, and I can see the reflected effigy burning in his eyes. But while I see it hanging there, while I fly around it, I'm thinking very different thoughts: suddenly, I know that the dangers lurking in the ice aren't the real reason for the tower. Because whenever we aren't in the middle of a puppet-burning, Shackleton stands up there on the small platform over the ice for hour after hour, just as he used to do in the crow's nest. And he's always looking south, to where the wreck is.

I think back to previous fifths of November. Guy Fawkes! That's the man who, three hundred years ago, wanted to blow up the whole British parliament with King James in it. At least that's how Dad explained it to me. In Emyr Blackboro's opinion, Guy Fawkes can only have had one motive for his gunpowder plot: must have been a Welshman. On Guy Fawkes Day, everyone has a big family meal, goes to the bonfire and takes a stroll in the countryside, even though on Guy Fawkes Day in Wales the rain's always coming down in buckets. That old Welsh rain makes sure that very few guys ever really burn, which means they get reused the year after. I can't remember a single sunny Guy Fawkes Day; today is my first. And it's happening in spring. For Mam, Guy Fawkes is the beginning of winter; all the fruit gets preserved and the bills get paid, otherwise something goes wrong in Gwen's accounts. Bakewell, who I'm telling all this, gasps for breath. Our celebrate-the-puppet day doesn't mean anything to an American; to him it's just another quirk of these eccentric island monarchists. Nonetheless, there's something that he, too, can associate with the date: on the fifth of November a year ago, we arrived in Grytviken on the *Endurance*.

"Where was your puppet then, huh? You didn't all forget your Guy Forks Day by any chance?"

Apparently so. And I think I know why: a year ago, we were

thinking about foreign coasts, the coasts that seemed to be waiting for us. Today we're on our way home. But I can't say that to Bakewell. He doesn't know what it is to have one.

I ON THE OTHER HAND KNOW ALL TOO WELL. AS BAKIE AND I LEAVE Guy Fawkes in the early evening to go to the wreck on Hurley's sleds, I'm wallowing in thoughts of my family for the first time in a long while.

But luckily I'm soon distracted. The drive across the floe requires all our concentration. Again and again, we have to get off and examine a suspicious strip of snow. And more than once it turns out to be loose powder with a nasty fissure waiting below it. We drive wide detours around these traps and finally reach the wreck after several hours. We unharness and stake out the dogs. Then we're standing in front of the lightly groaning field of wreckage that used to be our ship.

Hurley's thinking only of his negatives. And he knows exactly where to look for the soldered, watertight tin canisters they were kept in, in the Stables, the old officers' mess between midships and the bow. Unfortunately, that part of the middle deck is no longer where it used to be. Parts of the galley walls are thrusting up into the sky over the foredeck, a few naked bunks are lying abaft on the ice and the stairs that used to lead below now don't lead anywhere. They're standing upright between the squashed kennels and all that climbs them is the leisurely ice.

"Okay," says Hurley, "I'm going to go on inside. We'll see what we can do." He reaches, jumps and is over the gunwale. The *Endurance*'s sides are no higher than those of our dinghies.

"Good luck," we call after him, and Hurley waves before he pulls the goggles down over his eyes and hefts his pickax for the first swing.

Bakewell was planning to salvage some more warm clothes, but the state of the crew quarters makes him forget that pretty sharpish.

By the time we're on the main deck ourselves, Hurley has already found a route below. We can hear him smashing everything to pieces in the Ritz on his way into the officers' mess. But pushing on into the sailors' cabins is out of the question. Stunned, we stand at the rim of the crater left behind when the ice pulled the vanished foremast into the deep. We look at icy gray porridge slapping around a shattered room where boulders of moving ice have crushed bunks and lockers. I forbid him to go down there.

After all, he's got other tasks to take care of. For McNeish, Bakie has to bring back some planks of a particular width, which are needed for converting the boats. Kerr needs couplings and clamps to finish his tent oven. And although he denies it exists, Green has nonetheless requested the crate of corned beef that the last group supposedly saw somewhere on deck. And finally, the constructors of the Antarctic clock have expressed a wish that it be brought to camp. Bakewell wants to find the wooden disk for Marston, in particular. Our artist was able to salvage almost none of the things that were precious to him, and so he sits around in camp like a bearded ghost with big glassy eyes and gets in everyone's way. Repairing and restoring the clock is sure to cheer him up.

Where does he want to start looking? I ask Bakewell, and he shrugs. But I sense how strongly he's tempted to go below decks, into the former Ritz with Hurley, who's hacking and hammering and could surely do with a bit of help.

"I think I'll go below first of all and get the clock. Who knows how long that'll still be possible. How about you?"

"Och," I say just as innocently as him. "Might go have a look what's left of that stuff out on the ice."

"You've got your eye on that Bible, don't you, you little royalist?"

Bakewell squats and peeks down over the rim of the hole into the dark interior. I should have known: where my bunk used to be, an impatient floe has bored its tusk through the hull. A damp chill is rising from the pit and it smells like the cellars of St. Woolo's.

"Yeah, the Bible, why not?" I lie. "And maybe I'll pick up Shack-leton's jewels as well"—the watch, cigarette case and the coins that can stay lost for all I care about them.

He climbs down over the rim.

"Bakewell! You're not going down there."

"You bet your ass I am. And it doesn't look like anything's going to stop me. You go do whatever you want. Just don't get caught. And look out for cracks, okay? Take a stick. See you later."

He lowers himself down. The last I see of him are the fingers clutching the frozen planking. Then he lets go.

THE QUEEN MOTHER'S BIBLE, SHACKLETON'S GOLDEN WATCH AND ALL the other discarded things are no longer there. In the ten days since the *Endurance* was evacuated, the floe has absorbed and carried them off. All the photographs, the souvenirs, gone. I go back to the ship empty-handed.

Anyway, I've got other fish to fry.

To get to the stern, I first have to clamber off the wreck. The way abaft across the deck is blocked by a barrier of ugly gray-green ice. Planks, ropes, spars and all kinds of unrecognizable junk have been encased in the wall and dragged along with it. The ice has climbed to twice my height up the mast and, at the top, the deserted crow's nest, which has broken from its setting, is rocking in the snowy wind.

I carefully make my way abaft on the floe and circle around the stern. It's in a bad way. Where the sternpost and the rudder have been torn out, a wide, crooked wound gapes open. It's white inside, because the whole afterbody is full of ice pressing outwards in all directions. It's breaking out through the ship towards the bow, bursting the hull out sideways, and here, in front of me, pushing back out of the stern. The ice has transformed our magnificent transom into a tattered wooden wall and rubbed out half the name that was written on it:

236

*END      NCE*
Lo    on

I climb up the starboard rope ladder and arrive on the afterdeck, as I'd hoped, behind the wall of ice. The gunwales, capstans and cabins here have been just as smashed as those amidships and forwards. The mizzenmast has snapped halfway up. The upper part and the yardarms have come down on the cabins, and the roof of Worsley's has collapsed under them. But to my great joy, the ice hasn't yet reached the deck, and Shackleton's cabin seems to have been left undamaged.

I can't hear anything of Bakewell and Hurley from back here. The icy cuff over the midships repels all sound from further forwards. Whenever the pressure on the wreck builds, there's a creaking and then an accelerating knocking. The *Endurance* shivers and rattles under my feet, and in the pauses between the squeezes, the noise of scraping and squelching comes at me from every angle. The ice is very near. We're probably only separated by the finger-width planking I'm standing on, and the thought of those two lunatics down there in their ice mine gives me the horrors.

My first glance into the corridor between Shackleton's and Worsley's cabins doesn't bode well. The corridor is twisted, like it's been crushed and then pulled apart again. The white-painted wainscoting has splintered off the walls, and the roof is gone. Against the uncovered sky I see the fallen mizzenmast that has destroyed the roof and smashed Worsley's cabin door off its lock and hinges. The floor's slippery. I crouch and stroke my hand across the thin film that the massed ice below is pressing up through the planking.

The skipper's cabin has been turned into a shattered scrap heap. It's now barely chest high, and dim light hangs in the squint, drafty room where I once, as wet as if I'd fallen overboard and wrapped in a woolen blanket, ceased to be a stowaway. Where has

237

Worsley's desk got to? And has he taken the folder with the newspaper clipping?

*Men wanted for hazardous journey.*

"Would you be good enough to finally dry yourself off. I'm not going to do it for you, you know."

Book pages and towels are floating in the icy broth, maybe even the one he handed me then, thirteen months ago.

The room is too small for me to have a look around in, and anyway, there's nothing that seems intact enough for me to bring to the captain. The half-sodden, half-frozen pages are from *David Copperfield*.

Also, I can't wait any longer. I'm dying to find out what's happened to Shackleton's books.

But the door to the cabin won't open; it's warped and something seems to be jammed against it from the inside.

It won't budge, no. I give up.

To both port and starboard, the portholes are tightly fastened and curtained from within. What can I do? I go forwards onto the deck and search through the ice for a long bit of scrap metal. And once I've managed to heave a piece of the mount for the deck railing out of the ice, I clutch this crowbar and scramble on all fours across the suspension bridge formed by the mizzenmast and onto the cabin roof. Shackleton's side really is undamaged. There's not even any ice on it.

Breather.

From up here, I hear the Prince call something and Bakie shout something back. They're doing fine.

The camp to the north is concealed by snow and fog, and only where the remnants of the effigy are smoldering on the watchtower do I see a thin thread of smoke coiling upwards in the distance. Though that could also be from the oven. When we left, Green was threatening to make blubber pudding.

To the east, west and south, nothing but ice.

Ice. When I've levered up three planks and pulled away enough insulation to make myself an entrance, light falls into the room and I realize immediately that it would have been better not to open this crypt. The whole space right up to just under the ceiling is filled with a blue-white mound, so that I, having only stuck my legs through the entrance, am standing directly on ice.

I rip more planks out of the roof, and once the hole is big enough, I begin to dig, more out of anger than expecting to find anything. The deeper I get, the looser the ice becomes. And in it are stuck all kinds of things that it has trapped and then moved around the room. I find Shackleton's hat and his typewriter, and I pull out the first books, three volumes of the encyclopedia. Then another two, frozen together into an uneven trilogy with, of all things, Dalrymple's *An Historical Collection of the Several Voyages and Discoveries in the South Pacific Ocean.* I started reading that tome shortly after we sailed into the ice and soon gave it back to Shackleton, horrified that Dalrymple, despite Cook's discoveries, continued to write about a temperate, inhabited continent in the south. Now I have the book in my hands again and won't ever be able to read any more of it. The ice has frozen the pages into a solid block. Part of it has broken off and has disappeared. But I can't take much with me anyway. Actually, everything should stay here, the books my spike digs out just the same as Shackleton's galoshes and the small metal horse his children gave him as a talisman on his journey. I put the little horse on the ice, give it a push and it skids off into a dark corner of the cabin.

I've dug a hip-deep hole in the ice in the cabin when my left hand grasps a length of bookshelf pulled out of its fittings and transported intact up to this height. Removing stratum after stratum of the ice across the books' spines, I make out, heart thudding, that it's the right one: explorers of the nineteenth century. But apparently not all the books have stayed on the shelf during its migration. I find von Bellingshausen, Weddell, Dumont d'Urville and Ross, but there are wide gaps between them. Two volumes I read recently are missing: Kemp's report on his voyage through the Southern Ocean in the *Magnet* in 1833 and the logbook of the United States Exploring Expedition under Lieutenant Wilkes. Also missing, unfortunately, is the book that I would have liked to take away with me.

A glance up through the hole in the roof tells me that it's getting time to leave. The dusk is gathering. The dogs' howling has got much louder, as if the dwindling daylight and the distance to cover were making them feel the danger of the journey back. I clamber up and spread myself out on the deck, hold my hands to my mouth and call out.

Nothing. The other two are still below.

Still time for one last look.

I rip the books off the shelf, sling them all up out of the hole and try to penetrate as deep as possible into the ice behind the empty shelf. I find Wilkes after a few seconds. I cautiously scrape around the book to free it. It's fastened to another, a yellowish-red volume on whose spine I can already read the expedition dates.

oh   al  ny

D  ove es f  e  IZA S  TT and t S   NA

1839  n  he S  th    ar S  s

1839, that must be it. I scratch off the white crust, breathe on the book and watch the shimmer of golden letters emerge through the ice:

*John Balleny*

*Discoveries of the ELIZA SCOTT and the SABRINA*

# 32

## TWENTY-EIGHT FISH FOR PATIENCE CAMP

ANYONE WHO SLIPS OFF THE FLOE AND INTO THE THREE-DEGREE water in the hole where Captain Worsley makes his depth soundings does end up with a very clear sense of the passage of time, feeling on his own skin how slowly it moves. The clothes take fourteen days to dry.

Day in, day out, I lie on my gradually disintegrating mat in my freezing tent and cling to the book. They sit in a semicircle around me, Clark, Hussey and Bakewell, black, gaunt, long-haired figures with toothaches and chilblains. They tell one another jokes, think up songs or invent recipes, and these phantom meals turn our tent into such an attraction that everyone blows in sooner or later to taste the words that become fattier, creamier and sweeter with every passing day.

If Vincent comes in, it means hastily covering the spine of the book so that he doesn't see what I'm reading. I take the opportunity to stretch my legs, stuff the book into my waistband and go outside the tent. Was his grandfather really on board when Captain John Balleny, without realizing it, discovered the passage to the Ross Sea and with it the only navigable route to the Pole? Or were you lying, bosun? I sit on the crate of food by the dogloos and keep reading until Dr. Macklin drives me away from there, too.

"Saved a book, have you, Merce? Be generous with it; the worms are famished."

Mack's sled is the only one left. In one afternoon on the day we abandoned Ocean Camp and moved ten miles northwest across the floe, Wild shot his and then also Crean's, Marston's and McIlroy's dogs. And once Hurley's remaining seven had hauled the last of our things from Ocean Camp into the new "Patience Camp," he took them, too, out behind a hummock. Dogs there was no more food for and that now serve as food instead. Skinny, with shaggy, matted fur, Macklin's six beasts look at me with large questioning eyes.

Vincent comes out of the tent. Sated by his figment of pie, he lugs his bellyful of air over to our small boatyard. His friend and paternal consoler Chippy McNeish is there with his pipe in the angle of his mouth, caulking the dinghy. And his sidekick and whipping boy, Stevenson, is leaning against the propped-up *Dudley Docker* and speechifying about something that only the scrawny ship's tiger is listening to. But Mrs. Chippy doesn't mind who plays the big man—as long as there's a chunk of seal meat in it for her. I wait for Vincent to rejoin his own kind, then stroll back to the tent and get comfy with John Balleny on my meltwater mattress.

Bakewell: "Do any of you know doughnuts?"

Hussey: "Course. What're you thinking?"

Bakewell: "Very easy to make. I like them best cold, with raspberry jelly."

Wordie: "Jam, no. I think I'd rather have that on toast."

It's a typical morning in Patience Camp when I first read the name of Balleny's ship's boy. He wasn't called Vincent, but, of all things, Smith, which doesn't mean a thing.


IT'S ALSO THE MORNING WHEN TIME STANDS STILL FOR ALL OF US. ON this, the twenty-first of November 1915, the 301st day since we were sealed in by pack ice off the Antarctic coast, the *Endurance* sinks.

Summer has returned. The warmth melts the ice, and where the floes, rubbing each other thin and thinner, finally break, water rises licorice-black. For weeks, Shackleton has been nervously waiting for the day when the icy trap opens and the vise that crushed our ship lets her go. When that day finally comes, he's standing alone up in the tower, and his shrill cry is both a lament and a command, so we drop whatever we're doing, come out of the tents and look to the south.

"She's going, boys! She's going!"

So back out again. Yes, she's still there. She's lifted her stern out of the ice. But her bow and midships are already completely submerged and waiting to swim down into the deep.

"Look at her."

"She's going" comes again from above, and this time it sounds satisfied, like when at a deathbed someone says, "It's almost over."

Sir Ernest climbs down the ladder and stands in the middle of the men.

"Pray for her," says Alf Cheetham. "She protected us like a mother; she was a good ship."

And we give her three cheers: hip, hip, hurrah; hip, hip, hurrah; hip, hip, hurrah!

Her stern up in the air at an even higher angle, she pauses for a long while, as though to let us savor this last image of her and fix it forever in our memories.

You'd like to call to her not to give up, because she's about to drown.

In an eyeblink, she's gone, zoomed into the depths like a child on a slide. A shout runs through us, and over there, miles away between the ridges, the ice is empty, and I can't help but imagine her gliding into the blackening deep.

Farewell, *Endurance*.

Weigh anchor!

SO WE'VE SAVED OURSELVES ONTO THE ICE AND SAVED EVERYTHING ON board that we need for our survival, but we weren't able to save our ship and now she's gone under. The new camp makes a strange impression: it looks like a ship without a ship. Everything that should be there is there: deckhouse, galley, funnel, boats, mast. Mack's dogs are lying around lazily like they used to do on deck, and we're all still busying ourselves with whatever smaller or larger tasks we've been given. Even though Shackleton assigned men to the tents with sensitivity and good intentions, the sailors, stokers and machinists have nonetheless formed one group; the doctors, scientists and artists another; and the bosses, that is, the skipper, the officers and veterans, a third. And Green, the grouchy cook, and I, the daydreaming steward, are still in a class to ourselves: we cook for everyone and bring everyone his food. Nor is it phantom food made of words; that is, it tastes foul, but it keeps us alive. Now and then there's dog on the menu, and not all of the men have the heart to push a chunk of Sailor or Shakespeare down their gullets. Otherwise, the ship's routines are preserved, the only difference being that there's no longer any ship.

WHEN I WAS A BOY, THE OLD BETHEL CHURCH IN PILLGWENLLY'S neighboring town of Mynyddislwyn was demolished to expand the Newport docks. I remember the discombobulating feeling I had while running across the space that stayed unused a whole summer long: that with the church, time, too, seemed to have disappeared. The leveled-off churchyard on the bank of the Usk that the hot summer wind swept across seemed like a hole in time where every mood, whether sad or happy, persisted limitlessly. Regyn and I stripped between the privet hedges, and the crabs that we pulled out of the river looked in their red boots like bandit captains.

We never forgot the stink of the privet and the taste of the wild strawberries on the sloping riverbank, not even when the memory of Mynyddislwyn had become embarrassing. No matter how much Regyn, at least, wanted to erase that time, the feeling of that summer didn't die away, in neither her nor me.

When time stands still you can't reach the future. You save your-self either from moment to moment, by waiting and hoping that some-one'll be inclined to pass the time with you, or you dream yourself back into the past, to sweets, strawberries red as the boots of the river crabs, or to a ship's boy named Smith. Then, as the child that I was, the present meant nothing to me. All I sensed was that time was stand-ing still, and I wasn't especially surprised. But in the ice, there's almost nothing worse than feeling lethargic old time falter and freeze up. That's why the men who kept diaries on the *Endurance* now note their tent-mates' every word and ailment. From the tent poles dangle obscurely marked calendars that survived the evacuation, and Wild and Worsley insist on continuing to enter our daily position, depth soundings and speed in the logbook. A thick line of ink divides the book into before and after: this is when she went down.

December passes. The Sundays of Advent melt together into a single afternoon with four servings of seal steak and penguin pudding. And after every meal, the phantom cooks in my tent put on a general-knowledge quiz with the couple of pages that had fallen out of the encyclopedia and that Hurley stuffed into his canisters long ago to cushion his negatives, unintentionally saving them from the ice: What does *ormolu* mean? Where is Ormoc? And the Christmas seal ragout and penguin pie have just been gobbled up when Bob Clark gets a decisive break in the trickiest of the puzzles: Who was Eleanor A. Ormerod?

"Was she a scientist?"

"Yes," says Jimmy James.

"I knew it! A biologist?"

"Yes," says Jimmy James.

"Ha! Didn't she do work on the dinosaurs?"

Justice is done to Mrs. Ormerod on New Year's Eve: she wasn't only an entomologist, she was the archetypal natural scientist and even, as Jimmy James reads out loud, "the Demeter of the nineteenth century."

We drink to that over our seal steak and penguin dessert. And already it's 1916. But it doesn't change a thing.

In the first six weeks of the new year, we drift a good hundred and twenty-five miles to the north. Paulet Island is only another hundred and fifty miles to the northwest, but there are still innumerable fissures and ridges between us and solid ground. The distance could just as well be to Wales. Until the ice releases us and we can switch into our boats, we're staked to our floe and have got to go wherever the drifting pack ice takes us.

"Things that exist but not in the ice" is the name of a game that keeps us busy through the warm summer days of January and February. The idea for it came from Sir Ernest, who'd been impressed by the entertainment and relaxing effect of the encyclopedia game. Once, when I'm bringing him and Hurley some tea in their tent and peek over their shoulders at their game of poker patience, Sir Ernest is on a run of luck and having, on paper, already won a silk umbrella, a mirror and a collector's edition of Keats, has now also taken from Hurley the camp's most hotly contested chip: dinner at the Savoy. Sir Ernest casually admits that he loathes every form of quiz. But if it's for the happiness of the men, he'll gladly take a bite of that bitter apple.

The game is very simple: someone thinks of a thing that exists somewhere but not in the ice, and the others take turns to try and guess it. Since there are twenty-eight of us, we have twenty-seven questions to zero in on each thing and name it. Whoever manages first gets to choose a prize of either a biscuit or a piece of one of the last two bars of chocolate. If no one guesses correctly, the prize goes to whoever thought it up.

We strike a problem right in the first round. A tense discussion develops about if there are pines in the ice. Jock Wordie propones that there are no trees within the Antarctic Circle and hence no pines, either. Orde-Lees, on the other hand, argues that parts of the ship and the sleds are made of pinewood and, the way he sees it, pine is pine.

It's almost the same with the thing that Greenstreet enters into the race for a piece of chocolate: grass. No one guesses it, but he's denied nonetheless when Dr. McIlroy pulls his rock-hard emergency reserve out of his breast pocket: a quarter-slice of white Grytviken bread from Stina Jacobsen's oven.

"There's good Norwegian grain in this, and grain, my dear Greenstreet, is nothing other than grass."

The game stretches out for weeks, just as Shackleton intended. Sometimes there's serious argument, for example between Vincent and Orde-Lees about gramophone. Vincent claims that there's no gramophone in the ice since ours, thank God, went down with the *Endurance*. Orde-Lees contradicts him. No one can know where his gramophone now is. Maybe it's floating around the sea on a block of ice. Maybe we'll find it again one day, totally unscathed.

"No," says Vincent. "It's gone forever. Satan's fetched it back."

We decide that the game isn't working. But the next day a small group has already formed, and when the first biscuit prizes are paid out, everyone else is gradually drawn back in to try their luck.

Hussey wins by guessing Cheetham's hornets, Holie manages to steer his Tower Bridge to victory and grasp his piece of chocolate, and the greatest uproar is created by, of all people, Tom Crean, who has been as good as silent since the shooting of his dogs and who, after twenty-seven unsuccessful questions, reveals that he had been thinking of Amundsen.

Shackleton announces the end of the game by proclaiming a bonus round. It's to be reserved for a single topic: women.

"Everyone who takes part and names a woman who's dear to him," he says, "will receive a biscuit or some chocolate. And because this piece of shortbread, unmarked by any tooth, is smiling at me the way it is, I'll be the first to earn myself one."

With that, he reaches into the biscuit tin brightly decorated with painted riders, dogs and forests. "In the name of my wife, Emily

Shackleton," he says and, while we all watch silently, takes a bite of the golden shortbread. "And in the name of my lover, also Emily Shackleton."

The first to imitate him is the skipper. "Theodora Worsley," says the captain, and takes a biscuit. "Mmhmm! Yes, gentlemen, that's her smell exactly."

And while we're still laughing, Marston's fingers are already stretching into the tin, as colorful as it is with flecks of paint. Not a day passes that Marston doesn't work on the names, figures and pictures he's using to beautify the recovered Antarctic clock. "Hazel Marston, God protect her."

"Yes, George, he will," says Shackleton. "I'm sure of that."

The names of wives, brides, mothers and daughters are spoken in turn. Some of the men even pull out photographs of their respective ladies and girls. But some are secretive. Holie says only, "Rose."

And Wordie says, "Who she is won't be revealed, only that she's called Gertrude Mary Henderson. Does that count?"

Every name counts. Bakewell gets a bit of chocolate for a Brooklyn barmaid named Lily, Crean stays true to Stina Jacobsen, and Mick McIlroy names all eight forenames of Her Majesty, the consort of our King: Victoria Mary Augusta Louise Olga Pauline Claudine Agnes, Princess of Teck.

One of the last to get his hands on a biscuit is me. After hesitating for a long time over if I should even say a name, my hunger for something sweet is stronger than my doubts, and so I follow my heart and, to my own surprise, name my sister, Regyn.


PLAYING THE GAME, THE SUMMER GOES BY, EACH DAY JUST LIKE THE LAST, and the only way we can tell that time is passing is by how much thinner we are. We're like the ice of the floe we're drifting on across the circular Weddell Sea. Ponds of meltwater form wherever we cook and sleep for longer than a few days, and often it's not long after we've moved on that the ocean nibbles through the ice and eats another hole into our frozen raft.

This perforation has its advantages: now and then, one of the few crabeaters wandering the periphery of the polar region at this time of year pops up out of the water and, before the confused seal has understood that it's stumbled into a gang of seal eaters, Wild already has the rifle at his shoulder. Frank Wild's shooting saves Stornoway's life one day at the start of April, when the Scotsman sprints towards a hole, pulling his knife and thinking he's sighted a magnificent Weddell seal. Less than ten yards from him and presumably motivated by exactly the same mistake, a gray-and-black-striped leviathan heaves itself onto the ice. It stares out of dead eyes, it has flippers for feet and it shrieks from a maw lined with spikes.

"McLeod! Get back! Stornoway, no!

Twice as big and twice as fast as he is, the leopard seal, in a flurry of sliding, waddling and slithering, shoots forwards towards Stornoway, who yells like a child, and the predator seal has almost reached our stumbling able seaman when Frank Wild fires the rifle, not even needing to reload.

Sir Ernest, Green and I discover that the leopard seal's belly is full of weird white fish. They're ice fish, Bob Clark explains, whose blood is white, not red. And there are thirty-one of them, which minus three half-digested ones make precisely twenty-eight, so that we get a fish supper each.

A miniature leopard seal, silver with black dappling, beside it the date and the number of our 435th day in the ice . . . George Marston lovingly preserves our feast in Patience Camp on the Antarctic clock.

We're usually so preoccupied with our thoughts of food that it's a wonderful change to tramp along the shore of a meltwater lake with a full belly and dream of the open sea. It can't be much further. Especially because it's been with us all this time. Fifteen hundred fathoms deep and licorice-black beneath my feet.

# 33

## A White Patch
## in the Snow

"WHAT'S SO TRAGIC ABOUT NOT DISCOVERING A SEA? JUST answer me that."

He doesn't understand what my problem is. Of course he can imagine very easily that one would be named after him, the Bakewell Sea, and if it doesn't happen: "So what? I can live with it."

We sink the ice picks into our trouser pockets and shoulder the blocks of ice we've cut out of the ridge. Back to camp.

"Well, listen," I say to Bakewell. "Don't interrupt me and I'll explain it." I start at the start. If it was Cook who discovered the house of the Antarctic, it was Ross who found the door that Scott, Shackleton and Amundsen used to enter it—the Ross Sea. But the discoverer of the keyhole, that was an old, incidentally very pious, seal hunter called John Balleny.

On board his schooner *Eliza Scott,* Balleny shot the sun with his sextant on the first of February 1839. He calculated that he was nearly three hundred miles further south than any human being before him. Hidden beyond the horizon, two days' clear sailing away and unbeknownst to Balleny, was the entrance to the sea that's now named after Ross.

Pack ice and fog forced the *Eliza Scott* and the smaller *Sabrina* to sail to the northwest. After ten days' sailing, Balleny discovered a group of volcanic islands. The commander of the *Sabrina* had himself rowed across to one of the desolate shores to collect rock samples.

251

Thomas Freeman was the first person to set foot on land within the Antarctic Circle.

I also tell Bakewell about the two days when the fate of Vincent's grandfather was decided, the thirteenth and twenty-fourth of March 1839. On the thirteenth, Balleny wrote in his logbook: "Captain Freeman came aboard this morning, bringing the ship's boy Smith and taking the ship's boy Juggins with him." Eleven days after this unexplained swap at sea, the two ships were sailing just north of the polar circle when they hit heavy weather. The *Sabrina* lit a distress signal during the night. But Balleny was in no position to rush to the aid of Freeman's men. The blue light was the last he saw of his accompanying ship. The *Sabrina* sank, and down with her went Captain Freeman and the ship's boy, nicknamed Juggins.

The *Eliza Scott* sailed back to London just in time for someone else to copy her logbooks and take them on his own expedition: Ross's ships *Erebus* and *Terror* followed Balleny's course and managed to sail through into the sea that had stayed hidden from the seal hunter. "So," I say, "that's the whole story."

Bakewell drops his block of ice at the entrance to the tent. Slush squirts out to the sides; that's how sloppy the ice is.

"Rotten luck. But at least they all got home. And you're certain this Juggins was Vincent's grandpa? How old was he? He must have already been a father."

According to the hiring list, Jacob "Juggins" Vincent was exactly the same age I was when Vincent and I first met, seventeen. And he was from Birmingham, same as our bosun. If Balleny knew that his ship's boy was already a father or if Juggins even knew, there's nothing about that in the logbooks.

While it becomes more obvious from day to day that the floe is disintegrating and that we're starving, I read Balleny's report over and again to fix all the important details in my memory. But I ask myself why I'm bothering. The smoothness has vanished from Vincent's face, as has his pride. The same limp, dirty consternation has etched itself into him as it has into all our faces. What can I tell him? That I've checked his claim and read in his family history about how his granddad died? Shall I say, I'm sorry, Vincent, but the terrible truth is that Juggins drowned seventy-five years ago because of an unlucky coincidence?

If we didn't have to sift through our rubbish for scraps of meat that even the dogs and the cat have refused, and if we didn't have to think day and night of the ice breaking under our feet and dropping us into a sea that could close again over our heads, but were instead sitting sated and cheerful with a cognac and tobacco in the hut on Vahsel Bay, waiting for the men of the glorious on-foot traversal . . . perhaps then it might be possible to talk to John Vincent and convince him of the worth of this slim little book.

It lies in my hand as orange as an orange. It was frozen stiff for weeks, and for that long again I carried it next to the fish by my heart, so that it would thaw and dry. Who he was, Juggins, John Balleny's ship's boy, is known only to his grandson, to me, my friend Bakie and to this book. I throw it off the shore of the ice and it sinks in an instant.

Bakewell's right: why should I worry about the dead when what matters is that we live? A narrow margin, slimmer every day, divides us from starving, freezing or drowning. We've been living off the belief that we were managing to survive, but we are gradually having to recognize that all we've been doing these months is drawing out our deaths. It's the start of April. Another winter is ahead of us. The giant petrels and skuas are still flying, a sure sign of open water. And at night we can hear the whales bursting the ice and blowing out spume. But Mr. and Mrs. Seal are playing at other latitudes. Our supplies are almost exhausted. Since there's no more blubber, we can't light the ovens and are eating the remaining scraps of penguin and seal meat raw, half spoiled, half frozen. As disgusting as they taste and as debased as you feel eating them, the hunger is stronger, and even stronger than that is the fear of getting so weak that, in the moment of departure, you won't be able to clamber from the ice into the boat. Hunger and fear, the two together lead to a naked despair that can't be alleviated by any phantom recipe, any game or any Ernest Shackleton. In all the months, all the time on board and in the two camps on the ice, not so much as a crumb of cocoa has gone missing from the ration crates. But as the floe breaks up and we find ourselves on a flooded chunk so small we couldn't play football on it even if we weren't too feeble to do so, the last pieces of meat go missing one morning from Green's ice-box. And even Wild's roaring can't change anything about the fact that there's no way of recognizing the thief. Because we all look the same: worried and appalled and scared and hungry.

Wild shoots the last dogs. And after a lot of resistance, McNeish gives up the cat's hiding place. Wild shoots her, too. After that, our daily ration consist of 200 grams of dried dog meat, three sugar cubes, a biscuit and half a beaker of milk powder in water. The rest of the water is untouchable. It's being saved for the boat journey and is placed under guard. Whoever wants a drink takes a tobacco tin full of ice into his sleeping bag and lets it melt in his body heat. On the same day, Shackleton strips Vincent of his bosun's rank and reduces him to ordinary seaman.

"They're calling me a dirty Jew," says Orde-Lees at night in the tent, "and Wild is letting it happen."

The morning after a night of rain, the boats are sunk halfway down into the softening floe. McNeish refuses to help drag the *James Caird* back onto the firmer ice.

"What's going on over there?" bellows Shackleton from the *Dudley Docker*. With a couple of strides, he's next to our main boat.

Worsley reports, "McNeish here thinks . . ."

Shackleton interrupts him for the first time: "Keep your men at their work, Captain. And you, McNeish, move it, that's an order."

McNeish doesn't move. The only light parts of his face are the whites of his eyes, which stare at Shackleton.

And he says, "You've got no right to give me orders."

And Shackleton: "Don't talk to me about rights! Who gave you the right to let twenty men stand around freezing? Or the right to put these men's lives at risk while you tell us what you think?"

And McNeish: "I think the boat'll break apart."

And again Shackleton: "What do I care about the God-damned boat? I care about the God-damned men and keeping them alive! That's what I'm responsible for."

"Well, I'm responsible for myself," says McNeish, "and it cuts no mustard with me if some bastard who sticks flags in the snow wants to tell me what to do."

Vincent comes around the boat and tramps across to the carpenter. "No ship, no contract. We don't give a monkey's what you order."

Shackleton goes for the two of them. He stops only when they step apart, and shouts at them, "I am the leader of this expedition! Your contract is with me and not with the fucking ship. Do as I tell you and I will make sure you survive. But if you put the lives of the men in danger, I will shoot you here and now."

But it can also work another way. In our tent, first Macklin and Clark, then Orde-Lees and Worsley get into an argument that goes on until Greenstreet's beaker of milk falls to the floor. He spins around and blames Clark for causing the misfortune. When Bob Clark protests, Greenstreet shouts him down.

We're all standing there, emaciated and bearded, staring at the patch where the milk has seeped into the snow. Clark is the first to pour a glug of milk from his beaker into Greenstreet's, and we all mutely follow his example.

The Prince, on the other hand, tries to make use of the disbanded mood. He wants to find space on the boat for as many of his negatives as possible.

Sir Ernest wants to know precisely how many pictures Hurley has salvaged from the *Endurance*.

"Five hundred, sir, five boxes."

"Good, we'll take perhaps a hundred with us," says Shackleton.

And Hurley: "That isn't enough. Two hundred. And you make the selection."

Shackleton holds out his beaker under the light snowfall. "It's not letting up, look," he says. He peers into his beaker and sips the milk. "Let's say a hundred and fifty, we'll make the selection together and I'll write you an affidavit saying that if I die all the rights revert to you."

Hurley agrees with a broad smile.

And Shackleton says, "You haven't spotted the catch, have you? You see, I've got no intention of dying."

*Part Four*

## THE NAMELESS MOUNTAINS

# 34

## THREE BOATS

FOUR HUNDRED AND FORTY-ONE DAYS SINCE OUR SHIP WAS LOCKED into the ice and sixteen months since we left the island of South Georgia, on the morning of the 9th of April, the man on lookout sights land. To the northwest, around sixty miles away, what we can clearly make out as grey cliffs reach up above the expanse of fractured ice and water we're drifting across.

Kneeling on the floe in heavy rain and held steady by two men with staring eyes, Worsley shoots the sun. His calculations allow only two possibilities: the peaks are either those of Joinville Island, the northernmost extremity of the Antarctic continent, or what we're looking at out there on the horizon are already the Clarence and Elephant Islands, which lie out in the ocean. What characterizes all three last outposts of the Antarctic is that the sea races between them as if through an open gate. All of us know that if we don't succeed in landing on one of the islands, the current will carry us out into the hurricane latitudes of the Drake Passage.

Shackleton wastes no time. After a hasty breakfast, the tents are dismantled and the boats made ready to launch. The same rules apply as when we were leaving the ship. The captain can take his navigation instruments, the doctors their medical equipment, Hurley the camera with the agreed number of negatives, and Hussey can take his banjo. The rest of us are left only with what we're wearing on our backs.

The places in the boats are assigned. In the largest, the *James Caird*, Sir Ernest, Wild and eleven other men. Worsley and nine others make up the crew of the *Dudley Docker* and Crean is put in command of the little dinghy, the *Stancomb-Wills*. The four riding with Crean are Vincent, Holness, Bakewell and me.

By early evening, we're ready. The boats are lying keel up a safe distance from the lip of the floe. We wait until the drumming rain relents to a drizzle, then turn them over one after the other, haul them to the water's edge and float them. On Sir Ernest's command, he, Worsley and Crean climb in, the last ones on board. The sea in the lead is black and the rain is picking up again. We take a last look across the floe and cast off.

"I once crossed Alaska on a train like a hobo," says Bakewell, next to me at the oars. "The abandoned gold-rush towns in the Klondike, that's just how they looked."

I'm not in the mood for talking. Because we're in the smallest boat, we're supposed to stay between the other two, and they've set off at a decent lick. Rowing. It's not my world. But anything's better than staying on that ice any longer and waiting for it to melt under your feet. By the end the floe was no more than a foot thick. Over Crean's shoulder I can see the shroud of fog that the rain streams through before it's whipped into my face. Where's the floe? Disappeared. And with it our former home, Patience Camp.

"Easy," Tom Crean says suddenly. "You're sailing with Shackleton, not with Scott. Nice and easy, Merce."

It's the first time I hear Scott's name from his mouth and, in fact, it does calm me down.

The dark-gray turbid sea is strewn with ice boulders. The floes groan and crack as they rock in the current. Our little fleet has settled into a smooth, rapid tempo, and for a few hours we pull regularly across the sea and through the evening rain. Sir Ernest gives the order to slow down only when the lead becomes too narrow and threatens to trap one of the cutters, or when a slab of ice slips off a berg that we haven't been able to make a wide enough detour around and sends rushing towards us a wave bearing sharp thorns of blue ice.

"Hands in the boats! And duck!"

The wave crashes over us, pours itself into the boat, soaking everything and everyone. Lumps of ice thwack into necks and backs and stay lying at our feet when we've bailed the boat dry. Sopping wet, we carry on. Rowing and sucking ice. And again Shackleton's voice from the *Caird,* ahead of us.

"Everyone duck! Hands in the boats!"

It's a wonder that none of the oars snap. Vincent swears behind me and Holie gasps for air. Bakewell isn't speaking anymore, and it's got so dark I can't see his expression.

Shackleton calls a stop. First our and then Worsley's boat come alongside. We're back together. Gloved hands are shaken across the thickly frozen gunwales, faces patted, jokes made.

A floe for the night. Wild paddles off and spots an even slab about fifty paces long whose point is directed straight into the current. Green and the little blubber stove are put ashore, then my oarsmen bring the *Stancomb-Wills* to the edge and heave me up onto it. The ice is firm and wonderfully clean.

"Ach!" Green spits a glob of chewing tobacco. "Don't stand about. Blubber in, fire on."

By the time the unloaded boats are lying keel up on the floe and the tents have been constructed, the evening meal is ready. The dog stew warms our stiff bodies, and in two of the tents you can hear songs and laughter. While Uzbird plays his banjo, Bob Clark and I go to look at the night sky. There's a weak light in the south and a sparse meteor shower.

But this first night at sea becomes a nightmare. Cradled to sleep by the gentle rocking of the current, we're woken by a smack and shudder. With flickering storm lamps, we swarm out to find that an iceberg has rammed our floe and spun it to lie directly across the current. Nor are we alone. A family of killer whales is on the lookout for a midnight feast; we can hear the big orcas blowing in the dark and the baby ones making obedient little puffs in response.

In the middle of the night, a heavy breaker hits our floe, which rocks once up and down, then snaps. The rent in the ice runs through our tent, rips out the pegs and in seconds has become a yawning chasm, yards wide, full of black and lapping water.

Everyone who's managed to scramble to safety in their sleeping bags starts roaring, "A crack! Help! A crack in tent number four!"

Wild and Worsley bolt across. They want a head count. But there's too much chaos. And Shackleton doesn't wait for it to calm down. He strides along the edge of the crack and shines his lamp into the water.

"The tents, pull them away. I want to see!"

Three men pull the tent material onto the ice.

Wild shouts, "Twenty-six! Two missing!"

At the same time, the beam of lamplight gliding across the crests of the waves falls on the outline of a man.

Holie. It's Holness who's floating there. He's thrashing with the one arm he's managed to free from the sleeping bag. Shackleton drops to his knees. The lamp falls into the water. He grabs the sleeping bag and heaves Holness onto the ice with a single jerk.

A second head count shows that Wild had made a mistake in the tumult. With Holie's rescue, we're all present. Nor would there have been a chance to rescue anyone else. Hardly have we moved to safety but the two halves of the floe crash back together. Splashed water freezing in the lamplight is the only sign the chasm was ever there.

I lend a hand and help carry Holness in his sodden sack of ice water through the mist of spray.

"You know what?" he says. "I was just about to roll myself a smoke. Now all my baccy's with Davy Jones."

His big, empty eyes are bloodshot and wet locks of hair are plastered crazily to his forehead.

But he's laughing again. Because Hussey says, "Might be a good moment to give up, then, don't you think?"

• • •

To REDUCE THE WEIGHT IN THE BOATS, WE HEAVYHEARTEDLY GIVE UP ALL
sorts of things that would be useful to us on land. Picks, shovels,
planking and three crates of dried fruit stay behind on the floe. For
stuff that none of our stomachs can tolerate, we've lugged these dried
plums and dates a very long way.

There's a strong and freshening easterly wind. Sir Ernest gives
the order to pull in the oars and set sails. McNeish's weeks of toil in
furnishing our three nutshells with masts now pay off, and all of us
are grateful to the carpenter for sparing us a second day at the oars.

The wind rolls heavy seas ahead of it. Waves break against the
edges of the floes. The spray freezes as it falls and lands as hail in our
lurching boats. Everything is sheathed in ice. I watch Crean's midnight-
blue overcoat turn white and stiffen, and each time he shifts to correct
the rudder, I hear his overcoat crunch and crackle.

While the land to the west disappears in fog and the darkness of
the second night, we flee the bergs and orcas onto a floe that's drifting
across a large, open lake. Apart from Holness, whose legs and feet
are showing signs of frostbite, each of us has got to keep watch for
twenty minutes. We all get a few hours' sleep and are at least a little
rested when in the morning we peer out at the arena that the bleak
new day has prepared for us.

We've reached the extreme northern end of the Weddell Sea.
Driven forwards by the quick southerly current and thrown back by
the powerful swell from the open ocean to the north, the ice is
churned into wreckage around our floe, which rocks and wobbles as
it's carried forwards. For as far as we can see, the water's surface is
laden with fragmented drift ice rising and falling on the waves. The
ice collides and smashes until its remnants are washed out into the
endlessness of the Pacific or the Atlantic. Inexhaustible streams of ice
that have pushed from Antarctica's glaciers and shelf ice into the Weddell Sea and been carried north now collide with the quick warm cur-
rents of the Drake Passage. All the ice that hasn't yet managed to

wreak any havoc in the wider world is shattered, heaped and battered by the maelstrom of the waves.

No ice floe escapes the monstrous grinder. Switching to a berg, as a group around Greenstreet and Hudson suggest, is brusquely dismissed by Shackleton, rightly, as it turns out. Three tabular icebergs capsize one after the other in front of us, and their deep blue juts into the sky for hours before they disintegrate and disgorge their masses of ice into the sea. Our flight again hinges on finding the right moment to move. Sir Ernest has us wait for hour after hour on the floe and watch as we drift unstoppably into the grinder.

We hold the three boats ready, waiting for our melting raft to break up. We're soon crouching on no more than a narrow white tongue. Waves break and rinse chunks of ice across it.

"Are you sure you want to wait any longer?" even Wild eventually asks when he comes back from an inspection. "The edges are soft. It'll be difficult to haul the boats across them."

"I'll wait."

Two hours later, Wild is again standing next to him and Shackleton says, "I'm waiting for that lovely beauty over there to discover us."

The beauty is a narrow lead of open water breaking its way through the jagged landscape. Wider and wider and soon so close that we can hear it, the lead is splintering the ice and showing us the dark water lying beneath.

The lead is with us quicker than expected.

And just as quickly, Greenstreet shouts, "She's breaking up!"

We tip the boats. Shackleton gives the order to smash the edges of the floe until we hit solid ice. We kick a bay into our floe and launch the three boats onto it, and as the lead arrives, the floe breaks down the middle with a single loud crack.

But we're away, suddenly on open water, perhaps a hundred strokes separating us from the ocean and the end of the ice.

. . .

THE LAND THAT VANISHED INTO THE FOG DOESN'T REAPPEAR, AND MIST and snow make it impossible for Worsley to determine our position. For a day and a night, it looks as if our plan to follow the border of the pack ice northwards to the Clarence and Elephant Islands will be changed again. Instead, Shackleton risks setting a course for Hope Bay on the Antarctic Peninsula. Sailing to the northwest towards the coast of the mainland has the advantage that we'll strike land whatever happens. Otherwise it would mean trying, in high seas and without a crow's nest, to find two rocky islands, both minuscule, as dark as the night and the sea, and encircled by wreaths of reefs uncharted even by Cook. And if we missed, there'd be nothing for us beyond them but the fury of the waves that race around the polar cap.

For fear of being dragged back into the maelstrom on a floe, we spend the night in the boats, moored to a berg, and in the morning we're frozen and close to death under a layer of ice and snow. Hours pass before the icy cuffs, as thick as my calf, have been chipped off all the oars. Green and I scramble up to a plateau above the heads of the others. We rope up the stove and the things we need to prepare a warming breakfast, but our lamentable scraps of blubber don't get the stove hot enough. Everything has to go back into the boat, where the little Primus cookers do what they can to make our milk and dog lukewarm on the spoons.

Shackleton is suddenly tormented by sciatica that, however, relents when Mick or Mack puts a needle in him and I or someone else he asks massages the spot. Crean, Worsley, Wild, Bakewell and I are the only ones still in reasonable condition. The other faces are divided by the morning light into those broken open by misery and those that are hardened and resentful. Holie's feet don't seem to want to recover. His boots are too thin and can't dry out, and when Sir Ernest orders him brought onto the *Caird* so that a doctor can take care of him, Mack establishes that three of Holie's toes are already irredeemably frostbitten.

"Set sail!" The order comes through rain as hard as hail.

We come out from the iceberg's shadow and see at once that the drift ice is hard at our heels. The plan to sail for Hope Bay is dropped. The stream of ice is pushing itself up the coast and blocking off the peninsula. It leaves us no other choice than to sail north, and so we do, after all, set a course for the two pinpricks in the vastness of the ocean.

# 35

## THE GLOVE

BUT HOW WONDERFUL IT IS TO DASH ALONG THE EDGE OF THE ICE over open water. The seabirds accompany us out onto the ocean and lone seals or small penguin groups sleep gently on cruising floes. At last we can again determine our speed of movement ourselves and take our progress into our own hands.

In all three boats, the masts withstand the ocean gusts. As soon as we moor against an iceberg to eat and care for Holie's foot, Chippy McNeish clambers from boat to boat and, with an expressionless gaze and paws that run gently across the wood, checks the joints at the mast's base, the hang of the spars, the mobility of the rudder, the turn of the capstans and everything else. Wide-legged and muttering, Chippy stands in our boat as it rocks from side to side, his legs clutched fast by two others. They throw their arms around him as if he were a venerable and sage old graybeard when he moves to sit down and tonelessly mumbles that "it'll hold." McNeish the carpenter; our skipper and navigation genius, Worsley; and Sir Ernest are the three our lives depend on. We watch hawklike over them, and when, pressed tight into one another against the cold and wet, we can't doze off, our taciturn exchanges under the tarpaulins and blankets center almost exclusively on these three and the miraculous interaction of their talents.

Since his cat was killed and his argument with Sir Ernest on the floe, McNeish has retreated fully into himself. He speaks only when it's unavoidable. Shackleton watches each of his movements and isn't too grand to thank the carpenter for every one of his masterfully simple adjustments. But the bond between the two has been as completely severed as that between Sir Ernest and his degraded bosun, and no amount of admiration can hide that the crew of the *Endurance* is no longer what it was. Our common aim, survival, has divided us after all and alienated us from one another. And even though it probably isn't clear to most of them, Sir Ernest expends more than a little of his strength and stamina on keeping them all in line.

The fourth April night since leaving the camp we spend in the boats. The only floes floating across the ocean are half flooded, and even the iceberg we moor against seems to Wild and Crean, who check it thoroughly, to be a treacherous haven.

With the onset of darkness, the temperature falls to twenty below zero. Sleep is out of the question. The boats rock in a chain, fastened end-to-end against the wall of ice. Slabs of snow break off and drop onto us. It rains, hails and snows one at a time or all, wildly, at once, and when another berg steams past in the dark, waves rush up to gush into the boats and—despite the tarpaulins, sailcloth, blankets and overcoats we've crawled beneath—soak us to the skin.

To replace poor Holness, Shackleton has put the frightened and exhausted How in the *Stancomb-Wills*. He, Bakewell and I hunker against one another under layers of fabric and tarp, unmoving and trying to let as little body warmth as possible escape to the outside. I have my arms tight around Bakewell. Between us, on the naked wood, cowers How, whom we keep warm, whispering reassurances before cold, hunger, exhaustion and the murderous lack of sleep get the better of him. Shuddering, How slides into a blank slumber.

At the beginning, Crean asks every hour if we're still alive.

"Yes," someone answers, and we listen to hear if Tom Crean's bass will sound another time.

"Good," he says a moment later.

I ask after Vincent, who's sitting next to Crean. "Is he still alive?"

"Don't you worry about me, Blackboro" comes straight back out of the blankets.

In the second half of the night, we go quiet and even the ringing calls of the three boat captains stop. Only the drumming of the rain, the breakers and the falling snow still reach me. I sit there for an eternity in motionless frenzy, holding on to my friend and trembling along with his shivers.

I don't want to close my eyes. The evil sleep waiting for me is an abyss that whimpers to me with my own voice. Hownow's hot skull scours the skin between my legs raw. But nor do I want to move his head aside. And even if I wanted to, I couldn't. I can't move a finger.

Bakie's mouth is close to my ear. He snores for a while but mostly just wheezes. It hardly sounds different from the low whining of the wind.

Only once, as if from far away, do I think I've understood two words.

"The fish," breathes Bakewell. Is he dreaming? Or was it just the wind?

The fish! Yes, as it flutters through my mind, I take out Ennid's fish. When if not now?

Read her greeting, be brave and at least this silent misery will be over.

And in my thoughts I reach for it with fingers whose cuts and chilblains have all healed. I swiftly unbutton the pocket and hold the trout in my hands. Bright light falls onto its colorful wood, and my heart beats in my throat as I open the flap. In the belly, there's no note; there's a tiny red book in there instead. I recognize that I'm in a nightmare by the miniature copy of Mr. Muldoon's accounts ledger, and yet I can distinctly see the seven pages, the little book holds no more than that, and read what's written on them:

*Hell isn't hot, it's cold as ice,*
*you devil,*
*and I who was a boy called Juggins,*
*my God,*
*I'm freezing still. So tell me,*
*you devil,*
*why did I die?*

In the morning, the fog hanging over the sea is so dense that I can't make out the faces of the men in the bow of the *Caird*. Holie's moaning is low under the quiet. Tom Crean inspects How for frostbite, then sits down behind him and encloses the sailor in his coat. In both their expressions, in Vincent's, in Bakewell's, in every feral expression, I can see traces of nightmares like my own.

Shackleton has everyone count off. He has slung an arm around the mast of the *James Caird* and listens to each name in turn.

And each of us, who have our brows so tightly pulled by pain that it seems our eyes are bound shut, every one of us calls, coughs or raises his voice to a croak.

It is a surprise to us all, but we are all still alive.

MARKED BY CHILBLAINS, OUR LIPS AND GUMS SWOLLEN UP, DEAD-TIRED and agonized by the fear of having missed the islands, we sail through fog and snow. When it clears for a short time in the afternoon, Worsley heaves the *Dudley Docker* to and shoots the sun. These are fearful minutes in which no one in any of the three boats, tied together and almost still on the gentle swell, dares say a word. The captain wordlessly repeats the calculation. But then he turns to Sir Ernest and both their faces brighten.

We're on course, only twenty-five nautical miles from Elephant Island. If we maintain our pace, we'll reach the island at nightfall. There's no cheering. We exchange glances, and some of the men look up to the overcast sky. The doctors wake Holness from his personal twilight.

"Land, Holness! We'll be there in a couple of hours! Holness!" Macklin holds Holie's face between his hands and after a while he responds.

"Yes," he says weakly. "Land. Aye, aye. Understood."

We've made a mistake in that, wanting to keep the weight down, we've taken too little meltable ice with us into the boats. We pay for our error with unendurable thirst. It gives us temporary relief to suck on chunks of raw seal meat thawed out under our coats and swallow the blood. But the meat's saltiness soon redoubles our thirst and the torment. As McCarthy in the *Docker* and McLeod in the *Caird* break out in yells and, thrashing around furiously, howl for water, Shackleton orders that the raw meat be given only at mealtimes or when thirst is about to deprive a man of his sanity. McCarthy and McLeod are both given a chunk. While the splashed blood crusts on their mouths and fingers, they stare aghast and horrified at themselves into the sea. The rest of the provisions are transferred into the dinghy and our boat, now impractically heavy, is attached by a towrope to the *James Caird*.

At early evening, a stiff breeze rips the skies open. Between the snow clouds, seven soft snow- and ice-capped peaks appear against the rosy firmament. There can be no doubt. Ahead of us lies Elephant Island. A swarm of gulls comes to greet us. The powerful birds plummet from the sky, fly briefly at eye level beside our boats and then tip suddenly into the wind, which catches and lifts them up into the dusk. The offshore breeze that the gulls know how to use so skillfully makes heavy going for our boats. Because as good as it feels to see the deepblack shape of the island grow and grow, the boats are no less helplessly exposed to the riptide that thunders around the reefs, or to the breakers that also grow as we near the island.

When the darkness becomes total, a new shower of thick snow falls. Worsley and Shackleton consult in shouts from boat to boat, and the skipper eventually gets permission to sail ahead with the *Dudley Docker* and search for a place to land. In the bow of the *Caird*, Shackleton directs the beam of the ship's lantern onto the sail to give Worsley's boat a seamark. For a while, a light flickers back from the *Docker*, and through the flurrying snow that races down into the crests of the waves, I see the illuminated sailcloth under the island's high-towering cliffs and peaks. But then the light goes out. For a long time after, Shackleton stands at the mast and stares out into the snow. The light is not relit. But Shackleton turns away and climbs back to the stern only when Greenstreet roars that Wild has passed out at the helm.

The *Caird* takes in the sail and with that gives up contact to Worsley's boat. Only with the boat steadier can the men of the *Caird* separate the frozen Wild from the tiller and lie him down in the boat's middle. Bakewell and I stand at the mast on numb legs and peer towards our flagship. Several men have to rub warmth into Wild from the chest downwards before they can bend his limbs apart from his body.

He regains consciousness. Beside him, propped halfway up and staring wide-eyed into the dark, lies Holness. As Wild groans, Holie groans, too, and begins to weep.

"Twelve hours that man's been sitting at the tiller," Tom Crean says to us, seeming to have forgotten that he's done the same. "Mr. Bakewell," he calls. "Loose the towrope. We're going alongside."

"Alongside, aye."

Wild lies stretched out in the boat and his face blinks out of his hood. His Burberry snowsuit is aglitter with snow crystals. He turns his head and looks across to the five of us in the *Stancomb-Wills*. When he recognizes Crean, he tries to stand up.

Shackleton holds him down. "You will stay lying down there, God damn you, until such time as I give you permission to move!"

"Enough of that rubbish," says Wild, incensed, and sits upright. "I'm just fine. We've got to get going." His voice is hoarse and his swollen tongue slows his speech.

Shackleton is no less incensed. "Show me your hands!"

Wild doesn't want to. He looks across at Crean again instead, as if not understanding how Crean can manage to sit outside the boat.

"Your hands. Show me them, you stubborn fool!"

Crean nods. "Show them to him, Mr. Wild," he says calmly.

A breaker rolls over the boats and soaks us for the thousandth time. Once the spray has settled, Shackleton directs his lamp onto the hands that Wild is holding up. Only one is in a glove. The other is bare. It's mottled red and blue and puffy with boils and chilblains, more like a stump than a hand.

Shackleton takes off a glove and holds it out for Wild to stick the hand into.

Wild doesn't want the glove.

"Take it, Frank," several men shout.

And Shackleton: "Take it, Frank, or do you want to lose that hand?"

"I will not take it," says Wild. "I lose mine, and because I'm too stupid one of you has to replace it? Not a chance. You keep your glove, Ernest, and I'll go back to the tiller. I'm fine." Wild wants to stand up.

Shackleton holds him down by the shoulder. "Go back to the tiller for all I care. But you won't go without this glove. You can choose: either you put it on or I throw it overboard."


OUR TWO BOATS PLOUGH THROUGH WAVES THAT SHINE WITH MOONLIGHT. What with the reflective fog banks and the snow showers, it's so bright that I can make out individual rocks on the black cliffs we're whizzing underneath. I push my face over the gunwale and into the wind. Scraps of fogs caress me. The *James Caird* is on a breakneck run. She's towing the little dinghy behind her ever closer to the island. The massive stone projects blue-black wedges into the surf. I lean outwards and try in vain to see its peaks. Dark, narrow rifts and caves appear, open and vanish again into the blackness behind us, along with glacial streams and waterfalls, foaming white and silent, so close that it seems I can feel their cool breath on my face. But it can't be, because every offshore breeze is swallowed by the salt spray over the ocean.

For two hours, we shoot through the night and along the north coast of Elephant Island. Frank Wild is again at the helm of the *Caird*. At the helm of the *Stancomb-Wills* sits Tom Crean. He hums. His tongue must be just as swollen as mine, and the breakers wash over him just as they do over me. The salt is eating away at the skin on our faces, and our lips are thick and black, like slugs in wet grass. Crean hums. He's my brother's hero. Like Tom Crean, says Dafydd, that's how you've got to imagine Sétanta, the Celtic Achilles, who launched a hurling ball down the throat of Culain's savage guard dog, killing it, and offered himself to the heartbroken man in replacement. The great hero became Cúchulain, the hound of Culain, and even took on the knights of the Round Table in a fair fight. Except, says Dafydd, that a fair fight is asking a bit much of an Englishman.

And it's Crean who spots Worsley's boat. He grabs me by the shoulder and points out its position. Almost invisible in the haze of spray and fog under the steep rock wall, a thin streak of light is wandering across the crowns of the waves towards us.

"The skipper," rasps Crean. "Get up to the bow. Go tell them, Merce. But hold on tight, you hear me? Nod if you've understood."

I nod. The safety rope knotted around my chest, I lower myself onto the floor of the boat and crawl under the benches towards the bow. When I surface there, the wind tears the hood from my head. I can hardly breathe. But there in the stern of the *Caird,* as if he were holding the towrope we're hanging from in one hand, I see the outline of Frank Wild. Close over his head, the wind knocks the boom with the billowing sail back and forth.

I know I only have the strength for one shout.

What to say? I have to draw his attention to both myself and the relocated boat; it's sailing on our port side, only a short half mile from the deep gray wall of a glacier, holding course for a fog bank that will engulf it before any of the men in Shackleton's *Caird* can notice.

I pull the glove off my left hand and roar as loud as I can: "Ahoy!"

And as Frank Wild spins around at the tiller and tears open his eyes, I stretch my bare hand out over the dinghy's gunwale and point: to port, look out!

IN THE QUIETER SWELL BEHIND A PRECIPICE OF ICE PUSHING OUT FLAT INTO the sea, the *Dudley Docker* comes alongside. Her sail has a makeshift patch and the hull has sprung a leak. Worsley's men have been bailing for hours without a break. Only Greenstreet and Orde-Lees are sitting turned motionlessly towards each other in the frozen white bow and are staring across at us. Orde-Lees has stuck a foot under Green-street's pullover to save it from frostbite.

The skipper has other news. The *Dudley Docker* has sighted a landing on the northeastern tip of the island. Only a narrow, stony strip of shore at the foot of impassable cliffs, a desolate corner exposed to the storms, but a landing nonetheless.

"We should try it, sir!" Cheetham translates Worsley's croaking. "Sir, what do you think?"

Shackleton looks east across the fog-shrouded seas. Day is breaking, the 445th unwanted day in the Weddell Sea. He nods in agreement.

Captain Worsley is ordered to sail ahead with the *Docker* but to remain in sight at all times. Close under where a glacier is pushing itself out into the ocean, our three boats turn north. It's a morning with showers of heavy, furry snow at minus ten degrees. Again and again, great gusts thrash in off the sea, many times colder and so powerful that the *Caird*'s sail bursts from the mast, forcing us to seek shelter in the bay of the glacier. And for the next hours, we suck this unexpected and wonderful thirst quencher, shoving the numbing lumps of ice around our mouths from one wound to another.

A treacherous curve of reefs shields the beach where we want to land from the onrushing breakers. Sir Ernest decides that the dinghy will be first to pass through the narrow entrance and that it will make a depth sounding in the bay inside. The *Stancomb-Wills* is released from the towrope. More rowing. We go alongside the *Caird* and take Shackleton on board.

We pass the portal in the reef and slide into the bay. We pull in our oars under the rock walls. Of the groaning of the storm and the thunder of the surf, all we can hear between the cliffs is a ghostly echo. It rises and falls almost as fast as the blood pumps in my hands after rowing.

Crean's sounding shows enough depth for the two bigger boats, and so Wild and Worsley receive the signal they'd hoped for from the storm lantern. They maneuver cautiously into the bay and come alongside. Our three boats glide through the now-still water.

No one says anything. Only Shackleton sometimes quietly calls out the course. And as the keel beneath me scrapes into the black gravel, he determines who will be the first person ever to set foot on Elephant Island. From the *James Caird* he calls out, "Gentlemen! Lift Mr. Holness onto this beach."

# 36

## On the Black Beach

NOWHERE CAN WE SEE A SINGLE TREE, NOT A SHRUB, NOT A
tuft of undergrowth, not even a tussock of the pale yellow grass that grows on South Georgia and chirrups
softly in the wind between the rocks. There is no plant life on Elephant Island, or none visible to the eyes of an ordinary castaway.
Bobby Clark, however, discovers mosses and lichens the moment
he sinks onto the sodden gravel. His spindly legs spread apart, he
sits on the beach and scratches his fingernail across the stones he's
heaped in front of him, which are dark and yet glimmer like his
eyes behind their glasses. In some months of the year, he tells us,
chinstrap and Gentoo penguins live on this island in enormous
colonies. And the island didn't get its name for nothing. There are
such enormous elephant seal rookeries here that even the mechan-
ical whaling ships haven't yet managed to wipe them out. But there
are no animals in sight. A reconnaissance group made up of Crean,
Hussey and Bakewell returns to the camp disconsolate. Even the
skuas departed into the fog over the sea when they realized there
was nothing to be had from us. Maybe it's like Vincent says, maybe
the world kept turning while we were fallen off its edge, and war
and progress have put paid to the elephant seals after all. Well,
could be. Apart from us, who lurk on the beach and enjoy the feeling of solid ground under our feet, there's not a thing moving on
the island. The shadows of clouds flit across empty cliffs and
through empty crevasses. Nothing but rock. Over it a shell, some-

times dozens of feet thick, of snow and ice. Elephant Island. Isn't that why it's called that?

In the west the sunset. In front of the darkening skies, a golden semicircle flat on the sea, a fiery and serrated half-disk soon wider than the whole island. If there were wood, we could sit around a campfire to watch it. But the only piece of wood on the island that isn't from a boat, or at least not from one of ours, is a plank that was washed through the reef into the bay and that Frank Wild fishes out of the water. The plank is green, it must have been floating the seas for months, and yet its wood is unmistakable. This board used to be part of a cherry tree.

Wild tramps back down to the water.

"Frank, stay near the camp," Cheetham calls after him, and then more quietly tells those of us gathered nearby what we already know, namely that there's a storm, if not a hurricane, in the air.

"He can't get over it," says Orde-Lees, not without looking around to see if Shackleton is near enough to overhear him.

Shackleton is with Chippy McNeish by the boats and supposedly discussing the necessary repairs with him.

The way Frank Wild is standing down there by the water reminds me suddenly of something familiar and beloved. His hand folded onto his back in Shackleton's black glove, he looks like the Napoleon portrayed in my dad's office.

"What is it you think he can't get over?" Hurley wants to know. He doesn't take his eyes from the sunset; his camera is ready for the shot.

"Don't ask me." As usual, Orde-Lees immediately feels offended. He takes a stone and closes his fist around it.

Hurley doesn't take the photo. Since the pictures of the landing, he only has enough equipment for fewer than a dozen more. He says to Orde-Lees, "Frank knows exactly what he can expect. Or has he told you something different?"

Orde-Lees glowers at Hurley but doesn't contradict him.

Hurley puts the camera aside. "So stop trying to play the oracle."

Shackleton and the carpenter come over from the boats in the dusk. Halfway to us, they separate and Shackleton goes down to the water to Wild.

"Chippy, come take a seat," Vincent calls to McNeish without taking the cigarette from the corner of his mouth. "It's just getting fun over here."

But McNeish stops, waves once and disappears into his tent. What I wouldn't have given to have listened in on his conversation with Sir Ernest. I'm sure that the discussion can have been about only one thing: the cat. But anyone who wandered into the vicinity of the boats was chased away by Greenstreet.

Orde-Lees sulks. This would be the first time he took a telling-off that didn't come from Shackleton or Wild. Vincent no longer exists for him, not even as a sailor, since he once left him lying in the snow. Hurley, on the other hand, has always been lower in the hierarchy than Orde-Lees, who still thinks of himself as either an engineer or a quartermaster. All of us seem to be finding it difficult to maintain our respect for a man who loses one position after the last. There are no machines for Aunt Thomas to tend and no provisions for him to check, organize and distribute.

He lets the pebble roll from one hand into the other while he listens or doesn't listen to who Vincent's mockery will strike next.

It's Marston's turn. "What is it, really, art?" asks Vincent while swatting at Marston's shoulder.

He says: "A lot of work, John, a damned lot."

And Vincent again: "And always blue balls, huh? And for what? In the end everyone dies like a dog. And just like a stinking mutt they forget you."

Cheetham comes to Marston's aid. The dead should be left in peace, he says to Vincent.

Vincent caterwauls. "Do you know why we forget the dead, Mr. Smart-Arse? Because we don't need them anymore."

For a while it's all quiet again, maybe because we're watching the sun melt onto the surface of the ocean, and only then does Orde-Lees attack. He goes off at Hurley so suddenly that the photographer flinches and lifts his arm in defense.

"There are very good reasons for it if I see fit to draw your attention to something, Mr. Hurley!" Orde-Lees shrieks, lifting himself onto his long legs. "And if it's all right with you, I will not tolerate any further insubordination of that type. You are the ship's photographer; either keep yourself in the background commensurate with your position or, if your need for admiration makes that impossible, please be so good as to open your trap only when among those of the same rank."

Ready to shout down Hurley's objections as soon as they're voiced, Orde-Lees has opened his trap good and wide. He's the one who's lost the most teeth. He hardly has incisors or canines anymore. The Prince, by contrast, has stayed in relatively good condition. His face is only lightly swollen with boils, though on the side of his head nearest me his hair has fallen out.

He doesn't have the strength to pit himself against Orde-Lees. He says nothing, and locks the camera between stiff hands in his lap.

The shapes of Shackleton and Wild emerge from the darkness of the shore and come towards us. They've heard the sudden noise from the tents. Everyone stands up. Some of them, including, to my astonishment, Vincent, move themselves out of the firing line.

"Trouble, Alfred?" Shackleton turns to Cheetham when he and Wild are standing in front of our sorry group.

"Not worth mentioning. There was a misunderstanding that, as far as I know, has been cleared up."

"Is that so, Mr. Orde-Lees?"

"Sir, you would have to ask Hurley, sir."

"I'll ask you both. Would that be all right with you?"


WE CAN'T SURVIVE ON ELEPHANT ISLAND. BOB CLARK DOES MANAGE to convince Shackleton that there must be a better campsite somewhere else, one from where we'll be able to hunt penguins and elephant seals. But the prospect of ending our starvation alters nothing about our helplessness against the hurricane winds that pick up on the day after our landing and howl across the island. Hussey can only estimate their strength. He puts them at more than twelve, which is meteorologically impossible. Uzbird admits that he's never heard of gusts of this magnitude. The main tent is ripped into tatters and flies off over the bay and the reefs and out to sea, where we see it flap off like an enormous bird. Plates of ice thick as the volumes of the encyclopedia sail across the beach and burst against the cliffs. Pots, pans and a grill vanish from the kitchen Green has set up in a rocky niche and fly past again hours later as if spun once around the island. Even Mr. Green himself is blown over and dragged off. Shaking and tugging, the wind hauls him down to the bay and is about to hurl its prize into the water when Crean, Vincent and Bakewell catch up and brace their combined strength against the theft of our cook. We pull the tents back right under the cliffs. The large boats are tipped. They now serve as accommodation for the men whose tent has been destroyed. We're all in need of some reassuring warmth, but these eight require it more than the rest. Piercingly fine snow forces its way through the cracks between the gravel and the hulls, blanketing the men and their possessions, and laying ever-new traps for weary feet.

Although Frank Wild's hand is anything but healed, Shackleton gives him the task of taking the *Stancomb-Wills* and four other men on a reconnaissance mission to the west as soon as the blizzard slackens. As crewmen, Shackleton assigns him Crean, Marston, Vincent and Bakewell. Wild takes the order as a punishment, a reaction that's still mysterious to me when he says to Shackleton that he'd hoped to be able to rest for a few days and let his hand get back to normal in time.

In time for what? Amid the clamor of the storm, this question won't leave my mind.

The third day on Elephant Island, the day when the dinghy

puts to sea again to search for food and a campsite on the west coast of the island, is the sixteenth of April. It's our 448th day in the ice. We escaped it for five days, but today the ice is back. Greenstreet is the first to spot it from his lookout in the cliffs. He shouts as if he's lost his senses, as if what's out there were the most unlikely of all things in these latitudes. But what he sees isn't a ship, it's a gray, undulating wall. The drift ice is drawing itself into a belt.

"Antarctica wants to go into hibernation," Shackleton says behind me. I didn't hear him approaching over the singsong of the wind sweeping across the beach.

He's alone. Surprise inspection. Spot test of the oven.

"It looks that way, sir. Good morning."

"You're cleaning the blubber stove, Merce; that's commendable. And it indicates a hope that we'll soon have something to cook on it again. I was just thinking about our books. I suppose you don't read anymore?"

"Sir? No. There are no books left."

"Other than the logbooks, navigation tables and the men's diaries, that's quite true." He stretches out an arm and tries a smile. "Walk with me a little, Merce."

The wind has relented back onto the scale. And the snow is no longer coming from all sides. Down at the water, it's falling almost vertically from the woolly white sky. The man relieving Greenstreet clambers up the cliffs. It's Rickenson. Whippet-thin, he feels his way over the outcroppings, easily recognizable by the outwards-turned seams of his snowsuit.

Shackleton sets an ambling pace. He wants to know if I've brought my researches about Balleny and the *Sabrina* to a conclusion, and I say yes.

"And have you already spoken to Mr. Vincent about your discovery?"

I don't want to let him see my surprise that he's in the picture.

McLeod probably couldn't keep to himself that I sent him to Vincent. Or perhaps Green slipped a hint about my questioning.

I say no, that I decided not to. Vincent's family's got nothing to do with me. "Balleny's book stayed back on the floe, sir."

He stands still. Both of us stand still. Ahead of us, on the side of the bay that's turned to the open ocean, is the passage through the reef. A few hours ago, the *Stancomb-Wills* sailed out through it, and even now, when there's nothing there but water, to me it seems that Bakewell's waving out of the rapidly departing boat.

"We can't shake off the ice," says Shackleton. "It ought not to be here at this time of year. But it is here." He presses his lips together. "In four weeks, perhaps only three, the island will be locked in. Is that enough time to lay in sufficient stores of meat for us to last the winter? What do you think?"

"We haven't even found the animals yet, sir."

"Let's hope that Bob Clark is right. And if there do happen to be animals on this island, Mr. Wild will find them." He sets off. I take two long strides and am level with him again. Shackleton clasps his hands behind his back and says, "I can't wait until we've gathered sufficient stores of meat. The risk of being trapped here before we've finished is far too high. Wintering here without supplies is something I don't even want to imagine. Desperate. Mr. Holness's foot requires urgent hospital treatment. The nerves of more than a dozen men are shot. All reasons why I've decided to sail one of the boats east and go for help before we're all frozen in for a second time."

After a few steps in silence, he gives me a clap on the shoulder and lets his hand stay where it landed. "Does that surprise you? You've gone pale."

"I'm thinking of the charts, sir. And if I'm not wrong, there's no land anywhere to the east."

We've paced off the whole length of the beach. We turn around in front of a huge boulder still glittering from the flood tide. Shackleton doesn't want to walk back along the waterline. He points diagonally up the beach towards the tent.

"Come with me," he says. "I want to show you something." His hand is still on my shoulder.

Greenstreet jumps down onto the gravel from the last outcrop. Out of breath and his teeth chattering, he reports that the ice lying off the island has made no significant movement. The hour on watch in the cliffs has marked him: he's shuddering and it takes all his effort to keep himself upright. For the first time I feel something like affection for our first officer. In all this while there's never been so much as a trace of condescension or scorn in the way he's treated me, and that remains the case as I walk up to him alongside Sir Ernest.

"Get some rest, Lionel," says Shackleton. Greenstreet stalks over to the boats on stiff legs and folds himself inside.

Shackleton leads me in the other direction, to a niche in the cliffs that's completely dry but far too small to be useful. In the gravel, much lighter than on the beach, is a circle of stones and pebbles arranged to portray figures, images and even numbers. And outside the circle is what must be a dozen little heaps, each built up out of more identical-seeming rocks. Even before Shackleton says anything, I know what I've got at my feet.

"Unbelievable. He put it back together out of stones."

"Yes," says Shackleton, "and did it from memory. As far as I know, Marston didn't take any sketches with him."

"No, he wanted to leave everything on the ice. It's beautiful, sir."

Shackleton crouches beside the Antarctic clock at the quarter-face been nine and twelve.

"And now look at this, Merce," he says, and points to two small black stones in the gravel. "This is Clarence Island and we're over here, on Elephant Island. To the south is the Weddell Sea that we've just come from, which is jammed with pack ice right up to where we are. There's no way back through there. And the north is equally closed to us, here. In a little boat like the *James Caird,* we would never manage to cross the Drake Passage and reach Tierra del Fuego or the Falklands."

"But to the west, sir, there's the peninsula, if we went westwards around the tip, we'd be sure to make it to the bays where the whalers are," I say, full of enthusiasm for my idea, because, no matter what, I cannot get into my head why he never sees what's nearby but instead always, in the end, having added a few more obstacles, plumps for the most difficult solution of all.

Shackleton gazes for a long time at the gravel before he turns his face to me. He's got old. I notice it as he says, "I'd gladly do you that favor, but we can't sail to the west, Merce. It can't be done."

"Why not? I don't understand. Cook did it. He went . . ."

"Cook sailed west, you're quite right. But he wasn't coming from the Weddell Sea and so didn't have to sail west through the Drake Passage. Going through the westwards current there is something we might attempt with a ship like the *Endurance* and a well-rested crew. In a thirty-foot tender it's completely impossible. Didn't you tell me yourself that you know what a killing storm can do?"

Our conversation about the sinking of the *John London* is a year and a half in the past, but he hasn't forgotten.

"Here," he says and points to the long flat stone shaped like a feather that Marston has placed underneath the twelve o'clock mark. "This is where we set off. That is, South Georgia. How far do you think it is to there?"

I've got no idea. But I do have a terrible foreboding. He wants to sail to there. Pastor Gunvald was right: he's mad. Between Elephant Island and South Georgia, there's an hour and a half on the Antarctic clock, a handful of stones. But in reality it's an uncrossable distance, a desert of waves.

"Six hundred sea miles," I say, staring at him.

And Shackleton: "Eight hundred, but well guessed. The current and the wind will carry the boat there practically all by themselves. The crew—I'll take five men with me—will only have to fulfill two tasks: we must keep the boat seaworthy and we must keep the navigator alive. If we succeed in that, the journey can be done in seven days. And in two weeks' time, we can all be saved."

You could feel sorry for them, the four who'll accompany Shackleton and Captain Worsley—he can't mean anyone else as navigator—on this suicide mission. But I'm even more worried about the twenty-two who'll be left behind in the desolation of Elephant Island, who'll have to see to it that they find enough meat and blubber to survive. To say nothing of the fact that, if the *Caird* doesn't make it to South Georgia, not a single soul on earth will know or will ever know where we twenty-two desertees have been deserted. With the best will in the world, I can't swallow these fears and surrender myself to the destiny that the man crouching there on the gravel has assigned me.

"Sir!" I say loudly, and stand up. "I'm not saying this for my own sake, but aren't you leaving twenty-two men to their fate?" I don't have the courage not to frame the sentence as a question.

Shackleton takes a deep breath. He, too, stands up. "No," he says. "I'm not leaving twenty-two men to their fate, I'm leaving them in the command of Mr. Wild and Mr. Greenstreet. No matter how much it may displease him, Frank Wild's hand injury means he will have to stay on the island. He'll lead the crew until my return."

That's what Orde-Lees meant on the beach: not being able to go on the voyage because of losing his glove, that's what Frank Wild can't get over. That's also the reason for this morning's despondency. Wild hopes to nurse his hand back to health, and instead Shackleton sends him out on reconnaissance. Did he ever intend to take Wild with him?

I shiver as we step out of the niche in the cliffs. The wind that's blowing across the abandoned beach knocks the hood onto my head, and I feel the blood shooting into my face. Will the four men with Wild in the *Stancomb-Wills* also be the four who sail with Shackleton and Worsley to South Georgia? Crean, Marston, Vincent and Bakewell. Is the reconnaissance also a practice run?

"If I can ask a question, sir, have you already chosen your crew for the voyage?"

"Yes. All apart from one already know and—no one will be forced to come—they've all declared themselves willing and ready."

Apart from one! If Bakewell has been chosen, he's that one who doesn't yet know about his misfortune. Because he'd have told me. He definitely would have said something.

The snow is thickening again. Up by the tents it's already a blizzard that envelops the group of stick figures huddling there. In their fur-gloved hands, they're holding out bowls and cups for cold portions of dog soup and a swallow of milk.

"Just wait for it, you rabble." We can hear Green scolding and then the grumble of the men answering back.

"I can't expose six men to that danger while I stay here and wait to be rescued," says Shackleton. "That's why I will lead the undertaking. Captain Worsley is the most important man. If anyone can navigate that tiny boat to South Georgia, it's him. As helmsman, and as the most capable seaman I know, I'll be taking Tom Crean. You were with him in the dinghy and you know what efforts he's capable of, by which I also mean on a human level, and that in particular is what it'll all depend on. Having six of us penned up in that space for a week will make extreme demands on our nerves. The sailor who, during the entire expedition, has shown himself the equal of any strain, and whose loyalty and esprit de corps I've never had cause to doubt, is . . ."

". . . Bakewell," I say tonelessly.

"Your friend, correct." We come to a stop in front of the two hulls that are gradually being painted with snow. "I'm very glad that Mr. Bakewell, too, has declared his readiness to sail with me."

"I'm pleased to hear it, sir."

He doesn't believe me for a second. "There's no choice. In order for everyone to be saved, the boat must reach South Georgia, and that will only happen if the six crew members' various skills complement and harmonize with each other. But that's only one side of it, Merce. And you're damned right: in all of this I can't forget about the twenty-two who are staying here."

Shackleton looks around to reassure himself that no one is listening. He stares at me with fire in his eyes. And says tensely, "I can't leave Vincent, McNeish and Stevenson here together, not unless I want to risk violence and mutiny. And I won't risk it, Merce! I'll take the biggest troublemaker with me. Mr. Vincent is a very strong man, perhaps the strongest of us all, and he wasn't made bosun for nothing. I'm sure he'll be useful on the crossing as long as he's kept in his place."

"Yes, sir. It won't be easy, but I'm sure Crean and Bakewell together will manage to keep him in check."

"Mr. Crean and Mr. Bakewell will be otherwise occupied. It will be you, Merce, keeping Vincent in check."

His arm speeds out and holds me by the shoulder. And I need it. I'm tipping. Tears spring to my eyes. I fall forwards and he catches me and holds me in his arms.

"Merce," he says quietly. He holds my head and shakes me softly. "I need you! We all need you! You're the only one in whom Vincent has a personal interest. You're the thorn in his flesh, and just for a week I want you to give that flesh a thorough stabbing. You'll see: his anger will help us survive. Also, my dear boy, we need you as a cook. Yes, and quite apart from that, you're a fantastic oarsman."

# 37

## Instructions for the Period of our Absence

THE BEACH THAT FRANK WILD'S SEARCH PARTY HAS DISCOVERED lies ten miles to the northwest in a bay sheltered from the wind. Bob Clark's prediction proves to be bang on: not far away is a colony of Gentoo penguins. But these birds with two big white patches over their eyes and rosy blades on their bills turn out not to be very fastidious about where they choose to nest. The quiet and uninhabited beach with the bare and strangely smooth rocks reveals itself to consist, under its snow layer, of guano. As deep as we dig, the spades bite into nothing but mushy yellowy sludge, and such a horrendous stink rises out of the holes and ditches dug for the tents that you can hardly stand it for longer than a couple of minutes.

A hail of swearing comes from the men at the shovels, and Frank Wild earns himself bitter complaints from the others. But that does have its good side. For the first time in a while, the mini-boss stops sulking to stick out his elbows and defend himself.

Shackleton presents the first dozen penguin carcasses to their advantage. "Admittedly," he says, hooking his arm through Wild's, "it's an astringent smell. But, gentlemen, the Gentoo penguin is among the meatiest of its genus. We can count ourselves lucky!"

"Hold your nose and be happy, got it," coughs Green, and even Wild has to laugh. Neither he nor Sir Ernest seems to notice that Green's joking isn't gallows humor. And even I, who've been exposed to his increasing bitterness every day, have only just started to understand that the exertions of the boat voyage have affected him more than the rest of the crew. I notice it by the way he holds himself upright on my arm while we're setting up the field canteen.

"It's all right again." He coughs. "Now, let go of me!"

A hundred feet from the base of the cliffs to the waterline and around two hundred yards in breadth, that's the size of the stony, ice-bound beach, curved in the shape of a crescent moon, where we put up the tents. Although the camp will have to provide space for six fewer men, the order is still given to tip the two smaller boats. A socket of stones will hold the dwellings fast in the wind. We make them watertight with the half-dozen seal skins we've managed to keep and the sails that are no longer needed. By the time darkness begins to close in, the camp is ready and the men who are to wait on the island are choosing where they're going to eat and sleep for the next two weeks. They do it without complaining, almost impassively.

What are two weeks! Two weeks have gone by since we left the floe. It's the 454th day in the ice, Good Friday 1916. Chippy McNeish reckons it will take him two more days to make the *James Caird* seaworthy. She'll put to sea on Easter Monday. I try not to think about it and am in a ferment nonetheless, almost the way I was before the departure of the *John London* from Newport. Bakewell's right: apparently I haven't learned anything since. When I ask him what he's more afraid of, leaving his comrades to themselves or sailing a patched-up rowboat into the unknown, he just shakes his head and says, "Neither. I'm just worried that I won't be able to stick it out. That the boat won't make it because of me. And that because of that, Wild and the others won't get a chance of ever getting back." His voice is hard and flat; he's nervous, agitated and tense. I'm disturbing him while he's preparing himself. Soon he won't say anything at all. Then he'll be ready and his worries not worth mentioning.

But he's not there yet. He cups my jaw between his palms.

"Come on, kiddo, think of it like this: the six of us can take it in our own hands. And whatever we do with it, it's gotta be better than waiting here in the penguin shit for a day that might never come. Don't say this to anyone else, but just that thought is stitching a silver lining into every shit-stinking second on Frank Wild's beach, even if it nearly makes me crazy thinking of the others."

Shackleton has us assemble for morning milk in the main tent. He announces the order of precedence and the jobs he has assigned on the island or the boat. I stick to my task and observe Vincent's reaction. The news that Sir Ernest has chosen not him but Bakewell as bosun catches him unawares. He's so disappointed that it disperses all his satisfaction about being one of the six on board. Worsley as navigator, Crean as helmsman, Bakewell as bosun and now even I am made quartermaster—Vincent is sailing as no more than a deckhand. As such, he knows, he's got to carry out any and every order from the other five of us. As the company breaks up, his eyes flash with the anger of someone who's seen himself passed over, but, if I'm not wrong, there's also a glimmer of sadness, the sadness of the patsy.

Shackleton hasn't failed to notice Vincent's reaction and he gives me a challenging glance before nodding in Vincent's direction.

"Mr. Vincent," I say with a quavering voice, because in my whole life this is the first order I've ever given, "report to the ship's carpenter and lend him a hand. Then report to me as soon as we can begin loading the supplies."

Vincent bares his teeth in the entrance to the tent but doesn't let himself be provoked into responding. Crean's bass tells Vincent to acknowledge my order. He does so. And as soon as he's out of the tent, Crean gives me a wink.


TOGETHER WITH BAKEWELL, WHO'S RESPONSIBLE FOR LOADING THE ballast, I go in the drizzle to inspect the boat. McNeish and Vincent have transformed the whaler's pinnace into a fully fitted miniature sailing ship. The *James Caird* is less than twenty-five feet long, but she now has a mainmast and a jib boom. McNeish has raised the gunwales and fashioned a cover out of sled runners and sailcloth that's supposed to partly protect the crew and provisions against the swell.

There are two entrances into the interior of the boat. One is abaft by the tiller, the other in the fore-ship, between the masts. I lower myself down and see for the first time my abode for the coming weeks. The space is so dark, so narrow and so low that it crushes my breath. How are two giants like Vincent and Crean supposed to fit in here, along with a beanpole like me and three other men? And that's before any of the provisions have been stowed. Even now it seems impossible for me to get through from bow to stern without crawling on my hands and knees. The crepuscular room is crossed by four benches halfway up, which are no more than planks and could provide storage space only as shelves for odds and ends.

Bakewell crouches in the stern entrance. "It ain't exactly the luxury cabin we always dreamed of."

Now that the conversion work is complete, the *James Caird* belongs to us for the time being. We use the little time when it's just the two of us to freshen up some favorite swearwords. And at one point, while Bakewell is calculating the amount of ballast from the volume of the stowage space, he asks me about Ennid's fish and if I'm planning to take it with me.

I say, "Yup, of course," though it hadn't crossed my mind till then. "Why do you ask?"

"No reason. Two years is a pretty long time, is all I was thinking."

"There was a war. Lots of people will have been away."

He is genuinely flabbergasted. "Wait, do you really think she's waiting for you?"

I shrug my shoulders, shake my head. "No idea. Hey, Bakewell, this nagging is really getting on my nerves."

"Sorry, sorry," he says, exaggerating. But right away he's serious again. "And if you go the same way as Juggins? And you've given her a kid? Have you ever thought about that?"

"Thousands of times."

"Let's hope so." He holds out the measuring tape, and we both know it's better if we change the subject.

It hadn't occurred to me that I might already be a father.

I get started drawing up a list of things we'll need at sea, sit in a patch of light at the forwards entrance where the rain doesn't reach me, and write. Bakewell crawls around at my feet in the half-light and stacks the stones that Hussey, Kerr and Cheetham deposit every minute or so on the cover above us. When the stone carpet has been laid out, Bakewell calculates the ballast weight at around a ton. Between the floor and the benches there's just enough space for a person to squeeze through. Most of the stones have woundingly sharp edges and we'll have to lay something over them. But I still have to wonder how we're supposed to lie on this in heavy seas, let alone sleep on it.

Shackleton and Worsley check the trim and nod. Bakie goes to bed, but not without first giving me a powerful clap on the chest.

The blow hits the fish and hurts. Bakewell is still in a serious mood: "Leave it here," he says, and jumps down onto the gravel. He grins up at me. "Just a piece of advice from man to man, Merce."

"So you're ready, are you?" says Worsley. "Excellent."

"Yessir." The bosses move on to my list of stores. Shackleton reads every item out loud and waits for Worsley's agreement before moving on to the next. The three of us stand in the narrow entrance, and Worsley bends over every time to imagine everything Shackleton reads out going in its place, a necessary, an unending procedure that takes so long that the sky goes dark and a man has to bring a storm lamp to shine onto my list:

Food:
300 sled rations, 200 rations of nut paste, 30 packets
of powdered milk, 600 biscuits, 1 box of sugar,
1 tin of Cerebos salt, a box of Bovril cubes, plus
130 pounds of ice and 2 18-gallon casks of water

Equipment:
1 Nansen stove, 2 Primus stoves, wicks and spare parts,
40 liters of petrol, a tin of spirit, 10 boxes of lighters,
1 box of flares, 7 candles, 20 cartons of matches,
6 sleeping bags, 6 spare pairs of socks

"Wonderful," Worsley says finally. He's just imagined stowing the spare socks in the bow. "You've thought of everything except the nautical clobber. Or would you recommend sailing without a compass and sextant, Mr Blackboro?"

"No, sir. I've got that stuff in my head: compass, sextant, telescope, charts, navigation tables, ice axe, aneroid barometer. It's all ready, sir."

BUT THAT'S NOT ALL WE TAKE ON BOARD. OVER BREAKFAST ON EASTER Monday, Shackleton asks the twenty-two staying behind to each give him one of their personal possessions. Everyone is to send something as small and light as possible with us on the journey, and anyone who wants can write a letter that we six promise we'll post home on the first boat from South Georgia.

Many are too weak to write. How and McLeod look at me with enormous eyes lined with red after spending the whole night melting ice and pouring it into two casks of drinking water for the *Caird*. Hownow passes me a photo of his wife with a message he's scribbled on the back, and Stornoway hands me a comb still in its paper wrapper.

Orde-Lees waits till we've collected all the tokens. He stalks nervously across the beach. Eventually, he takes heart, steps in front of Shackleton and salutes. "Sir! I hope not to relinquish too much of the deep respect I owe you in asking you to take this with you to South Georgia. It's yours." With that, he pulls out Shackleton's gold watch and passes it into his open palm. Shackleton is too nonplussed to say anything. He takes the watch and holds it to his ear.

"It's still going, sir." Orde-Lees bursts into tears.

WHILE THE BOAT IS BEING LOADED DOWN AT THE WATERLINE, SHACKLETON gives final orders in the main tent, "instructions for the period of our absence." He makes two provisions. In Hurley's diary he writes that, in the case of his not surviving, all the rights to film material shot during the expedition will become Hurley's property. He also bequeaths his large telescope to the delighted Prince.

In the logbook he writes a letter to Frank Wild, transferring all the men remaining on the island to his command. Wild is also empowered, in the event of Shackleton's death, to give lectures in his place as well as, together with Orde-Lees and Hurley, write a book about the *Endurance*'s voyage.

"Dear sir," it says at the end of the letter, which any of us is allowed to read, "I have and have always had the utmost trust in you. May God bless your work and your life. Please convey my most intimate greetings to my family and assure them that I love them and have done my best."

I accompany Shackleton to the men who are too weak to watch the boat's departure from the beach. Rickenson is recovering from a mild heart attack. McIlroy sits beside him, laying out a game of patience on his abdomen and forbidding him, as if for no other reason, to move an inch. Next to him lies Green. He's refusing food and, precisely because McIlroy has obviously been given the job of softening him up, Green is indulging fully in his rancor. Shackleton sits down beside him on the mat. He asks Green to name my successor.

Green coughs. "A successor for him! You'll never find another lazy good-for-nothing like that one. Quartermaster!" He laughs malevolently before being shaken by an equally malevolent coughing fit. He nearly chokes, but only nearly.

"Come on, Charlie, tell me. Who would you like to give a good tongue-lashing? I know you must have your eye on someone."

"Me? I'd let them all go to the devil."

"Stevenson," says Shackleton. "How about him?"

"Give me a cigarette, Merce," squeaks Mother Green, and sits himself upright.

Holness is no longer conscious. Dr. Macklin is keeping watch by him. He reports to Shackleton that while putting together the supplies for the boat last night, he found the chloroform that had been supposed lost.

"We'll be able to amputate with that, sir."

Holie's breathing is shallow. Pearls of sweat form on his temples, and from time to time a gentle twitch tugs at his body. Shackleton bends down to him and, while I do the same in my thoughts, squeezes Holie's trembling hand.

Wild collects us from the tent. The boat is ready. "Everything's on board, Ernest." I walk behind the two men and, through the snow drifting lightly over the bay, I see Worsley and Bakewell sitting at the forward, Vincent and Crean at the stern entrance. A semicircle of men has opened in front of us and another dozen are standing ready to push the *Caird* into the water. Hands, I don't know whose, help me on board, and only there does it occur to me that I haven't said goodbye to anyone. I wave and find that I can't stop waving, while Shackleton shakes every man's hand. I'm still waving when he takes Frank Wild in his arms and seems not to want to let him go.

# 38

## ROLLERS

WHEN I OPEN MY EYES, I SEE CLOUDS MOVING ACROSS THE SKY. They're faster than our boat because they don't have to reach the summits of these mountains of wave, don't have to sink into these troughs and don't have stones in their bellies.

While I lie around on the makeshift deck and let the sun dry my damp things, words pour out of me like a waterfall. The book I read about Sir Francis Drake, I say, was as gray as this ocean. Its pages were yellowed and closely printed, and the *Endurance* was puttering down the Forster Passage alongside the ice barrier when I crept into my bunk and, my heart in my mouth, read about that belligerent seaman who, lest we forget, was originally a privateer.

"In what year exactly I can't quite remember anymore, but it was sometime close to the end of the sixteenth century. Drake reached the southern tip of Tierra del Fuego, and when everyone thought that the land mass would just carry on stretching southwards, he found a passage instead. Imagine that. He was sailing onto a nameless sea. No one had seen it before him. Drake must have felt like he'd just pulled two continents apart. Admit it, Vincent, that's not bad, is it?"

Vincent seems not to be listening. Since we've been at sea, he hasn't dignified me with so much as a look.

"You can assume that Mr. Vincent also appreciates Drake's contribution," Crean says drily. He nods at me.

So I continue. "'It is a large and open area' is what Drake wrote in his logbook, and that he'd lain on his belly on a cliff and stretched his arms and torso out over the drop. Do you know what the cliff is called today? That's Cape Horn, and the sea that Drake discovered is what separates America from the Antarctic. It's the Drake Passage."

"Really?" says Vincent. "I thought it was the Caribbean."

After three days' sailing, the *Caird* has covered a hundred and fifty nautical miles. Since we rowed through the belt of drift ice and set sail on the open ocean, Drake's sea has been bathed in sunshine. I, too, am bathing in sunshine on the boat's cover, dozing away my two hours off and letting images pass through my head as pale and quick as the clouds streaming east above us. We can stay in the open air, can stretch ourselves out, which is even more of a relief for those below.

Crean hums at the tiller. Worsley reads columns of figures in the nautical almanac. Vincent sews. There's a tear in the jib. Three men are on watch, three are resting. Three sleeping bags are occupied, three are drying in the wind. That's how it goes for shift after shift, for roller after roller that comes up from behind us, lifting the boat and lifting it higher and carrying it along on its crest until releasing it to glide down into the next valley. As threatening as the giant waves appear at first glance, we've long since stopped finding them frightening. I hang my arm over the gunwale. Gray, the waves are nothing but gray, as gray as the book about Drake. He was the first to call them Cape Horn rollers, and without my saying anything, that's what John Vincent calls them, too.

"The first to sail through it, two hundred years after that, was Cook. The *Adventure* sailed eight hundred nautical miles towards the northeast in three weeks. Cook said that the storms they met in the passage were 'impressive.' If you know how Cook spoke, you'll know what he meant."

Worsley looks up from his book. "Impressive," he says. "That's great. I wonder what the old slave driver would have made of what we're up to."

Vincent's face doesn't change. But in his gaze, which wanders from the skipper to the helmsman and back, there's a deep incomprehension. What Crean and Worsley are trying to achieve, what can interest them in a gobshite like me, is a mystery. He wipes his paw across his face. It's beyond him.

It can't stay as nice as this. We all know it. It's on the fourth day that the wind changes. It comes from the south and for two long days it drives icy gusts through the valleys of the waves. The only one who stays outside in the freezing drizzle is whoever's sitting thickly swaddled at the helm. He's got to hold out there for eighty minutes before the two who aren't lying in their sleeping bags pull him down through the opening and below deck, where one towels him dry, rubs him warm and feeds him while the other has already slipped above to the tiller and is binding himself tight so as not to be washed overboard. Every day, there are eighteen stretches at the tiller to be occupied, three times a day each of us cowers at the helm. Each has to hold the *Caird* on course, come what may. Nothing more is required. The helmsman has to do nothing other than use all his force to defend himself against the wind, which wants to snatch him up and throw him into the sea, and brace himself against the current, which shakes tirelessly at the rudder as it tries to break it from the stern.

At some point on the sixth day, it's got so cold that the rain turns into snow. Soon it's tumbling from the sky like an endlessly high wall. We tack blindly though an unceasing blizzard for a day and a night, deafened by the noise of the flakes rushing into the ocean, harried always by the fear of running into a floe or an iceberg, and with no chance of measuring our position or depth. The snow makes a second deck watch necessary. Scrabbling back and forth on the speeding boat, held on only by a rope, this man has to do his best to keep the deck, sails and rigging free of snow. The snow that a third man is shoveling up from the entrances constantly gets in his way: the shovelful either lands in his face or on the patch he's just cleared. And as soon as you've hurled this sludge overboard and are resting, stretched facedown on the cover, one arm clamped around the mast, just for the blink of an eye, every inch on board and you yourself are again lying under a thickening blanket of snow whose weight endangers the boat and the six lives from which another twenty-two are dangling. The snow man is hardly left enough time to look across to the man at the helm. Where is he? The entrance is nothing but blizzard. Whose sleeve is that? Half a dozen times, it's me who's sitting there being snowed in. But just as often I'm the man who's got to watch the one at the tiller being buried under the snow. And because I know how he feels, I, on snow man duty, crawl over to him, wipe a breathing hole around his mouth and breathe easier, as if I were sitting there myself.

The men below deck don't have it any better. The snow swirls down through the entrances and into every corner. The body warmth of the three who're sleeping, dead to the world for the next hour and a half, is enough to melt the snow as it enters. The resultant water collects between the ballast stones, where it stays and sloshes back and forth with the boat's movement. The water's icy and could only be scooped out by removing the stones. In the few exhausted moments we have between the fifth and sixth days, we try again and again to take these black rocks, most the size of a head and lying amidships in snow-clogged water, and shift them to the bow or the stern without jeopardizing the trim. But neither Bakewell and Vincent nor Shackleton and Crean manage it. Each time, the *Caird* lists so unexpectedly to one side or lifts her bow so abruptly that the two men, who've got just enough space to pass the slippery rocks around themselves, tumble into each other and injure their arms and legs on the sharp points. Suffering from both sciatica and lack of sleep, his face deeply furrowed, Shackleton looks older and older every day. But we probably all look like that or, as Vincent puts it, like we've been living for months in a leaky shack. In the end, it's Crean, in place of Shackleton, who puts his foot down: the water stays in the boat. The following day, it stops snowing and the three spare sleeping bags that we lay across the stones as mattresses suck up the water greedily, passing on its chill.

It's so cramped below deck that there isn't space for two people to crawl into their sleeping bags at the same time. Even the movement of one person who wants to take off his wet clothes and put on some less damp underwear below them has to be coordinated by someone else. It's usually Shackleton or Worsley who crouches in an entrance and gives the instructions: "Now move your foot to the left, Tom, and you, Bakewell, pull your knees up to your chin. Hold on!" Whoever's above calls out that there's another breaker rushing towards us: "It's going to hit to starboard!" And down below Worsley barks: "Mr. Vincent, stay lying down, Blackboro next to him, Ernest, hold on God damn it, or do you want to . . ." Time and again, everything that isn't lashed down or stowed in a crate flies around the interior. Stoves, navigation charts, socks, letters, candles, all have at some point been in the broth slopping between the stones, which has long since ceased to be just water. Powdered milk is dissolving in it, biscuit mush is floating in it, and we don't always succeed in bringing the contents of Mother Green's blue porcelain casserole, which we relieve ourselves into, up to where we empty it overboard. The stink coming off the bilgewater is different from that on Elephant Island; it reeks less of filth than of decay, and we can't get rid of it, even when we've scooped all the old mess out of the water and taken pains to make sure anything new is removed at once. It stinks nonetheless, and every day it stinks more.

Since our seventh day at sea, Shackleton has been apologizing ever more frequently for having calculated that we'd reach South Georgia within a week. That is now patently untrue. The Drake Passage provides no landmarks we could orientate ourselves on. There's no reef, no island, not even the smallest of rocks stretches above the waves. And after eight days we still haven't seen either seaweed or birds, nothing that would indicate land within two or three days' journey. The sea is gray, stormy and endless, a single wave rolling up and down below an overcast sky. Once, as we're sitting on deck with Crean and talking about my brother, Shackleton asks me if I can imagine that someday aeroplanes will be able to cover these kinds of distances. My mouth is clacky with hair, fine little nonhuman hairs, which are everywhere below decks and whose origins no one can explain, and because I'm busy getting them out and spitting them into my glove, I just say, without thinking about Shackleton's question, "Yes." A yearning suddenly flares up, not so much to be able to fly as for Dafydd, Regyn and my parents. But right now those are one and the same, and, while Tom Crean hums his eternally unchanging song behind us, Shackleton, who is just as plagued by the tiny hairs, can also say only, "Yes. It's bound to happen."

On the ninth day, Worsley uses a gap in the cloud cover to shoot the sun. He comes unspeaking back below deck carrying the soggy navigation tables and the folded plate-sized charts, then crawls headfirst as far as possible into the bow. It's the only halfway dry corner on board, the only one where he can calculate undisturbed. In the sleeping bags at his feet, Vincent and I are lying so close together that we can hear each other breathing despite the heavy seas. Each clasping one of the skipper's legs, to hold him steady for when the *Caird*'s bow lifts, then tips on the crest and plunges into the roaring body of the wave, we put our heads together and wait for Worsley's command to pull him back out of the cavity. Like all of us, the skipper is wearing woolen long johns, duck trousers and Burberry coveralls on top. Each of us is wearing two pairs of socks and, over them, knee-high felt boots. Over those we're wearing finneskos, with a high tongue made of reindeer skin with the hide on the outside. Worsley's Finnish boots, clattering back and forth around me and Vincent, are limp, soaked through and have, like all of ours, long since lost their covering of hide. They used to have these fine, silvery hairs. But the ones that are now sticking to everything are too many to come from just six pairs of finneskos.

They've formed a layer of fur on the inside of the boat's walls; they shimmer in the bilgewater and float in the milk.

The boat rolls lightly to port, and one of my father's sayings occurs to me: that you've got to seize an opportunity by the hair, before it goes bald. Into the sudden quiet I say out loud what I've been thinking at the sight of Worsley's shoes. I ask Vincent, who's staring into space so as not to have to look at me, if he's read *Robinson Crusoe*.

"Yes," he says, "when I was a boy." He looks at me. "Weren't expecting that."

He's not wrong there. "Impressive," Cook would have said.

The next wave rolls up, breaks against the bow and knocks it up into the air. We hold on.

"Almost!" shouts Worsley. "Dear God above, what a . . ."

"I was thinking," I say to Vincent, "that, when his ship goes under, all that Crusoe can rescue from his crewmates is three hats, a cap and two shoes . . . two that don't go together. So six things from six different men."

"The same number as us," says Vincent. His voice sounds suspicious and defensive, but there's no hostility in it.

"Exactly."

The skipper wriggles. "Pull me out," calls Worsley. "How can anyone take it in here?"

We pull. Across Worsley's legs, Vincent says, "And now here's what I'm thinking: it can't just be the shoes. It has to be the God-damned reindeer hide we got from those bastard Scandinavians."

"There's an unimaginable noise in there," pants Worsley while he sits upright between us. "There's a droning from every direction like gongs being struck. I think my head's still ringing. But I've got them, I've got the figures. And you know what . . ."

"Just a minute, please, sir," I say, confused. "Vincent was just . . . he's discovered something."

Worsley is so surprised he isn't even annoyed.

"The stink, Frank, sir," Vincent says quickly, his enormous face blushing red. "It's coming from your shoes, from the reindeer hide, and that's what's in the sleeping bags."

TO BE TOTALLY SURE, WORSLEY TWICE REPEATS HIS CALCULATIONS WHILE Vincent and I hold on to him and make peace with each other. Even hours after we've crawled out of the bow, the skipper is still deaf in the ear he couldn't cover, but even though he can't understand what we're saying, you can see how nonplussed he is that Vincent and I are suddenly on speaking terms.

Vincent's suspicion is confirmed when he and I examine one of the three sleeping bags we've been using as mattresses: on the outside it's almost dry and undamaged, but the fur lining on the inside has disintegrated almost completely, and it's the remaining naked leather, rotting into mush, that stinks so sour-sweetly of decaying meat. It's not easy to convince Crean and Bakewell, who're sleeping as deeply as the stones beneath them, of the need to take away their soft mattresses. But after all our words have been in vain, glancing into the sack and shaking it slightly is persuasion enough. Vincent and I throw the sleeping bags overboard and, a few hours later, the smell has dissipated.

Worsley's calculation shows that after ten days' sail we've covered around five hundred nautical miles. And what's even more important, it shows that other than a ten-mile drift to the northeast, we've stayed right on course for South Georgia. If the westerly wind keeps up, it could drive the *Caird* all the way to her goal within forty-eight hours, assuming that we don't miss the island. If we do, we'll skip past its northern tip, past Willis Island, Bird Island and all the further-flung rocks of South Georgia losing itself in the sea, and then there'll be no chance of turning round for our little nutshell, then it'll be out on the ocean where the waves roll uninterrupted all the way to Australia. Worsley, the Kiwi, says he wouldn't mind. But Shackleton and Crean decide to obviate this risk before it occurs. We drop the plan to sail north around the island and maneuver the boat into Stromness Bay to reach Leith Harbour or Captain Sørlle's whaling station. Our new goal is the island's south coast, which is wide enough for us not to miss it even if our course deviates further than we can see. There are lots of bays there that are protected from the wind, and glaciers, and streams of clear, bright water. But there's also something else. A spine of hills blocks the way to the whaling stations on the north coast, a range that no one has named because no one has ever crossed it.

"That, gentlemen, is about to change," says Shackleton, and in his eye there's already the glitter of the snow on the South Georgian peaks. Though all around us there's nothing but the sea and the few figures that Worsley has assembled into an island.

54° 38 south, 39° 36 west, sixty nautical miles from the coast of South Georgia, that's our position on the eighth of May, a Monday. For us it's the fifteenth day at sea, for those on Elephant Island, the 470th trapped in the ice.

The sea becomes wilder again. The Cape Horn rollers are back. They push up mountains so high they create their own microclimates. In the valleys between the waves, the air is so saturated with the water raging on every side that it pours rain, while it snows evenly up on the crest. For hour after hour, the *Caird* plunges out of the fluttering snow into the downpour and then climbs back up into the flakes. And although it's always the same dirty clouds that scud across the sky, it seems for two long days as though autumn and winter, winter and autumn are fighting over us and that the two seasons aren't seasons, but two kingdoms at war over which is worse than the other. Both, the cold and the wet, soak into our bones. We all have saltwater burns on our wrists, ankles and knees, and Vincent seems to be suffering from rheumatism. All that the onboard half of McIlroy's medicine box can offer against it is a little bottle of tincture of witch hazel, which Vincent greets with no more than a tired smile.

Convulsed by shivers, he turns his emaciated body in the sleeping bag. For a while he carries on shuddering but then falls asleep and lies quietly as long as the boat's rising and falling doesn't throw him onto the rocks. The snow sweeps in through the entrance and the rain pours in behind it.

At the end of his break, Vincent goes back to his post. Shackleton was wrong about him. He as little as any of us needs any special motivation to do his duty. Even when he almost can't move with pain, he goes before the mast, lashes himself to it, and directs his salt-encrusted eyes to the horizon. It's him who, standing there around midday on the sixteenth day, spots a large clump of seaweed halfway up the side of a rising breaker. It's the first sign of land.

From then on, we scour the skies for a glimpse of birds. And they come. In the few seconds that our boat pauses on a crest, we can see the flocks wheeling over the ocean to the southwest. What kinds of bird are they? We make bets. Bakewell discovers a small carpet of jetsam: spars connected to each other by rigging thick with algae, the sight of which makes us fall cheering into each other's arms. But where's the island? The mountains are so high, why can't we see them? The clouds are chasing too deep and too dark across the skies ahead.

"Aim for the birds!" shouts Worsley. They're soon so near that we can distinguish them, fulmars, blue petrels and terns. Crean, who doesn't leave the tiller, follows their course, and his singsong at the helm becomes louder the louder the birds announce our arrival.

"There!" shouts Sir Ernest. "There, the clouds are parting; it'll clear and we'll see the peaks."

A broad stripe of sky flies out of the west; he's right, the weather's changing.

In the same second, Crean roars a warning.

I've never heard him scream like this, and it's as if he's lost his head, because, just like with his song, no one can understand what he means. "It's coming!" he screams. "Hold on!"

It's not a rip in the cloud cover that's racing towards us from astern. It's the white and foaming crest of a wave whose height far outreaches anything I'd ever imagined. Its roaring envelops every other sound, and for a few instants, while the *Caird* is still slicing down into the preceding trough, all the noises of the ocean are subsumed in it.

There's no time to reef the sails. Nothing matters in the seconds we have left except finding somewhere to hold on and clamping ourselves fast. Crean wraps the rope at the stern around himself and lashes himself to the tiller. The man at the mast sinks onto the deck; it's Worsley. He slings his arms and legs around the mast. Vincent plummets down through the forward entrance, I down through the stern with Shackleton behind me.

"Three men below," he shouts, and I see that his forehead is bleeding. There's no answer from deck. "Tom," he screams, "Tom! How many?"

And I scream, too: "Where's Bakewell?" Then the *Caird* starts to hop; she hops up and down like a flea. Shackleton and I fall into each other. Stones fly through the boat, the water casks roll over us and I see Vincent lying in the bow, his head thwacking again and again against the underside of a bench until it splits with a bang. The shaking stops and the boat's bow is lifted, swiftly, easily, totally silently it climbs ever further, as if it had grown wings and were sailing up off the water. In a flash I realize where we are, on the crest of the wave, with the descent into the valley ahead of us.

As the bow tips, water rushes in. The boat floods in an instant. The water is icy and so powerful that it sluices Vincent and everything that was with him in the forward part of the boat in a single spate back to the stern. The *Caird* plunges. The water runs backwards and gathers in the bow. Shackleton, Vincent and I wedge ourselves together amidships, each trying to hold on to the others and bracing, gasping, for the crash.

It takes a long time, so long that I can say, "Bakewell! Oh, God, Bakewell!" a dozen times.

The impact pushes the boat under water. Every noise stops, and the color of the water changes without the light. Drake's gray sea goes glassy-green.

All at once, I know: we're going under.

"We're sinking," Vincent groans into my arm.

But Shackleton, his faced smeared in blood, knows better: "It can't be," he gasps. "It won't be. I forbid it."

# 39

## THE FOURTH MAN

A DAY AND A HALF LATER, THE FIVE OF US HAUL THE SHATTERED boat as far as we can up a shingle beach deep in the interior of King Haakon Bay on South Georgia.

No one has said a word for hours, and even now, at the end of our crossing, we make no sound other than deep, ugly groaning. We haven't drunk anything for thirty-six hours, since the wave smashed the two casks, and Shackleton, Vincent and I in the belly of the *Caird* had to watch our drinking water pour out into the onrushing sea. My tongue has swollen into a gag. I barked when I saw the cliffs of Cape Demidov stretching out of the swell ahead of me, I yowled for joy like our late Shakespeare in front of Hurley's sled and still, in the lap of the beach, the trickling of glacier water in my ear, I can't stop thinking about the agony that Scott wrote about and that I've now experienced for myself: the mortal fear of being suffocated by your own tongue.

It's only at the sight of the little stream splashing down from the ice overhang to the rocky shore that we fall into one another's arms. The water makes our survival certain. Worsley and Vincent, who is swaying with exhaustion, are ordered by Shackleton to go and drink at once. Crean, he and I first go back to the boat to salvage Bakewell and carry him to the rivulet.

Behind a curtain of icicles twice as high as a man, and a few paces above the tideline, Worsley discovers a cave in the cliffs that's large enough for three sleeping bags, the one functioning stove we have left and the rest of our supplies. We retreat into it once we've tied up and unloaded the *James Caird*. I prepare a stew of dried seal meat, and now that we have fresh water everyone can have as much milk as he likes. Shackleton makes the sleeping arrangements: Vincent, who is unresponsive for minutes at a time with the pain of rheumatism, gets a sleeping bag to himself. Crean and Worsley share the second, and the third goes to our patient and me. Sir Ernest takes the first two-hour watch, pacing between the cave and the boat. Darkness falls outside the icy curtain and in our shelter it soon becomes black and silent.

Our boots rest against one another at the bottom of the sleeping bag. I hold Bakewell in my arms.

"Shhhh. Easy . . . nice and easy . . ." I say close to his ear, and I stroke his sweat-pearled forehead when a new wave of pain breaks inside him and his body seizes up.

"It's all right," I whisper. "Everything's going to be all right. You've made it, mate. Bakie, we're off the water."

He jibbers and mumbles. The arm that saved his life is as hard as a piece of wood under his overalls, and where the boom fell on it and held him fast, the flesh has swollen as thick as my leg. He moans out loud with every shiver, until I have to move.

"Bakie, hey, I have to sleep," I wheeze. "I'm dying of exhaustion. And you've got to sleep, too, do you hear me? Now, sleep! It's all finished, we've got through it, there's nothing left for you to do. You can just lie here and rest. And tomorrow your things'll be dry and the sun'll be shining, then we can cool your arm and make it a splint. I'm not going away, I'm just going to sleep a bit."

Now and then, I'm woken by his shuddering or by a particularly loud groan, but otherwise I sleep, sleep as deep and sound as I never have before in my short but hardly sleepless life. When Worsley wakes me, it's not quite day. It's raining. In the cave entrance, a number of icicles have dropped from the ceiling, and the wind is whistling in mockingly through the gap. Crean, who took the second watch, is asleep, snoring in the crook of Shackleton's arm.

"Got your strength back?" Worsley asks with friendly eyes, and when I nod, he checks on Bakewell. He's pale but sleeping, and his forehead is cool and dry.


FOR THREE DAYS, WE ONLY LEAVE THE CAVE TO SECURE THE BOAT OR look for food. There are albatrosses nesting on a ledge above the cliffs. Shackleton shoots a young bird and then its mother. The bird is so big and heavy in my hands that I imagine this is how it must be to pluck an angel. Crean and Worsley bring a whole sailcloth full of tussock grass back from the cliffs. They line the cave's floor with it, and I snap off a couple of handfuls and cook them in the pot with the albatross. We eat and sleep, eat, drink, sleep. We eat, drink, smoke, chat and sleep for days. On the third evening in the cave, we still look like long-haired skeletons. Shackleton, Worsley, Crean and I, however, are well-enough rested and recovered not to find it a great effort to remove McNeish's wooden upper works and deck covering from the *Caird*. Even though it destabilizes the boat even further, we've got to do it, because Shackleton has decided to give the two sick men only one more night of rest before we penetrate six miles deeper into King Haakon Bay and sail through to its tip. The chart shows a more hospitable area, like a fjord, with beaches flat enough for four of us to pull the much lighter boat up past the tideline. Protected from the wintry gusts off the sea, the three staying behind are going to wait under the inverted hull. Thirty-five miles, ten fewer than from the cave, is how far Worsley calculates the distance from the tip of the bay over the mountains in the interior and down to the whaling stations of Stromness and Husvik. Worsley also declares that he's a sailor and not a mountaineer. All he means by that is that he's willing to stay behind with Vincent and Bakewell. Shackleton, Crean and I will attempt the march.

We spend another day of rain and storms inside the cave, where I replace the splint on Bakewell's arm and tell him and Vincent a little about the books that I've read about Captain Scott's march back from the Pole. Time and again, just like I once interrupted my brother, one of them asks why it was that Scott, Bowers and Wilson died. Why, in the protection of their tent, did they lack the strength to wait out the blizzard? Where was the mistake? These unanswered questions make Vincent so furious that he retires swearing to his sleeping bag. I don't have an answer, not without the books. And Crean, whom Scott ordered to go back and who only survived the tragedy at the Pole for that reason, Tom Crean, who listens to what I whisper while I care for Bakie's arm, the Irish giant, as Scott nicknamed him, Crean darns his trousers in the flickering light of the stove and says nothing.

FOR FOUR HOURS WE SAIL INTO THE ISLAND. THE NEARER WE GET TO THE innermost point of the bay, the more birds we see in the air and on the cliffs of the rocky coast. Shortly after midday, we drag the *Caird* up onto a gently rising beach of gravel and black sand. A colony of elephant seals has set up its winter quarters in the vicinity. The animals immediately send over two young bulls to investigate. There are so many that Worsley, Bakewell and Vincent will be provided with food and fuel throughout the foreseeable future. Should the other three of us fall into a crevasse in a glacier, if we freeze or starve or all of the above, these three will be able to hold out through the winter. It'll be eighty sea miles in the boat around the ice-free island to Stromness. The question is, how many men on Elephant Island will still be alive come spring.

We turn over the *James Caird* a safe distance from the tideline. The wooden cave is fitted with a thick base of stones, a carpet of tussock grass and a wall to protect it against the wind. Worsley names the place Peggotty Camp, after the family of David Copperfield's wet nurse.

For three days, fog, rain and driving snow prevent us from setting off. We use the time to make Peggotty Camp as snug as possible, lay in stores and check and recheck the equipment for the march. To reconnoiter potential routes, Shackleton undertakes long trips along a steep, snow-covered slope to the northeast and thinks things over while he wanders, discussing them, as he says, with Frank Wild. He misses Wild so much that he often, without noticing, calls even Crean by the mini-boss's name. During our seventh night on South Georgia, the night of the seventeenth of May, under a full moon whose light Shackleton had counted on having on the march, he's so restless that instead of sleeping he spends hour after hour pulling nails out of the boat's superfluous planking. Hardly are the rest of us awake, but he asks me and Crean for our shoes and hammers the nails into their soles, eight in each boot.

Crean and Shackleton agree that we'll set off the following night regardless of the weather conditions and will do so with only the minimum of luggage. The three sleeping bags will stay with those waiting behind; the overland crew will sleep in shifts during the three-day march, always watched by one who can't fall asleep under any circumstances. Each of us will carry his own share of the rations and biscuits. We'll distribute the combined weight of the Primus stove and enough fuel for six warm meals, as well as a small cooking pot, a box of matches, two compasses, a telescope, a fifty-foot rope and the ice ax. No personal possessions are allowed.

He'll permit no exceptions, says Shackleton, and points to my heart, to Ennid's fish. "That goes for your talisman, too, Merce."

Then he reads out what he's written in Worsley's diary.

"Captain, I am shortly to attempt to reach South Georgia's east coast in order to fetch help. I transfer to you responsibility for Mr. Vincent, Mr. Bakewell and yourself. You have plenty of seal meat, which you will be able to complement with as many birds and fish as you are diligent enough to collect. I leave you, *inter alia,* a double-barreled shotgun and fifty cartridges. Should I not return, I advise you to wait out the winter and then sail to the east coast. The route that I will take to Stromness is east by the compass. I expect to bring

313

you help within a matter of days. With great respect, Ernest Henry Shackleton."

Bakewell and I again crawl into our sleeping bag. Crean wakes us around two in the morning. While Worsley warms up the rest of the albatross stew for everyone's breakfast, I switch jackets with Bakie. He slips into mine and gropes for the fish sewn into the breast, then, moving as well as he can with his splint, clamps me in a hug.

"One, two, three," he says, trying to look relaxed. "Three days and you'll have gotten there. Then you can come back in the motorboat and pick us up. Bring a beer along. And now get going so I can finally read what it says on this note."

Vincent has his fun by whacking me across the shoulders.

The three of them go with us out of the boat. They stay standing there, Bakewell on the right, Vincent left and Worsley in the middle. And they're still standing there when I look down through the morning from a snowfield high above. I can see the ocean and the beach, and I see the small, inverted boat, Peggotty House in a garden of stones.

SHACKLETON'S CHART ONLY SHOWS THE ISLAND'S COASTLINE AND EVEN that's incomplete in many places. Again and again, it's interrupted by the mapmaker's blue of the Southern Ocean. The interior of this sketched crescent is as white and empty as the country in my old dream, and although the mountains are visible from far out at sea, not even they are marked on the chart. No one before us has ever dared climb them. No one knows how high they are and no one has given them names.

Shackleton stuffs the map into his breast pocket, though, at best all we can use it for is to confirm what we know from the compass. He tramps ahead across the snowfield's swiftly rising ground. It's foggy and the snow is loose; we sink in up to our knees. We rope ourselves together to catch anyone who falls into a hidden crevasse.

Shackleton walks ten yards ahead of me; Tom Crean is ten yards behind. When we stop to catch our breath, I see myself mirrored in his
snow goggles; my beard, my long mane. Under my tatters and swad-
dles, I'm skinnier than skinny Holness ever was.

Crean notices how out of it I am. "What's wrong, Merce? Hungry already?"

"None of that," Shackleton calls from above us. He's out of
breath but wearing the broadest of grins. He's in his element, all eu-
phoria. "We've got to get up there first, gentlemen."

I call back, "Sir, that's not it, I wasn't . . ."

And Crean calls, "We were just admiring the view," which must
be a joke, given the fog. That would make it Tom Crean's first joke
since Montevideo. If it was, he's turned serious again. "We've already
finished."

The rope goes taut. We carry on. From behind me I can hear the
same melody as out on the floe, in the boats and on the *Caird*. Crean
hums.

Our first break, the one I didn't even want, is postponed again.
From the crest of the snow-covered slope, and through the slowly dis-
persing fog, we can make out a large, white and hence frozen lake,
only a little to the left of the eastwards course of our march. Shackleton immediately pronounces it a stroke of luck, since the lake does
seem to have a flat route along its further shore.

We traipse effortlessly for a good hour down the other side of
the ridge. Then we encounter the first rips in the crusted snowfield. At
first, they're narrow and not particularly deep. But these are soon followed by ever wider fissures, whose depths are out of sight and which
can be nothing other than crevasses. They can mean only one thing:
that we are not climbing down the shoulder of a hill blanketed in snow
and ice, but across a glacier. Crean and Shackleton see it the same way
I do, I who have never stood on a glacier before but have read about
hundreds of them and know fine well that a glacier is a flow of ice and
that it flows into the sea. On an island, at least, it would never flow

315

into a lake. What looks so invitingly white and smooth down there at our feet cannot, with the best will in the world, be a lake.

Crean stops humming and says, "It's not a lake."

Sir Ernest pulls out the chart and unfolds it. "Yes, Tom, I'm afraid you're right. The shorelines match. It's Possession Bay. It's the damned ocean."

The chart shows four large bays to the northeast: Possession Bay, Antarctica Bay, Fortuna Bay and, the only inhabited one, Stromness Bay, our destination. Between them, the coastline consists of nothing but glacier-riven walls of rock, cliffs and, opposite them, reefs. Even though we've crossed the island at its slimmest point after only eight miles' marching, it doesn't help us a bit. There's no route from the tempting white plain at our feet through to Captain Sørlle's station.

We turn around and climb back up the slope of the glacier. Crean goes to the front, Shackleton to the back end of the rope. And, between the two of them, I ask myself if Scott would have risked a descent to the bay or if he would have turned around just like we have.

If he were still alive, I conclude, and if it were a race against Shackleton to get to the bay at Stromness, Scott would never have turned back. As Dafydd would put it, Scott would rather have cut off a hand and then, the ax between his teeth, hacked off the other.

Why does Crean never talk about Scott? I can imagine Drake or Cook, men who've been dead for centuries, more easily than I can this man who froze to death four years ago. And that despite knowing his diaries and believing that I can hear his voice when I read: "All this struggle—for what? For nothing but dreams that have now ended." Where was it I read that Scott, alone with two other men in the hut by the Ross Sea, is supposed to have said to one of them, "You and the idiot now do this and that"? Where the one Scott wasn't talking to was Shackleton.

EVENTUALLY, AFTER SIX HOURS OF UNINTERRUPTED MARCHING, WE HAVE our first break at around nine o'clock. A low mountain chain rises into the morning light to our east, right across our route. Its four rounded peaks are connected by near-horizontal ridges and look like the knuckles of a clenched fist. At the foot of the slope that leads to the first ridge, we dig a hole in the ice, put the Primus stove in it and stir together a mixture of sled rations and biscuit, which we eat burning hot. Half an hour later we're back on the march. When the slope becomes too steep for us to work ourselves upwards through the snow with our hands and feet, we take turns to cut steps into the ice every second yard.

Shackleton is the first who can see over the ridge to the other side, shortly before midday. He waves me and Crean up to join him. I scramble to the crest on all fours and look over the top.

There's no way down. Like Lilliputians on the brim of Gulliver's hat, we're lying on our bellies over an almost vertical cliff. The bare blue-gray slopes below are littered with ice boulders that must have broken off from our lookout point and dropped into space. An impassable landscape of crevasses and ridges stretches all the way to the sea.

Inland, to the east, however, Crean makes out through the telescope a soft slope mantled in even snow. Shackleton estimates that it leads perhaps nine miles into the island's interior. He passes me the telescope and says, "That's the route. No matter how we do it, we have to be down off that slope by nightfall. Let's try it over the second ridge. Do you trust yourself to go first, Merce? Then let's go, back the way we came."

I only have to follow the steps and then, further down, our tracks. After an hour or so, I've guided us safely down to the foot of the second slope. The air is clear and cold; it's early afternoon. There's hardly any wind. But we can see that the storms often play here and that they're none too dainty. I lead us through overhanging ice cliffs and along the fissured edge of a glacier. The route is the right one, but my heart pounds nonetheless when I go first along a scythe-shaped gully, miles long and at least a thousand feet deep. It must have been cut into the ice by the storms that have been raging here for who knows how many centuries.

Nor does the second crest bring us any luck after I have led us up it. Every twenty minutes we lie in the snow with our limbs stretched away from us, sucking in the thin air and recovering from the effort of climbing, pulling the rope and cutting steps. At around three in the afternoon, Shackleton looks over the ridge, capped with light-blue ice, and, the telescope to his eye, just shakes his head. Again it's Crean who notices something essential. Fog banks are forming in the valleys to our east, and behind us, too, the evening fog is coming in from the sea to the west. Crean estimates our altitude at 4,500 feet. We're too high, far too high to survive the plunging nighttime temperatures without sleeping bags, in only our shredded snowsuits.

"What would Frank Wild do now?" Shackleton asks the wind, and when neither I nor Crean answer, because I, for one, don't have the feeling that Shackleton expects us to, Sir Ernest says as quietly and as lovingly as if the mini-boss were really lying nearby, perhaps in a strangely small snow hole at our feet, "Come on, Frank, give me a clue, you old bloodhound."

Despite the risk of being surrounded by the fog, he decides not to climb back down to reach the third ridge. Instead, after a short rest, we start cutting steps into the ice that leads around this peak. It is, as Cook would have put it, an impressive piece of work that we've taken upon ourselves, to build a walkway around the back of a nameless mountain on the last island on earth. Our causeway curves around softly towards the last ridge. I cut every third step, and Shackleton and Crean finish theirs so quickly I can hardly gasp for breath before it's my turn again.

In threes! Always in threes! goes around my head again and again during the hours of exertion. We had three boats. We left three men behind. The mountain has three ridges. Scott, Bowers and Wilson were a three, a three just like we are.

The third ridge forms such a narrow crest that Shackleton can sit astride it. Panting for lack of oxygen, he looks through the telescope. The fog has engulfed the valley; I can see that much with my naked eye. The sun is setting; the cold is starting to cut.

"All right, come on, let's go, this way it is."

He climbs over and immediately starts stamping the first step into the ice on the other side. Crean follows him, then I do. My legs feel like they've died.

After only a few yards, the solid crust gives way to softer snow, which, according to Crean, is a sign that the slope might be easing. But he wouldn't bet on it. We need to make steps only rarely, but our progress through the dense clouds rising up the mountain is hardly any faster than before. After only a few more minutes we're surrounded by fog.

Shackleton looses the safety rope from his belt and indicates that Crean and I should do the same. Crean protests, but Shackleton brooks no argument.

"You'll do what I order," he barks at Crean, whom he's never spoken to like that before, and in a hardly less severe tone says to me, "The same goes for you, Frank. Take out your tin plates. Coil the rope into a circular mat. Put it on the plate and then sit on it. We're going to sledge."

"That's insanity," says Crean. "We don't know what's down there."

But he obeys nevertheless, folding the rope and placing it on the plate just as Sir Ernest demonstrates.

"If we don't want to freeze, this is our only chance," says Shackleton. "We'll go together, me first, so that if I fall, you might with a bit of luck be able to save yourselves. Is that acceptable to you, Tom Crean?"

Crean nods.

"Frank?"

I nod, too. "Agreed. But I'm not Frank Wild, sir."

"I'm sorry. All morning I've had the feeling that we're not alone. As though there were a fourth man alongside us. Tom thinks the same, don't you, Tom? Don't you, Merce?"

Since he's said it, I don't see a reason to conceal it any longer. "Scott, sir."

"Yes, Scott perhaps. Though I'd prefer Frank Wild." He laughs. "Let's hope that it's really the one with the same initials as the *James Caird*. Are you ready? Then pray take your places, gentlemen. God be with us. On my command. On three. One, two . . . !"

# 40

## GHOSTS

FASTER AND FASTER WE RACE DOWN THROUGH THE FOG ON THE frozen slope. We clutch onto one another, my arms are slung round Shackleton's chest and I can feel Crean's skull on my shoulder. The ice we're speeding across on our plates and ropes spurts up at us, cracking and whooshing, and leaps to sprinkle us in tiny glittering splinters. Shackleton is the first to start shouting against the noise and the speed. At first he just roars as if the buffeting air were rushing through him. I feel his chest expanding, feel him drawing himself together and blowing up again. But then he lets out a loud, joyful yell that keeps breaking up into laughter and only goes quiet when we fly over an escarpment of ice and he holds his breath in my arms. The waves that run through him go on into me, and his laughter carries me with it, and for a while I ask myself why it is that I'm not laughing, too, why I can't do anything but cling to him, until I hear my own laughter without knowing how long I've been laughing for, and wish suddenly that this ride across the breaking, jangling ice would never stop.

Crean sings. He sings right in my ear and I recognize the melody; it's the one he's been humming for months, but now I finally believe I can make out every word:

> "From the wave-tops, from the breakers,
> Splashing over troughs and haar,
> From atop the water's acre
> Speaks the horse of Uíbh Ráthach."

That's what I think I can hear Tom Crean singing. He bellows the verses into my ear so loud that Shackleton must hear them, too, from where he's hunched in front of me, and as we race downwards and drive deeper into the fog, he sings along in his far more stilted Gaelic:

> "There is none in water, land or sky,
> Not a soul and not a star,
> That existed longer here than I,
> Me the horse of Uíbh Ráthach."

We plummet, three Celtic skeletons, two warbling Irishmen and me, the Welshman who doesn't notice when he laughs.

But I do notice that the hillside's getting ever flatter. The slope smoothes out until it's almost level, and we lose speed rapidly.

They're still singing:

> "All you birds, and people, man and jack,
> Live the day you live and are."

And as we slide into a snowdrift that brakes us and finally brings us to a halt, my laughter stops and I join in with Crean's final verse:

> "Don't live forward, don't live back!
> Do not ride to Uíbh Ráthach."

We clamber off our plates, stand up on wobbly knees and fall, giggling and sobbing, against one another. Rising high above us out of the fog is the line of the crest we were climbing on only a couple of minutes before. All at once, I remember my father's pony, our old pony Alfonso, which I haven't thought about for years. I see his huge sad eyes in front of me. Crean grabs me, laughs and won't stop clapping me on the back until I stop crying.

"It's only," I sob, "only because of that song, nothing else."

• • •

AFTER A MEAL OF SLED RATIONS AND BISCUIT EATEN STANDING UP, WE pack away our utensils and ropes and get back on the march. Minute by minute, our tiredness increases. There's no time to lose. The snowfield, which runs deep into the island's interior and that looked flat from the crests of the hills, proves to be a soft but rising slope. The further we march east in the light of the full moon, the higher we reach and the colder we get. Shortly after midnight, we've been tramping through the crusted snow for five hours without a break. Crean estimates our altitude at four thousand feet and the temperature at below minus twenty.

A mute hour later, the incline ends and the snowfield begins to fall off and snake down to the northeast. We follow it down under the yellow moon for another hour, happy to be going downhill and secure in the belief that we'll soon see the water of Stromness Bay on the horizon. "There it is," one of us will shout, maybe even me, and maybe we won't just spot the shape of the bay from up here, but also the lamps on ships and boats, the lights in the houses and the faint threads of smoke rising straight from chimney pots in still air.

Instead, come between three and four in the morning, we're exhausted, hungry and frozen, going back up the slope we've just descended. My tiredness has ossified into a paralysis that stops me moving any part of my body but my legs. Disappointed and full of dumb resentment against every lump of ice that juts out of the twinkling light-blue snow and forces me to step over it, I trudge behind the two others, stumbling along the shore of Fortuna Bay, which we in our hopeless enthusiasm had taken for the bay of Stromness. They do indeed resemble each other, as Shackleton, seeming to need to apologize, shows us on the map. There's a largish island in the middle of the bay and some other landmarks that he and Crean pointed out excitedly, so familiar did they seem. But in truth, no soul on earth can be familiar with Fortuna Bay. It's a bleak, naked slash into the island's armor, a never-inhabited, ever-barren patch of waste. In cold so cold it makes my eyes burn, I think: nothing has ever happened here. Even Cook must have mapped it without going ashore. And why *would* anyone want to wander around it? There's nothing here. Was Cook so cynical that he named the most desolate of desolate spots after the goddess of luck? No, it must have been someone like me, a day-dreamer, keeping a longing lookout for chimney smoke and lights where there's nothing but rockfalls and ice. We stagger uphill again, following our own footsteps back up the snowfield. It takes hours, and the bay disappears only very slowly at our backs.

We are so despondent that no one can talk. Crean has stopped humming. We trudge across the snowfield, as mindless as the moon and as weak as the glimmer of the stars in the Great Bear. Only Shackleton speaks, at some point after the deceptive water has vanished behind the tongue of a glacier: "Fortuna Bay lies behind us. That means it can no longer lie ahead."

IT'S STILL ALMOST COMPLETELY DARK WHEN, AT ABOUT FIVE IN THE morning, I've got to admit that I can't go any further. The tiredness is making me start to despair. With every step I feel my hope that we'll reach Stromness subside a little further, and for the first time in a long while, I feel the fear that I'll never see any of them again, neither Bakewell, Worsley and Vincent on the other side of the island nor Wild, Holness, Clark, Orde-Lees, Greenstreet, Hurley, Green, neither them and all the others on Elephant Island nor my brother, nor my brother-in-law, Herman, nor ever my family nor old Simms nor Ennid Muldoon. I drag myself along between Shackleton and Crean for an endless few more minutes, but I notice that I'm swaying and staggering ever more often. I'm shattered by the thought that I might no longer have the strength to open my mouth and ask for a rest, and the panic that that spreads in me keeps me walking for another few minutes, gasping with my mouth wide open in dismay.

I come back to myself in a niche in the rocks under a deeply snow-covered ridgeline. Crean's shredded glove is stroking across my forehead. Shackleton's hair must be as long as my mother's; it falls out of his hood across both of his cheeks when he leans forwards, his face dark with concern, and demands that I take the half-beaker of milk and the biscuit that I've apparently been refusing. The three biscuits we eat in the niche are our last three, and although it leaves us without any more to eat, we demolish the two remaining sled rations. Pressed against one another, each with an arm around the man beside him, our slurping and chewing faces as tight together as we can get them, we sit in the niche with our backs to the cold of the breaking morning and wait for the calories' warmth to stream through us, for our courage to return and the world to lose its horrors.

"It can't be much further," says Shackleton. "Just this ridge, then it's downhill to the coast, I can feel it. I promise you, we'll see the station in six hours at the most. We can't slacken now! Merce, are you already feeling better?"

"A bit better, sir."

"You're doing excellently. Everyone has his dead point. What's important is that you respect that limit and don't demand anything impossible of yourself. I need you. Aren't you in the mood to tell us a little anecdote from one of our abandoned books, one that'll cheer us up or at least give us something to think about?"

What occurs to me is only an image, an image of biscuits in the snow. Particularly because it's bound up with Scott's disaster, it's an image of ease and happiness, which is why it seems right to me, even if I might hurt Crean in his undimmed love for his captain.

I tell them about Amundsen. While Scott was starving to death in his tent, Roald Amundsen had traveled to the Pole and back so quickly and saved so many supplies that he organized a biscuit-fight with his men on the ice. Each of the polar explorers was given a box of biscuits as ammunition. And, at the end, the Norwegians loosed the dogs from their sleds and let them gobble up the battlefield.

Shackleton and Crean are silent, but on both sides my arm is squeezed. We've eaten everything; the beakers are empty. Shackleton takes out the chronometer; it's quarter to six. He tells me and Crean to sleep for half an hour before we try to climb the ridge. Crean leans back against the rock, encloses me under his arm and Shackleton wakes us up.

I rub my face awake with a handful of snow.

WE LEAVE THE PRIMUS STOVE IN THE NICHE, ROPE OURSELVES TOGETHER and begin to stamp steps into the slope. The half hour of sleep has refreshed me more than expected, and I find the ascent up to the ridge comparatively easy; sometimes I even help Sir Ernest stay on his feet. Shackleton now seems completely spent; he's panting and he avoids my gaze. Crean goes first, I hear him humming again, not a soul and not a star. And so we've almost reached the ridgeline, which runs across above us, light-blue in the dawn, when we hear a noise. It sounds like a very distant whistle, but not like the cry of a petrel or a skua. We stop and look at one another.

From above, Crean asks distinctly, "What time is it?"

It's an effort for Shackleton to suppress his panting. Once he can speak, he pulls out the chronometer. "Half past six precisely."

How can it be half six, Crean and I want to know, if we've slept half an hour since quarter past and also climbed halfway up a snowy slope?

Sir Ernest, still panting, explains, "The two of you feel rested, Tom, don't you? I woke you after five minutes because otherwise I would have fallen asleep myself. It's half past six."

"At half six," says Crean, "the siren wakes the men at the whaling station."

And Shackleton: "That must be what we heard."

"If that was it," says Crean, "we'll hear it again in half an hour. At seven, there's the signal to come to work."

And Shackleton again: "That's exactly right. We only have to wait. And what can we do better than that, eh? Let's have a look over this ridge."

WHEN STROMNESS'S STEAM WHISTLE SOUNDS FOR A SECOND TIME, WE'RE standing on the falling slope we've been walking down into the valley for the last half hour, and we throw our arms around one another.

"It's too good to be true," Shackleton says once to Tom Crean and once to me, before we carry on our way through the ankle-deep snow. In the distance, at the other end of the valley, are the high peaks that lie to the west of Stromness and Husvik, blue-white summits that shimmer in the thin morning air. They are Coronda Peak and Mount Cook. Mountains with names.

We walk all day. Shortly after noon, we climb over a small chain of foothills and look across the level line of its crest. Lying in the light ahead of us is a black bay. A motorboat is crossing quite far out. The boat pulls the water into chevrons. And moored at the Stromness dock is a sailing ship, a three-master like the *Endurance*. I can see men on the decks; they're tiny from here, but the variously colored jackets they're wearing are clearly visible. There are others between the docks and the sheds. They're walking around. Some of them are carrying things, tools perhaps. How wonderful. We lie on our bellies for several minutes in the snow of the crest. Now and then, when a gust of wind blows against the shore, the flag on the village's mast unfurls and shows us the blue, white and red of the Norwegian cross. It looks like the flag is being woken by the wind coming over the bay, and when it slumps down, like the wind is letting it drift off again.

I haven't seen a stranger in seventeen months. I pass the last hours that we need for the descent to the Stromness coast in a state of such tension that it almost rips me apart. I lock it up inside me, unable to bring out so much as a word of relief and share the common happiness with Crean and Sir Ernest. We share it in silence and by knuckling down. Nothing must happen to one of us now. Each hand-clasp makes me blissful, and any touch from either of the two who help me stay on my legs, and who use helping to stay close to me, fills me with trust and makes me forget a little more of the fear that I'm only dreaming, that I've gone under with the *James Caird*, that I'm dreaming as I drown, that I've fallen asleep and am freezing to death in the snow on the mountains, freezing because there's no one left to wake me.

What does wake me, and violently, is the cold torrent of an icy waterfall. We rope down through it. Since it's the last obstacle on the way that leads directly to the whaling station, we leave the rest of our equipment on the bank above. We divest ourselves of the tatters of our Burberry snowsuits and climb down one after the other through the booming water.

Trembling in sodden rags, our faces black with smoke and filth, we're tramping down the slope an hour later. Only this snowfield still lies between us and the world. Crean suddenly stops walking and asks me and Shackleton to wait. He gropes for something in his breast pocket and pulls out a couple of safety pins.

"I want to at least stitch myself together a bit," he says with a sad smile, and begins to take the shreds that are hanging around his legs and pin them together at his knees and ankles. Once he's finished, we're to tell him if we think he looks different. I can see his hands quiver, but when I go over to make him not feel that he's kept the pins so long for nothing, I notice that it's not just his hands, but the whole Tom Crean that's shaking. Crean's chin, with the matted beard hanging down over his chest, is quaking as much as his knees, and I bend towards them in total astonishment.

We walk towards the houses. There are already lights on in the windows. Hammer strikes on metal ring out from a small, rust-red shack on the shoreline, and once we've almost reached it, the door to the shack flies open. Children come running out. There are three small children. When they notice us, they stop short, and I see that they are two girls and a boy, siblings perhaps, because all three are wearing identical red oilskin jackets. They run off, and the three of us, who were just as frozen, set ourselves in motion again and, for the first few steps between the sheds and houses, seek out one another's faces and in them the comfort for the children's horror.

The children huddle around the legs of a foreman who's standing at the jetty and overseeing a couple of his men unloading a boat. It's hard for him to stay on his feet, so hard do the children tug at him. When he spots the reason for their panic, when he sees us, tattered ghosts with women's hair and beards, approaching slowly along the landing stage, he shouts an order and right away two men leap from the boat. It must be the motorboat from the bay. They calm the children while the foreman, a young man, taller than Crean and as broad as Crean once was, with widely set eyes, white-blond hair and a red face, comes bravely towards us. Then he stops, crosses his arms and blocks our way.

Shackleton, for his part, spreads his arms out wide and so signals for us not to go any further.

"Would you please be so kind as to bring us to Captain Sørlle?" he calls across, forcefully and in English.

The Norwegian is hardly older than I am. He hesitates before answering. And he looks around just as hesitantly to check on the children.

"Please, sir!" Shackleton calls to him.


CAPTAIN SØRLLE EMERGES FROM HIS HOUSE AT THE CENTER OF THE settlement. He's in his shirtsleeves. Roald Amundsen's brother-in-law has a napkin in his hands and an enormous, gleaming silver mustache on his face. He's visibly baffled by this evening crowd. More than two dozen workers, plus their wives and children, have followed us at a respectful distance to the steps that the station head is now walking down, a dark look on his face as he comes to submit us to inspection.

329

The young foreman comprehensively explains the situation to him, and eventually the captain has gathered himself sufficiently and wiped enough crumbs from his mustache to stand in front of us.

"You've come from the mountains, they tell me. Is that true?"

Shackleton nods.

"Impossible," says Sørlle. "Where precisely have you come from?"

"Our ship was wrecked. My companions and I started from King Haakon Bay thirty-six hours ago. It's true, Captain. Don't you recognize me?"

"I know your voice. You're the helmsman of the *Daisy*. Tell me your name."

Sir Ernest answers calmly. "My name is Shackleton."

Thoralf Sørlle looks at me and looks at Crean before his gaze returns to Shackleton. He moves aside and spreads his arm towards his front door.

"Come in," he says, "come into the house." He goes ahead of us. But the captain hasn't yet reached the steps that lead up to his brightly lit home when he turns away and begins to weep.

*Part Five*

## THE FLYING ENNID

Between the Ebbw and the Usk
Hail and Farewell

# 41

## BETWEEN THE EBBW AND THE USK

O N ONE OF THOSE DAYS WHEN THE NEWS IS GOING AROUND THE
world that Shackleton has succeeded on the fourth attempt
at rescuing all those shipwrecked on Elephant Island, I'm
sitting with Mrs. Simms on the veranda of her bungalow by the Ebbw
and drinking tea. To keep her sorrow at bay, I have to tell Mrs. Simms
all about what I've been doing despite my thoughts being quite elsewhere. I think of a ship that I'll never see, of which I only know the
name.

The elm's crown of autumnal gold whispers by the riverbank
when no one's talking. A large bird, a magpie or a rook, hops from
branch to branch, and beside it, hardly smaller than the elmen crown,
stands the disk of the deep sun, cool enough to look at.

One more hour till nightfall, says a glance at the sky. I've got to
be off soon. My sister, who's as heartbroken as Mrs. Simms, Regyn
needs me, she and the little one are waiting.

"I don't have a light on my bicycle," I say, without looking at
Mrs. Simms. "It'll soon be dark."

"Why did that captain . . . What was his name?" she asks with
an apologetic smile before reaching for the teapot. "You'll have another cup of tea, won't you, Merce? Raspberry-leaf tea is very good
for the kidneys."

I tap the cup to show my agreement. "Thank you. But then I'll
really have to get going."

My face flits across the polished silver like a moon. But as Mrs.

Simms lifts the teapot to pour me some more, my gaze falls on her sun-browned hand. On her middle finger, one above the other, she wears the two wedding rings, and her skin is full of furrows, full of those strange deep wrinkles that by the end were all over Tom Crean's haggard legs, which I was just talking about.

"Sørlle," I say with the cup at my mouth. "Captain Sørlle."

"They've all got unpronounceable names, these Norwegians."

I nod and Mrs. Simms, my teacher for all subjects except P.E. from the first form to the fifth, notes it with a confiding twinkle.

"One more biscuit, Merce, you'll have to have one, I insist. Look at you, how long have you been back from this gruesome corner of the earth where there's nothing but Norwegians and Russians?"

"Nearly three months, Mrs. Simms."

"And still no meat on your bones. You're as thin as a lamppost. Mr. Simms wouldn't have stood for that. He'd have insisted that you stay for supper. And he'd have had some words with your mother about making sure her son gets a double helping as long as he's still just skin and bone, every meal, and for at least eight weeks. Eat, for my sake, lad. That biscuit. And another, here."

The October breeze carries in the smell of fruit rotting in the grass of the pear orchard. Ducks quack beyond the banks of the Ebbw. The stream passes a stone's throw from the house before it narrows under the brick bridge of the old Pillgwenlly road and disappears.

*Yelcho*. The name has been fluttering around my head for days. It's the name of a small Chilean cutter that all the reports say was totally unsuitable for taking into the ice but that Shackleton used to finally break through to Elephant Island after three months of failure. *Yelcho*: having to chew the name over without having a mental image to connect it to makes me nervous. I know it isn't true and that I'm imagining things, but alongside the stream's swooshing and plashing, the cawing from the elm branches, now quieter, now louder, sounds to me like *Yelcho, yelcho, yelcho!*

While Mrs. Simms tells me anecdotes about myself and my former classmates, I think of the notice that my dad found in the *South Wales Echo,* namely that Shackleton is about to return to London and . . . Dear God, I'm being tormented by my bursting bladder, so much so that it hurts when I bite into the hazelnut biscuit.

The noise of my teeth sounds like the magpie's cawing.

"Mmh. You were asking about Captain Sørlle, Mrs. Simms?"

"Yes, quite right. Why did Amundsen's brother-in-law, this Captain Sourly, start crying? Can you explain that? They didn't exactly sound like tears of joy."

"They thought we were dead," I say, under pressure, but regret the sentence immediately. Last November, around the time the *Endurance* sank, old Mr. Simms died. His widow, offering me biscuits, is still in her mourning black.

Under the gaze of her green eyes, I hurry to add, "But seeing us alive, it wasn't just that. I think Captain Sørlle realized all at once that the three of us had no idea how much the world had changed since we'd fallen out of it."

"You mean how devastating the war had become."

"We didn't even know the war was still on. When he saw Sørlle crying, Shackleton asked him when the war had ended, and the captain said to us, 'The war isn't over. Millions of men have fallen on Europe's battlefields and tens of thousands are still dying there every day.' The whalers showed us some old newspapers that they translated for us. That's how we found out all at once about the *Lusitania* being sunk, the poison gas, flamethrowers, Gallipoli. You see, we could hardly believe it. The evening after we got to Stromness, there was a blizzard, we were hunkered down in the house, eating as much as we could, taking baths, shaving and having to keep retelling the story of what had happened. But as soon as it was just us, all we could talk about was the war. That there's supposed to be a hot breeze on the battlefield before the mustard gas comes. And the blizzard didn't stop. It was as if . . ."

"It's snowed a lot here, too, this year," says Mrs. Simms.

I nod. "Yes, Mam told me."

"The grave was white all over. Very peaceful."

"It's a lovely grave, Mrs. Simms."

"Isn't it? Sorry, I interrupted you."

"Well, after two days, Tom Crean could finally go and pick up the three others on the south coast. But about the war, well . . . He didn't tell them the truth. He said it was finished, that there were peace talks. He didn't have the heart. Mrs. Simms, I'm sorry, but I've really got to . . ."

"They must have been so weak, that was probably the right thing," Mrs. Simms says quickly, and just as quickly reaches across the table with both hands. "You learned about it soon enough. Just as we all learned about it soon enough. Have some, Merce. Don't worry about taking too many." She holds out the silver platter with the apparently undiminishing biscuit mountain. "As a very small boy, do you remember, you were fixated on eating. A right little podger you were then."

"I must have changed quite a lot since then, Mrs. Simms, I'm sorry to say. Shall I help you clear this away?"

"Yes, it's getting dark," she says, turning her head and looking out into the pear orchard as if the darkness waiting for me were only in that little corner. She's got no intention of dismissing me, my old schoolteacher.

Instead, she says, her expression neutral, "One of those three who didn't go with you on the march over the hills . . . What were they called again?"

I tell her their names.

"It was Vincent, I think. In the papers, it said that he'd torn off his upper lip on a frozen cup of milk?"

She looks at me. Fear and sorrow speak from her eyes. And yet her desperation has nothing to do with John Vincent.

"Yes, Mrs. Simms, I'm afraid it's true."

"What happened to that man?"

With a loud *yelcho,* the bird swings up into the sky and flies away.

"I don't know. He went to hospital in Valparaiso. That's the last time I saw Vincent. He'll have gone back to England."

She makes a hand gesture that means nothing, unless that she wants to drive something away, a wisp of fog, a bad daydream, perhaps, or her fear.

"Wait a moment. I'll be right back," she says, but doesn't even make as if to stand up.

I stand. Pain hammers in my lower abdomen and I can't think of anything but the relief when I'll lean against my dad's bicycle in the dark and hear the water splashing into the grass.

"Bobby Cooper, the rugby coach, you don't know him. He lost his arm in the battle at the Somme. Mrs. Cooper told me yesterday that the shrapnel was as big and black as a bat, but much faster, and that it just flew right through his arm and sliced it off. The Hutchinsons, too, who live a few doors down. They got three telegrams in six months. All of their sons, I taught all three of them: fallen heroes. Dead men in every street, Merce, in the village, too. Your brother-in-law, Herman, no one knows what happened to him. Mustard gas, my husband said, now they're using a gas that's ten times deadlier than chlorine. And then he started complaining, oh, if only I could go, if only I could put on the uniform myself, I'd soon show those German devils. And one morning, Merce, he was lying there dead with his head on the pillow."

Mrs. Simms stays seated, unmoved by the person opposite her, just the way she always was when she sat with her back arched behind her desk and got one of us in the sights of her green eyes.

It's a mild evening I cycle relievedly through back to Pillgwenlly. There's not a soul on the road. They say there's a clan of giants that's lived in the woods at Dasshebdn since King Arthur gave them the hill with the poplars and birches as a way of thanking a young giant for carrying him across the Usk. The woods are still there, and from the stubbled fields that climb towards it creeps the fog, the cloak worn by the giants of Dasshebdn. A herd of deer on a fallow field listens and chews and isn't bothered by the squeaking of my bicycle.

I used to come here with Dafydd. When I was ten and my brother fifteen, we were both taught by Mrs. Simms. The older pupils sat at the back, the younger ones on the benches at the front. Once school was finished, we streamed along the stone walls and walked across country to the Usk to go swimming. It must have been the year that Blériot flew across the Channel, because I can still remember us searching the clouds with our eyes whenever it said in the *Echo* that in Wales, too, someone was going to take to the skies. I've forgotten his name, but there was a businessman in Swansea who ordered a Blériot monoplane from France and spent a summer trying to fly the single-decker that none of us ever saw across the Severn to Portishead. I remember a shameful feeling of insincerity, because all this flying around didn't mean much to me in itself, I was just imitating my brother's excitement and would probably have done the same if he'd been ready to cut off a leg for horses or mushrooms instead. It was Dafydd's dream to experience just once what every boy at that time, even I, could recount in every detail, the story of how Wilbur Wright lost his way while flying over France, made an emergency landing in a field and invited a presumably chalk-white fruit farmer to jump in behind him.

Of course, the Swansea birdman, as my Dad called him, never did come to take Dafydd for a spin and even "Wilbur," as my brother always called him, isn't flying anymore, but is building aeroplanes instead in his factory in America. Only in July 1915, when I was drifting over the Weddell Sea on the trapped *Endurance* and a remarkable Antarctic derby was taking place on an ice floe, were Dafydd's dreams of flight finally realized. Working at night, he screwed a decommissioned triple-decker back together, and William Bishop, whose problems with the propeller and the machine gun Herman and Dafydd had now solved, proved to be as grateful as King Arthur was to the Dasshebdn giants. He gave Dafydd a few hours of flying lessons and then let my brother do whatever came into his head with the old Sopwith triplane.

Dafydd did what I would have: he flew over Pillgwenlly and turned loops over our parents' house until my mam ran inside screaming. It didn't bring him the expected recognition. When I told my dad that Shackleton had named a seal-inhabited islet in South Georgia's King Haakon Bay after me and had even telegraphed the King to tell him, my dad turned to Dafydd, clutching me under his arm, and said, "You hear that? That's seafaring! And you're rattling about in midair like a Frenchman!"

And Herman, where's Herman, who managed to give my intolerable sister a purpose for her life? Herman isn't rattling around in midair. My brother-in-law came back home from Merthyr Tydfil to Pillgwenlly by train and bicycle every weekend after the start of the war to see Regyn and the baby they named after the pilot and after me, William Merce. Herman got to see his son and heir for three months. His unused bicycle has been in the woodshed for almost twice that.

I lean dad's bike against it.

The big kitchen window is dark; the lights are on in the sitting room and upstairs in my sister's bedroom. The lantern on the veranda flickers. But it only looks like that because the chestnut tree's branches are swaying gently up and down, interrupting its beam. The gravel path that my dad has redone still leads under the chestnut, and I know what'll be waiting for me when I go along it: the bats that live in the tree and launch their nocturnal flights from its branches.

Just as much has stayed the same as has changed. The gravel is new and Regyn has a baby. The lantern has been hanging there under the roof of our veranda since before I can remember. Herman managed to send a card from Paris: "I'm going to see the Arc de

Triomphe and the Pantheon, might go for a walk in the beautiful sunshine." A few days later, his troop of engineers were ordered to the Somme. I think of Mrs. Cooper, her husband the rugby coach and the splinter of shrapnel that supposedly resembled a bat and tore off his arm. But bats never fly into people; they sail high over their heads, where they're sure of finding only air and insects. The shells, I've read, explode into jagged spikes. The fragments of the largest calibers the Germans use are so heavy that two men can hardly lift them. And yet they scream through the air at hundreds of miles an hour to tear open a soldier's belly, or rip off a leg, an arm or a jawbone.

WILLIE MERCE IS SLEEPING IN HIS COT AND REGYN IS LYING ON THE BED. She's pulled the quilt up to her chin and is slumbering. I sit down and examine her. She cried for weeks. And she's again as thin as back when her arms and legs wouldn't stop growing and she was suddenly taller than I was.

But Mam says she's been doing better since I got back. On the nightstand is a photo of Herman. He's wearing a suit and hat and looks proud. Beside him is a wooden propeller that stretches two feet above his head.

Willie Merce is sleeping peacefully. He lies there in his cot like a calm miniature of our dad and snores lightly. In the kitchen is a plate that Mam has left out for me. I eat a few mouthfuls standing up and then go to wash. I hear Willie croaking from the bedroom, and when I go to check on him, both are already sitting on the edge of the bed, the little one on Regyn's knee and looking at me.

"Hey, look who it is. Everything all right with you two?"

I'm to tell her all about Punta Arenas again. She lies in the crook of my arm and her eyes keep falling shut. But sometimes a smile dances across her lips, so I carry on talking and breathing in the milk smell that flows off her. I tell the story of the bright-blue June day when we arrived from the Falklands and met the unbelievable welcome that the Chileans gave us. And to make her laugh a bit, this time I also tell her how Shackleton had telegraphed anonymously ahead from another port further south to announce his own triumphant return.

Dozens of ships and boats came sailing out to meet us from the harbor at Punta Arenas, and the largest and finest of them, I tell Regyn, seemed in the light and in the noise of their horns and whistles like envoys, envoys not just of the countries whose flags they were sailing under, but as if one had been sent by each of the twenty-two comrades who were still waiting to be rescued from Elephant Island. For me, the boats sailing out towards us were the *Greenstreet*, the *Wild*, the *How* and the *Holness*.

"There were fifteen big steamers and seven sailing ships, believe me. I counted them three times; there were exactly twenty-two."

"Like the fish," she says, almost inaudibly, into the pillow.

"What fish?"

She opens her eyes and looks at me. "The all-white fish in the belly of that monster."

"Oh, the leopard seal, right; then there were still twenty-eight of us."

"Like a whole February," she says, and strokes her thumb across my lips and the beard that I've grown to hide my ruined skin. "And now everyone who was there has been rescued and is safe."

Something, my sweet, that sadly isn't true. At the same time as we twenty-eight were fighting to survive in the Weddell Sea, three men from the Ross Sea group died on the other side of the Antarctic, including the *Aurora*'s captain, Aeneas Mackintosh. He, Hayward and Spencer-Smith lost their lives trying to lay depots that we'd never have got anywhere near.

Regyn doesn't need to know anything about that for the time being. Once she has her strength back, girlfriends of hers whose husbands read the papers will soon tell her how much doubt there is about Shackleton's glory. The article in the *Echo* that Dad found about Shackleton returning to London finishes by saying:

> *As this man makes every effort to conceal the fact of his comprehensive failure, we offer him the advice that he give up looking at icebergs and finally put on a uniform instead.*

I TELL HER A BIT MORE ABOUT OUR FAREWELLS IN VALPARAISO AND THEN about my crossing with Bakewell. But Regyn soon falls asleep, and I stay lying where I am and wait in the dark for Willie Merce to wake up, to lift him from his cot and lay him down beside her. Later on, our parents come home and tiptoe, whispering, up the stairs and along the corridor. Emyr Blackboro giggles, he's tipsy, and my mam hushes him, but she wouldn't be Gwendolyn, his Gwen, if she didn't start giggling herself.

It goes quiet in the Blackboro house and I, too, fall asleep. When the baby begins to whimper, Regyn jerks upright, but I've already got the little one in my arm and pass him to her. She turns to the wall, and Willie Merce drinks and smacks his lips.

I've fallen asleep again when Regyn turns back to me. She rests her head on my shoulder and drapes an arm across my chest.

We lie next to each other in silence for a while, then she suddenly strokes her hand across my nose and forehead. She's wide awake, her voice clear, when she whispers, "And Ennid? Are you very sad about it?"

# 42

## HAIL AND FAREWELL

I N A CLOUDLESS AUTUMN SKY, THREE AEROPLANES CLATTER TOWARDS
us from the direction of the hills to the north, William Bishop's
green-and-white Sopwith Camel, Albert Ball's sky-blue Nieuport
Scout and the blazing orange of Micky Mannock's triple-decker.
My parents, my sister and I sit in our Sunday best under woolen blankets in our new pony trap. Alfonso II pulls us unhastily along the
bank of the Usk. I watch the three machines reach the suburbs of
the town and start flying loops between the tower of St. Woolo's and
the mistletoe-shrouded poplars that fringe the town's fairground.

Mick Mannock, up there in the air, is hardly older than I am
and already a greater idol than Tom Crean ever was. He's one of
the most accurate and most feared pilots in the Royal Air Force. I
don't know how she got to know him. Dafydd says he's an all-right
guy, very shy, probably because of the patch he uses to hide a dead
white eye.

The fair where Ennid fell in love with Mick Mannock wouldn't
have been a fair like the one that half of South Wales is on its way
to see today. But, I've been told, it was a flying show with not a
little glamor, with lots of uniforms and a dance afterwards. It was
on the meadows at Caldoen, at the other, equally green, end of the
town, on a lovely warm day in August. To be precise, it was the
fifteenth of August 1915, I've since found out. Ennid looked rav-
ishing, wearing a white bonnet with a scarf and a flowery dress
long enough for her leg brace to be barely noticeable. They chatted,

343

my mam, my sister and Ennid, who told them she was thinking of moving to Merthyr Tydfil like Dafydd had, and as if that had made her think of something else, the three of them then spoke briefly about me.

Where was I on that day? That's the question. Where, Merce Blackboro, were you on that fifteenth of August fourteen months ago, eh? For weeks I've been wondering if I should regret not keeping a diary in the ice.

But no, I don't regret it. In the mirror of the Usk, I can see tree-tops flaming red and yellow. My dad's loving eye will be examining them while he clicks his tongue in appraisal. From time to time, the water's surface splits and puckers. There are pikes hunting below it. What does it matter if, on the day that Ennid met Mick Mannock, Bobby Clark was telling me about macaroni penguins, or if I was reading Biscoe's descriptions of the Southern Ocean when Miss Muldoon stepped up into the train to Merthyr Tydfil, to leave her stunted life in her dad's shop behind her?

The fifteenth of August 1915, as far as I can work out, was my 203rd day locked in the ice. It was a Sunday, I was drifting across the Weddell Sea and it was dark for twenty hours a day.

Dad steers our cart onto the outer ring road. We loop around the town center, whose alleys make dangerous driving for horse-drawn vehicles even when it isn't a holiday. The motorcars that are wildly roaring and hooting back and forth are enormous, and their drivers wear wide, fearful expressions as they race past. "Like logs in a current" is how my dad describes the motor traffic in town. And even on the avenue that runs through the eastern suburbs to the fairground we can hear the thrumming and banging coming from the streets between cathedral and harbor. I think of what Dafydd said, that he was thinking of opening an automobile work-shop after the war. If I want and don't think I'm too good for it, I can be his partner.

Blackboro Bros.
AUTOMOBILE MECHANICS
reasonable FANTASTICALLY reasonable
and faster than you can drive


THROUGH THE AIR MOVING LIGHTLY IN THE WIND I CAN HEAR THE
clashing and parping of the Newport Policemen's Brass Band. We
rock as we turn onto the meadow and Dad climbs down from the
box. He takes Alfonso's halter as the pony nervously tosses his blond
mane. Dad leads us to a line of trees that the carriages are parked
under, and I jump down onto the grass and help the women.

It's Regyn's first outing since Herman was listed as missing. She
purls her arm through mine and asks sadly, "Are you sure I don't
look silly?"

The motors are parked under the poplars opposite. I don't see
the white Morris Oxford Bullnose that belongs to Ennid's parents. But
it's still early in the afternoon, and ever more cars are rolling up across
the churned grass to pause and let out a loud bang, then go silent as
abruptly as if Frank Wild had laid them out with a single rifle shot.
It's unlikely that the Muldoons would miss this festive heroes' farewell,
especially because it's in honor of their future son-in-law. Bishop, Ball
and Mannock, our three boys, are flying to the aerial battle for Paris.

"You look very nice, *très* chic."

Regyn screws up her eyes, tries a smile and squeezes my arm.

When we meet Bakewell at one of the first stalls, a red-and-
white-striped one selling horns, flags and souvenirs, Regyn doesn't
want to let go. She doesn't want to follow our parents into the bustle
and noise of music and propellers. As far as I can see over the hats
and partings, the crowd stretches all the way to the barrier where the
aeroplanes and the brass band are. Behind it I can see grass, a wide
green lawn.

"Who knows who'll waylay me over there," she says, "No, no, not for anything."

Bakewell has scrubbed up. He's wearing a white shirt and a strange cardigan and, until he notices us, has a new peaked cap on his head. I know he's very keen on Regyn and, well, just look at him, rotating the hat in his hands and staring at it like my sister had just given him it as a present.

"Good afternoon, Regyn." Words his lips form but that you can't hear.

"Reg," says my mam, who's the only one to call her that, "there's no need to be anxious. Your brother and Mr. Bakewell would like to have a look around. And we'll do the same. Say hello and wave good-bye."

And Dad: "Come on, poppet, I'll look after you."

BAKEWELL HAS TO HURRY TO KEEP UP WITH ME. EVEN WHEN HE SEES HIS latest employer standing in a group of young suits just before the barrier, I push forwards and call over my shoulder, "Come on, he won't run away, and Mannock's about to take off."

Mr. Klein from Boston has made Bakewell, the only American to sail with Shackleton, the head of his Newport office. Slightly taken aback, he lifts his bowler hat as we press past him and his business associates.

"Mr. Klein," says Bakewell, "sir."

"Mr. Bakewell?" asks Mr. Klein. He doesn't say "sir," though he probably should, even if my friend's wearing neither gaiters nor tails, but a bizarre cardigan.

To me, as soon as we're out of earshot, Bakewell says: "Holy hog's butt cheeks, he's going to fire me, you know that? I'm gonna lose the best job of my life just because you want to transport a wooden fish halfway round the world."

"You won't. And if you do, you'll find something else. Come on."

"I should've burned that thing on South Georgia. Read the note and then into the fire and good-bye. Tell me why I didn't do that."

"Because I'd have ripped your arm off and you know which one."

"And you know, I hope, what you've got to do. Where is it?"

I pat my heart and my heart answers with a patter of its own.

"Good, so take it out."

"That's why we're here."

We haven't reached the barrier yet, but there are already uniforms all over the place, air force officers, trombonists. The closer we get to the aeroplanes, the fewer women there are, but the ones who've come this far despite the mud are exceptionally elegant. They must have been carried; you can't see so much as a fleck of mud on the hems of their dresses, only a crease here and there from sitting through a long journey in a motorcar.

I can't imagine Ennid in that kind of lower-body armor or in a vast borrowed flying hat worn at an angle, covering half her face, or in a strawberry-colored jacket with long ribbons and metal clasps on the back. I keep watch for a summer dress with a floral print.

But, of course, it's too cold for that. It's October. I haven't seen her for two and a half years, and then there she is, standing in front of a giant orange-red aeroplane, surrounded by men in overalls or uniforms and wearing the same raincoat she was then in my dad's office.

She wears her hair longer now. I recognize her cool, keyed-up expression. *No* articulates itself in my head, and something in me builds, half panicked and half rebellious. No, she hasn't changed. It's only that time has run on and made her into a woman. No, she doesn't love that tall, skinny child in the ridiculous flying hat, how could she! She still has the same face, the same face that I saw when I looked into the ice or lay at night in the meltwater squeezed out of my mattress. I haven't lost her, no. No one and nothing should ever be given up for lost, Shackleton's right, and why should it be me rather than someone else who gives up my girl, why should I be the one who gives up Ennid?

347

Both my fear of having lost her and my resistance to it disappear as soon as our eyes meet. She's less than ten yards away on the other side of the barrier and clutching the arm of the one-eyed pilot who's going off to war, whom she loves. It's an exchange of glances between two people who've never met. That's why she's even prettier than I remember; she's taken on the beauty that strangers have. Me, on the other hand, with my beard and the skin that's been eaten by the frost, she doesn't recognize.

Run away, come back another time when I've regained my strength, when I can hurt her instead of suffering this useless hurt myself.

It's me, your little monkey!

Beside me, Bakewell says nothing, but he notices what's going on. So that must be her.

"Give it to me." He holds out the palm of his hand.

"No," I say, despite how tempting his suggestion is. I take out the fish, almost all its color has faded.

After I duck under the barrier, it's only a few paces further. A mechanic, like Herman was, stands at the top of the ladder leaned against Mannock's plane and closes a flap. Written on the board is the reality, the name of love, written in script as yellow as the sun: *The Flying Ennid.*

*Ennidurance,* I sometimes called our ship, just to myself.

You're going to fly to France, I tell my fish. You've been to the end of the world, now you can go to war as well.

And I've not yet reached him when I call, "Mannock! I've got something for you!"


NONE OF US, INCLUDING ENNID, SEES MICKY MANNOCK AGAIN.

I'd have liked to have told that boy who looked at me so well-meaningly from his one eye on the fairground at Newport but who nonetheless seemed completely absent, as though already flown, I'd have liked to have shouted through the racket of the motors what Pastor Gunvald shouted to us explorers in the snowed-in little church at Grytviken:

"Turn back, Mannock, if you don't want to end up like King Sverre!"

I don't know why that phrase in particular leaped into my head when I gave Mannock the fish, and Ennid, standing crying beside him, finally recognized me. Stumbling back towards the barrier in the wind from the propeller, I suddenly realized what the reason for my good luck had been. I knew all at once, without having to read it, what was on the note in the fish's belly and knew at the same time that the words couldn't mean any more than the fish itself. It was terrible, but since it didn't come from her, the fish wouldn't bring Mick Mannock anything. And nor would my decency. It was like Ennid's crying, like her tears: he would remember, but he wouldn't be able to hold himself on to them.

Of the three pilots, only Willie Merce's first namesake, William Bishop, comes back alive. He actually sits in our kitchen one afternoon after the war and tells my dad how proud he can be of Dafydd's work. Albert Ball is shot down at the start of May 1917 by Lothar von Richthofen's fighter squadron. Mick Mannock dies fourteen months later, in July 1918, in the fire of German infantry, when he makes his trademark dive to snatch a trophy from an opponent he's shot from the sky. I read in the *South Wales Echo* that the fallen hero has immediately been awarded the Victoria Cross and that the medal's been presented to his father.

Nor does Pastor Gunvald survive the war. I learn about his death from a book of Frank Hurley's photographs that my parents give me for my twenty-first birthday. Next to a picture that must have been taken shortly after his turbulent sermon, which shows Gunvald posing with a smile beside Captain Jacobsen and his wife, Hurley has written tersely that the ship on which the pastor had hoped to reach Chile from the Falkland Islands was torpedoed by a U-boat and sunk.

"There have been," according to Hurley, "no further signs of life from this man of the cloth."

Another photo in Hurley's book, which, like his later film, is called *In the Grip of the Polar Pack Ice,* shows the strangely coincidental pairing of Alf Cheetham and Tim McCarthy. It's a day on board the ice-encased *Endurance* that I remember well, the day of Orde-Lees's bicycle excursion, and in the picture you can see the contraption leaning against Mother Green's cool-box.

McCarthy is the first of the old crew to lose his life to the war. I find out about it much later in a letter that Tom Crean sends me from Ireland. Tim McCarthy, who in all that time in the ice I never really spoke to, dies at his gun in the Channel less than three weeks after coming back to England. In Hurley's picture, they each have an arm around the other, McCarthy and Cheetham, and I think I can remember the ring of Alf Cheetham's laugh when he was in a good mood and no one was undermining his ice-veteran status. But despite the bicycle and the frost over everything, I don't remember when the photo was taken, no matter how many times I look at the picture of these two ghosts. Alfred Cheetham was a famous personality. No other explorer crossed into the Antarctic Circle as often as he did, and so his death a few weeks before the Armistice earns a notice even in the *Echo*.

GERMAN U-BOAT SINKS

MINESWEEPER IN THE HUMBER MOUTH

*ENDURANCE*-VETERAN CHEETHAM DROWNED

DAFYDD CAN'T BELIEVE HIS EYES WHEN HE REALIZES WHAT HE'S GOT IN his hands. In spelling that comes from the heart, Tom Crean tells me in his letter that he has gone home to Annascaul and opened a pub there. As if they were all meeting there every evening at the bar and telling the landlord about the progress of their lives, Crean knows all about what has happened to Orde-Lees, Wild, Clark and many of the other men of the *Endurance*. They, for their part, write him letters or send pictures, or it happens that one of them is on a lecture tour and makes a detour to the South Pole Inn that belongs to the Irish giant of Annascaul.

Having entered the Royal Air Force on Shackleton's recommendation, Orde-Lees is largely responsible for the pilots' now being equipped with parachutes. To demonstrate their effectiveness, Aunt Thomas leaps off Tower Bridge. Hurley, made a captain in the Australian Army, takes many famous color photographs of the trenches at Ypres. Expeditions lead him to Papua New Guinea and Tasmania, from where he reports to Crean that he's married a young, dazzlingly pretty French-Spanish opera singer. Worsley, as the captain of a clandestinely armed merchant ship, sinks a German U-boat and is highly decorated. From Worsley, Crean hears hints about a supposedly secret mission that takes Shackleton to Spitzbergen and finally Murmansk, a mission where Sir Ernest is again in command of our old skipper, alongside Wild, who sinks into alcohol in Archelansk, and McIlroy, who was badly wounded at Ypres. Until the Bolsheviks chase them away, Shackleton, Worsley, Wild, Hussey and Macklin maintain an Arctic outpost whose purpose no one knows. "Lennon," writes Crean, "has scattered the core of the old crew back to the winds," and it takes me a long while to realize that this mysterious and powerful figure can only be Lenin.

I wouldn't have asked him more about it on my own account, but to fulfill a long-held wish of my brother's, I write to Crean in the first summer after the war and ask him to explain what happened to Scott. Months pass before Crean responds with a postcard, months when Dafydd fulfills another dream and opens his motor workshop near the Alexandra docks. On Tom Crean's card is a pale-blue picture of Annascaul. He'll always admire Sir Ernest, he says. But it's Captain Scott he'll always love.

In that rainy summer, my sister, after long hesitation, gets engaged to Bakewell. Regyn's resistance outlasts all fraternal ruses, and totters only when Bakie offers to adopt Willie Merce. She first tells Bakie she loves him after he insists to Mr. Klein on being allowed to take her and the boy with him on his business trip to Boston, Mexico and South America.

I see Shackleton one more time.

*South,* his book about the voyage of the *Endurance,* comes out in 1919. Reading tours take him all over America and Europe until, on one of the first days of spring, he shows up in Newport. We blend into the audience in a hall that's less than half full. The gentleman in the immaculate pinstriped suit, who was once my Bakie, Mr. Bakewell and I—he'll always be Bakie to me—have decided to reveal ourselves only once Shackleton has finished his lecture.

He's been marked by the strain of scraping together the money to pay back what he borrowed for the failed expedition, as well as by the journeys over the Andes, the Appalachians, the Alps; by the vain attempts to win everyone over all at once and still be a war hero; by all that's been printed in the gossip press about him and his wrecked marriage, about his drinking and his gluttony, his addiction to adventure and his American lover, Mrs. Rosalind Chetwynd. He's forty-two and looks sixty. But he still doesn't look as old as he did then, twisted by sciatica on board the *James Caird,* which is now, he tells us, being transported all over the world.

While he reads, I think of John Vincent and try to imagine who that beast of man has tormented since then. What happened to Stevenson, who, of the two of them, was doubtlessly the bigger rat? And did How, the shadowy Hownow, find his way back to his Helen and the son named, like him, Walter?

"Those men were held captive in the ice for six hundred and thirty-five days," says a woman wearing a flowery hat in the second row. "How long will it be, sir, before they can forget that time?"

Shackleton's answer confuses the lady, and the flowers on her hat tremble. "Ice, madam, is the memory of water, it isn't water itself, and in that it resembles the state of many people today."

He doesn't have time to stay and eat with us. He has to move on. Tomorrow Cardiff, Swansea the day after. Despite how tired he is, his happiness at seeing me and Bakewell again is obvious and completely genuine. After Wales, he's got Ireland on his schedule, the new Ireland, independent for eighteen months and perhaps now his homeland after all. By the motorcar that waits for him with its engine running, a short conversation about Easter weekend of 1916, when the rising was crushed. While it was happening, we were sailing the *James Caird* from Elephant Island to South Georgia.

He shakes our hands, then lays his on my shoulder and gets into the car. What was I expecting?

A moment. A connection. A not letting things be lost.

He knows or feels it. And other than Crean, who has good reasons of his own, I don't just admire him, I love him for not turning the bond against me.

"Farewell, Merce," he says through the car's open window. "Don't forget that it was you who rescued yourself. Build yourself something. But please be clear that one day I will come to you again and ask you to leave it all behind."

We walk through the port, I to my bicycle, which is by the chandler's, and Bakewell to his own motorcar. We're impelled down to the Usk as if to check it's still there. The trees on the banks are still leafless. But a huge number of birds have already arrived, a swarm of finches that rises into the evening, lands on the naked branches of the plane trees by the water and at every loud noise sprays back into the air, scolding and singing. For an instant, I'm back in La Boca and looking out of the window of our hotel at the bare tree in the street that stinks of guano and leads down to the harbor of Buenos Aires. The way the finches fly, quick and flitting this way and that before they float and let themselves drift, so, too, swim the Weddell seals.

Members of the Imperial Trans-Antarctic Expedition
1914–1916, Weddell Sea Party

Sir Ernest Shackleton, expedition leader
Frank Wild, second-in-command
Frank Worsley, captain
Lionel Greenstreet, first officer
Hubert Hudson, navigator
Thomas Crean, second officer
Alfred Cheetham, third officer
Louis Rickenson, chief engineer
Alexander Kerr, second engineer
Dr. Alexander Macklin, ship's doctor
Dr. James McIlroy, ship's doctor
James Wordie, geologist
Leonard Hussey, meteorologist
Reginald James, physicist
Robert Clark, biologist
Frank Hurley, photographer
George Marston, artist
Thomas Orde-Lees, motor expert, then quartermaster
Harry McNeish, carpenter
Charles Green, cook
John Vincent, bosun, then able seaman
Walter How, able seaman
William Bakewell, able seaman
Timothy McCarthy, able seaman
Thomas McLeod, able seaman
William Stevenson, chief stoker
Ernest Holness, ordinary stoker
Merce Blackboro, stowaway

# ACKNOWLEDGMENTS

THE CHARACTERS AND EVENTS IN THIS NOVEL HAVE BEEN FREELY invented. Although much of what I describe does correspond to historical fact, my intention was not to write a maximally accurate retelling of the voyage of the *Endurance,* but rather to embark on a storyteller's adventure of my own and set off into the temporal as well as geographical unknown. In contrast to my alter ego, I have never been to the Antarctic. On the other hand, Perce Blackboro, the real name of Shackleton's stowaway, never read his way through an Antarctic library nor fell in love with a girl like Ennid Muldoon. I therefore took the liberty of altering his initials to my own. Alongside much else, I changed the name of the ship on which Blackboro sailed to South America; the chapter "Shipwreck" uses motifs from John London's stories, which is why the *Golden Gate* was baptized the *John London.*

My thanks go to Robert Schindel for his company and important suggestions. I thank Norbert Hummelt for rendering my epigraph from Eliot's *The Waste Land* into German, as well as Nuala Ni Dhomhnaill and Sean O Riain for help with Gaelic and the person of Tom Crean.